ACOUSTIC ALCHEMY

Richard Gradner

Richard Gradner - Acoustic Alchemy

ISBN-13: 978-0-639-81940-2

richardgradner.com

facebook.com/richardgradnerauthor

instagram.com/richard_gradner_author

About The Book

Tracy Barnes. Milwaukee High-schooler. Music lover. Oracle. On a perilous quest to prevent her nemesis from fulfilling an age-old doomsday prophecy.

Right before her seventeenth birthday, Tracy awakens the power of prophecy, a supernatural ability inherited from a long line of ancient seers. She journeys with her father to a 12,000 year old temple site in Turkey, where they discover a mystical flute designed with the ability to counter the effects of gravity.

Tracy's riveting discovery attracts the unwanted attention of Sabine, another powerful oracle, responsible for a spate of gruesome, gang-related murders. Armed with the magical flute and her powerful intuition, Tracy must traverse the spiritual realm and confront Sabine in an acoustic battle to save the world from a terrifying Armageddon.

About The Author

Richard Gradner is a Director at Mustard, a Creative and Digital agency based in Cape Town. He was the first Red Bull Marketing Director in South Africa and has a passion for brands and branding. Richard trained and taught Kung Fu and Tai Chi for over 12 years and currently runs his own massage therapy practice called GLVTE. He has a deep connection to all things spiritual and maintains a healthy mind and body through the daily practice of Power Yoga. He is also an international, bestselling author of fantasy novels, Return to Lemuria, Unicorn, Servant of Memory and Acoustic Alchemy, all available on Amazon.com. To find out more, please visit richardgradner.com.

To my late Dad, for whom music was everything.

Richard Gradner - Acoustic Alchemy

1 ~ Naming Rights

The sound of silence consumed her like a suffocating shroud. It was all around her and deep inside her head, buzzing inside her ears from both the inside and out. She squeezed her eyes tight to banish the maelstrom and clear her mind from its scrutiny. An inquisition by the psyche. That's what it was. An inquisition. Why *was* she so inquisitive? She couldn't help feeling this way.

It's in my nature, she said to her mother when she scolded her for asking too many questions.

Tracy blinked her eyes open in the darkness. She massaged away the sleep with the knuckles of her left hand and then pushed her right arm out from beneath her, reaching for her phone on the bedside table. Her fingers tingled with a mild bout of pins and needles as her thumb found the home button. The LCD screen sprang to life, blasting the blackness away, along with the pressing silence of her thoughts. She squinted. 4.33am. She took a deep breath, sighed it out, and turned over in her bed. She was wide awake. There was no way she was going back to sleep. It was the fourth time this week that she woke up before the crack of dawn. It was as if there was a nagging feeling tugging at her mind, pulling her to do something, always

6

just beyond her grasp like the tendrils of a dream that faded into memory as soon as she opened her eyes. She closed her eyes once more, trying in vain to see the visions, straining her mind, stretching it taut like a rubber band that came back to snap at her, leaving nothing but a welt of frustration deep inside the synapses of her brain.

The buzzing from her phone startled her. A wave of apprehension that threatened to engulf her like a restless spirit washed over her entire body, sending jittery tingles down her spine.

Why's my alarm going off so damn early?

Tracy twisted around in her bed, reaching for her mobile again. She tapped the red, blinking snooze button, killing the annoying sound and checked the time. 6.45am. She closed her eyes and smiled, relieved that she had somehow managed to succumb to the elusive succour of sleep. Today was going to be a good day. She sighed out heavily, and the stifling wave receded, leaving her exposed in the warm sunlight on a sandy atoll. She stretched out her body beneath the covers and yawned, enjoying the feeling of her muscles tensing from her fingers all the way down to her toes. Her foot popped out of bed, and she quickly pulled it back beneath the duvet as the wintry air in the room stung her toes with an icy kiss. She curled into a foetal position, pressing her head into her soft pillow, savouring the warmth beneath the covers. Thoughts of the day ahead flooded through her mind like a relentless torrent.

Friday.

Two more days until my seventeenth birthday.

She tensed her body in anticipation of the exciting occasion and then realised that she was still holding her phone. She pressed the Home button and opened Instagram, quickly scrolling through her feed, absorbing the content, getting lost in the pretty images and the fascination of the lives of others.

"Good morning," whispered Tracy. She closed her eyes and breathed in her mother's familiar, reassuring scent. She wrapped her arm around her mother's waist and shifted her body closer beside her, snuggling into a comfortable spooning position.

"Morning, angel," whispered her mother. "How did you sleep?"

"Much better, thanks."

"Good."

"Mom." She kept her voice to a whisper. "I love you."

"Love you too, baby."

Tracy hugged her mother affectionately and smiled deeply. She felt safe. Safe from the world and its complications. Safe from the anxiety she experienced when she spoke to Josh. Safe from that weird-looking homeless man who sat on the corner of Pine and Grove watching Tracy as she drove past him in the mornings. Safe from Veronica Lipman, that bitch who just wouldn't leave her alone, even when her bestie, Lisa, told her off several times. Stupid cow. Tracy sucked in a deep breath.

Focus on this moment, the here and now. Free your mind from the shackles of the past. Stop worrying about the future. Breathe in all those memories. Breathe in all those feelings that are making you tense and just let them go. I want to hear your breathing. I want to hear the sound of your breath as you breathe.

The soothing voice of Denise, her yoga instructor, echoed inside her head as she pulled herself away from her racing thoughts and focused on the present. She took pleasure in her mother's scent and the rise and fall of her ribcage as she breathed, the softness of the pillow beneath her face and the warmth she felt as she cuddled in the safety of her embrace.

"Can I make you some coffee?" whispered Tracy into her mother's ear.

Her mother nodded. "Thank you."

Tracy squeezed her mother one last time before letting her go. She rolled out of the bed and tiptoed into her own room, pulled on her slippers and threw her gown over her shoulders, shivering as she made her way into the kitchen. She peered out

8

of the window, gazing up at the morning sky as she brewed two mugs of piping hot coffee, savouring the aroma that filled the air. It was a clear winter's day with not a cloud in sight. Morning sunlight streamed into the kitchen, bouncing off the counter-top in a bright, white light without much warmth.

"Here you go," said Tracy placing the hot mug on her mother's bedside table. She propped a cushion up against the headboard and climbed back into bed beside her, sitting up to sip gingerly at her hot coffee, enjoying the feeling as it warmed her body up from the inside. She turned on her phone in her free hand and opened Whatsapp. Her class group chat was out of control again. 147 messages. She scanned through the conversation. Mrs. Perkins was seen at a nightclub again. Oh, the drama! Avril Perkins was a fifty-three-year-old English teacher at Milwaukee High. Brenda Descartes always said that she was a twenty-one-year-old trapped in an older body. She had her boobs done. More than once. It was likely the only reason that she was hired by Dean Anderson. That perve. She always wore short skirts and low-cut tops, shamelessly showing off her heavy assets, and spent more money bleaching her hair to maintain its white-blond look than Veronica did on her highlights for an entire year! Tracy smiled. She was still trying to understand who saw Mrs. Perkins at the club. It could only have been Paul Williams. He always boasted that he used his fake ID to get into clubs. To his credit, he did look way older than twenty-one.

Camilla slowly pulled herself into an upright position. She brushed her dusty-blond hair away from her face, the same dusty-blond colour as Tracy's, only a little shorter, and picked up the mug of hot coffee from her bedside table. "Hmmm, this smells good," she said with her eyes closed, as she breathed in the aroma. "Thanks, Trace. Dylan still asleep?"

"Must be," replied Tracy without looking away from her screen.

"Trace, please go and wake him. You know how he is in the mornings. He needs time to wake up and get ready for school. I don't want to have to rush to get him ready again."

"Yes, but you know that no matter what time we wake him up, he still manages to do everything last minute."

"Just go and wake him, please. And bring me his phone. That's the reason he is late, actually. He lies in his bed playing games and watching videos before getting ready. And put yours down too, please. As the older sister, you need to set an example, little lady."

Tracy sighed. "Yes, mother." She stretched out her words, lacing them with enough sarcasm to cause her mother's eyebrows to rise in alarm. She took another sip of coffee before throwing her legs out of bed.

"Dylan, Dylan!" Tracy shook her brother awake.

He turned over with a groan. "Uhhh."

"It's time to wake up, little bro. Come on. Don't make us late again, okay?"

Dylan groaned again. His eyes were still closed. They looked as if they were glued shut. He screwed up his face as if he had just eaten a bitter lemon and then rolled over, away from his sister.

"Oh, no, you don't," said Tracy, pulling her brother over again.

This time, Dylan opened his eyes. "What?! Leave me alone! I'll get up, just leave me alone."

"Okay, okay. Calm the fudge down." Tracy unplugged her brother's phone and left the room.

"Here," she said, handing the phone to her mother.

"Thanks, Trace," said Camilla. "These electronics," she murmured. "They're gonna drive me to drink."

"Don't drink and drive, mom."

"Ha-ha. Very funny."

Tracy smiled. "Speaking of which, I'm driving to school today."

"Okay," said Camilla with a smile. "Just make sure Dylan gets to class. I don't want another call from the school asking if he's sick at home." She looked at Tracy askance. "Can't believe

10

that you're seventeen come Sunday. Where have all the years gone? Come sit here so that I can brush your hair." Camilla patted the bed. "You know," said Camilla, as she pulled the brush through Tracy's long, blond hair, "my mother used to brush my hair just like this before I went to school."

Tracy sighed. "I know, mom. You've told me this story hundreds of times."

"There *is* one story that I've never told you about."

"Which one?"

"It concerns your second name."

"Sybil? I know that you named me Sybil after Granny Sybs."

"Yes," whispered Camilla. She was silent for some time, deep in thought. The steady raking sound of the bristles through Tracy's hair filled the room.

"And so? What's the story?" Tracy was intrigued. She'd never really cared much for her second name.

"Do you know *why* your grandmother was given the name Sybs?"

Tracy scratched her head. The bristles tickled her scalp. "No. What's the significance?"

"It's a Greek name."

"Greek? Now that's something I never knew. Really?"

"Yes. Her mother - your great-grandmother - was Greek."

"She came from Greece?"

Camilla smiled. "Yes, Trace. Greeks come from Greece."

"Duh-uh. Obviously. I was just surprised because you never told me any of this before."

"Sybs, short for Sybil, comes from the Greek, Sibylla, meaning prophetess. Your grandmother's name was passed down a long lineage of women dating back thousands of years."

Tracy turned to look at her mother. "Interesting. So, the first Sybil was a kind of seer or something? In Greece?"

"Something like that." Camilla smiled.

"How come *you* don't carry some form of the name?"

"The naming skips a generation."

"Why?"

11

"I'm not really sure. What I do know is that the first Sybil was a powerful oracle. She could see the future. Through prophecy. There were others too. Angels communicated through them, predicting great events like famines, the outcome of great battles and the fate of men. Some regarded them as deities themselves."

"What's a deity?"

"A divine or supernatural being."

"Wow. What about Granny Sybs? Can she see into the future?"

Camilla placed her hands on Tracy's shoulders and whispered, "Yes. And you will too."

Camilla's words created a strange, tight feeling in the pit of Tracy's stomach twisting her insides like a knot.

"What do you mean?"

"As I said, it skips a generation."

"Why… haven't you told me this before?"

"Because you're not seventeen yet."

"What's that got to do with it? You still could have told me. When? How do I?…"

"Trace. Relax. Everything will be fine. You're not the first and certainly won't be the last."

"Granny Sybs? Really?"

"Yep. She's been able to foretell the future since she was seventeen. That's when it starts happening."

"So *you* can't? It skips a generation?"

"Uh-huh." Camilla nodded.

"And it's been like this for thousands of years?"

"Exactly."

Tracy's mind raced. "Geez. I have so many questions. Ha-ha-ha." Tracy laughed out loud.

"What's so funny?"

"Now that I think about it, every single time that I visit Granny Sybs unannounced, she has tea and cookies ready and waiting like she's expecting me! And remember that time we couldn't visit her because she said it was dangerous? You just

12

agreed with her but when I asked you why, you just said, 'Granny Sybs knows best.' It made absolutely no sense to me. Then that very evening, there was that shooting at Dixon High, right near where she lives." Tracy felt a cold shiver run down her spine. "So weird."

"We must pay her a visit," said Camilla. "Tomorrow. We'll leave early. Spend the day there."

A look of distress crossed Tracy's face.

"Don't worry; I'll make sure we're back in time for your party."

"Yessss!" Tracy fist-pumped the air. "Can we go to Navy Pier? Please?"

"Sure. We can take Granny Sybs there for lunch."

"What about Dylan?"

"He can join us unless he wants to go to a friend."

"I'm sure he'll stay. He hates driving to Chicago. He always says it's boring."

"We'll see. In the meantime, you'd better get ready for school, young lady. You're going to be late. And get that brother of yours out of bed. Otherwise he'll soon be at another detention."

"Yes, ma'am!" Tracy stood up and saluted. "Love you, mom," she said, giving her a squeeze.

"Love you too, baby." She kissed Tracy on the cheek.

2 ~ School Daze

"Mizz Barnes!"

Tracy jumped in her seat.

Mrs. Perkins had her hands on her hips. Her icy-cold stare bore down on Tracy like the piercing yellow eyes of a great horned owl, penetrating the very depths of her soul. "What are you doing, young girl?" Her words stung Tracy's ears as if someone had set them on fire.

"Um, nothing, Mrs. Perkins."

"Is that a mobile phone under that desk? What did I tell you about using phones in my class?" She surveyed the rest of the students, twisting her head around almost 180 degrees. "If anyone is caught using a phone in my class, it will be confiscated for the remainder of the week. Is that clear?!"

Tracy discretely swiped her finger up the screen on her phone to close the meme that someone had created of Mrs. Perkins, with her head superimposed over a girl dancing on a table in a nightclub, surrounded by a group of guys staring up at her in fascination. She had one leg high up in the air, and her arms stretched out in opposite directions like she was completely spastic. The bold white text read, **DANCE LIKE NO ONE IS WATCHING.** Tracy quickly squeezed her

14

phone between her leg and the chair as Mrs. Perkins turned her gaze back towards her.

"And wipe that smirk off your face Miss Barnes otherwise you will find yourself in detention."

"Yes, ma'am."

"Now, class," continued Mrs. Perkins. Her bright, yellow v-neck shirt exposed her cleavage, but her pink skirt was quite modest today, extending down almost to her knees. This didn't stop more than half the boys from staring wide-eyed at her bust as she pranced around the room like a peacock on display at the zoo. "Today, we will focus on learning about participles. Who knows what they are? Tracy?"

"Um." Tracy stared at the ceiling. "A participle is a verb?"

"Be more specific. You are only half right."

Tracy looked at Mrs. Perkins blankly.

"Anyone?" she gazed around the room. "Participles are *formed* from verbs and used as adjectives or used to form verb tenses in a sentence." Mrs. Perkins began typing on her laptop, and the words appeared on the smart-board. "So, if you burn the toast, the verb, burn, is formed into an adjective when you say that you have burnt toast. Who can give me another example? Yes, Mr. Gordon?"

"When you dance in the club," said Danny Gordon.

There were giggles from one corner of the class. Mrs. Perkins' face turned as pink as her skirt. "Now, that's enough!" she screeched. "Right, Mr. Gordon, stand up."

Danny rose reluctantly from his seat.

"Okay, young man. You think you're so clever. How many types of participles are there? Hmm?"

Danny quickly scanned the room, looking for some support from his class-mates.

Rick had two fingers stretched out over his jeans.

"Two."

"Very good. What are they?"

This time Danny shrugged his shoulders.

"Present and past, Mr. Gordon. Now, give me an example

15

of a past participle."

"She danced in the club?"

Yvonne Gomes clapped her hand over her mouth to hold back her laughter. Others in the class weren't so lucky.

"Sit down Mr. Gordon." Mrs. Perkins typed furiously away at her keyboard, ignoring the mixed reactions from her students. She switched back to the toast example. "Mr. Gordon was right. A past participle ends in -ed, -d, -t, -en, or -n. So you can have burnt toast, or you burned the toast. A present participle only ends in -ing. So, you are burning the toast. Finally, these modified verbs that can be used as adjectives are also called verbals."

Brenda had her hand in the air.

"Yes, Miss Descartes."

"What is a gerund?"

"Very good question, Brenda." Mrs. Perkins stared at Danny. "Are you listening Mr. Gordon? You may actually learn something today. Gerunds are very similar to present participles because they are also formed from verbs ending in -ing. The difference is the function that they provide in the sentence. Even though gerunds, once converted from verbs, end in -ing, they function as nouns, not adjectives."

Tracy zoned out, her mind casting back to the conversation she had with her mother. For the first time in her life, her second name felt important, like it meant something. Up until now, she had always been embarrassed to use her second name. Sybil sounded so last century. When she said it, all she could picture was Granny Sybs, a much younger version, mind you, in the olden days, in those black and white photos she had in the album that lay on the coffee table in her living room. So, Tracy tried purposefully never to use it, unless she didn't have a choice, like when she was filling out an important form. When she wrote it down, it stared back at her mockingly, taunting her. And then she wondered, if she just left it out, even on important forms, what would happen. Would the cops bust in on her and demand that she use it or face the consequences?

Was it a crime to not use your middle name? Sybil. She ran the name over in her mind. The Greek Prophetess. She smiled. She liked the sound of that. She imagined Granny Sybs standing inside the Acropolis in Athens, wearing one of those long, white Greek robes fastened with a golden sash, surrounded by people listening intently to her while she related her prophesies over to them. The sound of the bell brought Tracy back from her daydreaming. She closed her laptop and slipped it into its pink neoprene cover.

"Trace," said Lisa. "You ready for tomorrow? I can't wait." Her brown eyes lit up as she spoke and she squeezed her fists together, pumping them up and down in excitement.

"Yep, I guess so. Can't believe the day has come."

"Can I come through early to help set everything up?"

"Thanks, Lis, but I'm going to Chicago tomorrow, and I'm not sure what time I'll be back."

"Chicago?"

"Yeah, to visit my gran."

"Oh, Okay."

"We're taking her out for lunch, and we'll be coming right back after, so I'm sure it'll be around three-ish. I'll tell you what; I'll let you know as soon as I'm home."

"Cool."

"Everything's mostly organised, but it would be great for you to come through early to help. Thanks."

"Don't mention it, bae. Let me know if you need anything."

"Thanks, Lis." Tracy squeezed her hand. "I really appreciate it," she said with a smile.

"How was Danny Gordon?!" Lisa's eyes were wide.

"Savage."

"I know, right?! That look on Mrs. Perkins' face!"

"Priceless. I'm surprised he didn't get detention."

Lisa grinned. "I think she was too shook to be dishing out punishments back there. What a head case."

"Yeah. I'm just glad *that* lesson's over."

"Come," said Lisa. "Let's go and sit by the court. What you

bring for lunch?"

"Um, just some salad," replied Tracy peering into her bag. "Oh, and a protein bar."

"You're such a health nut."

"Am not."

"Yes, you are. I don't think I've ever even seen you eat chocolate."

"Sure I have. Besides, chocolate is good for you."

"Whateverrr." Lisa slapped her forehead with the palm of her hand.

"In moderation, of course."

"Yeah but not when your definition of moderation is, like, never."

"Listen, let's not get started. At least I don't starve myself," said Tracy.

"It's called I.F. - intermittent fasting - and it's a thing."

"What do you mean a thing?"

"I mean there's millions of people doing it. Even Hollywood."

"Ha-ha. That's reason enough *not* to do it."

"No, listen, for real. There are books on it. I just read *Eat Stop Eat,* and it was totes amazeballs. It's the future, Trace."

"Okay. I'm listening. How does it work?"

"Well, you fast for a set period of the day."

"How long?"

"For like sixteen to twenty hours."

"Jee-zuz. In one stretch?"

"Yeah. And then you like eat a small meal or two during the other four to eight. And during the fast hours, you're allowed to drink coffee, tea, and water. Some people even eat vegetables, but I don't."

"Sounds like torture."

"In the beginning it's hard, but after about a week, it becomes like normal. The worst is a few tummy pangs, but they eventually go away."

"So when do you plan that sixteen to twenty hour fast in

the day and how long should one be on this diet?"

"Well, they say that the best is from about eight at night till four the next afternoon. The longest I've ever done it is two weeks."

"And?"

"I lost four kilos."

"Wow!"

"Yeah, but I put back three in just four days." She hung her head.

"You look great, Lis. You always look good."

"Thanks, Trace. I gotta work hard to maintain this booty." Lisa twisted her hips and flicked her hair with her hand.

Lisa was such a beautiful girl. Her thick, dark brown hair matched her sultry eyes and her fine features, and pouting lips reminded Tracy of Mila Kunis.

"Not as lucky as you, though," said Lisa. "You've never even seen the arse-end of a diet. I mean, just look at you! Skinny as a runt. I *wish* I had your body."

"Don't be ridic. Have you seen the way the boys look at you? I mean, even Paul Williams."

"Paul Williams is a dick."

"Okay, let's not get started with the boys."

"Just don't tell me you've invited him to your party, Trace."

"He's mates with Josh. If I didn't invite him, he would have asked Josh to ask me if he could come."

"Aah. Guess you're right. How is Josh anyway?"

Tracy blushed. "He's okay, I guess. We don't see each other that much, you know."

"Yeah but you chat on Whatsapp all the time. I know you do."

"I guess." Tracy inadvertently checked her phone. "We're not officially dating, okay."

"Yeah, whatever."

"What about Deon, Lis? How's that going?"

"Oh, that's definitely overs."

"I thought you were going to give him a second chance?"

19

"Nah. Caught him in the act again."

"Don't tell me…"

"Yeah. It was actually in the girls' toilets yesterday. He walked out with Dorothy Spengler. She was giggling. He had this surprised look on his face when he saw me. That prick. Him and Paul Williams can go suck balls." Lisa spat out the last few words of her sentence.

"So sorry, Lis."

"Ah, no worries. Like my Dad says, 'there's plenty fish in the sea.' By the way, how is *your* Dad? I still think he's hawt!"

"Lisa!"

"What? It's true! I actually love older men. I dream about Ryan Reynolds all day. Ahh. Just imagine."

"He's back tonight?"

"Who?"

"My Dad."

"Oh. Where's he been?"

"At some kind of scientific congress or something in New York."

"Cool. Just in time for your birthday. So is he going to be there?"

"Maybe just for the beginning. But who wants their parentals at their birthday party? Yuck."

"Maybe I do. I mean just your Dad." Lisa laughed out loud.

Tracy smacked her hand. "Stop it."

"Love you, Trace," said Lisa, a big smirk stretched across her face. She kissed Tracy on her cheek, affectionately. "Come, let's go. I betcha Josh is playing ball."

The basketball court wasn't that busy. It was pretty chilly, so most of the students remained indoors. Aside from the basketball players, there were only a handful of students in the stands. Tracy pulled her beanie down over her ears and then removed a pair of woolen gloves from her pocket. She sat down next to Lisa and opened her lunch box. She scanned the players. Josh was there. He played point guard position because he was the best ball handler, dribbler and passer in the team. His job was to bring the ball down the court and coordinate the attack on the opposition, leading the team with assists and steals. Josh hadn't seen her yet, and she never expected him to because he was really focused on the game. She hoped he would, though, so she tried to keep an eye on him out of the corner of her eye in case he happened to glance up at the stands.

"Can't believe it's March already," said Lisa in between a mouthful of food.

"Yeah. It feels like just the other day we were in Times Square!"

"That was by far the sickest New Year's I've ever had."

"Yeah, was so extra," said Tracy. She took a bite of her protein bar.

"Is that chocolate-flavoured?"

Tracy turned the bar around to look at the wrapper. "Sure is. Told you I eat chocolate."

"Yeah but that doesn't count."

"It's still chocolate."

"No, it's not. It's just chocolate-flavoured. Like if it was banana-flavoured, it doesn't mean that you were eating a banana."

Tracy laughed. "Lis, you're too funny." She quickly looked up at the basketball players. Josh was on the attack. A wing from the opposition tried to steal the ball from him, but he deftly side-stepped him and thrust the ball to the ground. It bounced between his attacker's legs and out the other side. Josh was there, quick as a flash. He grabbed the ball and thrust it across to his shooting guard who was standing within three feet of the basket. He took one step and then pushed himself up into the air. An opposition player also jumped in an attempt to block the shot, but the shooting guard was taller, higher and closer to the basket. He flicked the ball out of his hand; it hit the backboard at an angle and bounced right into the net. Josh's team ran back to their starting positions, high-fiving each other along the way. Josh turned to face the opposition and then looked up into the stands. Tracy's heart exploded. Josh gave her a quick wave. She

21

returned the wave and then he was back in the game, focused on the ball and his team-mates.

"Well, look at you," said Lisa. "All flustered and pink in the face."

"It's just the cold, Lis."

"Don't think I didn't see that exchange."

"So, what of it?"

"It's so cute. And I'm envious. Josh is so nice. I just seem to attract the bad boys like Deon and Paul. What a bunch of pricks."

"Paul? I never knew he liked you."

"Since third grade. He told me."

"Yeah but he's been with Brenda for like three years."

"Exactly. Then why tell me that? Agh. Boys. They're all the same. They think with their dicks. Except maybe for Josh."

Tracy was mesmerised as she found herself staring at Josh once again. She just loved the way he moved across the court. He looked like an ice hockey skater, gliding across a frozen lake, twisting and weaving in between players with the ball magically stuck to his fingers as he played.

3 ~ Welcome Home

"Daddy!" Tracy threw her arms around her father as he stepped through the door. "You're home."

Harold's eyes lit up, and his heart sang. He closed his eyes and smiled, returning the loving embrace from his daughter. "Hiya, Trace." He whispered into her ear as he breathed in her sweet, familiar scent. "It's so good to see you as always."

His beard tickled her cheek. She released her grip. "How was your conference?"

"Symposium," he corrected her.

"Same difference."

Harold smiled. "Very interesting. You would have enjoyed it. Some very interesting speakers. Doctor Miley Rinpoche spoke about the sound of dark matter."

"The sound of dark matter?" Tracy's brow furrowed.

"Yes. Dark matter is everywhere, all over the universe, but it's also the most elusive element."

"You mean it's hard to find?"

"Exactly."

"Then how do we know it's even there?"

"Because scientists have the results of the gravitational effects that it has on its surroundings. Oh, it's there all right, it

23

just hasn't been identified as yet."

"You mean it hasn't physically been found?"

"Yeah. No one has been able to see it because, as its name implies, anything that we throw at it in order to measure it, comes back empty."

"So, we're all in the dark. Ha-ha-ha." Tracy threw back her head. It felt good to laugh, especially at one of her Dad's serious conversations.

"Ha-ha. Yeah, you could say that. To measure particles such as gases and other elements in the universe, we look at the radiation that they give off. Dark matter neither absorbs nor emits light, so we can't see it, but Doctor Rinpoche says we should be listening instead. Everything in the universe - all matter - is made up of waves. She believes that dark matter can be detected by searching for its frequency or sound wave."

"Fascinating."

"Indeed."

"What about *your* talk. How did it go?"

"Oh, I don't want to bore you with the details." Harold sucked the air in through his nose. " Hmmm… what's that I smell? Your mother's cooking?"

Tracy smiled. "Of course. And I helped her. Maaahm!" Tracy shouted down the passage. "Dad's home!"

Dylan came running out of his room.

"Dylan!" yelled Tracy. "Put on some clothes!"

Dylan was wearing a pair of checked blue jocks. He looked at Tracy and stuck his tongue out, then ran up to his father and hugged him.

"Dylan, my boy. Good to see you. Aren't you cold? It's freezing outside," said Harold hugging his son affectionately.

"Nah. Just had a hot shower. How was your trip?"

"Good, thanks." Harold smiled. "Your sister tells me she cooked up a great meal."

Dylan looked at Tracy and shrugged his shoulders. "Since when does she cook?"

"You!" Tracy raised her hand.

24

Dylan backed away, laughing. "What? Seriously, since when do you cook? I've only ever seen you make eggs and toast."

"Mom's been teaching me, okay?"

"Now, you two," said Camilla walking down the passage. "Stop your bickering. Hi Darling," she said, kissing Harold on the lips. "Welcome home."

"Hi, Hon. Good to be back."

"Dylan," said Camilla, "Dad's right. Go put on some clothes, young man." She turned back to Harold. "How was it?"

"Good, good. Was just telling Tracy about some of the interesting talks."

"Let's chat about it at the table. Dinner's almost ready."

"Yeah. Smell's delicious. I'm famished. Let me drop my stuff and wash my hands," said Harold, wheeling his bag to the bedroom.

"Dylan! You're still just standing there," said Camilla, raising her voice. "Go-and-put-on-some-clothes." Her voice took on a slow and condescending tone, implying that there were serious consequences ahead.

Dylan bolted as if he was being chased.

"And clean your room!" she yelled. "It looks like a pigsty! Trace, please lay the table while I finish off in the kitchen."

"Sure, Mom," said Tracy, making her way to the dining room. She pulled open the top drawer of the dining room server, removed four place-mats and four plates, and carried them to the table. She went back to get the cutlery, serviettes, and glasses, humming a familiar tune as she worked.

Camilla placed two Corningware dishes on the table. "Trace, please get the salad from the kitchen for me. Thanks."

"Sure thing."

"Harry! Dylan!" called Camilla. "Dinner!"

"Coming, Mom!" replied Dylan.

Harold walked into the dining room and sat down at the head of the table.

Dylan was hot on his heels. "Aaah. Smell's delicious," he said, rubbing his hands together. "Chicken?"

25

"Chicken curry," said Camilla. "That's the curry, and the other one is rice. Here's some banana, ground coconut, and raisins."

"Yummy," said Dylan, helping himself to a generous portion of rice and curry.

"Dylan," said Harold. "I think you've grown in the week that I've been away."

"I'm sure he has," said Camilla. "He's eating me out of house and home. Must be one of those teenage growth spurts."

Tracy laughed.

"Hey," remarked Dylan. "Who you laughing at?"

"Nobody," said Tracy, helping herself to the sumptuous-looking food.

"Now, you two," said Camilla. "That's enough for one day." She looked at Harold. He winked at her.

"So, tell us about those talks at the conference," said Camilla.

"Symposium," said Harold.

"Same difference," said Camilla.

Harold looked at Tracy, and they both broke out into fits of laughter.

Camilla was taken aback. "What? Did I miss something?"

"Tracy said exactly the same thing to me," said Harold.

"But there's not much difference, is there?" said Camilla. "Not really…"

"Exactly. Now, tell us about the talks."

"Daddy was going to tell me about *his* talk," said Tracy.

"Let me guess," said Dylan, his mouth full of food. "It was about sound and music. The sound of music."

"That's a screenplay," said Tracy.

"Dylan's right, of course," said Harold. "I spoke about music."

"Du-uh. Ob-vee-us-lee," said Tracy, dropping her jaw for an extra dash of sarcasm. "You are a professor of music."

"Archaeoacoustics," said Harold.

"Huh?" Tracy's mouth hung open again, but this time, her

26

face took on a confused look.

"My talk was entitled archaeoacustics."

"What's that?" said Dylan.

"What do you think?"

"Um. The archaeology of music?"

"Close. It's the study of the way that sound was used in archaeological sites and archaeological artefacts. And I'm not really a Professor of music, Trace. My title is Professor of Cultural Anthropology."

"But you study music."

"Yes, as a subset or subculture of ancient peoples. It forms an integral part of what I do. It's a big part of my research. Music helps to shape my understanding of these age-old cultures. How they applied it to their everyday lives is what interests me. I spoke about bluestone dolerite."

"Cool," said Dylan, scooping some more rice and chicken onto his plate. "What's so special about bluestone dolerite?"

"Bluestones are a kind of naturally occurring volcanic rock made from crystals deep within the Earth's mantel. The best part about them is that they ring when you strike them."

"They ring?"

"Yep. There's a place in Pennsylvania called Ringing Rocks Park."

"There's a park of ringing rocks?" said Dylan. "Where did they come from, Aliens?"

Harold smiled. "That's a good question, Dylan. Some believe that the rocks are fragments of a meteor that crashed to Earth."

"Ha! Told you. Aliens."

"Well," continued Harold, "not exactly. The majority of bluestone is made up of diabase, which is the main component of the Earth's crust. But there is still no conclusive evidence as to how these particular rocks in Pennsylvania got there because they are on the top of a hill where it's unlikely that they came from a mountain slide collapse - the usual result of a boulder field. Additionally, there is no plant life, and animals steer clear of the area."

"How do you think they got there, Dad?" said Tracy.

"Well, it's estimated that these rocks are over 200-million years old. They could have been pushed out by a volcano long since eroded."

"Or aliens," said Dylan.

"Or aliens." Harold grinned.

"And why or how do they ring?" questioned Tracy once more.

"Now *that* is the most interesting question, young lady. How and why do these stones ring? Once again, there's no conclusive evidence. I believe that it's due to millions of years of weathering. You see, the rocks in Ringing Rocks Park that are under the shade of trees do not ring. Same goes for rocks lodged deep under others or rocks under the soil. Only those rocks exposed to the elements ring, pointing to my theory that over millions of years of being exposed to the sun, rain, and wind, has somehow altered the composition of the rocks, allowing them to ring when struck."

"Fascinating," said Camilla. "Are there other places around the world where one can find these ringing rocks?"

"Yes. There are some in New Jersey, Montana and, believe it or not, Stonehenge."

"Stonehenge?" said Dylan. "Has to be aliens then. Come on, it's obvious."

"The stones at Stonehenge are also made from dolerite. And most interestingly, almost all of the rocks have scuff marks where they may have been struck."

"So they were used to make music?" said Tracy.

"Exactly," said Harold. "Stonehenge was erected almost 5,000 years ago. Its builders made the effort to transport the rocks from a site hundreds of miles away. Why? Because these rocks were special. Even back then, the people at the time must have believed in the power of the sound that they made and decided that they had to form part of the construction at Stonehenge. The ringing rocks, both at Stonehenge and in

Pennsylvania, have been considered sacred across different ancient civilisations. These civilisations - from the American Indians to the people who constructed Stonehenge, believed that the rocks contained powerful spirits that, when made to ring, communicated with the gods in ancient rituals that they held back then."

"I'm sticking with aliens. You know that they're here?"

"Where exactly?" said Tracy.

"Here. Among us. You might even be one of them."

"Stop talking shit, Dylan."

"Hey, young lady," warned Camilla. "Language."

"But, he…" Tracy folded her arms in silence.

Dylan stuck his tongue out at his sister.

"So, how was your week?" said Harold, quickly changing the subject. He flashed his teeth around the table. "I believe there's a birthday coming up." He squeezed Tracy's hand affectionately.

Tracy's face turned pink. She looked coyly away, despite the firm, warm grip of her father's hand in hers. She hated being the center of attention. She looked up at her father. "We're going to see Gran tomorrow," she blurted out, quickly changing the subject once more.

"What?" said Dylan, his mouth filled with food.

"You don't have to come," said Tracy. She turned to her mother with an I-told-you-so look.

"Good because I have other plans."

"What plans?" said Camilla.

"I'm seeing Kyle."

"Kyle Brody has been grounded, my friend."

"I know, mom. That's why I'm going to visit him."

"What'd he do?" said Tracy.

"Dylan can tell you," said Camilla, folding her arms.

Dylan deftly avoided his mother's remark by pushing a fork filled with rice and chicken into his mouth.

"He crashed his father's car," said Camilla.

"He did not!" blurted Dylan. Bits of rice flew from his

29

mouth. "It wasn't his fault."

"It wasn't his fault that he took the car, or it wasn't his fault that he crashed it?" said Camilla.

Dylan swallowed. "He… um… Someone drove into him."

"Dylan. It's irrelevant who drove into whom. Kyle is fourteen years old. He doesn't have a license. He shouldn't have taken the car in the first place. I know he's your friend, but there's no need to defend him. He's guilty. Plain and simple. And I don't approve of you hanging out with him."

"Mom!"

Harold squeezed Camilla's hand.

"What? He's a bad influence on our child, Harold."

"I'm sure the punishment fits the crime," said Harold. "How long is he grounded for?"

"A whole month," said Dylan. "He's not even allowed to play video games."

"Good," said Harold. "Then maybe you two can do more constructive stuff together. That's how real friendships are built. Face to face time, not via a headpiece and a television screen."

"Dad's right," said Tracy. "You do spend too much time playing games."

"Who asked you, Tray-cee?" Dylan whined. "You're also on your phone, like all the time."

"Am not!"

"Are too!"

"Okay, kids," cautioned Camilla in her stern voice. "That's enough. Let's have a nice family dinner for once."

Tracy folded her arms and huffed. Dylan went back to feeding his mouth in silence.

"Wonderful dinner. Thanks, honey," said Harold with a smile.

"My pleasure," said Camilla, returning the smile.

Tracy wished her brother fell off a cliff or something. He had a way of pushing her buttons that made her so mad. She cast her mind to the days ahead and smiled. She was looking forward to seeing her grandmother.

4 ~ City Limits

Tracy gazed out of the window as the first rays of sunlight clipped the horizon. She looked at her phone. 6.48am. It was early. She stretched her arms into the air above her head, pressing her hands backward against the roof of the car and yawned. The I-pass transponder made a barely audible beeping sound as they drove through a toll on the interstate. Tracy pulled the lever on the side of her seat, tilting it back so that she could lie down in a semi-horizontal position. She closed her eyes and drifted off to her mother singing to the song *When Doves Cry* by Prince on the radio. It must have had an effect on her because she dreamt she was flying like a bird through the clouds. The wind tickled her face and wrapped itself around her body like an unseen force keeping her afloat. It felt strange because she knew that she should be falling and yet, somehow, she possessed the ability to propel herself forwards, while at the same time, resisting the effects of gravity. She navigated through the currents, adjusting her speed and altitude, sensing the way that the wind moved as she flew. She knew that if she pondered too long over the physics of this phenomenon, she would end up falling, so she smiled instead and concentrated on her goal. She looked down and the sparkling reflection of the

31

sun on the sea below, shimmered like millions of tiny diamonds, winking up at her as she whizzed across the sky. The smudge on the horizon ahead became more distinct, growing larger as she approached. She squinted. She could make out tiny buildings now, nestled neatly on the slopes of the mountain peak, cast in shadow by the sun rising on the other side. She slowed down her trajectory, and the whistling wind in her ears softened to a whisper; a whisper that became more discernible as she approached the mountain. It was a voice, a familiar voice, a woman's voice, repeating the same words in her ears. At first, the words sounded like an indecipherable cacophony of multiple voices chanting as one, that gradually became clearer until they burned themselves into her brain like a branding iron. It was a song that played itself over and over in her mind. She knew the words but just listened as the enchanting voice sang to her, guiding her to her final destination. Her feet touched down gently on the Earth. She looked up and watched as thousands of leaves drifted down from the sky above. The words of the song were scratched onto the leaves, the letters glowing eerily in an unfamiliar language, gradually fading away as the leaves touched the ground.

Tracy lurched forward as the Earth beneath her feet moved. She turned her head and opened her eyes, finding herself back in the car, curled up on her seat. She rubbed her eyes, twisted her body around and stretched it out, extending it nice and long.

"Good morning, sleepy-head," said Camilla.

"Hi."

"You were out for almost an hour."

Tracy pulled on the seat lever, and the seat swung back up to a vertical position. "We there yet?" she said, looking out of the window.

"About another thirty minutes."

The highway looked much busier now as they approached the City of Chicago. Thank goodness it was Saturday. Tracy imagined that it was probably gridlocked at this time during the week with all the commuters on the road. She looked up at the sky. It was grey, filled with big, puffy, clouds. "Is it going to rain?"

"The weather report didn't say so," said her mother. "I'm sure it'll clear."

"Hope so." A leaf smacked the window, and a bout of vertigo hit Tracy like a wave. She drew in a sharp breath as the memory of the dream came back to her.

"What is it?"

"Nothing. I'm fine." She closed her eyes and tried to visualise her dream. She remembered floating. The sun was in her eyes.

The leaves.

She shook her head and then realised that she was holding her breath. She let it out with a sigh and gazed out of the window at the passing traffic. A couple of kids had their faces pressed against the window of a car as they drove past. Tracy smiled and waved. They looked so cute. Camilla changed lanes and left the interstate, taking them onto Walter Payton Memorial Highway and into the village of La Grange Park, in Cook County, Illinois, just a short drive west of Chicago city centre. The tree-lined streets were quiet as they made their way deeper into the village, finally arriving outside a familiar, quaint house with a white picket fence adjacent to La Grange Park woods. Granny Sybs was standing outside with a great big smile on her face as they parked the car.

"Granny Sybs!" Tracy wrapped her arms around her grandmother in a warm embrace. "It's so good to see you!"

"Tracy, my darling."

Tracy breathed in her grandmother's familiar scent.

"Mom," said Camilla kissing her mother on the cheek. "You okay?"

"Happy as a clam," grinned Sybs. "And how are the two of you? Let me look at you, young lady." She took a step back to look at Tracy. "My you are looking beautiful today. Simply glowing."

Tracy blushed. "Stop it, Gran."

"Come, come inside. I've just made some tea and cookies."

The smell of freshly baked cookies filled the house as Camilla and Tracy followed her grandmother inside.

Within a few minutes, Tracy was biting into one of her grandmother's famous cookies, still warm from the oven. She swallowed it down with a sip of hot tea. "Hmm, Gran. These cookies are delicious as usual. I was just telling Mom yesterday how you always manage to have them ready and waiting for us, fresh out of the oven, each time that we visit you like you know precisely when we'll walk through the door. And then we got talking about your ability to see into the future!" Tracy grinned.

Granny Sybs scrutinised her granddaughter for a moment and smiled. "I see you're getting straight to the point, my child." She turned to Camilla. "How much have you told her?"

"Hey, I can talk for myself, you know," interjected Tracy. "Are you really an oracle? Why haven't you told me before?"

Sybs smiled warmly. "Because the time was not right," she said simply.

"Mom said it's because I wasn't seventeen yet."

"Your mother's right."

"But I'm seventeen tomorrow. What's a few hours or days or even weeks difference?"

"Have you experienced any visions lately?" said Sybs.

"No." Tracy thought of her dream. That could hardly be called a vision. Or was it? She scratched her head as if she could stimulate the memories to return. "Well, I had this weird dream in the car on the way over here."

"Tell me about it."

"I can't. Can't seem to remember. Just flashes. Leaves…"

"Leaves?"

"Yeah. Words scratched on leaves. And there was this song. Someone singing. A woman."

Sybs' eyes widened, pushing her brow into deep furrows like a dried-up river bed. "That's it," she whispered. "It's happening. You have it."

Goosebumps erupted all over Tracy's body like a rash. She

34

shivered. "Have what?"

"The gift."

"What do you mean?" Tracy looked at her mother, who just shrugged her shoulders imperceptibly.

"She sang to you."

"Who? Gran, stop being so cryptic!"

Sybs took a deep breath and sighed. She closed her eyes for a moment as if she were searching for a memory deep inside her head. She opened her eyes, reached out her hand, and placed it gently on top of Tracy's hand. It was warm to the touch. Tracy looked into her grandmother's grey-green eyes. They were the same colour as hers. On a cloudy day, they were grey, but when the sun shone, they sparkled green like twin emeralds.

"Did your mother tell you about the first one? The first Sybil?"

Tracy nodded her head and swallowed. She opened her mouth to speak, but words failed her.

Sybs continued. "The first Sybil came from the family of Noah. Her name was Sambethe. It was she who's song you heard."

"But... how?"

"It is as I said. You have inherited the gift of sight. When I turned seventeen, Sambethe also came to me in a dream. The words of her song burned their way into my head."

"Yes!" Tracy jumped in her seat. "The words. They were like fire. On the leaves. So bright! But why leaves?" Tracy frowned.

"Sybils of old used to write their prophecies onto leaves and stones, and often in code. Do you recall where in your dream you were when you heard the song? When you saw the leaves?"

Tracy closed her eyes. "I..." She cast her mind back to the dream. "...was on a mountain. I think."

"A cave, perhaps?"

"Maybe at the entrance to a cave. I dunno." Tracy turned her hands palm side up and shrugged her shoulders.

35

"Sybils preferred to live inside caves or near springs. If someone approached the Sybil with a question, they would have to come to the cave of the Sybil to find the answer before the wind blew the leaves away. The Sybils believed that the questions asked of them were of great importance. They took them very seriously."

"I have so many questions." Tracy's mind raced.

Sybs sighed. "Ask away, my child. We have all day today, but first, I need to fetch something." She stood up. "I won't be a moment," she said, leaving the room.

"Mom," said Tracy. "Who else knows about this? About Gran and everything?"

"Obviously your grandfather knew. *I* know."

"What about Dad?"

"Yes, he knows."

"Still can't believe that you've never told me. Never said anything." Tracy turned her head slowly from side to side. "After all these years you kept it a secret from me."

"It wouldn't have meant anything to you if we had told you sooner. Also, this information is not something that we share unless we have to. This gift can be a dangerous tool if it falls into the wrong hands. I mean, imagine if a Sybil was used to predict the outcome of a war. This world would be a very different place, Trace."

Tracy pondered over her mother's words. "I guess so, but I still believe that I could have been told sooner. I know that I only inherit this gift or whatever you call it when I'm seventeen, but it suddenly feels as if it's something that I have been cheated out of my entire life! I don't know who I am anymore. Mom, I don't want my life to change." Tracy looked to her mother in despair and threw her arms around her, burying her face in her shoulder. She squeezed her eyes tight, hoping that when she opened them, everything would return to the way that it was.

"Don't worry, Trace. Nothing will change." Camilla gently pushed Tracy away. "Look at me. You are still Tracy Barnes. My daughter. And I love you very much. Look at Granny Sybs -

36

she's okay, isn't she? Up until now, you never knew about her gift and now that you know, has *she* changed?"

"Well, I guess not."

"There you go." Camilla smiled. "It will all be fine. I promise."

Her mother's soothing voice calmed her somewhat. She took a deep breath and lifted her head as Granny Sybs returned.

"Here," said Sybs, "this is for you." She held out a small black box.

"What is it?"

"Open it," said Sybs with a grin.

The small, rectangular, wooden box felt heavier than Tracy expected. She turned it over in her hands. It looked old like the wood had darkened and hardened over the years. She felt the soft resistance of the magnet that held the box closed as she pulled it open to reveal a beautiful crystal with a black leather cord pressed inside a dark, velvet inner lining. "Wow," she whispered, gazing at the stone. "It's beautiful."

"Happy birthday, Tracy," said Sybs. "Here, let me put it on for you." Granny Sybs lifted the crystal by its cord.

Tracy was caught in a trance by the light that danced through the crystal's multifaceted surface, sparkling like the flicker of a thousand candles in hues of pink. She looked down at the stone suspended across her chest, as her grandmother fastened the cord behind her neck.

"There. How does it feel?"

"Heavy," she looked at her grandmother, gauging her reaction to the question.

Sybs smiled. "You'll get used to it."

"Where's it from?"

"It's a family heirloom, passed down from generation to generation. It's made of amethyst. My grandmother gave it to me when I was your age and her grandmother before her. It's old. Very old. One day, you will pass it on to your granddaughter."

"What if I don't have any?"

"What? Granddaughters?" Granny Sybs laughed. "You may have sons, but you *will* have a granddaughter."

Tracy's mouth dropped. "You've seen my future?"

Sybs smiled. "Every Sybil, since the very first, has always had at least one granddaughter."

"What if there is more than one? Do they all become Sybils?"

Granny Sybs smile quickly disappeared. She was silent for a moment, deep in thought. She looked deep into Tracy's eyes. "Only the first-born receives the gift of sight. Only the eldest." Her voice was a whisper. "The first Sybil was born a twin. Twin sisters. Both possessed the gift. Both were Sybils. One was pure of thought, pure of mind, pure of heart. The other..." Her voice drifted off. "The other was bad. Corrupt. Evil. She was the cause of much pain and bloodshed. She was banished forever. Never to be seen again."

Tracy shivered. She dropped her head and gazed at the pink crystal around her neck. "It's beautiful," she said.

The warm smile returned to Sybil's face again. "Yes. You will begin to recognise its power as it helps you focus your thoughts."

5 ~ Revolution

The thirty-minute drive to Navy Pier on the I-55 was around twenty miles from La Grange Park. Tracy sat in the back, gazing out of the window as they drove, deeply lost in thought. Granny Sybs and her mother were reminiscing about an event that took place a long time ago. They sounded like two young girls as they laughed together. Tracy absentmindedly fingered her crystal and smiled.

"Trace," said Camilla. "Please go online to that parking garage like last time and book a spot for me?"

"Sure, Mom." Tracy opened the *Spot Hero* app on her phone. Their payoff line came up as the app loaded: *Save up to 50% when you book a great parking spot. And get everywhere, easier.* She typed '500 North Lake Shore Drive Parking.'

"It's seventeen bucks, Mom."

"Okay, please book us a spot. We're almost there."

"Done."

"Thanks, love."

The walk from the garage to Navy Pier took them just a few minutes. Tracy was excited. She hadn't been to Navy Pier since she was fourteen. She was looking forward to seeing all the shops, parks and restaurants again. "Shall we go for a ride on the Ferris wheel?"

"I guess we can," said Camilla. "Mom?"

"Ahh, the Ferris wheel." Said Sybs looking up at the large piece of machinery jutting up into the sky like a mechanical Godzilla. "Last time I went up there…"

"Was with Gramps, right?" said Tracy.

"Yes. Seems like just the other day. Oh, how I miss him." Sybs sighed. She turned to Tracy. "I see that you're coming into your powers," she said with a grin.

"Huh?"

"You just finished my sentence. You knew what I was going to say."

Tracy was flabbergasted. "No, I, Uh… just thought… You've told me before how Gramps took you for rides on the wheel."

"Just pulling your leg, Trace," said Sybs with a giggle.

Tracy laughed, wrapping her arm around her grandmother's shoulder in a warm embrace. "You're so funny, Gran. But seriously, is that how it will happen?"

"What?"

"Like I'll start saying random predictions and stuff."

"No. It doesn't quite happen like that. I'll explain everything to you later."

"Oh, okay. Mom, where should we go for lunch?"

"What do you feel like?"

"Oh, I dunno. How about you, Gran?"

"I'm easy."

"Last time we went to that pizza place, remember?" said Tracy.

"The one where Dylan threw up?" said Camilla.

Tracy laughed. "Yeah. When he barfed into the sea."

"How could I forget? My car stunk out all the way home. It was disgusting."

They laughed together.

"Okay, then let's try that burger bar along the pier. What's it called again?"

"Not sure," said Camilla. "I think it's down there," she said, pointing.

"DMK Burger Bar," said Tracy squinting into the distance.

"How on earth can you see that sign?" said Camilla. "It's so far away."

"20/20 vision Mom." Tracy grinned. "Let's hit the wheel first. Can't wait to see the view."

The Ferris wheel loomed above them as the ladies approached the ticket booth below.

"Three, please," said Camilla to the ticket sales lady.

"We have a special offer on the VIP gondola today, ma'am. It features a glass bottom with space for four."

"Please, Mom," said Tracy. "Please can we go?"

"A glass bottom? Are you crazy?"

"It's very safe, ma'am."

Sybs looked up at the wheel. "It looks bigger."

"It was replaced in 2016," said the ticket seller. "It holds 180 more riders."

"Thought so."

"The ride is twice as long now at twelve minutes and three revolutions per ride. The gondolas also feature padded seats, air conditioning, and televisions."

"Come on, Mom. How often do we do this?" said Tracy imploringly.

"Ah, okay," said Camilla, giving in to Tracy's whining.

The VIP gondola was nice and cosy as Sybs, Camilla and Tracy sat down on the plush, padded seat inside.

"Wow. It's nice and warm in here," said Tracy, gazing through the glass between her feet.

"Don't do that, Trace," said Camilla. "You're making me nervous."

"But it's the best part," she said, as the wheel started to move. She squeezed her grandmother's hand in excitement as the ground fell away beneath them. "It feels like we're flying." A memory popped into her head. She turned to Sybs. "It's like in the dream I had this morning. I remember flying over the sea."

She looked out of the gondola and across Lake Michigan.

"The one where Sambethe sang to you?"

"Yes. Before I heard her sing, I was flying like a bird. I remember looking down at the sea below. It was sparkling in the sunlight. So pretty."

Sybs squeezed her hand. "It's part of your awakening." She smiled. "It was the Mediterranean. The sea. She came from Greece."

"Who?"

"Sambethe. She called to you. She will call again."

"What do you mean, called to me?"

"We are both connected to Sambethe, the first Sybil. It's the gift that we carry deep inside of us. The gift of sight. The first Sybil awakens this gift within us with her magical song."

"The words on the leaves," whispered Tracy.

"Yes. It was a familiar song that you heard wasn't it?"

Tracy nodded. "I thought I'd heard it before."

"That's because you have," said Sybs. "In a previous life. It's the song of prophecy. A powerful, magical song that will stay with you for the rest of your life."

"Do you still hear the song?"

Sybs smiled her warm smile. "Always, my love. It's part of me, and soon it will be part of you. You will learn to embrace it. It will guide you on your path. It will show you the way."

"Do I have any choice?"

"What do you mean?" Sybs' brow furrowed.

"What if I don't want to be a Sybil? What if I choose not to listen to the song?"

Sybs smiled. "You can choose to ignore it, but it will always be there. You will always hear its calling, and you will still see."

"You mean the future, right? I will see the future?"

Sybs nodded. "It's your destiny. This is who you are."

"So I don't have a choice."

"Well, you do, and you don't."

Tracy looked confused.

"Let me explain. Firstly, you must see that what is

happening to you is a gift. A gift that has been passed down for thousands of years, from grandmother to granddaughter. Don't ever see it as a curse because this will only bring you despair and ultimately, madness. You don't have a choice in this matter, this thing that is happening to you. You will receive this gift, whether you like it or not. And I suggest that you learn to like it. You do have a choice to do nothing with this gift because you have free will, but I'd like for you to see it as an opportunity to use it to do good in the world. You have an opportunity to help others, Trace. There aren't many that have this opportunity in life. See it as a jump start over everyone else. Imagine what a positive impact you can have on the world around you. Being in a position to help others avert tragedy, loss, and danger is honestly the best thing that ever happened to me." Sybs closed her eyes and smiled. "I remember them all. All the people that I helped. All the people whose lives I saved. Saving a life is the most rewarding thing you can ever experience."

Tracy sighed and stared out across the water as the wheel reached its pinnacle. She twisted around in her seat, taking in the spectacular 360-degree view with Chicago to her left and Lake Michigan out in front.

"Ooh. I think I'm going to be ill," said Camilla on their third and final revolution.

"Last one, Mom. Don't look down! It will make it worse," said Tracy.

Camilla sat back in her seat and looked up at the sky as their gondola made its final descent to the ground below.

Tracy stared down at the ant people below. They gradually grew larger as the wheel turned, slowed, and finally came to a stop. Tracy felt a bit giddy as she stepped onto the platform. She helped her gran out of the gondola and down the steps. "I'm famished," said Tracy. "Funny how a Ferris wheel ride can make you hungry all of a sudden."

After a short walk down the pier, the trio arrived at DMK Burger Bar.

"Good afternoon," said a friendly waitress. "Table for

three?" She reminded Tracy of Yvonne Gomes. She had a set of teeth that seemed slightly too large for her mouth when she smiled. Her hair was tied up in a ponytail, and she wore a pair of blue dungarees over a white vest. Tracy balked. A name badge with her name on it stared back at her mockingly. Another Tracy. Why? How rude. What made things worse was that her mother opened her mouth.

"Tracy, look, she has the same name! My daughter's name is also Tracy."

Tracy, the waitress, bared her over-sized canines in a wide-toothed grin that made Tracy feel sick to the core. She pulled her face into one of the fakest smiles she could muster.

"Oh, wow," said waitress Tracy. "What a coincidence!"

"Yeah," said Camilla. "Amazing. Is there a table available outside?"

"Yes, of course, follow me," said the waitress, leading them to the top side of the outside deck. "Here you go. What can I get you ladies to drink?" she said, handing them each a menu.

Sybs sat down first, followed by Camilla and then Tracy on the other side of the table.

"I'll have an orange juice, please," said Sybs.

"How about you, Trace?" said Camilla.

"A strawberry shake, please. Can you make it double thick?"

"Sure. And for you?" said the waitress. There was that over-sized smile again.

Camilla glanced at the menu. "I'll have a diet cola, please."

"Sure thing. I'll be right back," said the waitress.

"Aaah," said Sybs, sucking in a deep breath. "I just love the taste of the air down here as it comes off the water. It's so refreshing."

"What do you feel like eating, Trace?" said Camilla. She had her reading specs on and was scrutinising the menu carefully.

"Hmm. I think I'll have number two. Chilli-rubbed onion rings, Amish blue, whatever that is and spicy Chipotle ketchup with fries."

"You sure? Looks pretty hot."

44

"Yeah. I love hot and spicy. Besides, I have my shake to cool things down if it gets too much."

"Okay. I'm gonna have number five."

"Hoo. Grass-fed bison," said Tracy.

"I'm just going to have a salad," said Granny Sybs, placing the menu down on the table. She looked up at Tracy. "So, young lady, I can't believe that you were born just the other day and now you're turning seventeen!"

Tracy smiled. "Neither can I. She looked down at the amethyst crystal hanging from her neck. Shades of the colour pink seemed to swirl deep within its depths as if it were alive. "Thank you so much for my present, Gran. It's so beautiful. Is it really as old as you say?"

"Yes. As old as time. I'll tell you an interesting story that my nana told me when I received the stone from her. It's a story about how the stone got its name. In the Greek language, Amethyst means, 'not drunken'."

"Not drunken? That's weird."

"That's exactly what I thought," said Sybs. "There's a Greek myth that tells of the son of Zeus, Dionysus, the god of wine and agriculture. He became angry because a mere mortal insulted him. He swore that he would kill the next mortal that crossed his path by setting a group of tigers upon him. It just so happened that a beautiful young woman walked by to pay her respects to the goddess Artemis. When Artemis realised that Dionysus' tigers were going to devour the young devotee, there was not enough time to save her life, so all she could do was turn her into a statue of pure crystal quartz. When Dionysus realised what his actions had caused, he was overcome with grief. He wept tears of wine. His tears poured all over the quartz statue, and the statue turned purple. The young woman's name was Amethystos. All amethyst is said to have come from this statue, and because of Dionysus' tears of wine, the wearer of amethyst is protected from drunkenness."

"Oh, wow! So does that mean that I can drink and drink and not get drunk?" said Tracy.

45

"Now don't go and get any funny ideas, young lady," cautioned Camilla.

"Just kidding, Mom. It's a super-cool story, Gran. I have to wonder though, if there's any truth to it? I guess I'll just have to find out."

Camilla eyed her daughter.

"Whoa, Mom. If looks could kill! Chill, I'm only pulling your leg."

"Actually," said Sybs, "the ancient Romans and Greeks adorned their wine goblets with Amythyst, believing that it strengthened their resistance to becoming drunk, allowing them to drink even more."

"You're not helping, Mom," said Camilla. "Rather teach her about the other stuff."

"What stuff?" said Tracy.

"Your mother is referring to your gift and how the stone is used to enhance it."

"You mean my visions?"

Sybs nodded. "The stone will still your mind, allowing you to focus on your objective. It stimulates the third eye, enhancing your perception of things, thereby speeding up the development of your intuition and psychic ability. It's a powerful talisman of focus and will create a protective light shield around you when harnessed properly. This will all take time to develop, but as your powers awaken within you, and with consistent practice, you will experience this in abundance."

Sybs' words hung in the air like they were magically alive with energy. Tracy just sat there in silence, absorbing the meaning of her grandmother's explanation. She gazed down at the crystal again but this time with a deep sense of appreciation as she began to understand its true purpose.

"So how do I do this? How do I develop all the stuff you're talking about? How do I create a forcefield of energy?"

"A light shield," said Sybs.

"What's the difference?"

Sybs smiled. "There are some things that cannot be taught.

46

They can only be explained. It's the experience itself that will teach you. When you experience your visions, only then will you learn. There's an ancient saying that goes as follows: When the student is ready, the teacher will appear. Tomorrow, you will be ready. On your seventeenth birthday, your birthright will be revealed to you, and your teachings will begin."

6 ~ Get Ready

"Mom, why does the ride home always feel quicker?" said Tracy as she gazed at the moving skyline out of her window. Granny Sybs' voice still echoed inside her head. *There are some things that cannot be taught.*

"I dunno, Trace. I guess it's because the route is more familiar after you've just ridden it in the opposite direction?"

"Maybe. I think it's also because there's more anticipation to get back home again. Like you've accomplished what you set out to do - to get to your destination, and now the return leg doesn't feel as much of a chore."

"Could very well be. I'm sure there've been experiments conducted on this type of thing. Ask your Dad. I'm sure he'll know."

Tracy was silent, lost in contemplation. Familiar landmarks appeared, signalling that they had entered the outskirts of Milwaukee and then all she could think about was her party. She pulled out her phone and started typing furiously away.

I'm almost home.

Tracy switched to Candy Crush while she waited for a response to her message. The familiar sounds of the game popped out of the phone's tiny speakers.

"Please turn that down," said Camilla.

"Sorry, Mom," said Tracy, adjusting the volume. Her phone vibrated. She switched back to Whatsapp. It was Lisa.

Cool. How was Chicago?

Great! I should be home in about 15min

Ok see you soon bae x

Tracy switched back to Candy Crush, and before she knew it, they were turning into the driveway.

"Hi, Dad," said Tracy as she stepped into the house.

Her father held open the door. "How was it? How's Granny Sybs?"

"She's great," replied Tracy.

Harold smiled and opened his arms wide. Tracy stepped into his warm embrace. She closed her eyes and breathed in his scent. She felt safe.

"Hi love," said Camilla, kissing Harold on the cheek. She shut the door and went into the kitchen. Tracy heard the kettle begin to warm up.

"Well? What did she say?" said Harold.

"It seems that I've inherited her Gift."

"So it starts tonight at midnight? As soon as you turn seventeen?"

"Yeah, I guess. Well, actually it's kinda started already."

"Really. When? What happened?"

"I had this dream in the car on the way there. About this woman singing to me on a mountain somewhere. Granny Sybs says it was Sambethe, the first Sybil."

"Wow. Okay. Did Sybs say why she sang to you?"

"Come to think of it, no, not really." Tracy scratched her head. "The words she sang were scratched onto leaves. They were familiar like I knew them but didn't. You know what I mean? Granny Sybs said that the first Sybils used to write their prophecies onto leaves. This was how she knew that it was the first Sybil who sang to me. This is how she knew that I had inherited the Gift."

"I see," said Harold.

"She said that I was to keep it a secret. Should I tell Dylan?"

"I think it's best to keep it hush for now," said Harold. "Your grandmother always told me that this gift of hers was on a need to know basis and Dylan doesn't really need to know right now."

"Yeah. That's kind of what Gran said. She said that this information could be dangerous if the wrong people knew about it. Dad, do you think my life is in danger because of this Gift I've inherited?"

"No, pumpkin. Don't be silly. Just think of it as our little secret, okay? If there's anything you need to talk about, your Mom and I are here, all right? And you can call Granny Sybs too. Anytime."

"Okay, Dad. Oh! Look at this!" Tracy held up her crystal. "Gran gave it to me. Said it was a family heirloom and that it would enhance and focus my powers."

"It's beautiful, Trace," said Harold reaching out to touch it.

"Uhh." Tracy's mind reeled. Her legs buckled. She instinctively placed her hand on her head and squeezed her eyes shut.

Harold caught her as she lost her balance. "Trace. You all right?" Concern mirrored his voice.

"My head. It hurts." She opened her eyes. "When you touched the crystal, a sharp pain tore through my head. I saw you in a strange-looking room with shelves. It wasn't clear but you were examining something inside a box." Tracy rubbed her head. "I'm fine now."

"Trace, you want some tea?" Camilla called from the kitchen.

"Uh, yes, please, Mom."

"You going to be okay? You sure?"

"Yes, Dad. I'm fine. Just a little shaken."

"I guess I shouldn't be touching that thing." Harold pointed at the crystal.

"Yeah, maybe not."

The doorbell rang. Tracy turned around and pressed her eye

to the peephole. "It's Lisa," she said, opening the door. "Hi, Lis."

"Hey, Trace. Hi, Mr Barnes. Um, I mean, Professor."

Harold smiled warmly. "Hi, Lisa. Harold. Just call me Harold."

Lisa smiled coyly.

"Come," said Tracy, tugging Lisa's arm, quickly pulling her out of her stupor. "Let's go and set everything up."

"Bye, Prof... Harold!" blurted Lisa as Tracy dragged her from the room.

"Thanks for coming, by the way. I appreciate it," said Tracy.

"Oh, don't mention it. Hey, nice crystal," said Lisa stretching out to touch the stone around Tracy's neck.

Tracy took a step to the side. "No. Don't. Sorry Lis, but I read somewhere that you shouldn't touch other people's crystals, especially while they're wearing them."

"Oh. Okay. Soh-ree. It's just a stone."

"Yeah, but they say that crystals have this kind of energy that gets messed up when other people touch them or something like that."

"Whateverrr. Where'd you get it?"

"My grandmother."

"Sick. It's really pretty."

"Thanks."

"Oh, hi Lisa," said Camilla handing Tracy a mug of hot tea. "Can I get you something to drink?"

"Hi, Mrs. Barnes. Yeah, sure. Some tea would be great! Thank you."

Camilla popped back into the kitchen.

"Okay, bae. Let's smash this. Where's all the stuff?"

"I told you that it's mostly ready," said Tracy. "Just needs to be hung up. Here, let me show you." Tracy took Lisa into the lounge. The dining room table was piled high with decor.

"Cool. So we just hang it up around the house?"

"Um, mostly here in the lounge and dining room and some in the garage."

Dylan walked into the room. "Hey sis, Lisa, what's going on?"

"Just setting up for my party," said Tracy. "Thought you were at Kyle's."

"Yeah, I was," said Dylan. "Was pretty boring. Couldn't play computer games or anything."

"Why didn't you just go to a movie or something."

"Couldn't do that either. Kyle's grounded, remember?"

"Oh, yes. Too bad."

"How was Chicago?"

"Nice. Gran sends her love. Wanna help us set up?"

"Thanks but no thanks. I need to finalise tonight's playlist. Bye. Bye, Lisa."

"Hi and bye, Dylan." Lisa waved.

"He's doing the music?" said Lisa as Dylan left the room.

"Yeah. He's been preparing all week. We're going to use the garage as the dance-floor."

"You've got a cool brother."

"Glad you think so. He's such a pain. He's fourteen, but he acts like he's five. He's always on my case. I hate him sometimes. No. I hate him most of the time."

"Ah, he's not that bad." Lisa grinned sheepishly.

"Hey, don't get any funny ideas."

Lisa giggled. "I think I prefer your Dad."

Tracy slapped Lisa on the arm. "Stop it! That's just plain weird. He's my Dad!"

"Are they gonna be at the party? Your folks."

"I think just for the beginning. Then they're going out for dinner. They said they'll be back by 1am."

"So that's your curfew? 1am?"

"Uh-huh. Here, help me with this." Tracy stood on a small ladder. She pressed the corner of a silver-foil, happy birthday sign up onto the wall near the ceiling. "Use that chair to fix the other end to that side of the wall."

Lisa grabbed the other end of the banner and climbed up onto the chair. "Okay. 1am. That's not too bad. My folks would

52

never even let me have a party at home. They're so boring."

"What you planning to do for your party, then?"

"Oh, probably just dinner with the girls or something. Haven't thought about it that much. It's still three months away. How many peeps you expecting for yours?"

"Around fifty or so."

"Aah, Trace. I can't wait. It's gonna be so much fun!" Lisa bounced up and down on the chair and almost fell over in the process.

"Careful, Lis. Can't have you breaking your neck before my party."

"Here you go, Lisa," said Camilla, placing a hot mug of tea on the table. "That's starting to look very nice, girls."

"Thanks, Mrs. Barnes," said Lisa.

"Is there anything I can do to help?"

"Thanks, Mom, but you've done more than enough already," said Tracy.

"Nonsense. I haven't done that much."

"Oh, come on, Mom. Don't be so modest. You only organised like *everything*. Okay, I did the invites, but you organised the decor, the balloons, the food, the drinks…"

"The drinks was Dad's department," interjected Camilla.

"I hope he bought some alcohol."

"You know the rules, young lady."

"Yes, I know. Was just kidding. Beer, cider, and wine. Did he get some of that at least?"

"Yes, I believe so. I hope you told your friends no driving."

"Sure, Mom. Don't worry. They all know."

"Okay, great, because we will not be held responsible for anyone leaving this house drunk and then driving home. This is your responsibility, and it's no joke. Understand?"

"Yes, Mom. I understand."

"Good. Lisa, please take care of my baby while we're gone. I know it's her birthday, and she wants to party, but you girls must look out for one another. Just don't overdo it. You know what I mean."

"Yes, Mrs. Barnes," said Lisa. "Don't worry; I'll take good care of her." Lisa gave Tracy a consoling hug.

"Oh, and one more thing, Trace." Camilla brought her voice down a notch. "Keep an eye on your brother. He knows not to drink, but if I so much as hear that a drop passed his lips, you will be held responsible." Camilla pointed her finger at Tracy.

Tracy nodded. "Don't worry, Mom. I'll keep an eye on him."

"We'll be back at 1am. That's cut-off time."

"Yes, Mom. I know. You've already told me."

"Just reminding you, Trace." Camilla smiled. "I'm not trying to stop you having a good time. You just need to be responsible, that's all."

"Thanks for the reminder. Now please let us finish here. I still need to do my hair and makeup. What's the time, by the way?"

Camilla looked at her wrist. "Just before four."

"Damn. It's late."

"What time is everyone coming?"

"Eight."

"Okay. Don't worry," said Camilla. "Everything will be ready. The food is being delivered at 7.30."

"What time you leaving?" said Tracy.

"8.30'ish. I'll make sure that everything is set up before then."

"Thanks, Mom."

"See you later," said Camilla waving as she left the room.

Tracy and Lisa continued to set up the decor around the house. It was only over an hour later that they finally finished. They pushed all the dining room chairs against the wall and moved the table to the other end of the room.

"We'll put all the food on the table, and then everyone can help themselves," said Tracy.

"Great!" said Lisa. "What about the garage?"

"Dylan was supposed to sort that out. Let's go and check it out."

54

Lisa followed Tracy as she led her out of the lounge and into the patio outside. She opened the side door to the double garage. A silver foil-like fabric was suspended around the room, and rows of string-lights adorned the walls. Lisa spotted a strobe light hanging from the ceiling and a strange-looking, rectangular black box on the floor next to a table with Dylan's mixer and amplifier.

"Wow, Trace. This looks am-a-a-a-zing! What's that box for?" She pointed at the black box.

"It's a smoke machine."

"Sick!"

"Yeah. Dylan organised it."

"I'll say it again - you have the coolest brother."

"I'm just surprised he pulled it all together. I bet my Dad helped make it happen."

"Hey," said Dylan as he stepped into the garage.

"Speak of the devil," said Tracy under her breath.

"You ready for the sound-check?" he said, plugging his laptop into the mixer. "So, what do you think?" he said, waving his arm about the room. "Sick, hey?"

"Yeah. Looks cool," said Tracy.

"It's rad, Dylan," said Lisa.

"Thanks. Okay, listen to this." Dylan fiddled with the mixer. There was a high-pitched screech, and then the music blasted through the speakers without warning.

Tracy clamped her hands over her ears. "Not so loud!" she shouted above the din.

Dylan adjusted the controls. The bass from the deep house track reverberated around the room.

"I said, turn it down!" shouted Tracy, pushing her hand through the air in a downward motion.

Dylan finally turned it down a notch. "So? How does it sound?" he said, bopping up and down to the rhythm.

"Great!" said Lisa, thrusting her thumb into the air.

"I hope you're not playing this doof-doof stuff all night long!" said Tracy. "My friends like more of the songs that they play on the radio."

"Yes, I know," replied Dylan. "This is for later. When the party really gets going."

"Just don't play any heavy metal or dark stuff."

"Don't worry, Trace. It's all upbeat and happy." Dylan continued to bounce to the beat. He adjusted the mixer controls. His teeth flashed in a great big smile across his face.

"He's in his element," said Lisa.

"Yeah. You'd think that this was his party, not mine."

Lisa glanced at her phone. "Shit. It's getting late."

"What?!"

"I said it's getting late! Gotta go and get ready."

"Oh, thought you said it's almost eight. I nearly had a heart attack! It's still so loud in here. Couldn't hear you." Tracy left the garage with Lisa in tow.

"Thanks, Mrs. Barnes!" said Lisa at the front door. "See you later."

"Bye, Lisa. Thanks for helping Tracy," said Camilla, opening the door.

"By Lis." Tracy kissed her friend goodbye.

"Okay, birthday girl," said Camilla. "Let's get you ready for your big night."

"Mom. I'm a little worried, to be honest." A look of concern crossed Tracy's face.

Camilla placed her hands on Tracy's shoulders. "Why? What's wrong?"

"It's this whole prophecy thing. I keep wondering what will happen to me at midnight? I feel like Cinderella waiting for the clock to strike twelve. The worst part is, you guys won't even be here."

"Trace, if anything crazy were going to happen, Granny Sybs would have said something. I wouldn't worry. Besides, we'll see you at one, unless you want us to come home earlier?"

"No," said Tracy flatly. "I've already told my friends that the party is on until one. It's gonna be ultra weird if you rock up at twelve."

"Okay. We're a call away if you need anything. Don't worry; everything will be fine. You've got all your friends with you, and you're at home. Just enjoy yourself and have fun." Camilla gave Tracy a consoling hug.

"K, Mom." Tracy closed her eyes, savouring the warmth of her mother's embrace. The warmth seemed to be emanating from the centre of her chest. Her heart? She felt the press of a hard object against her breast bone. The crystal. Of course! As soon as she brought her attention to it, she could see it in her mind's eye. It floated just out of reach, in front of her, turning slowly on its axis. It pulsed, gently, like it was alive with energy. Just beyond the crystal, it's glowing light illuminated a face. Granny Sybs! She smiled, and Tracy smiled back. The glow from the crystal expanded until it blotted out everything around it including Granny Sybs' face. It filled Tracy with energy; a fresh, clean, burning energy that she couldn't explain. Her smile widened until her cheek muscles burned from the strain, but it was a good burn, a cleansing burn, a burn that enveloped her head like a cloud and lifted her up and away from the anxiety that she felt before. She was happy. She felt somehow enlightened and at peace.

7 ~ Party On

The doorbell rang.

"Trace!"

"Got it, Mom!" shouted Tracy as she ran down the stairs. She checked her phone. 7.56pm. "Lisa! You are looking hot, girl," said Tracy as she opened the door.

Lisa wore a pair of ripped jeans; a bright yellow cropped top and a matching denim jacket. Bright, red lipstick and dark, black eyeliner had transformed her face into a work of art.

"Thanks, but you don't look too bad yourself, birthday girl. I've never seen your hair looking so beautiful."

"You like it?" said Tracy, turning around. "My Mom did it for me." Tracy's dusty-blond, blow-dried hair bounced off her shoulders.

"She's a pro! Next time I'm definitely coming over for a blow. This is for you." Lisa held out a small, orange-coloured paper bag adorned with a beautiful, yellow daisy on one side.

Tracy smiled from ear to ear. "Thank you, my bestie!" She hugged Lisa.

"Open it, open it!" said Lisa, with far more excitement than Tracy could ever muster.

Tracy pulled open the bag and reached inside. "Oh-em-gee!

Is this what I think it is?" She pulled out a small, green, and brown clutch purse.

"It's a Miu Miu!" said Lisa and Tracy together, jumping up and down as if they had just won the lottery.

"Oh, wow, wow, wow, Lis! This must-have cost you a fortune!"

"Oh, I've been saving up."

"Thank you so, so much." Tracy kissed her friend again.

"Anyone here yet?" said Lisa.

"Nope. You're the first."

"Cool. I'm glad. I wanted to get here early. Hi, Mrs. Barnes."

"Hi, Lisa," said Camilla, as she walked into the room. "You are looking lovely."

"Why, thank you." Lisa blushed. "Tracy looks incredible too. I love her hair."

Camilla smiled. "You girls have fun tonight. Lisa, I'm counting on you to look after my baby. You have my number, right?"

"Yes, ma'm. Don't worry; everything will be just fine."

"Will you two stop fussing over me already?" said Tracy. "I can look after myself. It's not like we're doing anything crazy. I mean I'm at home for goodness sake!"

"Okay. I think that's my cue," said Camilla. "Let me finish off upstairs so we can be out of your hair."

No sooner had Camilla disappeared upstairs, the doorbell rang again. "Yvonne! Stacy! Brenda! Good to see you. Thanks for coming," said Tracy as she opened the door.

The house quickly filled up with people. It was quarter to nine when Tracy approached Lisa. "Have you seen Josh?"

Lisa scanned the lounge. "Nope. Have you checked the dance floor?"

"Just came from there. Maybe he's in the loo?"

"Hmm. Don't think so." Tracy scratched her head.

"I'm sure he's just fashionably late."

The doorbell rang again.

"Bet you it's him!" Lisa ran to the door.

"Oh." Lisa's mouth dropped. "It's you." It was Paul.

"Hey, Lee-sa," chimed Paul. He waved his hand through the air and bent his knees as if he was about to let loose a rap-rhetoric. "Wassup? Where's the birthday girl?"

Lisa folded her arms and just glared at him. "Paul Williams. You had better be on your best behaviour tonight."

Tracy looked over Lisa's shoulder. "Oh, hi, Paul."

"There you are," said Paul, side-stepping Lisa. "Tell your bodyguard," he jerked his thumb over at Lisa and winked, "that I'm cool, okay?" He raked his fingers through his long dark fringe, pushing it back over his head.

"Oh, don't mind Lisa," said Tracy. "She's just a little over protective. My Mom told her to look out for me while she's out this evening."

"Well, tell her to lay off the crazy babysitter vibe," said Paul. "It's a bit disturbing."

Lisa spun around. "The only disturbing thing here is you and your attitude, mister."

"You know that you look more beautiful when you're angry?" said Paul with a mischievous grin.

"You... I..." Lisa was at a loss for words. Her face turned crimson.

"You seen Josh?" said Tracy, quickly cutting in. Somehow she knew that things weren't going to end well.

"Um, yeah," said Paul. "He was at school today."

"No, you dummy. Thought maybe he was with you. He's not here yet. He said he was coming."

"Ha-ha. Just kidding. I spoke to him a while ago. Said he was catching an Uber."

"Oh. Okay. Hope he's all right."

"Want me to text him?"

"Nah, it's okay. I guess he's on his way."

"Yeah, probably in the car right now. Happy birthday by the way. Here." Paul thrust a bottle of champagne into Tracy's hand, leaned forward, and gave her a peck on the cheek.

"Why, thanks," said Tracy.

"Cool. Enjoy. Now just direct me to the bar so I can get as pissed as a bum in a refinery." Tracy gave Paul a look of dread. He laughed out loud. "Just kidding!"

"Um, over there." Tracy turned and pointed towards the dining room. "And the dance floor is out back in the garage."

"Awesome! Later!" Paul left with a wave, darting over to the bar. He pinched Yvonne's bottom on the way over, and she let out a screech.

"Told you he was a pain," said Lisa, her arms still folded tightly across her chest. "Hope he doesn't wreck your place."

"I'm sure my crazy babysitter will take care of him for me," said Tracy laughing.

"Oh, shut up," said Lisa slapping Tracy on the arm. "Come, let's get something to eat. For some reason, that encounter has left me famished."

◊ ◊ ◊

A little while later, Lisa found Tracy sitting on a bench between the house and the garage. "Trace. There you are. Come, let's go inside. It's freezing out here."

Tracy looked up at Lisa with a despondent look on her face. "What's wrong?"

"He's not answering his phone. I'm worried, Lis. It's not like him."

Lisa looked at her watch. "It's almost midnight."

"I know. This is turning into the worst night of my life." Tracy hung her head.

"Come with me." Lisa grabbed Tracy's hand and pulled her to her feet. "We're going to hit the dance floor. Dylan is going to do a countdown to your birthday."

Tracy reluctantly put one foot in front of the other, as Lisa dragged her into the garage. Tracy led her past everyone, right to the front of the room. Her friends gathered around her as Dylan cranked up the music. Lisa disappeared, but the upbeat

61

music, flashing lights, and positive energy from her friends made her smile and she quickly forgot about her melancholy.

Tracy spotted Lisa again. She was pushing something onto the dance floor. She couldn't quite make out what it was in the dark room, between all the dancing bodies and flashing lights. Her friends gradually shifted away to allow Lisa through. Someone was lighting something on top of the structure. It was a cake! A giant cake! Tracy's mouth dropped, and her eyes widened in shock. She looked at Lisa, who just grinned back at her sheepishly. The cake was huge and round and set on top of some kind of trolley. Three big sparklers sent fiery sparks shooting high up into the air as Lisa pushed the cake into the middle of the dance floor. Dylan turned down the music and began counting backwards from ten to one over the microphone. Someone lit a string of Chinese firecrackers and threw them next to the cake, causing Tracy to jump back in fright. At the very same time, the top of the cake flew open and out popped Josh, wearing nothing but a pair of board-shorts and a black bow tie around his neck. Silver glitter covered his face and gold spray was in his hair. Tracy screamed as did so many others. The screaming turned to applause, and then her friends burst into song.

"Happy birthday to you, happy birthday to you, happy birthday dear Tracy, happy birthday to you!"

Tumultuous applause and several loud whistles rocked the room, before Dylan turned the music back up, sending everyone jumping up and down to the banging beats. Tracy just stood there, stunned, while her friends took turns to hug and kiss her amidst their jumping and stomping. She stared at Josh as he climbed out of the cake. She couldn't believe her eyes. She watched him push the cake off the dance floor and return to stand before her with a sheepish smile on his face. Tracy wasn't sure if she should slap him for allowing her to sit around worried about him for four hours or hug him in relief. She just stood there, immobile, like a statue, as the music washed over her, numbing her senses, the heavy bass pulsing through her body like a jackhammer.

Josh approached Tracy. He opened his mouth to say something and then closed it again. There was no way that she was going to hear what he was going to say amidst the din of the music. He leaned forward to speak into her ear. "Happy birthday! Sorry I'm late!" He took a step back, gauging Tracy's reaction. She took a deep breath and sighed it out with a smile. He smiled back and reached out his hand. She took hold of it, and he pulled her in close. She caught his musky smell, and her heart skipped a beat. Her feelings of anxiety and angst washed away like flotsam in a current as her world closed in like a cocoon with just her and Josh caught safely inside. The sound of the music became a dull throb and even the flashing lights seemed to dim and fade with every passing moment. Their foreheads touched, then their noses and before she knew it, Tracy was kissing Josh with fervour, and intensity. She closed her eyes and imagined him transporting her through space. Her Silver Surfer atop his otherworldly board of supernatural energy, his sparkling face and shiny hair illuminated by the stars in the universe as they traversed across its boundless expanse. She marvelled at the swathes of colour, smudged around her like the giant strokes of a galactic paintbrush, hues of yellow, orange, green and blue, shimmering in the sky like the aurora borealis, still wet and dripping with the cosmic energy of the Creator.

Tracy turned her attention back to the board, the silver bullet that transported them across the galaxy and realised that she was alone. Josh had left her to face the future by herself. The celestial winds buffeted her face as she sped through space, tearing into her skin like the sand in a desert storm, pulling back layer upon layer until there was nothing left but bone. White, polished bone. And then her bones began to wither and crumble, quickly becoming one with the dust of the universe. She was naked; her soul laid bare amidst the stars in the heavens. Her physical body had been taken from her, yet she could still see. She saw with the eyes of the oracle, the Sybil, the prophetess. She saw, and it was beautiful. She was awakened; alive with purpose and determination. Alive with a fiery energy that burned deep inside her, a voice that wanted to get out, to speak the words of the universe, of creation, of all that was, is and will be. It was the voice of the Sybil, translating the vibrational patterns of energy; the energy of creation, into something tangible, something real. The translation would make sense only to those wanting to hear, those wanting to listen to the voice of the oracle, to the words that spoke with hidden meaning and cryptic verse. Tracy gazed around in awe as the patterns of light energy washed over her in waves of throbbing colour, filling her soul with pure enlightenment and ancient knowledge passed down from those who came before her, right back to the very first that ever was. In what seemed like an eternity but was just a fleeting moment in time, Tracy had grown, evolved into who she was meant to be. She was the next Sybil, an old soul born into a new body, predestined to fulfil her role in this lifetime, to fulfil her duty, her purpose. She smiled an all-knowing smile, and for the first time in her life, she possessed a self-confidence that she never knew was possible. A self-confidence that gave her courage and strength. A fearlessness that knew no boundaries. Everything else in her life was meaningless in the face of this courage. She rose above it all, the mundane, the conventional, the same old. She was alive and she was free.

8 ~ Smoke & Mirrors

The owl's gown of soft, brown feathers provided insulation from the cold, wintry breeze that came from the easterly side of the evergreen cedar forest. Its golden-eyed stare pierced through the darkness like the twin headlamps of a ranger's jeep on patrol. The feathery shape pushed up and off the branch it was perched upon, releasing its talons to ride the current through the dark, dense forest in search of its unfortunate prey. Wispy, grey tendrils of smoke rose up and out of the forest canopy in the distance, dissipating into the night sky like spectres being released from an earthly prison. The owl flew on, oblivious to the unusual activities elsewhere in the forest, intent only on satisfying its instinctual desire to hunt and eat. Its short, wide wings gave it the advantage of maneuvrability beneath the treetops as it scanned the ground for the slightest movement with its razor-sharp vision. The predator's flight path took it nearer to the source of the smoke. The crackling sound of burning wood popped through the forest in fits and starts, frightening a squirrel hopping from tree to tree and into sight of the rapacious bird of prey. Without hesitation, the owl twisted its body in mid-flight and dropped from the sky like a stone, narrowing in on the furry creature below. The squirrel made one final jump into the air. Black-ribbed, razor-sharp talons clicked open, plucking the squirrel from its vault with deadly accuracy. The powerful talons dug deep into the mammal's soft flesh, quickly crushing its spine, terminating its life in their iron grip. The owl pushed harder, flapping its wings, rising between the treetops and the thick plumes of smoke, before finally disappearing into the dark, cold night.

The fire continued to crackle as the flames gradually fed through the damp wood, spitting and hissing like a venomous cobra defending its territory. Next to the fire stood a girl, completely naked, but for a dark, misshapen stone hanging around her neck that appeared to suck the very light out of the fire like a ravenous beast. Her long, dark hair was matted and filled with leaves and dirt as if she had been rolled around on the forest floor. Irregular, muddy streaks covered her body like swabs of thick, crusty paint from an old, over-sized brush. Her unflinching eyes stared wide into the flames as the shadows danced across her face to their own, silent tune. A hunched up figure swaddled in several layers of cloth sat unmoving against the trunk of a tree nearby, watching, waiting. The girl slowly began to open her mouth. It stretched taught at the corners and pulled at the skin across her face. She dropped to her knees, her mouth still wide open in anticipation of a sound much delayed. And then it came, a soft wail at first, like it was emanating from far beyond the depths of her lungs. It grew louder and louder, becoming a scream so deafening, the trees around her seemed to bend away in anguish. She screamed and screamed until there was nothing left in her to scream; until her voice faded away like it was the very last breath that she gave in this life. Her head dropped forward, and she slouched down onto her haunches, her energy depleted, her body exhausted from the ordeal. The crackling sound of the flames filled the silence, sending a shower of sparks into the night sky. The figure nearby began to shift, rising slowly, yet purposefully, towards the exposed girl beside the fire. Her hood dropped back to reveal a face filled with hundreds of deep furrows, exaggerated in the light of the dancing flames. Long hair, white with age, fell to her shoulders as she threw a thick, dark blanket over the girl. She stared into the flames and then dropped her head back to stare up at the stars in the night sky. She closed her eyes and moved her lips in a silent prayer for a moment, before making her way back to her spot against the tree. She settled down again, pulled her hood over her head, and closed her eyes. A cold breeze rustled the tops of the trees, and the stars turned in the sky.

Without anyone left to feed them, the fiery flames neared the end of their banquet, reduced now to mere embers. Hot coals in a dark pit hewn from the forest floor. The blanketed shape that was the girl began to move. She pulled the blanket snugly around her lithe frame as she rose to her feet and shuffled over to the older woman by the tree.

She opened her mouth to speak. Her dry throat produced a croaking sound. "Grandmother."

The old lady lifted her gaze. "Sabine," she said. "You are ready. You have been chosen. Sabbe has spoken."

The girl nodded her head in acknowledgement.

"Has she told you what you are to do?"

The girl nodded again.

"Good, good." The grandmother smiled. Most of her teeth were either missing or crooked. "The time has finally come, my child. You must fulfil the prophecy."

The girl extended her hand from beneath the blanket.

"No," said the old woman. "I am done here. I am tired." She sighed. "I have taught you what you need to know. I need to rest now."

The girl slowly lowered her arm.

"Sabbe will guide you. She is with you." The older woman smiled her toothless smile again. "Trust in the process, and your path shall be revealed to you. Give, and ye shall receive."

Sabine stood in silence for a moment longer and then turned around to shuffle deliberately out of the forest. A thin veil of white steam puffed methodically out of the blanketed figure as she gradually made her way back to the main road about three miles away. She closed her eyes.

Trust in the process, and your path shall be revealed.

Her grandmother's voice echoed deep inside her mind. She closed her eyes and pictured the car approaching, working out exactly where to stand. She made her way into the road and stopped. She waited - a dark, immobile shape on the tarmac.

Mark Landman focused on the road ahead. He gripped the top of his BMW steering wheel and glanced down at the radio as it blared out *Who wants to live forever?* by Freddy Mercury. It was at that moment that his side mirror clipped something hard with a loud snap. He swerved, hit the brakes and skidded to a halt.

"Shit! What the hell was that?" he said under his breath.

He opened his door and checked his mirror. It was twisted. He hadn't imagined it. He stepped out of the car, popped the mirror back into place, and turned around to look for whatever it was that he had hit. He turned on his phone-torch and took a few steps back down the road, trying to pinpoint the exact location of impact. He scratched his head and swung his phone around in an arc, looking for the mystery evidence that just wasn't there. He shrugged his shoulders and made his way back to his stationery vehicle. He dropped into the driver's seat and immediately jumped back in fright. There was someone sitting right next to him. There was a flurry of movement in the darkness. Instinctively, he raised his hands to his throat as it closed up, making it tight and difficult to breathe. He looked down. His hands were wet, completely covered in a warm, dark substance. He took a breath, but it was as if his mouth was filled with water that he struggled to swallow. He turned his head towards his passenger, and his eyes grew wide with fear. He choked as his mouth continued to fill with liquid. He clutched frantically at his throat again, writhed around in his chair for a moment and then was still. Sabine climbed out of the car, made her way around to the other side and pulled Mark's lifeless body out of the driver's seat. With some effort, she managed to drag him across the road and into the bushes nearby, leaving a long, dark, blood-stained smear across the tarmac. She returned to the vehicle, climbed inside and pulled down the visor. She slid open the mirror cover, and the light flicked on. Her mud-streaked face stared back at her. She smiled, staring at the flames still dancing in her eyes, swaying her head to their flickering, mesmerised by their hypnotic rhythm. She snapped the visor shut and, led by the voice of Sabbe urgently whispering to her deep inside the recesses of her mind, she started the car and drove off into the night.

9 ~ Surprise

"So, how does it feel?" said Camilla to Tracy at the breakfast table.

Tracy pushed her unkempt, dusty-blond hair out of her eyes and looked up at her mother in confusion.

"I mean to be seventeen."

"Oh, I feel the same. I think. Except..." And then it all came back to her like a wave, knocking her over from behind.

"Cat got your tongue?" said Camilla as Tracy reeled from the powerful memories of the previous night.

"I... I'm not..." she stammered. "It feels like a dream and yet..."

"Oh, it's all very real, Trace." Camilla smiled.

"No, I mean, yeah, it feels real to be seventeen, but last night I changed." She looked down at her hands cradling the hot mug of coffee, almost expecting to see someone else. Another person in another body. "I feel different." She looked at her mother. "She spoke to me again. Sambethe."

"What did she say?"

"It wasn't like she said anything specific. I could just hear her voice inside my head. She showed me stuff."

Camilla looked at Tracy expectantly.

70

Tracy shrugged her shoulders. "Ah, I dunno, Mom. It was all pretty surreal."

"But you're okay? I mean, you don't feel sick or anything?"

Tracy smiled. "I'm fine, Mom. Just a bit overwhelmed, I think." She absentmindedly fingered the crystal around her neck. "I kissed him," she whispered. She felt the blood rush to her cheeks. She looked up at her mother. "I kissed Josh."

Camilla smiled. "He's a lovely boy." She walked over to Tracy and wrapped her arms around her in a warm embrace. "Happy birthday, my baby. I love you so much." She kissed Tracy on the crown of her head.

Tracy hugged her back. "Love you too, Mom. Where's Dad?"

"Oh, he's been up since five."

"Let me guess. He's in his office working."

"He's busy with that research project."

"But it's Sunday. Doesn't he ever rest? Doesn't he ever sleep in?"

Camilla shrugged her shoulders. "You know your father," she sighed.

"Dad!" exclaimed Tracy as her father stepped into the kitchen.

"Morning my two beautiful ladies."

"We were just talking about you," said Tracy with a grin.

"Hope it was all good?"

"Only the best."

"Happy birthday sweetness," said Harold kissing Tracy on the cheek. "Good Lord, let me look at you." Harold took a step back. "Seventeen years old. I can't believe it. You are the most beautiful girl in the world."

Tracy blushed. "Stop it, Dad."

"No. I mean it." Harold looked around the kitchen. "Where's Dylan?"

"Still sleeping. Where else?" said Tracy.

Camilla's phone rang loudly. "It's Granny Sybs," said Camilla swiping her finger across the screen. "Morning, Mom.

71

Yes, I'm fine. How are you? Great. Yes, I know, it's cold here too. Yes, she's awake. Okay. Here she is," said Camilla handing the phone over to Tracy.

"Hi, Gran," said Tracy.

"Happy birthday, my angel," said Granny Sybs. "How was your party?"

"Oh, it was amazing. I had so much fun."

"You feeling okay?" Granny Sybs' voice took on a tone of concern. "I mean, has anything unusual happened to make you feel... um... different?"

"Yes. It happened. Last night just as you said. Like clockwork. I was flying through space. It was so beautiful. And then Sambethe..."

"She spoke to you again? What did she say?"

"Well, it was like she spoke through me, not to me." Tracy closed her eyes, trying to remember more clearly. "Her voice was all around me and inside me. It sounded like many voices."

"All the Sybils that have come before you," said Granny Sybs softly. "The voices that speak the language of the universe. The many voices that speak of the past, present, and future. Did you hear or feel anything else?"

"What do you mean?"

"Did you hear anything in the voices that made you feel uneasy?"

"No. I don't think so. Why?"

"Hmmm." Granny Sybs was silent for a moment. Tracy heard her take a deep breath and sigh it out. "There is turmoil."

"What do you mean, turmoil?"

"In the ether. Do you remember where you were when you heard all the voices?"

"I was amidst the stars. It was so beautiful." Tracy smiled, remembering.

"Is this the ether?"

"It is a reflection of the universe. As Sybils, we can step beyond the confines of this world and into a place where the rules that govern us mortals here on Earth do not apply. We can

72

step into the very fabric that makes up everything that we know - the stars, space, everything. The gift of the oracle is being able to translate the voices into something coherent; something that makes sense. It will take time, Tracy. Time to decipher what the universe is teaching you. Time to understand the language of creation. With practice, your gift will manifest. You will become stronger."

"But what did you mean when you said that there was turmoil in the ether?"

"I'm not quite sure what it means, but I felt a great shift last night. Something that I have never felt before. I thought that it must be your transition into becoming an oracle. But then, as I looked beyond the confines of this world, I sensed that something was different. The vibrations were truly magnificent at first, but then there was a distinct change, something not quite right."

"I didn't sense anything unusual." Tracy scratched her head. "Actually, the entire experience was quite unusual." She laughed. "It was ethereal like I've never felt before. So, if there was turmoil, or whatever, as you said, I guess it would have made no difference to me because I saw it all as a huge, fantastic experience." Silence greeted Tracy on the other end of the phone. "Gran, you okay?"

"Yes, yes, of course. Just got my thinking cap on. Trying to make sense out of this. When I try and see through it all, I find myself surrounded by flames with no clear way out. I cannot see anything else. I can't translate the voices as I normally do."

"Maybe it's because you are losing your powers and I am gaining mine?"

"No," said Sybs. "That can never happen. I fear that this is something a little more than that. For the first time in a very long time, I felt a sense of dread. My first instinct was to check that you were okay. It's probably nothing to be alarmed about. Just promise me that you will be vigilant, Tracy, okay?"

"Sure, Gran."

"If anything unusual happens, please call me."

"Of course. Thanks, but I'm one hundred percent fine, so please don't worry."

"Love you, Trace. Enjoy your day."

"Thanks, Gran. Bye."

"Everything okay, Trace?" Camilla took hold of Tracy's hand and squeezed it reassuringly.

"Yeah. All good, Mom," said Tracy with a smile. "Granny Sybs is just overprotective."

"Best to heed her warnings, Trace. She has saved me tons of trouble over the years. If it weren't for your Granny Sybs, I probably would never have met your Dad."

"What do you mean?" said Tracy with a frown.

"The night I met your father, I was on my way to visit Sheila Woodbridge, an old friend of mine from Chicago. I stopped at a gas station on the way over there, and the phone rang."

"But you never had mobile phones then?"

"It was the phone in the shop. The shop assistant called me. It was Granny Sybs."

"She knew you were there?" Tracy took a sip of her coffee.

"Yes. It wasn't the first time she called me at a strange number. It was like she had attached a tracking beacon to my body and could find me whenever she wanted to. I hated that. Anyway, she just said, 'Camilla, don't go.' I was flabbergasted. I argued with her. She was adamant. She had that sternness in her voice, that firm, unwavering tone that just made me obey her without question. I remember placing the receiver down. I was shaking, but not from the cold. I knew that after that call, something bad would have happened to me if I went to Sheila's."

"What did you do?"

"I went into the diner next door and ordered a coffee. This handsome young man next to me told me that I had beautiful eyes."

"Dad."

Camilla nodded and smiled. "He was so charming. He paid

74

for my coffee and then told me that his car had broken down outside. We sat down and spoke for over an hour." Camilla stared up at the ceiling. She had a glazed look in her eyes.

"What about Sheila? Did something happen to her?" said Tracy.

"Oh, no. She was all right, except that she didn't talk to me for over a week because she thought that I dumped her over meeting your father."

"So you never found out why Gran forbid you to go to Sheila's?"

"I did. There was an accident on the interstate that evening, not far from the gas station that I stopped at. A bus lost control and smashed into another car, killing the occupants. An elderly lady in the back and a young girl driving."

Tracy felt a shiver run down her spine. "That could have been you."

Camilla nodded.

"I wonder how she did that," said Tracy. "I wonder how Granny Sybs could find you. Just like that." Tracy snapped her fingers.

"It's her gift, her powers of sight. The same one that you have inherited. I don't know how she does it but she has saved me from embarrassing moments and dangerous situations countless times over the years. I have learnt to trust her instincts without question. It's real, Trace, this gift of yours. Use it wisely, and it will bring you only good things."

"Good morning," said Dylan as he stepped into the kitchen. He stretched his arms into the air and yawned. "What's for breakfast? I'm famished."

"Morning sleepy-head," said Harold.

"Morning Dyl," said Camilla. "Been waiting for you."

"What do mean, waiting?"

"Just sit down at the table," said Camilla. "Both of you." She gestured to Dylan and Harold.

Tracy watched as her mother went into the kitchen and returned with a large chocolate cake covered in candles.

Tracy clamped her hand over her mouth in surprise. "Mom!"

Camilla beamed. "Happy birthday Trace."

Harold started lighting the candles. "There you go."

"Looks like we need to call in the fire brigade," said Dylan.

"Oh, shut-up, Dylan," said Tracy.

"Just blow them out already. Otherwise I'm going to have to get the fire extinguisher."

"Dylan! It's enough," reprimanded Camilla.

Tracy took a deep breath and blew. She had to take another breath to blow out the remaining five candles.

"Make a wish," said her father with a smile.

"Just be careful what you wish for," said Dylan. "It may come true."

Tracy closed her eyes. The tiny, individual flames from the candles still glowed red behind her eyelids. She thought of her family and then Josh popped into her head. That kiss… Dylan's words echoed inside her head. 'Be careful what you wish for.' If only her brother knew about her gift. And then she began to wonder if her gift of sight influenced her wish. She dismissed the idea, wishing that she could travel to an exotic destination. She pictured a place filled with interesting people and fascinating cultures. She opened her eyes. "There," she said with a smile.

Dylan, Camilla, and Harold broke into song. "Happy birthday to you, happy birthday to you, happy birthday dear Tracy, happy birthday to you!"

Dylan continued singing. "Why was she born so beautiful why was she born at all? She's no use to anyone; she's no use at all."

Tracy stuck her tongue out at Dylan.

Harold handed Tracy a white envelope with her name written in bold on the front. "Happy birthday, my angel. May all your dreams come true."

"Thanks, guys," said Tracy, tearing open the envelope. The card was pink with a large 17 on the front in a silver-embossed

76

font. She opened it, and something dropped out and onto the table. It was another rectangular card. "Holy shit," said Tracy in awe. "It's a ticket. A plane ticket!" she exclaimed, picking it up off the table. She turned it over. "Istanbul!" She looked at the date. "Whaaaat!? This is next week! What about school?"

"Well, Monday 19th of Feb is a holiday, so you'll only be missing three days of school," said her father.

"George Washington's birthday."

Harold nodded. "We leave on Thursday and will be back Tuesday."

"Are we all going?"

Harold smiled. "No. It will just be the two of us. I need to visit Turkey for my latest research project. I thought it would be nice for you to join me. You've never been, and Turkey is a very interesting place with an amazing culture."

The hairs on Tracy's arms lifted. She shivered as Dylan's mocking words played over in her head once again.

"Thank you, Daddy," said Tracy hugging her father. "Thanks, Mom."

"Only a pleasure," said Harold and Camilla together.

"I'm so excited!" said Tracy jumping up and down. "What's the weather like this time of year?"

"It's winter, just like here," said her father. "About fifty degrees."

"Lucky fish," said Dylan with a long face. "I wish I could go overseas."

"Sorry, but there aren't any more wishes left," said Tracy. "I used them all up," she said with a wink.

"Yeah, whatever," said Dylan.

"Don't worry, Dyl," said Camilla. "You'll get your turn. Promise."

"Okay, now what's for breakfast? And don't say cake," said Dylan.

"Cake," said Tracy with a grin.

"Oh, shut-up!"

"Will you two ever stop fighting?" said Camilla with a sigh.

She shook her head. "Guess not," she mumbled to herself. "I'm making scrambled eggs," she continued, cracking several eggs into a bowl in the kitchen.

"Great!" said Dylan, whipping out his phone.

The back of Tracy's head tingled. She scratched it absentmindedly, closing her eyes for a moment. She pictured Lisa dialling her number. She opened her eyes and stared at her phone as it began to ring. She answered it without even looking at the screen. "Morning Lis."

"Good morning, birthday girl," said Lisa on the other end. How are you feeling?"

"Great, thanks."

"Ohhh. My head hurts."

"Too much to drink?"

"I think it was that stuff that Paul gave me."

"What was in it?"

"Dunno but it was green and tasted foul."

"Yuck," said Tracy, pulling a face. "He must have mixed a bunch of stuff together."

"Yeah. Anyway, I still had loads of fun. What you up to today?"

"Oh, just chilling I guess. You won't believe what my folks bought me for my birthday."

"What?"

"A plane ticket to Turkey!"

"No friggin ways Trace!"

"Yes, ways! And I'm going next week with my Dad. I'm missing school for a couple of days."

"Eeeeek! I don't believe it! Take me with you!"

"I wish."

"What you gonna do? Where you staying?"

"My Dad is busy with this research for work and stuff, so I guess I'll hang with him and maybe see some sights." Tracy shrugged her shoulders and glanced across at her father, who winked at her in response.

"He's only just told me, so we haven't exactly discussed the itinerary, but you'll be the first to know."

"I'll hold you to that, Tracy Barnes," said Lisa. "I want to know each and every detail."

Tracy giggled. "Yes, ma'am!"

"Just be careful of the Turks," said Lisa. "I hear they love blondes."

"Really?"

"Yes. It's because nearly all of the Turkish women are dark-skinned with dark hair."

"Okay, makes sense, I guess."

"But don't worry, you have Professor Indiana Barnes to take care of you."

Tracy laughed again, imagining her father in an adventurer's hat, a coiled up leather whip in one hand and a pistol in the other, ready to take on a horde of zombies from the Peruvian rain forest. "Just call me Lara. Lara Croft."

"Yeah, I can see the headlines now: Father and daughter team up to search the catacombs beneath the city of Turkey, discovering ancient tombs filled with long-forgotten treasures."

"Ha-ha! You crack me up, Lis."

"Okay, let me not keep you from your tomb-raiding. The world is at stake, and you gotta save us from a zombie horde!"

"Ha-ha-ha! Thanks for calling, Lis. Love you."

"Love you, Trace. Have the best day. Chat later. Bye."

"Bye."

"How's Lisa?" said Camilla dishing up a plate of delicious scrambled eggs and placing it down in front of Tracy. Hot steam rose up off the plate. Tracy's mouth watered.

"Oh, she's great. Crazy as ever. You know Lisa."

"Indeed, I do." Camilla's teeth flashed in a broad smile. She scooped the rest of the eggs into plates for Harold and Dylan.

10 ~ Up & Away

Tracy had a smile on her face all week. She was so busy at school that the days seemed to fly by. Before she knew it, it was Wednesday, and she was packing her bag for Turkey. "Mohhhhm!" She shouted from her room. "Where's my beanie?!"

Silence.

"Mohhhm!"

Camilla stepped into the room. "Will you please stop shouting? Are you talking about your black one?"

"No. The green and orange one. You know, the one that Gran bought me."

"Sorry, hun. Haven't seen it."

"Shit. I loved that beanie. It was so comfy. I've got this yellow one with a bright, pink pom-pom on top." She held up the beanie. "It's so kitsch, and the black one is so boooring."

"Do you *really* need one, though? Dad said that Turkish winters aren't that cold."

Tracy looked at her mother with an exasperated glare. "It's not about *that*, Mom."

"Oh, sorry. It's about the look, right?"

Tracy ignored her mother's question by turning back to

80

rummage in her drawers. "Ah! My drawers are such a mess!" she snapped.

"I'll check my cupboard," said Camilla. "Otherwise, you can borrow mine. My blue one?"

"Okay, thanks, Mom," grumbled Tracy, without looking up.

A few moments later, Camilla was back. "Here," she said, holding out a pale blue woollen beanie. "Couldn't find your green one."

Tracy took it, albeit reluctantly. "Thanks."

"Will it work?" said Camilla. "It goes with just about anything."

Tracy pulled the beanie over her head. She looked in the mirror and adjusted her hair. "Thanks. It's perfect," She smiled. "Better than my others for sure." She hugged her mom.

"You must be excited," said Camilla. "You're going to have so much fun!"

Tracy grinned. "I just hope Dad has some time to show me around. I don't quite fancy hanging around him if he is going to be working most of the time."

"Don't worry. He told me that he has quite a few nice things planned." Camilla smiled.

"He hasn't said a thing to me," said Tracy in dismay.

"Don't tell him I said anything but he wants to surprise you."

"I won't. Promise." For the first time, Tracy felt butterflies in her stomach.

"You are going to love Turkey. The first time I was there was with your Dad many years ago. We travelled around quite a bit. The culture is interesting, and there is so much to see."

"I know. I'm so excited!"

◊ ◊ ◊

Tracy gazed around O'Hare's Terminal 5. "Wow. It's like a giant shopping centre."

"Did you know that it's the largest international terminal in the US?" said Harold.

"Bigger than JFK?"

"The biggest. In fact, if you include domestic flights, O'Hare is the second busiest airport in the States."

"Shoo. Never knew that."

"Come, let's check-in, and then we can grab a bite to eat."

Tracy followed her father as he led them to the Turkish Airlines check-in counter. A friendly lady greeted them as they arrived. "Good evening. May I please have your passports?" She had a strange accent. Tracy glanced at her name badge. *Azra Polat.*

"Good evening," said Harold handing over their passports.

"Anything sharp or flammable in your hand luggage?" She pointed to a laminated sign on the counter that said, *Restricted Articles,* with thumbnail pictures of a gun, a syringe, nail clippers, scissors, a pen-knife, an umbrella and a set of tools on one side and a host of unrecognisable, flammable aerosol containers on the other.

"Nope," said Harold.

Tracy zoned out. She turned around to watch all the people moving about the terminal like a colony of ants all programmed to perform particular functions. There was a hum of excitement in the air that caused those butterflies to flit about again in her tummy.

"Okay, we're all set," said her father flashing the boarding passes in Tracy's face. "Let's go."

"Where to?"

"Swissport Lounge."

"We're going to a lounge?"

"Yup."

"Cool. Does that mean we get free food?"

"Well, technically, yes. You can eat whatever you like."

"Yesss." Tracy fist-pumped the air.

◊ ◊ ◊

The lounge overlooked the terminal on one side and the airport runways on the other. Tracy gazed out of the long, curved glass windows at the rows of aircraft parked below. They reminded her of Dylan's planes stacked across the windowsill in his room. Tracy watched as a Boeing touched down in a puff of white smoke in the distance and a tractor pulled a row of luggage carts across the tarmac just below.

"Here you go," said Harold handing Tracy a glass of ice-cold apple juice. "Your favourite."

"Thanks, Dad. You're the best!"

Harold grinned. "Go and get yourself something to eat." He pointed at the open fridge. "I'm just gonna sit here and catch up on my mails," he continued, pulling his laptop out of his bag.

Tracy grabbed a tomato, basil and Emmental cheese sandwich on rye and a small Greek salad and sat down across from her father. She popped her headphones into her ears, opened the music app on her iPhone, and Ariana Grande's sweet, melodic voice filled her head. She closed her eyes and took a generous bite into her sandwich, savouring the mouthful of flavours that exploded inside her mouth. "Hmmm. So tasty," she said, her mouth still full of bread and cheese.

Harold winked at her from the other side of the table and then turned his attention back to his screen.

Tracy washed down the sandwich with some apple juice and then began to pick at her salad. "Dad," she said.

"Yup?" Harold looked up again.

"What's our itinerary looking like?"

"I have some exciting things planned," he winked again.

"Okay, I get it. It's a surprise. At least give me a clue?"

"Well, since it's your first time in Turkey, we're doing some of the usual touristy things, but with a twist."

Tracy opened up her phone browser, typed *Turkey with a twist*, and hit *Search*. The first thing that came up was a tangy Turkey recipe. She erased the search bar and typed, *What to see in*

Istanbul. She scanned the results, tapped on *The top 10 things to do in Instanbul.* The screen went blank for a moment before revealing a list of familiar attractions. "Wait, we're going to Istanbul, right?"

"We're landing there, yes."

"So we're not staying in Istanbul?"

"We are, but we're also going somewhere else," said Harold with a grin.

"Da-ad! Why are you being so cryptic?"

Tracy wiped the search bar again and typed, *What to do in Turkey.* She waited a moment for her browser. "Aha! Sixty-four cool and unusual things to do in Turkey! That's it!" She tapped her screen. "Hang on. 64 things. That's way too much. I'll never guess. Let me see. Cappadocia, cities carved out of ancient, volcanic rock. Wowee. Pammukale water terraces, Basilica cisterns of Instanbul, Lycian rock tombs." Tracy smiled as she remembered her conversation with Lisa about raiding tombs. *Why not?* she thought to herself. She hazarded a wild guess. "Dad, are we going tomb raiding?"

Harold laughed out loud. "You've been watching too many movies. Sorry. No. We're not going tomb raiding. Number one, it's illegal and number two, there aren't any tombs to raid."

"Oh, I thought maybe…"

"You have a great imagination. Actually we're going somewhere better. Somewhere magical," whispered Harold.

"Dad, you're such a tease!"

Harold took a bite out of an apple and then glanced at his watch. "Why don't you grab some dessert? We need to get to the boarding gate soon."

"I'm pretty full, thanks." She eyed the open fridge and spotted a tray filled will mini chocolate brownie squares. "Ahh, I'm going on holiday, why not?" she said, standing up and making her way over to the delectable treats. She popped one into her mouth and took a second one for good measure. "Hmm. These are delicious. Try one, Dad." Tracy held out the other brownie.

84

"Thanks, but no thanks," said her father, taking another big bite of his apple.

"Dad, I'm surprised that Mom hasn't taught you how to make a girl feel better about herself."

"Huh? What do you mean?"

"If a girl offers you something sweet, you should always say yes. It makes them feel better about eating it themselves. Us girls are always conscious about our weight."

"But you're far from fat."

"Aah!"

"What?"

"Please try to never even say that word. It's evil."

"But I mean it."

"No. Stop. You're making it worse."

"Okay, okay, I'm sorry. Okay, let me try one," he said, holding out his hand.

"No. Now it's too late. Just remember for next time, okay?"

"Okay. Sure." Harold shook his head. "You girls. Always making the most trivial things so complicated. I guess I'll never really be able to work it out." He chuckled to himself.

◊ ◊ ◊

She stared out of the window. Millions of tiny lights flickered like fireflies from the ground below as the giant metallic bird rose up into the night sky. The deafening roar from the twin jet engines at maximum thrust drowned out all other sounds as the g-force pulled the butterflies right out of Tracy's belly. The gravitational pull subsided as the aircraft began to level off. Tracy settled back into her seat and pulled out *Skylife*, Turkish Airlines' in-flight magazine. She flipped to the entertainment schedule at the back and scanned through the list of movies and series available during the flight. She plugged in her headphones and skipped through the channels, finally settling on a television series called *Riversdale*, about a group of young school kids and their adventures. She read the synopsis in the magazine: Season 3, Episode 6: *Tensions mount when the closure of Northside High forces Mickey and his fellow classmates to transfer to Riversdale High. Nerine ensures Mark and Stephanie that she still approves of their plans for Jefferson.* Tracy glanced over at her father who was reading a book. He looked up and winked. She smiled in return.

◊ ◊ ◊

Tracy woke with a start. She vigorously rubbed the back of her stiff neck and pulled the flimsy, blue, aircraft-issued blanket up over her cold arms. She wondered why the airlines could never get the air-con temperature right. It was always a couple of degrees too cold. She remembered reading somewhere that most of the air inside the plane came from the engines' compressors that are used to warm and pressurise the much colder air from outside. She pushed up the window-blind and gazed out into the darkness. Her seat was just aft of the plane's wing. She stared at the tiny red light winking steadily back at her on the wing-tip. Something outside moved at the edge of her peripheral vision. Had she imagined it? She blinked and then pressed her nose onto the cold, plexiglass window. There it was again. This time closer. Closer. She jumped, quickly pulling her face away. Her eyes widened.

Impossible!

A leaf had come to land on the other side of the window, pressed flat against the glass like a piece of wet newspaper. She turned to her father, but he was fast asleep, his eye-mask partially covering his forehead. She turned back to the window, but the leaf was gone. She pressed her nose against the plexiglass and squinted into the darkness. She ignored the cold shiver that ran from her nose over her skull and down the nape of her neck. She rubbed her eyes and glared out of the window again. It was there. She saw it. And then her common sense kicked in. The aircraft must be cruising at around 40,000 feet.

86

There was no way that a leaf would be drifting about at this altitude, and even if by some miracle it was, how could it end up being pressed against the window of the plane? *Her* window! She craned her neck to look out and up into the sky. Darkness. Nothing but darkness.

Tracy pulled the plastic blind down and dropped back into her seat. Her mind raced. It was a sign. The leaf. Another sign from Sambethe. There was no other explanation. She pinched her arm. She wasn't dreaming. What could it mean? What was Sambethe trying to tell her? She looked at the blind. She was tempted to open it again. Instead, she pushed her pods into her ears and tuned into one of the music channels. She pulled up her blanket, closed her eyes, and tried to go back to sleep, but she couldn't get the image of the leaf out of her mind. The leaf became many. Thousands of leaves falling from the sky, falling like snow, drifting, floating down from above, spinning and twisting through the air as they fell. The leaves were so many that they began to rise around her until completely covered her. They were soft and comforting, gentle, delicate. She let the weight of her body go. She let it fall into the bed of leaves. She felt relaxed, cosy, safe. The leaves continued to fall until there was nothing but darkness, the deep, tranquil darkness of sleep.

This time she dreamed. She dreamed of a foreign place and yet she knew that it wasn't the first time that she had visited this place. It was dark. There was a light in the distance. A bright light. She had to shield her eyes from it as she approached. She had been in the darkness for a very long time. Too long. It was time to emerge. It was time to share her wisdom with others. It was all in her head, and it needed to be released, lest it explode with such force, she knew that she would not survive the tumult. She was the Sybil. She was the oracle that spent many long days and nights inside the cave of secrets. The cave where she went to receive the powerful visions that came to her in the darkness. The visions that spoke of things to come. Of things that were meant to be. Of things that were hidden to others but her. Of things that she was chosen to reveal to those that would listen.

She came forth from the cave, and the light blinded her, yet she could still see. She could see the words of prophecy. She could see the light of truth. It burned brighter than the noonday sun, painfully seared forever behind her eyelids. Her audience was there. Waiting. They chanted her name, and she responded by raising her arms. She dropped to her knees and lifted a limestone from the ground. She used it to scratch words onto the rocks around the cave. The light behind her eyes dimmed with each word released until her vision gradually returned and the burning pain subsided to a dull throb. She finally collapsed onto the ground, exhausted from lack of food, water, and sleep, her hands raw from her fervent scratching. Her devotees lifted her up, high above their heads, and carried her away to rest and heal her battered body.

11 ~ Evidence

Richmond field office Chief, Gregory Williams sat back in his leather-bound chair, lifted his black, shiny brogues onto the corner of his desk and casually crossed one foot over the other. "What do you make of it, Trudeau? Gang-related?" He instinctively smoothed his hand over his bald, brown head.

Special Agent Wesley Trudeau sat on the other side of the desk, scrutinising the gory images in the file. He frowned. There had been a spate of gang-related killings recently, which is why it was the first question Williams asked of him. The FBI team at Richmond had been tasked by the headquarters in Washington to root out anything related to gang-related activity in the area. "Could be, sir. The victim's eyes were missing."

"Missing?!" Williams jumped bolt upright in his seat. "What do you mean missing?"

"I mean they were gouged out and are nowhere to be found."

"Holy crap."

"Yeah, it's pretty creepy."

"Do we know who he is?"

"Mark Landman. 45. Car salesman from Montrose. Wife and one dependent. He has no criminal history. Nadda."

"His family been notified?"

"Yessir."

"So no leads or witnesses?"

"No, sir. Nothing. A farm worker found him yesterday just off the 288, right next to Pocahontas State Park. Autopsy report says his neck was cut from ear to ear around two days ago. The killer used a long, sharp blade in one, clean stroke. They found a few microscopic fragments from the blade. Here's where it gets interesting." Trudeau looked up at the Chief who swung his legs off the desk in anticipation. "It was made out of obsidian."

"Obsidian? Isn't that a type of rock or something?"

Trudeau nodded. "Volcanic rock."

"Fuck."

"Actually, volcanic glass." Trudeau held up his phone to read from his web browser. "Obsidian is a hard, dark, glass-like volcanic rock formed by the rapid solidification of lava without crystallisation. It's sharper than steel."

"Sharper than steel? Wow. Never knew that."

"Yes, apparently it says here that under a microscope, the sharpest steel blade is uneven, while obsidian is smooth."

"Huh! Just like glass."

Trudeau nodded. "The fragments have been sent to a special lab for further tests. They do something called obsidian hydration dating, which will determine the age of the fragments. This may help us trace the weapon's origin."

"So, the victim was a car salesman. Hmm. Where's his car?"

"We're working with the police who have an APB out for it. It's a silver BMW X5."

"So, the killer stole it?"

"Apparently. We're still working on the motive. Not many leads, unfortunately."

"Okay, Trudeau," said the Chief glancing at his watch. "Keep me posted if anything else comes up. I need to get to my next appointment."

Trudeau nodded. "Yes, sir," he said, turning back to the file as Chief Williams stepped out of the office. He scratched his head, trying in vain to figure out why an unarmed, used car salesman was brutally killed and dumped on the side of a highway. *Was the killer a disgruntled hitch-hiker? A psychopath on the warpath?* There were too many unanswered questions to warrant even suggesting a single reason that made any sense whatsoever. Trudeau closed the file, grabbed his keys from his desk, and made his way outside. He was itching to get to the scene of the crime like the craving for a cigarette. It had been a little over a year since he quit and the cravings hadn't diminished. There were those times that he thought he'd crack, like immediately after dinner, or followed by a couple of drinks at the bar. He looked up at the sky and silently prayed to himself. *God, give me strength.* He squeezed his hands into fists and popped a piece of mint-flavoured gum into his mouth. He ground his teeth into the tiny piece of gum, making a concerted effort to focus on the task at hand.

Trudeau checked the GPS coordinates and then stepped out of his vehicle. The first thing he noticed was the dark, blood-stained smear on the road. It began in the middle and stretched diagonally across in a snake-like pattern for about ten yards. He followed the smear until it came to an end where the tarmac met the gravel on the roadside. There were still traces of dry blood in the sand, but they were far less apparent. A red marker flag protruded from a thicket of bushes nearby, signalling where the deceased's body was found. Trudeau turned around and closed his eyes, trying to picture the scene of the incident in his head.

Okay. The victim was sliced. His car must have been stationary when it happened because there is no sign of an accident following the murder. Trudeau played out all the scenarios in his head. *He could have been killed somewhere else and brought here to be dumped. Possible, but unlikely because of all the blood in the road. Most of the victim's blood would have drained out on the journey over here. Instead, it's all over the*

91

road and in the bushes.

Trudeau took a deep breath. The smell of nature permeated his nostrils.

And if the victim was killed elsewhere, why would the killer not place the body in a bag or something? Why drag the body from the car and leave a fresh trail of evidence for us to find? The killer is either really dumb or incredibly bold. Trudeau worried deeply about the latter. *Boldness leads to fearlessness, and fearlessness leads to having complete disregard for the law. This had to be the work of a psychopath.* He wondered where the killer was headed next. He turned around and gazed into the forest. *Did the killer come from the forest or was he in the car already?*

Trudeau crouched down onto his haunches and examined the blood-caked bushes. Something glinting in the sunlight caught his eye. He stood up and pulled a pair of cream-coloured surgical gloves from his pocket. The snapping sound of the latex on his skin as he pulled them on, caused a startled bird to flee from a tree nearby. He reached down and picked up the shiny object. It was a ring, caked with dry blood. He dropped it into a tiny ziplock bag and placed it inside his jacket pocket. He pulled off his gloves, made his way back to government-issued black Buick and called Doctor Lloyton, head of the forensics department back at his office.

"Hey, Doc, what's up?"

"Agent Trudeau?"

"Yep, it's me. Any further clues on the Landman case?"

"Actually, yes. We found some foreign hair on the victim. Tests have just come in."

"And?" Trudeau's heart thumped in his ear pressed up against the phone.

"Caucasian. Female. Black hair."

"Hmm. Could it be his wife's?"

"We don't know that, sir. We would need some of her hair to corroborate that hypothesis."

Trudeau pulled the ring out of his pocket. He held it up to the light and peered at it through the plastic. *Or maybe not.*

"I found a ring at the scene of the crime," he said into his phone. "It's caked in blood. Must belong to the killer. And it's narrow and small enough to belong to a female." Trudeau squinted his eyes as he examined the ring, noticing an unfamiliar pattern on the outside.

"Bring it in, and we'll run some tests," said Doctor Lloyton. "I'm certain the ring will contain traces of DNA that we can compare to the strands of hair that we found."

"Any word on the age of those obsidian particles?"

"Sorry. Not yet. It's a very particular test that needs to be conducted off-site."

"Yeah, I know. Obsidian hydration."

"Yes, and the lab we sent it to has only just received the samples."

"Okay, great. Thanks, Doc."

Trudeau dropped the ring into his pocket and looked around the crime scene one last time before heading back to the FBI office in Richmond. He couldn't stop thinking about the new evidence. The killer was female. He pictured a psychopathic woman with black hair wielding a long, narrow obsidian blade.

Very interesting. Very interesting, indeed.

12 ~ First Night

"Wow. This is huge!" said Tracy gazing around the airport terminal. "Even bigger than O'Hare."

"Yes, it's Istanbul's brand new airport, the biggest airport in the world. Or it will be when it's finished," said her father, as they made their way towards the baggage hall.

"It's not finished?"

"Phase one was only opened recently. It's being built in stages over a period of over ten years."

"Ten years?"

"Yup." Harold smiled. "The final phase is due to be completed in 2030."

"That's just mad."

"There will be six runways, four terminal buildings, hotels, and even a state palace!"

"Huh? A palace?"

"Yeah. It's a thing here in Turkey. You'll see."

"How come you know all this stuff?"

Harold chuckled. "I read it in an article on the plane. When it's finished, the airport will have the capacity to service close to 200 million passengers every year."

"Jeez. That's a lot."

"There are our bags." Harold pointed at the baggage carousel. "Great, they're almost first out."

"Didn't you know?" said Tracy.

"What?"

"Bags belonging to cultural anthropology professors always come out first."

"Ha-ha. How'd you figure that one out?"

"Well, because we're in a city filled with a vibrant culture, of course!"

"Clever girl. How come I never thought of that?"

"Because it needs someone clever like me to work it out. Who other than the daughter of a professor?" Tracy took a mini curtsy.

"Trace, you bring a smile to my face."

Tracy grinned. "Thanks for this," she said, hugging her father. "I'm so excited."

Harold smiled. "Whoops," he said, turning around to grab their bags off the carousel. "Almost missed these," he huffed, lifting them up one at a time onto the trolley.

◊ ◊ ◊

"Welcome to the Intercontinental, Professor Barnes," said the hotel clerk at the check-in desk. "Mrs. Barnes." he said, turning to Tracy.

"Umm. That's Miss Barnes. This is my daughter." Harold winked at Tracy.

"My humblest apologies, Professor. Miss Barnes," he continued, bowing his head. "Please, help yourselves to some apple tea."

"Why, thank you," said Tracy. "Hmm, this smells nice," she said, almost dipping her nose into the dainty cup of hot, herbal tea.

"Our porter will show you to your rooms," said the clerk, gesturing to a man in a dusty orange suit and red fez, standing nearby. "I hope that you enjoy your stay with us. Don't hesitate to call me personally if there's anything that you need."

Tracy followed her father and the porter to the elevator. They ascended to the fourth floor, and then the porter took them down the passage to their rooms. Tracy opened her door and walked over to the window. The lights of the city reflected across a huge body of water. "Wow. Awesome!"

"That's the Bosphorus," said Harold, coming to stand next to Tracy. "It connects the Black Sea with the Sea of Marmara. It's part of the border between Europe and Asia."

"Cool. It's so pretty at night."

"How you feeling? You tired? Hungry?"

"Wide awake. Maybe a little peckish. Can we just order some room service?"

"Sure. My room's right next to yours. Let me know if you need anything else. I know your body's telling you it's morning but try get some sleep because we've got a busy day tomorrow."

"Sure, Dad. I'll try to. Goodnight."

"Night."

Tracy turned back to the window. She imagined how even more spectacular the view was going to be in the morning. She kicked off her shoes, lay down on her bed, and called reception.

"Hello, reception, how can I help you?" said a female voice in a Turkish accent.

"Hi. Please can I have the wifi code?"

"It's *bosphorus*. All lower case."

Tracy smiled. "Thank you. Oh, and can you please put me through to room service?"

"Certainly. Please hold." Some traditional Turkish music began playing in the background. She heard a violin, a flute, what sounded like a guitar and a few other unfamiliar sounds. A female was singing in Turkish. It was strangely melodic.

"Good evening. Room service. How can I help you?"

"Hi. Can I please order a burger and chips?"

"Yes. One burger and chips."

"Wait," said Tracy, all of a sudden. "What is your speciality? I mean, what is nice on your menu?" She felt stupid for asking such a random question.

"We have several Turkish speciality dishes," said the voice on the other end. "Do you like meat or vegetarian?"

"Um. Meat, please."

"Well, we have the kofte which is made with balls of ground beef, flavoured with our traditional Turkish sauce, served with flatbread. Then we have manti. Small, boiled lamb dumplings, served with yogurt and spices. We have kuzu tandir. Slow, roasted lamb strips, served with rice or potatoes and yogurt."

"Hmm. That one sounds good. Can I please order that last one, with potatoes please?"

"Certainly ma'am. Can I get you something to drink?"

"Yes, please. Can I get a Coke Light and some still water?"

"Yes. Of course. Anything else?"

"No, thanks. That's all."

"Very good. That will take approximately twenty to thirty minutes."

"Thanks." Tracy placed the receiver down and connected her phone to the wifi. She began typing out a message. *Hi Mom. Just arrived at hotel. All safe. It's evening here. Just ordered room service. Love you xxx*

Without waiting for a response from her mother, she opened up her chat with Lisa and began texting. *Hey girl. Turkey is awesome. Just arrived at hotel. Staying in sick room overlooking this huge river called the Bosphorus. Luv it here. How's school?* Laughing emoji.

Within seconds, her phone vibrated with a response from Lisa. *Bitch. Hate you,* followed by an emoji face with its tongue sticking out. *I'm sitting here in class with that Perkins cow, while you live it up overseas. Shit. Wish I was there with you.*

Tracy grinned and began typing out a response. *Please take notes for me, bae?*

Lisa replied: *You kidding, right? Jeez, I'm gonna kill you. Can't talk now. Chat later. Bye.*

Tracy's phone vibrated again, and a message from her

mother popped onto the screen. *Hi, my baby. Glad to hear you're safe. Please send me pics! Love you!*

I will. Promise, she responded.

Tracy switched to her camera, flipped to the front view and looked at herself on the screen. She ran her hands through her hair, pulling some of it across her face, pouted her lips a little and snapped a shot. She looked around the room, looking for something Turkish to use as a backdrop. A washed-out, watercolour painting of Istanbul was hanging on the other side of the room. *That will have to do,* she thought to herself. She snapped another picture and loaded the photo onto Instagram stories with the caption, *Istanbul. Living the dream.* She climbed back into bed and switched on the television. She turned down the sound, reached over for her backpack, and pulled out her book. She glanced at the cover image of a topless man in a pair of black denims that reminded her of Josh. She closed her eyes, and her mind drifted back to her birthday party. She smiled as she pictured Josh holding her. And that kiss. Tracy sighed deeply. She swooned, feeling quite giddy all of a sudden. She opened her eyes and gazed at the cover image again. *Lost in the Passion* was the title of the book. It was a typical teenage love story, about a young girl falling for an older man. She was about half-way through, and things were starting to heat up. She opened the book and began to lose herself to the story.

13 - Sights & Sounds

It was only at around 2am that Tracy finally fell asleep. She slept peacefully, waking to the ringing sound of the hotel phone next to her bed. A wave of disorientation washed over her. She shook her head to clear her thoughts and lifted the receiver.

"Good morning!" said her father, excitement in his voice.

"What time is it?" she heard herself croak.

"8am. How did you sleep?"

"It feels like I haven't slept," she said, rubbing the sleep from her eyes.

"I know. It's the jet-lag. Jump in a hot shower. It'll make you feel better. I'll meet you downstairs for breakfast at eight-thirty. Okay?"

"Yeah, sure, Dad." Tracy put the phone down and yawned. She stretched her arms up above her head and then wrapped them around her cushion, curling her body into a foetal position on her left side. She closed her eyes. It felt as if an invisible weight was pressing them closed. She fought the voice inside her head, telling her to go back to sleep. *Come on, Tracy. Into the shower*, she heard her father say, silencing her nagging thoughts. She rolled over, stretched her arms and legs out under the covers one last time before making her way to the bathroom.

The shower did make her feel better as her father predicted. She smiled as the heat from the hot water warmed up her body, washing away the last remnants of sleep.

◊ ◊ ◊

"So, where are we going today?" said Tracy, spooning some strawberry yoghurt into her mouth.

Harold grinned. "Today we're going to visit the Hagia Sofia and Topkapi Palace, and maybe somewhere else if there's time."

"And tomorrow?"

"Surprise!"

"I hate surprises," grumbled Tracy. She closed her eyes, trying to work out if she could 'see' where her father was taking her. Nothing. "Ughh! This is no gift."

Harold looked at her quizzically. He laughed. "You're trying to see into the future!"

Tracy glared at her father. "Well, it's not working. It seems that I can't. I'm not an oracle," she snapped.

"I think that being frustrated doesn't really help, Trace. Your grandmother once told me that for her gift to work, her mind had to be still."

"I still can't believe that no one's ever told me." Tracy shook her head. She looked at her father. "Okay. So my mind must be still. What else?"

Harold shrugged his shoulders. "Not sure, Trace. Didn't Granny Sybs prepare you for this?"

"No. No one did," she said, fingering the stone hanging around her neck.

"What about that?" he pointed. "What about the crystal?"

Tracy squinted down at the rock around her neck and remembered her grandmother's words. "Of course! She said that it would help me focus my thoughts."

"Well? Why don't you try? Just hold it this time as you close your eyes." Harold smiled.

The pink stone glistened silently. Tracy took hold of it in

her right hand and closed her eyes once more. She focused her intention on the crystal, visualising its texture, its hues, its shape - still nothing. Her mind wandered. Just as she was about to give up, something strange happened. The hairs on the nape of her neck rose. She felt a tingling sensation, like an intuitive feeling that began not in her mind, but her heart. Her chest felt restricted, under pressure. She had to force her lungs to breathe, to suck in some air. A single shape protruded from the mist inside her mind. It was blurred, misshapen. And then it became clear, recognisable. She saw the shape of an animal. It was a carving. A wooden carving. No. It was a rock carving. She ran her hand over the rough outline of the animal. Her fingertips grew hot as if they were being burned. She instinctively pulled her hand away to look at her fingers, but they appeared to be normal. The searing sensation disappeared. Tracy lifted her head. The mist was gone, replaced by an expanse of water. She was in a boat, and it was moving. She strained her eyes to see the horizon, but it was obscured, as if something or someone deliberately blocked her vision, not wanting her to see beyond a certain point. She opened her eyes and realised that she was swaying gently from side to side. She gripped the sides of her chair to steady herself.

"And? What did you see?"

Tracy looked at her father and frowned. "I was in a boat, on a river." She cast her gaze up towards the ceiling. "It was so... real, like I was there, like I could touch the water." She looked down at the floor, expecting to see the river as the current pushed her along.

Harold smiled. "Anything else?"

Tracy closed her eyes again. "An animal. I touched it. It was carved into stone."

"Wow," said Harold, aghast. "Remarkable. You could never have known."

"So it worked? Is this some of the stuff that we're going to see tomorrow?"

Harold grinned. "Maybe."

101

"Da-ad! I'm right, aren't I?"

Harold avoided her question. "Come on, finish up otherwise we're going to be late."

"I knew it!" She squinted down at the crystal again and smiled, bringing it to meet her lips so that she could kiss it. "Granny Sybs would be proud." She spooned the last few mouthfuls of yoghurt into her mouth and swallowed it down with the rest of her apple tea. She savoured the taste of the sweet tea and realised that she was quickly becoming used to the Turkish custom of drinking it. "Dad, please can we buy some apple tea sometime? It's so nice."

"Sure." Harold looked at his watch. "If there's time today, I'll take you to the Grand Bazaar. They sell everything under the sun."

"Thanks, Daddy. Love you."

Harold smiled. "I love you too, my munchkin."

◊ ◊ ◊

Tracy gazed out of the taxi window at the beautiful dome of the Hagia Sofia and the four minarets flanking it. It was an impressive sight.

Her father leaned over. "Beautiful, isn't it? It was first built in 537 CE."

"Wow! That's old," remarked Tracy.

"Remember Dan Brown's Inferno?"

Tracy nodded. "I saw the movie as well."

"The Hagia Sofia features in the story. Remember that?"

Tracy's mouth dropped. "Of course! Yes! I remember now." She looked at the structure in a new light. "I remember that scene when they went deep underground, and there was that fight in the water. Is there really water beneath the Hagia Sophia?"

Harold smiled. "The Basilica Cistern is about 160 yards southwest of the Hagia Sophia. That's what you would remember from the movie. It's a huge, cavernous chamber, filled with over 300 marble columns, and yes, it's filled with water, with the capacity to hold over 100,000 tons of it."

"Wow!"

"Currently, though, the Basilica only holds a few feet of water."

"Just like in the movie!"

"Uh-huh."

The taxi came to a stop.

"Teşekkür ederim. Keep the change," Harold said, handing the driver 40 Turkish Lira.

Tracy climbed out of the Taxi. She looked up into the sky, pulling her mom's blue woollen beanie over her ears. It was chilly. She smiled as she breathed in her mother's sweet, florally scent.

"Come, have a look over here," beckoned her father as he walked towards a garden adjacent to the entrance to the Hagia Sophia that towered majestically above them. "I want to show this to you first. These are the remains of the second Hagia Sophia." He pointed at several eroded marble blocks protruding out of the ground.

"What do you mean the second?"

"The Hagia Sophia was originally built as a Church on top of the foundation of a Pagan temple. There's nothing left of the first version. It was burnt down during some riots at the time."

"Wait, I'm confused," said Tracy. "If there's nothing left of the first version and these are the remains of the second Church, is that version three?" She pointed at the huge dome behind them.

"Correct," said Harold with a smile. "What's also interesting is that the Hagia Sophia is the only structure of its kind in the world that has served three different religions."

"You mentioned Pagan and Christian," said Tracy. "What's the third?"

"Islam."

Tracy face-palmed her hand to her forehead with a smack.

103

"Of course!"

"Some people dispute the Pagan link, but there are dozens of symbols and embossed columns scattered all over the structure depicting the trident of Neptune, dolphins and even an Ankh, the Egyptian key of life," said her father.

"Egyptian? But that's not Pagan."

"I know. It's a real mystery."

"What does it really mean, Hagia Sophia?"

"Holy Wisdom, referring to the second member of the Christian Holy Trinity."

"Dad, you're like an encyclopedia of facts!"

Harold smiled. "It's part of the work that I do."

"I know, but it's still pretty impressive."

"Come, let's go and explore inside," said Harold, leading Tracy into the massive structure. "Look. See?" said Harold pointing at the huge circular murals written in Arabic inside the dome.

"What do they say?" said Tracy.

"They depict the names of Muhammed, Allah, and several others."

"It's not still a mosque today, is it?"

"Ha-ha. No, Trace. It was converted into a museum in 1935."

"Oh! Okay. Makes sense," she said. "I can't get over the size of it. And the dome," she continued, tilting her head back to gaze in awe at the huge structure. "It looks like it's just floating up there. Just to think it's almost 2,000 years old. Incredible!"

"Yes. It was the largest man-made structure for over 1,000 years. When the daylight shines through all of those windows up there, it blots out the dome's support beams, making it look like it's just floating in thin air."

Tracy pulled out her phone and began to take some pics. "Excuse me," she said to a young couple walking by. "Please can you take a photo?" she held out her phone. "Dad, come," she beckoned to her father.

The young man, an Asian, smiled, bowed his head and took

her phone. Tracy put her arm around her father and smiled. "Thank you," she said after the man was finished. He handed back her phone, bowed his head again and returned to his partner, waving goodbye as he left. Tracy posted the photo to her feed with the caption, *Robert Langdon eat your heart out.*

14 ~ Diamonds

Tracy and her father finally stepped out of the Hagia Sophia after over two hours of touring through its magnificent structure.

"Thanks, Dad. That was really interesting. Now to the Topkapi Palace?"

Harold nodded. "Yep."

"I take it it's also been converted into a museum?"

"Yes. It was the Sultan's residence for a couple of centuries, first constructed in 1459."

"Are we catching another cab?" Tracy looked up and down the street.

"Nope. Topkapi Palace is less than a mile away."

"Oh, okay," she said, following her father in a northerly direction.

They soon reached a cobbled square with an ornately designed, small, square building about the size of a bus in its centre. Five small domes protruded out of the top of the structure.

"This is the fountain of Ahmed III, built in the early 1700s."

"Who was he?"

"He was a Sultan who loved Tulips."

"Ha-ha! That's funny. Tulips?" Tracy leaned over the low fence surrounding the building. She squinted her eyes. "What's that text inscribed on the sides?"

"It's poetry. Apparently in dedication of water. Come, I need to buy us tickets." Harold walked over to an impressive marble structure that towered high above them. "This is the Imperial Gate, the first gate to the palace. The ticket office is just through here."

"How many gates are there?" said Tracy gazing up at the gate in awe as they walked through.

"Oh, several." Harold paid for a pair of Topkapi Palace entrance tickets and led Tracy through another gate. "That was the first court," Harold pointed behind them. "This is the second court. In olden times, only the Sultan was allowed through this gate on horseback. Everyone else had to walk on foot."

Tracy looked around. The second court resembled a park with beautifully manicured grass and dozens of trees.

"The great Palace Kitchens are in that building to the right," Harold pointed as they walked. "And on the left is the Imperial Council Chamber. Come, let's go and look at the treasury. It houses the palace's arms collection."

The treasury building was as old as all the other buildings in the courtyard, but stepping inside, however, was a very different matter entirely. The interior was air-conditioned, modern and stylish, filled with dozens of glass-encased displays containing hundreds of headless mannequins in all sorts of attire. Tracy gazed through the glass at an ancient piece of metallic armour over one such mannequin, with a shiny, curved sword fastened to the waist.

"The armoury holds the richest set of Islamic arms in the world," said Harold.

"Wow! Look at these." Tracy looked up at a row of swords suspended on the wall in the centre of the room.

"That's a collection of the Sultan's swords. There are over

400 different types of arms from many different countries on display here," continued Harold.

Tracy saw daggers, helmets, shields, rifles, arrows, and many more swords on display. "Well, if we're under attack, I know exactly where to go," she said with a grin. "I think I'll take that." She pointed at a set of chain armour behind a glass case, with a black, slightly curved wooden scabbard attached at its side.

"Good choice. That's Japanese." Harold read the inscription on the glass. "Given to the Sultan as a gift in 1891. Very interesting."

Tracy snapped a shot. "Where's the famous Topkapi Dagger?"

"That's housed in the Imperial Treasury, in the third courtyard, the heart of the palace."

"But I thought you said that *this* was the treasury?"

"It used to be until it was converted into the armoury."

"Okay, so let's check it out."

"Sure," said Harold, leading Tracy from the armoury building and out into the courtyard again.

Tracy turned her face to the sun and closed her eyes for a moment. She welcomed the sun's warmth and smiled. But then something strange happened. Her eyes burned as if they were wide open and she was staring directly into the fiery orb in the sky. She dropped to her haunches and winced, bringing both palms to press against her eye sockets.

"Tracy?" said Harold, alarmed. "What's wrong? You all right?"

Tracy blinked her eyes open. The bright light and the sharp pain that followed had dissipated. She looked up at her father, who had one hand on her shoulder. All she could see was a blurry image of his face as it peered into hers. Gradually her vision cleared. She rubbed her eyes. They were tender.

"Tracy?"

"I'm okay."

"What... what happened?"

"I have no idea. One minute I was bathing my face in the

warmth of the sun, the next, it was as if I was staring directly at it and yet my eyes were closed." Images flashed through her mind. "The dream," she whispered.

"What dream?"

"The one that I had on the plane the other night."

A look of concern weighed heavily across Harold's face.

"The dream where I was a Sybil, and I stepped out of that cave." Tracy closed her eyes, and she remembered like it was yesterday. "It was so dark, so very dark, for a long, long time," she whispered. "And then it was over. It was time to go. It was time to leave the cave, to share the words, the words that filled my head. It was the only way to let go of the pain, to release the pressure. But I couldn't see. I needed to get out into the sunlight so that I could write down the words and release them. Only then could I close my eyes and rest. Only then would the voices inside my head quieten. Only then would the pain subside. But the sun blinded me. I was in the cave for far too long. I was blind inside the pitch black of the cave then I became blind outside in the bright light of the sun. My eyes burned from the brilliant sunlight and yet the only things that burned brighter were the words. With my eyes still closed, I could see them as if they were etched onto the inside of my eyelids with a pen of fire. I picked up a stone from the ground and began to scratch out the words onto the rocks around me. I wrote until my hands bled. I wrote until I couldn't lift my arms any longer. I wrote until I collapsed from the effort. And as I wrote down the words, they disappeared. They left my head. They faded from behind my eyelids, replaced by tears of relief that poured freely from my eyes, gushing forth like a magical spring."

Harold wrapped his arms around Tracy. She breathed in his familiar scent and sighed out again. She smiled. She felt so safe in her father's embrace. She knew he would protect her at all costs, and it made her feel good.

109

Tracy stared in awe at the magnificent dagger and its golden sheath suspended inside the glass case. "Wow," she whispered in awe. There were so many questions inside her head. She turned to her father, standing beside her. "Where exactly did it come from?"

"I believe it was designed by one of the Sultans in the 1700s as a gift for Nadir Shah, the ruler of Persia. By the time the dagger reached him, Shah was assassinated."

Tracy breathed in a short, sharp breath in alarm. "Why?"

"He had many enemies. He was a cruel leader. The dagger was brought back to Turkey where it has remained ever since."

"Fascinating. Are those diamonds?"

"Yep. There are over fifty diamonds on the sheath, and those three large green gemstones on the handle are emeralds. The emerald on top is a lid that flips open to reveal a tiny clock beneath the hilt."

"Huh! Really?"

"Trace, come and have a look over here." Harold beckoned Tracy over to the other side of the room where another glass case was suspended on the wall.

"The Spoonmaker's Diamond," she whispered. A large, pear-shaped diamond, the largest that she had ever seen, was suspended inside. It was surrounded by a double-row of much smaller diamonds. "Wow."

"They say it's like a full moon surrounded by stars, lighting the night sky," said Harold softly.

"It's magnificent."

"The fourth-largest diamond in the world."

"Where did it come from? Where was it discovered?"

"That's a mystery in and of itself. There are several tales. No one knows for sure. One story explains how the diamond got its name. It's said that a fisherman found it and traded it in for three spoons because even the jeweller believed that a stone of such a size was a worthless piece of glass."

"It does look like it could be made of glass," said Tracy.

"It's one of the purest kinds of diamonds. This is evident in its colourless appearance. It's 86 carats."

"What's the biggest diamond ever discovered?"

Harold stroked his chin. "Hmm. Not too sure. You're going to have to Google that. I think it's a diamond found in Africa or something."

"Dad! I'm disappointed. I always thought that you knew everything."

"Ha-ha," Harold chuckled. "Not everything."

"Okay, so where are we going next?"

Harold glanced at his watch. "Let's grab something to eat and then…"

"Wait!" Tracy held up her hand. "Let me guess." She closed her eyes and thought back to the visions she had at breakfast that morning when she tried to guess where they were going. She took hold of the stone around her neck and focused her attention on it. She drew in a deep breath and held it. She saw the sun again, but this time, it was bearable. The light moved. It was shiny, reflecting. She opened her eyes. "I know! I know!" she blurted. "We're going on a boat!"

"Ha-ha. Yes. You're right!" Harold laughed. "We're going on a sunset cruise."

"On the Bosphorus?"

"Yeah." Harold nodded.

"Awesome! Thanks, Dad."

"We need to make our way back to the hotel because we're getting collected there. There's this place we can grab some Turkish kebabs on the way."

Tracy took one last look at the huge diamond in the glass case as they turned to leave, while her father's words played through her mind like a broken record: *the full moon surrounded by stars lighting up the night sky.*

15 ~ Questions

Trudeau's phone rang. He looked at the screen. The number was hidden. *Probably internal.* He answered. "Trudeau."

"Hi, it's Lloyton."

"Doc! Watcha got for me?"

"Come down to the lab. You have to see it for yourself."

"Okay. On my way." Trudeau killed the call and made his way down to the forensics lab. A myriad of thoughts raced through his mind. Had the evidence led them to the killer? Was she female? What was her motive? What was the killer's connection to the victim? There had to be one. Trudeau ran his hand through his short-cropped hair and scratched the back of his scalp.

Doctor Isaac Lloyton wore a customary, white doctor's coat. He was short in stature; around 5"4, bald and clean-shaven. He reminded Trudeau of the rocket scientist in a television series he was watching - about a team of survivors stranded on an island somewhere in the Caribbean.

"Hey, Doc," said Trudeau as he entered the lab.

"Morning Agent," said Lloyton with a smile. "Come," he beckoned, "let's sit in my office. Can I get you some coffee?"

"That'd be great, Doc. Black, no sugar, please."

"Sure." Lloyton headed over to the coffee machine.

Trudeau followed closely behind him. "So, what you got for me?"

"The results of the tests on the ring," replied the doctor with his back to Trudeau. He turned a dial on the coffee machine and pushed a few buttons. The machine sprang to life. Lloyton sat down at his desk and flipped open a file. "Sit," he gestured, placing a cup of steaming hot coffee down on the table.

Trudeau sat down opposite the doctor. "Smells good."

"Colombian. The best," said Lloyton with a grin. He turned the file around to face Trudeau. "The ring," he said. "We analysed the blood caked all over it."

Trudeau poured over the close-up imagery. "And?"

"It belonged to the victim."

"What about the DNA on the ring? You said that you could match it with the hair you found."

"Yes. We examined it, and it's a match. My guess is, the killer lost it while she was dragging the victim across the tarmac. Her hand must have been wet with blood, which made the ring slip off her finger."

"And the ring itself? Anything unusual about it?" Trudeau looked up from the file and took a sip of coffee.

"Yes, yes," replied Loyton. He leaned across the desk, flipping over the photos in the file until he got to a page filled with data. "These are the scan results of the ring using an electron microscope."

Trudeau stared at the list of scientific names and associated numbers and then looked back at Lloyton with a blank look on his face. "What does it mean?"

"It's an antique. 14 karat gold. Handmade. There's also a tiny inscription pressed into the inside of the ring. It's a name. Alastor."

"Strange name. Is it perhaps the jeweller's name?"

Lloyton shrugged his shoulders. "I looked it up. According to Greek mythology, Alastor was a mortal who was slain by

Hercules and then became a demon. The name Alastor means *avenger*. He incited people to commit murder and other sins."

Trudeau flipped back to the images. "Hmm. Very interesting. So he wasn't one of Marvel's, The Avengers?"

"Very funny, Trudeau," said the Doctor. "No. He wasn't a comic book superhero. Very far from it."

Trudeau grinned. "Seriously though, you say the ring is antique? Any idea how old exactly?"

"Hard to say." Lloyton scratched his bald head and adjusted his wire-framed spectacles, pushing them up the bridge of his nose. "Couple of hundred years old at least, maybe even a thousand. Other than the inscription, it's quite a plain-looking ring."

"Oh, yes!" remarked Trudeau. His eyes widened, pushing his eyebrows up, creasing his forehead. "I almost forgot. Have you received the results back about the obsidian fragments?"

"Yes. Just came in this morning." Lloyton tapped on his keyboard and then turned the laptop around to face Trudeau.

The heading read, *Obsidian Hydration Dating Test.*

Trudeau scanned over the detail until he came to the summary near the bottom of the screen. He read it out loud. "Obsidian hydration testing on fragments submitted from case number RF673T yielded positive results. The hydrated layer is unusually thick at 12.5 microns." He looked across at Lloyton. "What does that even mean?" He pressed his eyebrows together, his skin creating furrowed lines just above the bridge of his nose.

"It means that the blade used to kill the victim was old. Over a thousand years old."

"Holy crap. So the age of the blade and age of the ring are of similar age."

"It appears that way," nodded Lloyton.

"So the murderer is a collector of ancient artefacts," said Trudeau thoughtfully. "Maybe even an antique dealer or something?"

"Could be."

114

"There's still no motive, though. What do you think, Doc?"

"This is a tough one," replied Lloyton. "I thought that it could have been some kind of antique deal gone wrong, but the victim has no history of buying and selling antiques, and the murder happened on the highway in the middle of nowhere. So what I really believe is the following. He's a car salesman, right?"

Trudeau nodded his head.

"I think that he was trying to sell her a car like his, so he let her take it for a spin. Something happened to piss her off, so she took out the obsidian blade and cut his throat." Lloyton made a throat-slicing action with his hand.

"Not bad, Doc, not bad," said Trudeau pushing his mouth into a sneer. "But it doesn't hold. I went to the crime scene. We know that the vehicle was driving in a northerly direction because based on the victim's sales route, he was on his way back home. The blood smear across the tarmac from the body being dragged from the vehicle begins in the middle of the road and continues across in a straight line to the left and into the bushes. If he was in the passenger seat, he would have been pulled out the right side of the vehicle and dumped into the bushes on the right, a much shorter and easier route for the killer to follow. Remember, the dead weight of a 180-pound body is no joke. But he was dragged halfway across the road from the left side of the vehicle, which means he was driving, right?"

"Makes sense."

"Exactly. So why would he be driving if she was interested in buying his car?"

"Good point," said Lloyton.

"Either she was hitching, and he decided to pick her up, or he was having an affair with her, and she lost her shit in the middle of the highway and decided to kill him because he didn't want to leave his wife."

"I think she's a time-travelling psychopath, come from the past to find John Connor," chuckled Lloyton.

"Ha-ha. So she's *terminating* everyone in her path until she

115

finds him!"

"Spot on."

"Ha-ha, Doc. You make me laugh."

"Quite a mystery, hey?"

"Yeah, that's for sure," said Trudeau. "We have an APB out for the car. I'm sure we'll find it soon enough."

"Unless it's stuck away in a garage or dark alleyway somewhere. Isn't there a tracker on the vehicle?"

Trudeau shook his head. "Nope." Trudeau glanced at his watch. "Shit. Gotta go," he said, getting up from his seat. "I have an appointment with Mrs. Landman. She's coming in to see me. Thanks, Doc, for your assistance."

"Sure thing."

"Let me know if anything else comes up, will you?"

"Of course. Good luck," said the Doctor, shaking Trudeau's hand. "Can you do me a favour, please?"

"Sure."

"Check her hair. The victim's wife. The colour."

"Oh, yes, of course. Will let you know. Thanks for the coffee."

"Pleasure. Glad you enjoyed it."

"That wasn't part of the contraband that came in the other day, was it?" Trudeau winked at the doctor. "The Colombian shipment?"

Lloyton smiled. "Yeah, sure. I've got a couple a kilo's of the good stuff in the back if you're ever in need."

Trudeau laughed. "Later, Doc," he said, raising his hand in farewell.

◊ ◊ ◊

She was waiting for him inside his office. She turned her head around as he stepped in. Her face was ashen, and her eyes puffy from crying. Long, red hair fell across one side of her face.

"Sorry to keep you waiting, Mrs. Landman," said Trudeau

116

extending his hand. He made a point of scrutinising her hair. She looked like a genuine redhead. She even had matching red freckles on her cheeks. Despite the state that she was in, she still looked like quite an attractive woman.

"Hello." She shook his hand and then pushed her chair back so that she could stand to greet him properly.

"No, no, no," said Trudeau waving his other hand in the air. "That's not necessary. Please sit." He made his way around to the other side of his desk and sat down. "I'm truly sorry for your loss, Mrs. Landman."

She pulled her chair in, nodded her head silently and bit her lip, her eyes holding back more tears. "Thank you," she whispered. "Jenny. Call me, Jenny." She dropped her head, wiped her eyes with a tissue, and blew her nose. "I'm sorry."

"No. Don't be sorry, Mrs… Jenny," said Trudeau. "I know that this is very hard for you. Thank you for coming in. It means a lot." He felt like giving her a consoling hug. "My name is Trudeau. I have been assigned to your um, husband's case. Can I get you something to drink? Tea? Coffee? Water?"

Jenny sighed heavily. "Just some water, please." She managed a wan smile. "Have you… found anything?" She looked up at Trudeau with big, teary, brown eyes.

"Yes. Yes, we have," he said, standing up to fill a polystyrene cup from the water cooler. "We know that the killer was a woman and that she took your husband's car."

"A woman?" Jenny's mouth dropped open.

Trudeau nodded. "That's all we really have at this stage. We are still looking for the vehicle. Here you go." He placed the cup of water down in front of her.

"It was a BMW. A silver X5."

"Yes, we know. I'm sure it will turn up soon."

"What else do you know about this woman?"

"Not much, I'm afraid. Preliminary forensic reports tell us that she was into antiquities."

"Antiquities?"

"Yeah. Really old stuff. Ring any bells?"

Jenny shook her head. "We… I don't know any antique dealers. It's not something we've ever really been interested in."

"Yeah. Thought as much." Trudeau scratched his head. "Is it okay if I ask you a couple more questions?"

Jenny nodded.

Trudeau took a deep breath. "Okay," he sighed. "When did you speak to your husband last?"

"Three days ago. At around 6pm."

"Okay, so the night of the incident?"

Jenny nodded again.

"So you were at home?"

Jenny nodded. "With my son."

Trudeau made a mental note. "And what did he say? Your husband. I mean, did he sound okay?"

Jenny nodded. "Yes. He sounded fine. He just called to tell me that he was on his way home. When I woke up the next morning, and he wasn't back, that's when I called him again. His phone just rang and rang. I left a message. I called again at about lunchtime - still nothing. That night, I logged into his iCloud account and traced his phone. The rest you know, I think."

Trudeau nodded. "You called the police who found his body."

Jenny dropped her head again. Trudeau watched the tears fall from her face and into her lap. Her body shuddered.

"I'm sorry, Jenny. I really am." Trudeau patiently waited for her to wipe her face again.

"Is there anything else that you can tell me? Did your husband have any enemies? Do you know if perhaps he had an argument with anyone recently?"

Jenny shook her head. "Mark was a good man. He never had a bad bone in his body. He was a salesman for crumbs' sake. It was his job to make people happy, and he was good at it. He never had any enemies. Everyone I know liked him."

"Okay, good. I just needed to know for sure."

"What does it mean, then? Why was he killed?"

"That's what I'm trying to work out. The more information that I have about your late husband, the closer we will get to find out the truth."

"The truth…" Jenny mumbled. Tears rolled down her cheeks again. She sniffed.

"Listen," said Trudeau. "We're doing everything we can. I promise you. We'll find the killer soon."

Jenny nodded silently. She took a sip of water.

"I know this is hard, Jenny, but I have a few final questions. Have you ever had cause to mistrust your husband?"

Jenny shook her head. "No. Never. We've always had an open and honest relationship."

"Okay. And is your husband the type of person who would stop to help someone? Would he stop to give a hitchhiker a lift?"

Jenny looked up at the ceiling and closed her eyes. She nodded very slowly and then buried her head in her hands and began to sob uncontrollably.

Trudeau pulled a few tissues out of the tissue box on the corner of his desk, rose from his seat, and made his way around to the other side of his desk. "There, there, Jenny," he said, placing the tissues down in front of her. "No more questions. You can go now. Here," he said pressing, his card down on the desk in front of her. "Please call me if anything else comes to mind. Anything. Once again, I am truly sorry."

Jenny grabbed a tissue and blew her nose. She picked up the other tissues, wiped her face, and then stood up to leave. "Thank you, Agent Trudeau," she said, shaking his hand.

Trudeau walked her to the exit, opened the door, and then watched her as she left the building.

"Trudeau, who's the babe?" said Agent Justin Sparks.

Trudeau turned around. "Oh, just the wife of a recent murder victim."

"The highway killing? You working on that case?"

Trudeau nodded. "Yeah."

"Strange one that. I heard there's no probable cause. You

think she was involved?" Sparks nodded towards Jenny as she walked away.

"Nah. Doubt it. No motive, no proof and she has an alibi. The killer was a woman, but she had black hair and was into old stuff."

"Old stuff?"

"Yeah. Antiquities. Jewellery. Weapons."

"Weird. Sounds like a real witch. A real bitch of a witch."

"Yeah. It's all pretty weird. The more that I think about it, the more it seems as if the victim was in the wrong place at the wrong time. The killer didn't make an effort to clean up or bury the body. She just dumped him on the roadside and took his car. Like he was in her way. Like she just needed to be somewhere, and his car was what she needed to get there. The question is, where? Where was she going?" Trudeau placed his hands on his hips and watched through the window as Jenny Landman climbed into her black BMW and drove away.

16 ~ Take the Ferry

The long, white boat was one of several double-decker ferries moored in the harbour. Tracy and her father climbed aboard along with close to 100 other tourists, and soon they were making their way across the Bosphorus. The ferry gradually picked up speed, passed under the Bosphorus bridge, and continued upstream.

"How long is the ride?" said Tracy.

"About an hour," replied Harold. "Look," he pointed. "The Hagia Sophia."

Tracy looked to where her father was pointing. The iconic minarets of the Hagia Sophia poked up into the sky like the fingers of a giant hand. The ferry made its way gradually down the coastline, and Tracy marvelled at the mix of old and new architecture as they passed by. She looked towards the aft of the vessel, and at the long, white wake of churned up water it left behind them. A red Turkish flag at the back of the boat waved in the breeze. They passed another ferry going in the opposite direction and everybody waved. Tracy waved back with a smile. She turned around to look at the coastline once again. There were several buildings so close to the water's edge that they looked as if they were about to fall right in, followed by what looked like another palace with several, much smaller minarets, surrounded by a long and very high stone wall. A tall, narrow spire rose out of one end of the structure with another red Turkish flag flying from on top.

Tracy cast her gaze to the horizon where the sun was beginning to set. The sky around it glowed a dusty orange, dimming to a dark purple the higher up she looked. Puffy white clouds dotted the sky, and a flock of birds sailed overhead. It was such a beautiful sight. The cold wind numbed her earlobes as they sailed across the bay, so she pulled her woollen beanie down tighter over her head. She took out her phone and began to film the voyage, turning slowly around, completing a full revolution, until she settled on the setting sun as it dipped closer to its final resting place on the distant horizon. After several, long minutes, she stopped filming and stared, while the fiery orb finally faded, as if the ocean itself began to gradually extinguish its light, sucking it down, deep into its watery depths. She took a deep breath of fresh air and sighed it out again.

Tracy turned on her phone again, snapped a selfie, and opened i-message. She sent the photo to Lisa and began to type out a message. *Sailing on the Bosphorus. What a blast. Miss you.* She sent the same photo to Josh with the note: *With luv from Istanbul xxx*

Josh was the first to respond: *Hey babe. Miss your smile. Crazy about u. When you back?*

Tracy replied: *Tuesday. Only 3 more sleeps. Miss you…*

Josh: *Sweet! Gotta go before Wang catches me texting in class!* Priscilla Wang was their science teacher. She was a mean old bitch.

Tracy laughed and quickly responded with a heart-emoji. Her phone vibrated and a message popped onto her screen from Lisa: *I'm so jellies right now. Have you met any nice Turkish hunks? Bring one back for me!*

Tracy: *Hun, all the men look the same. Like they've come out of a sausage factory or something They all have straight black hair and moustaches. A bit scary if you ask me. No hunks. Sorry :(*

Lisa: *Well, that totally sucks. At least your Dad is with you*

Tracy: *Sure. Wait. What do you mean?*

Lisa: *If I were you, I'd just be purving over him all day long*

Tracy: *That's disgusting. Shame on you!*

Lisa: *What? I said if I were you. I meant if I was in your place*

Tracy: *I know, but it's still disgusting. Ewww!*

Lisa: *Okay. I admit it. I have a crush on yr Dad. So what. I think he's sexy. Kinda like George Clooney sexy*

Tracy: *Lis. Stop.*

Lisa: *Oh, the things I would do…*

Tracy: *I think I'm gonna be sick. I said STOP!*

Lisa: *Okay, okay. Calm down to a sizzle. Oh, forgot to tell you. Paul asked me to the prom. What an idiot*

Tracy: *Williams? He likes you. What did you say?*

Lisa: *No, of course! He's such a dork*

Tracy: *Yeah, but in a cute kind of way*

Lisa: *WTF! Can't believe you would even think I'd consider Paul Williams as an option. Yuck!*

Tracy: *You know that underneath all that crap, he is actually quite a sweet guy?*

Lisa: *Whatever*

Tracy: *Seriously. It's all a facade. He just acts like a punk because it's his way of protecting his vulnerability. Do you know how much effort it must have taken him to actually ask you? And you just shut him down*

Lisa: *He deserved it*

Tracy: *So who'd you really like to go to the prom with? And don't say my Dad!*

Lisa: *Your Dad ;)*

Tracy: Angry-face-emoji.

Lisa: *I don't really know, hey*

Tracy: *Exactly. There isn't anyone else besides Paul…*

Lisa: *Okay now it's my turn to say STOP*

Tracy: *Lisa and Paul sitting in the tree. Kissy, kissy, kisseeeee!*

Lisa: *Cow*

Tracy: *Bitch*

Lisa: *I love our little chats. They're so special.* Funny-face-emoji.

Tracy: *You're special. Special needs!* Laughing-face-emoji.
Lisa: *Tracy Barnes. I'm gonna give you such a smack*
Tracy: *Ooooh talk dirty to me bitch*
Lisa: Zap-sign-emoji
Tracy: Red-heart-emoji
Lisa: *Luv you too much girl. Send more pics*
Tracy: *K. Bye. X*

Tracy turned off her phone and pushed it into her pocket. She held onto the chrome railing of the ferry as the boat slowly turned around to make it's way back along the river.

◊ ◊ ◊

Tracy made her way down to meet her father for dinner later that evening. She felt refreshed and rejuvenated after a long, hot bath infused with the hotel's aromatic bath salts.

"Good evening," said her father with a smile. He stood up from the table and pulled Tracy's chair back.

She kissed him on the cheek. "Hi, Dad. Thank you," she said before sitting down.

"You smell nice," said Harold. "Fresh."

"Thanks," said Tracy with a grin as she pulled her chair in towards the table. "I had a nice hot bath."

"If there's time, I must take you to a traditional Turkish bath. You'll love it. They physically scrub you down with soap. The first time I did it, I lost my tan!"

"No way ho-zay," said Tracy.

"But it's winter. You don't even have a tan."

Tracy lifted her arm. "Well, what little tan I've retained from summer, I'd like to keep, thank you very much."

"Trace, don't be silly. It's really good for you to shed some skin."

"Ewww. Gross, Dad. We're about to have dinner. I'm not some kind of snake, you know."

"No, I mean it. The Turkish scrub is a great way to exfoliate. Exfoliation leads to smoother, healthier, glowing skin.

124

It's the secret to anti-ageing."

"Dad, I'm seventeen. I promise you; I don't need to be performing any anti-ageing techniques on my body right now. My skin is already fresh and glowing."

"Okay, okay," said Harold, waving Tracy down. "I'll just shut up now. Let's see what's on the menu."

"Dad."

"Yup," said Harold as he peered over his reading glasses.

"Thanks for today. It was great."

Harold smiled. "My pleasure."

"Any clues as to where we're going tomorrow?"

"I'm sure you can work it out."

"How?"

"Remember at breakfast?"

Tracy gasped, clapping her hand over her mouth. "How could I forget?! The river. Of course. It worked!" She clasped the pink crystal hanging around her neck. "I visualised the river cruise. I was so caught up in the sights that I totally forgot about it. Wait." Tracy closed her eyes. "I remember the stone animal now. Yes." She opened her eyes. "But we never saw any stone carvings today as far as I can remember."

Harold smiled.

"So that's the clue? Must be…"

"We're catching a flight."

"We're flying there? So it's not in Istanbul?"

"Nope." Harold shook his head.

"It could be anywhere," said Tracy in exasperation. "Come on, Dad, just one more clue?"

"Why do I have the feeling that it's going to get harder and harder to surprise you with anything? Can I just have this one moment?"

"Good evening," said the waiter.

"Good evening," said Harold looking up from the menu.

Tracy turned towards the waiter. He looked like another typical Turk with dark, straight hair and a matching moustache. "Hi. Can I please have the kofte and a Coke Light please?"

"Yes, of course," said the waiter with a nod. "And you, sir?"

"I'll have the same, please." Harold winked at Tracy. "But a glass of fresh orange juice instead of a Coke."

"Yes, sir. Will that be all?"

"Yes, thanks," said Harold, handing the waiter his menu. He removed his glasses and turned to Tracy. "So, where were we?"

"You were having a moment."

"Ah, yes. Tomorrow's surprise. Let's just say that right now, you know more than you know and that even with your gift, it's nice sometimes to still get surprised about stuff. Especially when it's something exciting."

Tracy sighed. "I guess you're right. But just imagine if you have this... this gift, where you know that you can predict stuff and see into the future. It's hard not to want to know when you know that you can find out if you really tried. That sounded like a bit of a mouthful. Know what I mean?" said Tracy, raising her eyebrows.

"Sure."

"But imagine if you knew everything that was going to happen. Life would become mundane, boring. There'd be no more surprises; nothing to look forward to. Life would lose its spice."

Tracy thought about what her father was saying. "I hear you, Dad."

"What I'm saying is, that some things are best left to unravel on their own because maybe, just maybe, that event or occurrence that was going to be a surprise, may turn into disappointment and that's when things can become unpleasant for you. I wouldn't like to see your gift become a burden. It's a big responsibility, you know."

"Yeah, I know, Dad. I'm a big girl now. I can handle it."

Harold smiled. "I know, Trace. It's just hard to believe that you're seventeen. I still see you as my little girl. I'm so proud of you and all that you have become. It's just that this thing, this gift that you have acquired takes getting used to. I can only imagine what you are going through in that head of yours. I just don't want to see you get hurt. You gave me a fright today at Topkapi Palace, you know?"

"I'm fine, Dad. Promise," said Tracy. She squeezed her father's hand reassuringly. "Okay, no more questions about tomorrow."

Harold winked. "Okay. No more questions."

17 ~ Bazaar

The airport was busy. Tracy followed her father as they walked across the large terminal hall. "You still haven't told me where we're going, Dad," she said, as they stood in line to go through the security check-in.

"Urfa," said Harold.

"Urfa? Where's that?" said Tracy as she rubbed the sleep out of her eyes.

"Oh, it's still in Turkey. The flight is about an hour and a half."

She looked at her phone. 6.23am. "Flip, it's early," she said, stretching her arms into the air with a yawn. "This had better be worth it."

Harold grinned. "Oh, it will be, Trace. It sure will be. You'll see."

"What is this place, anyway?"

"It's an ancient city that is known by many names."

"How can a city have many names?"

"Well, a city as old as Urfa has been home to many civilisations with many different cultures and languages and so, over time, the name has changed each time it was inhabited by each of these people. From the Armenians and the Greeks to

128

the Arabs and the Turks and some say to civilisations even older than that. The Arabs and the Jews believe that Urfa was Ur Kasdim, also known as Ur of the Chaldees, the birthplace of Abraham, the patriarch of both of these ancient religions."

"Wow. Okay, now I get it. This is why we're in Turkey, right? Urfa is the reason for this trip. Your research project. It's why you know so much about this city."

"Yup," Harold nodded.

"Cool. So now I know. No more surprises." Tracy grinned.

Harold was silent.

"Da-ad," Tracy whined. "There's more, isn't there? Damnit! This is so frustrating." She absentmindedly fingered the pink crystal around her neck.

"Uh-uh," Harold waved his finger. "Remember, you promised."

"Oh, Okay," said Tracy in a huff. She let go of the crystal. "No more questions."

They made their way through the security check-in and then towards the boarding gate.

◊ ◊ ◊

Tracy switched her phone on as the plane touched down. 8.20am. She looked out of the window. The long runway looked out of proportion to the small group of terminal buildings on the other side. They disembarked and walked a short distance across the tarmac to the airport. "What time is our flight back?" said Tracy to her father as they stepped inside.

"4pm," said Harold without turning around.

Tracy hoisted her backpack over her shoulder as they continued through the airport building, Harold leading the way.

"There he is," said Harold pointing at a man wearing a pair of baggy, cream-coloured trousers, a red waistcoat with gold trim and a matching red fez on his head.

"Berat!"

"Professor!" said Berat with open arms. "So good to see

129

you again."

Harold hugged him. "This is my daughter, Tracy," said Harold, turning around.

Tracy smiled. "Hi," she said with a wave.

"Aaah, Professor, she is magnificent! Hello Miss Barnes. Welcome to Urfa!" Berat said enthusiastically. He winked at Tracy, and she blushed.

"Berat will be our guide," explained Harold. "He knows this city like the back of his hand."

"But Professor, I think with all of your knowledge, you can show us around this time," Berat said with a grin.

Tracy laughed.

"Berat, I have missed your humour," said Harold. "Come, let's grab some breakfast," he said, putting an arm around Berat's shoulders.

◊ ◊ ◊

After a brief ride into town, Tracy found herself led by Berat through Urfa's bazaar. He waved his arms animatedly about as he spoke to her father. The click-clack of backgammon pieces from a pair of Arabs playing the traditional game, mingled with the chit-chat of traders and hubbub of people crammed into the narrow alleyways, filled the air. The smell of sweet incense, along with the waft of pungent spices, assaulted Tracy's nostrils. She imagined that she had stepped back in time to a place steeped in history, filled with interesting stories of merchants and their adventures. She pictured Aladdin and his band of forty thieves being chased through the alleyways and corridors of the Bazaar by a troop of angry soldiers brandishing curved scimitars, barking commands in their native tongue. Berat led them through the narrow entrance of a store. The jingle of tiny bells signalled their arrival as the door shut behind Tracy, instantly sucking away the hum of the bazaar outside, replacing it with soft, melodic music, played out of several clandestine speakers. The air was surprisingly cool, and the interior was dimly lit with the soft, yellow glow of traditional Turkish lamps hanging from the ceiling. Tracy's eyes gradually adjusted to the darker environment as she followed Berat and her father to a small, round table in the corner of the room.

"Welcome to Aziz Urfa," said Berat, pulling back a chair for Tracy.

"Thank you," said Tracy as she sat down. "This place is so lit."

"It is a great traditional restaurant," said Berat in his thick, Turkish accent. "The food here is superb."

"Hmm," said Tracy, breathing in the spicy aromas. "Smells awesome." Her stomach rumbled in anticipation.

A waiter approached them. Berat rambled off some instructions in Turkish, and the waiter disappeared.

"Don't worry, Miss Barnes," said Berat. "I've ordered for all of us."

"This was the first place Berat took me to when I visited Urfa for the first time many years ago," said Harold.

"You are right, professor," said Berat. "And it's still the best. It has been around for almost 200 years. Fifth-generation."

"How old is the bazaar?" said Tracy.

"It was built in the 1500s," said Berat. "So, that makes it about 500 years old."

"Oh, wow," said Tracy, flabbergasted. She gazed around the cosy restaurant in awe, marvelling at the numerous old tapestries adorning the walls and unusual trinkets suspended from the ceiling.

"The bazaar was built by Suleiman the Magnificent," continued Berat, "the longest reining Sultan of the Ottoman Empire."

"Why was he called the Magnificent?"

"Because he ruled during a time when there was the greatest justice and harmony between people."

"Interesting."

Two waiters arrived with several plates of food that they placed across the small table until almost every square-inch was covered. Tracy breathed in the fresh aroma of cooked Turkish sausage, freshly cut slices of goat's cheese, boiled eggs, sliced tomatoes, cucumbers, and olives.

"What's that?" said Tracy, pointing at a flaky pastry dish.

"Borek," said Berat. "It's pastry filled with spinach, minced meat or potato. Try it. It's really delicious." Borat spoke to one of the waiters who quickly disappeared into the kitchen and promptly returned with a pot of hot tea.

Tracy got stuck into the food, while Berat and her father caught up over their tea.

"So, Professor, how's the lovely Mrs. Barnes?"

"She's fine, thank you. She sends her greetings."

"And your son? How old is he now? Twelve? Thirteen?"

"Fourteen," said Harold.

"My, how time flies," said Berat shaking his head.

"It sure does. And your daughter? How old is she?"

"Twenty-one!"

"Wow. She must be a beautiful young woman."

"Ai-yai-yai! She gives me nothing but grey hairs." Berat smacked the palm of his hand on his forehead. "All she wants to do is cause trouble. She won't leave the boys alone, and she spends all of my money on clothes!"

"Sounds like a typical young woman." Harold winked at Tracy. "You should be proud, Berat."

Berat's face softened. "I love her so much," he said with a smile. "I must introduce you to her," he said to Tracy. "Perhaps on our way back."

"On our way back from where?" said Tracy, her mouth full of sausage.

Harold looked at Berat, smiled and shook his head.

"Apparently, your father wants to surprise you."

"Apparently," said Tracy in a huff. She swallowed her food. "This sausage is delicious," she said to Berat.

"It's called sucuk. Traditional, fried Turkish sausage. It's made with cumin and garlic."

"Aah. That's why it's a little spicy," said Tracy, taking a sip of her tea. "Where are we going next?"

"You'll soon see," said Harold. "It's not far from here."

"That's a beautiful crystal," said Berat.

Tracy looked down at the pink stone around her neck. "Thanks. My grandmother gave it to me. It's really old." She fingered it as she spoke.

"There is a great shop just around the corner with some amazing crystals," said Berat. "It's owned by a famous fortune-teller. Maybe we can stop by there next." Berat looked across at Harold. "We have time?"

Harold looked at his watch and nodded. "About an hour."

"Great, then I can show you some other shops too. Do you have a boyfriend, Miss Barnes?"

Tracy nodded.

"Good, good. Then you must buy him some traditional Turkish Delight. There's a shop nearby that makes the best Turkish Delight in the whole of Turkey!" Berat spread his hands wide. "The best part is, you can to try the many different flavours that they have. And of course you must buy some Pismaniye."

"What's that?"

"It's like Turkish cotton candy. Really delicious."

"Yum," said Tracy, pushing some cheese into her mouth.

18 ~ Fortuna-tea-ly

The sweet shop was about two minutes from the restaurant. Trays of multicoloured Turkish Delights were on display. Their sweet, sugary smell tickled Tracy's nostrils as she bent down for a closer look. She was particularly interested in the pistachio-filled variety. The shopkeeper handed her a small plate filled with chopped up samples for her to try. She popped some into her mouth, and the flavour assaulted her senses. "Hmm. Very good," she said. "Can I please have some of this and this?" she said, pointing at the green and then the pink variety. "What are those?" She pointed at another tray of sweets that looked like thousands of little gems, sparkling in the light.

"That's Akide," said Berat. "It's Turkish, hard candy. Mint, lemon, rose petals, pistachio and cinnamon are added to the sugar during the production process.

"Here, try," said the shopkeeper, offering Tracy another plate filled with the colourful sweets.

Tracy popped a yellow one into her mouth. It was hard, just as Berat had said. She tasted cinnamon and mint.

Berat led them from the candy store, down another alleyway and through a cobbled area filled with people sitting at square, wooden tables, drinking coffee and eating some borek. They walked past a shop adorned with dozens of metallic teapots, jugs, and plates. A man sat hammering an intricate pattern into a brass plate. His hands were smudged black from his craft. He looked up at Tracy with a grin as she passed him by. She stopped and turned to snap a shot with her phone and then ran to catch up with Berat and her father. The clang-clang of metal on metal began again as the metalsmith returned to his work.

"Here we are," said Berat, stopping in front of a little shop with a purple awning. A black a-frame sign with fancy yellow writing stood outside. It read, *Madame Kezia, Expert Gypsy Fortune Teller. Past, Present, Future. Crystal Ball Gazing. Tarot. Palm Reading. Coffee Reading.* "After you, Miss Barnes," said Berat, raising his arm and taking a small bow.

Tracy stepped past Berat and her father. Strings of long, red beads hung down over the entrance. She pulled them aside and stepped into the store. They tinkled gently as she let them drop behind her. She breathed in the sweet, rose fragrance of incense as it clogged the air, savouring the smell as it enveloped her senses like an invisible cloud. Soft, melodic sounds trickled from the back of the room like a gurgling brook in a magical forest, and the warm glow from strings of fairy lights suspended from the ceiling filled the otherwise dark enclosure. The beads tinkled behind Tracy as Berat and her father stepped inside.

"Good morning."

Tracy jumped.

"I'm sorry, I did not mean to alarm you," said a voice to her left in a thick, foreign accent.

Tracy turned to face the voice's owner. Dark, round eyes stared back at her from a face with skin so smooth and shiny, Tracy thought she was looking at a mannequin. Thick, black eyeshadow framed her eyes, accenting their penetrating gaze and an emerald green turban was wrapped tightly about her head. "I... um... hi," Tracy managed to say.

"Good morning, Madame," Berat said, stepping past Tracy. "The young lady over here would like a reading, please."

Berat's intervention caused the woman's gaze to tear away

from Tracy's. Tracy staggered backwards in a heart-wrenching moment that made her head swim as if she was being dragged through thick mud that had congealed at her ankles.

"Certainly, Monsieur."

Tracy recognised the accent now - French. She surveyed the woman again; the fortune teller. Her flawless skin was darker than usual. Tracy remembered the sign outside. Gypsy. Her features were striking - high cheekbones and a long, narrow nose. She looked almost regal, yet there was something else, something that caused the hair on Tracy's arms to rise. A shiver ran through her body.

"Anything in particular?" said the woman to Berat.

Tracy visualised the sign outside once more. "What's a coffee reading?" she inquired, intrigued at the notion of being able to make a reading using someone's coffee.

The fortune-teller smiled, and Tracy was relieved to see her face produce wrinkles around the corners of her mouth and eyes. "Tasseography," she said. "The art of reading the signs found in the leaves of tea, the granules found at the bottom of a cup of coffee, and even the sediment left behind after drinking a cup of wine. It's a form of divination that has been around for thousands of years. We call it Fal here in Turkey. Come with me, and I will show you," she said to Tracy, turning to make her way deeper into the store.

Tracy looked at Berat and her father. Harold nodded his consent.

The fortune-teller pulled aside a long, black, velvet curtain so that Tracy could enter before her. Tracy stepped into a tiny, dimly lit room with a pair of low stools on either side of a table, covered in a black tablecloth adorned with stars, and interspersed with moons. A deck of tarot cards was positioned on one corner of the table. Several candles of different sizes, both in breadth and length burned from atop a shelf at the back of the room. The air was hazy and smelt of sandalwood. The fortune-teller walked over to a copper pot with a long handle and filled a cup with a dark liquid. Tracy caught the waft of coffee. She watched as the steam rising from the cup twisted into the air as if it was alive with purpose.

The woman turned around, placed the cup of coffee on the table, and sat down opposite Tracy. "Please, take a seat," she said, gesturing with her hand.

Tracy pulled back the chair and sat down.

"My name is Madame Kezia, but you can call me Kez," said the fortune-teller extending her hand. Her fingers were long and thin and adorned with an array of colourful gems.

"Tracy. Tracy Barnes," said Tracy, shaking her hand. She found herself inextricably pulled to gaze into Madame Kezia's dark, enigmatic eyes.

Kezia's grip was firm. It grew tighter. Even tighter. Kezia's penetrating gaze intensified, and Tracy felt her head begin to swim again. Her hand began to ache. She relaxed it, allowing it to go limp so that she could easily pull it free. Just as she was about to cry out in pain, Kezia let go.

"My apologies," said Madame Kezia, quickly retracting her hand. "But you have… an energy about you that is so… intriguing." She looked at the stone dangling from the black cord around Tracy's neck. "And that… that crystal. Where did you get it?"

"My grandmother," said Tracy, clasping the stone tightly in her hand.

"It's an amethyst."

Tracy nodded. "It's very old."

Madame Kezia's eyebrows pressed together in a frown. "Yes. I know. I can sense that. I can also sense someone else. Someone close to you. Your grandmother? It must be the stone. Did your grandmother have it in her possession for a long time?"

Tracy nodded again. "She told me that it was a family heirloom."

"That explains it then. I sense that this stone has channelled power before. Lots of it."

Kezia closed her eyes for a moment while Tracy sat silently

on the other side of the table. Kezia opened her eyes and spoke. "Drink. Please." She placed the coffee cup down in front of Tracy.

The coffee was strong. And hot. Her taste buds were on fire. She placed the cup down on the table and looked inside. "How do you do the reading?" she asked.

"Only once you've finished your coffee," said Madame Kezia with a smile. "But be careful not to drink it all," she continued. "Turkish coffee, unlike the western variety, is not filtered or strained, so there is always a thick, residue left behind. It's this residue that is most important when I do the reading."

"Now I know why it tastes so strong." She took another long sip. The effects of the caffeine rush was beginning to make her feel light-headed.

"Tell me about your grandmother," said Kezia. "I still have a very strong feeling about her."

"Well, she lives in Chicago."

"But she's not from there," said Kezia flatly.

"How did you know?" said Tracy turning her head askance.

Kezia smiled. "Oh, I know," she leaned forward. "And neither are you," she said, staring into Tracy's eyes.

Tracy tore her gaze away. "But I am," she implored. "I was born there."

Madame Kezia shook her head slowly from side to side. She stared at the crystal once more. Her eyes narrowed to slits. "There is something that you are not telling me. Your eyes - they do not lie. I can see it."

"What?"

"Your gift. It's so new. So fresh. I can feel it. She is with you."

Tracy looked into her coffee cup. There was a buzzing in her ears. She took another sip and looked up at Kezia. "Who is with me?"

"Let me see," said Madame Kezia pointing at Tracy's cup.

"Oh, here you go," she said, handing the cup to Kezia who glanced briefly inside.

138

"Good. That's enough. Now close your eyes and make a wish."

Tracy did as she was told.

Kezia placed her hands over Tracy's and also closed her eyes. "Your wish. It will come true," she said in a whisper. "Here," she said, handing Tracy a white saucer. "Take this and place it over the top of the cup."

Tracy did as she was told.

"Good. Now, make sure that you seal it well. That's it. Put some pressure over it."

Tracy leaned into the table, pressing her weight down onto the saucer.

"Now, pick up the cup and saucer and raise it to your chest. Yes. Now, make three circles clockwise, swirling the remains of the coffee around in the cup."

Tracy made clockwise, horizontal circles as instructed.

"Excellent. Now I want you to quickly flip the cup and saucer upside down. Okay, now pass it over to me."

Tracy handed the inverted cup and saucer to Madame Kezia who gingerly took it from her outstretched hands.

She placed it carefully down on the table and then turned back to Tracy. "Now, we wait."

"How long?"

"About five minutes or so. It needs to settle and cool."

"Oh."

"Now, where were we?" Madame Kezia furrowed her brow. "Ah, yes," she said, gazing deeply into Tracy's eyes once more.

Tracy shifted uneasily in her seat as Kezia's eyes bored deep into her very soul.

"You're no stranger to this, young lady."

"What do you mean?" The hair on the nape of her neck rose. She shivered despite the room being warm and cozy.

"I think you know exactly what I mean. Your grandmother is an oracle, and so are you."

"But, h… h… how…?" stammered Tracy.

Madame Kezia smiled. "It began early this morning. I woke

up at 3am after a powerful dream. A vision. I was expecting you. I knew you would come. At first, I wasn't sure. You are so young. But then my doubts were extinguished when I saw that crystal and felt its power. *Your* power."

Tracy was at a loss for words. She looked down at her lap. "It's true," she whispered. "My grandmother is like you. She can predict the future. I... I've only just discovered that I have the same gift."

"Who else? Who else in your family?"

"No one else. My gran told me that it skips a generation."

"Interesting. Very interesting. Okay. Shall we see what the coffee granules say?"

Tracy nodded, shifting forward over the table to get a closer look at her inverted coffee cup.

Madame Kezia gripped the handle and gently pried the cup from the saucer. Excess sediment slid out of the sides of the cup as she lifted it. She silently studied the shapes and patterns of the muddy remnants of coffee as it oozed slowly across the saucer. "Hmm. Light in colour. This is a good omen. It reinforces my prediction that the wish you made will come to fruition."

Tracy opened her mouth to speak.

"No!" Madame Kezia raised her finger. "Do not tell me your wish, otherwise it will lose its power." She tilted the saucer. "I read the signs in the saucer *and* the cup and then combine them to reach a conclusion." She swirled the contents of the saucer and closed her eyes for a moment. She opened her eyes and then brought the saucer up close to her face. "Hmm. Very interesting."

Tracy peered at the nondescript shapes. Her curiosity got the better of her. "What do you see? What do you see?"

"I must look at the cup first," said Madame Kezia, picking up the coffee cup and peering inside. "Ahh. Mmm. Yesss," she hissed, pointing at shapes in the sludge that Tracy failed even to fathom. "A mountain." She looked up at Tracy. "This represents an obstacle, but do not fear because I also see a bird. Yes. A bird." Kezia looked closer. "This represents that good news is on its way to you." She continued to scour the blobs of coffee, looking for the faintest signs. "What's this? A claw? Can it be?"

"A claw?" said Tracy. "What does that mean?"

"A claw means danger. It means that your enemy is closer than you think."

"My enemy?" said Tracy flabbergasted. "I don't have any enemies. Although, there was this young kid that embarrassed me once. Nah. There's no way that it's him. I'm sure he moved out of state anyway."

"An enemy that is close to you could mean something more than just someone in physical proximity," said Kezia. "Close, could also mean *like* you. In other words, this enemy could be somebody that is similar to you in age, looks, abilities."

"And you see all of this in that?" Tracy pointed at the muddy contents of the saucer and cup.

"Yes, of course," said Kezia. "But this is just scratching the surface. One has to look even deeper."

"Like combining the readings of the cup with the saucer, as you said."

"Correct! Now you've got it," Kezia said with a smile. Her pearly-white teeth flashed before Tracy. She placed the cup and saucer alongside one another and stared at them, her eyes shifting back and forth across the nondescript patterns.

Tracy rose up off her seat in anticipation. "What is it? What do you see?"

Kezia lifted her gaze, and Tracy sucked in a short, sharp breath. Kezia's smile had been replaced with a look of earnest. "The raven," she said quietly, glancing around the room uneasily. "It brings with it tidings of foreboding."

"So you mean something bad is going to happen? To me?" said Tracy anxiously.

Kezia ignored Tracy's question. Instead, she said: "I want you to press your right thumb down into the coffee granules inside the cup and twist it in a clockwise direction. This will produce a pattern that will help me determine your feelings and thoughts, which, when combined with all the other readings, will give me more of an accurate insight into the course of action you should take to combat these negative tidings. This is the final 'stamp' of the reading."

Tracy did as she was instructed. She pushed her right thumb down into the coffee-sludge at the bottom of her cup and twisted it in a clockwise direction.

Kezia quickly picked up the cup and peered inside. "Fascinating," she mumbled. "Fascinating." She looked into Tracy's eyes and gripped her arm once more. "Listen to me. You need not fear as long as you follow your instincts and stay on the path. You have the power of sight. It is a gift that you must treasure. It grows stronger each and every day. Use it wisely by helping others, and you will be helped in return."

"But… how?" said Tracy in consternation.

Kezia smiled. "I'm sure you've heard that with great power, comes great responsibility? And with practice, comes perfection? You need to practice, Tracy. You need to practice using your power of divination so that you can better prepare yourself for what is coming. I cannot tell you what it is, just that there are challenges ahead. The sooner that you come fully into your powers, the sooner you will be equipped to deal with these challenges, whatever they may be." Kezia handed Tracy a paper towel so that she could wipe her thumb. "That's it," she said. "I hope you learnt something valuable."

"Thank you, Kez," said Tracy. "How much do I owe you?"

"This one's on me," she replied. "It's not often that I get customers like you. I have learnt much today." Tracy opened her mouth to speak, but Madame Kezia silenced her by raising her hand. "Uh-uh. I will hear nothing of it, Miss Barnes. Why don't you purchase something from my shop instead?"

"Okay. Thank you so much," she said, getting up to leave.

"Wait," said Kezia grabbing Tracy's arm. "Here, take this," she said, pressing a small, blue-beaded bracelet into the palm of her hand. "It's only 100 Turkish Lira."

Tracy opened her hand. The shiny bracelet winked at her in

the candlelight. "Wow. It's so beautiful." One of the beads was larger than the others. It looked like an eye.

"It's a Nazar Boncuk charm bracelet," said Kezia. "The eye stares back at the world to ward off evil."

"So it's a protection bracelet?"

Madame Kezia nodded. "Yes. It will confuse your adversaries." Kezia smiled. "You should wear it. Always."

Tracy slipped the bracelet onto her wrist and laughed. "You keep talking about my enemies and adversaries as if there are people out to get me or something." She shook her head. "Oh, well, at least I know I have the protection of the Nazcar Bonk!"

"Nazar Boncuk," said Kezia, correcting her. "And remember, practice, practice, practice."

19 ~ Blow & Behold

Tracy glanced at her phone. 11.12am. She followed Berat and her father out of the bazaar and back towards the car. A cold breeze twisted through the alleyways as they walked. She zipped up her sweater and shivered. "Where we going?"

"You'll soon see," said her father.

"At least tell me how far away it is," said Tracy climbing into the car.

"About eleven kilometres, said Berat.

"That's about seven miles," said Harold. "Give or take."

The fifteen-minute ride took them northeast out of Urfa and through the countryside. Tracy watched a shepherd and about two-dozen, miserable-looking sheep make their way across a field as they drove past. She imagined that one stared up at her mockingly, bleating loudly, *dohhhn't gohhh*. Berat took them off the main road and onto a narrow dirt path that soon ended in a parking lot with about forty other cars at the foot of a hill covered in long, dry grass. It seemed that most of this region was pretty arid. Tracy stepped out of the car.

"Welcome to Gobekli Tepe," said Berat, pointing to a large, cream-coloured, oval-shaped canopy, protruding from out of the top of the hill.

144

"So, this is the surprise?" said Tracy. "A strange-looking roof, or whatever that is, in the middle of nowhere."

"Gobekli Tepe is Turkish for potbelly hill," explained Harold. "It's what's beneath the canopy that will surprise you."

"The name rings a bell," said Tracy. "I'm sure you've told me about it before."

"Yep. When you see it, you'll remember."

Tracy followed Berat and her father as they made their way towards the tent-like canopy at the top of the hill. She approached a solitary tree on the way that was adorned with tattered strips of cloth.

"What's with this tree?" she said.

"It's a mulberry tree," said Berat. "The farmers that used to inhabit this area used it as a wishing tree."

They stepped onto a wooden walkway that surrounded the canopy on top of the hill.

"*This* is Gobekli Tepe," said Harold, pointing down at a huge pit that had clearly been excavated below. Several, huge, t-shaped stone pillars that looked as if they had been purposefully inserted into sockets in the bedrock stood in concentric rings at the bottom. Some of the pillars were broken, while others were supported by makeshift wooden beams to prevent them from falling over. There were even some partially excavated pillars in the outer rings, where just their t-shaped tops protruded from out of the earth.

Tracy was gob-smacked. Her father was right. How could she forget? There was no mistaking the pictures her father had shown her of these strange stone pillars. At the time, she dismissed them as trivial, but now she couldn't believe her eyes. It was as if their very construction belied belief. They seemed out of place like they didn't belong here in this remote place, this potbelly hill. Questions flooded her head like a torrent. She turned to look at her father. She must have looked like she was in shock, judging by her father's impish grin.

"Look," he said, pointing at the pillars near the centre of the excavation.

Tracy squinted her eyes and then opened them wide as soon as she realised what her father was pointing at. Dozens of carvings in low relief protruded from the sides of the stone pillars; carvings in the shapes of animals. Tracy walked across the wooden walkway to get a closer look. A group of Chinese tourists was crowded around one section of the enclosure. They all had their cameras and phones out, snapping away at two of the biggest and most prominent of all the pillars. Tracy noticed what looked like a spider, a fox, and a long-legged bird carved onto the sides of the pillars. Jutting out of the side of one pillar in much higher relief, was a lizard with its tail curved to one side. She could even make out the creature's ribs that had been carved into its sides. She caught her breath. Her vision. The stone carving. This was it. Gobekli Tepe.

"Incredible, isn't it?" said Harold as he and Berat approached Tracy.

"I... I don't know where to begin," said Tracy. "This is exactly how I imagined it in my head. How long... when... how old is this place?"

"Really old," said Harold. "Any idea how old the pyramids are?"

"The Egyptian pyramids? Oh, I dunno. About 3,000 years old?"

"4,500."

"Wow!"

"Yes. Stonehenge is older at around 5,000 years. Gobekli Tepe is more than double that."

"Whaaat?" Tracy's mouth dropped.

"Yeah. Over 12,000 years old."

"Jee-zuz. But how? Who...?"

"Gobekli Tepe is considered to be the oldest temple on the planet," continued Harold.

"A temple?" Tracy turned to have another look at the huge stone pillars.

Berat nodded in affirmation. "Yes. A temple. Built by the ancient neolithic people."

"But didn't religion begin just a few thousand years ago?"

"That's what makes this site so interesting," said Harold. "Its discovery has challenged a lot of traditional thinking."

"When was it discovered?"

"In the 60s but excavation only began in 1994 by Klaus Schmidt, a German archaeologist."

"So, this is the project that you have been working on?" said Tracy.

Harold nodded. "Yes. Along with several other archaeological teams from around the world."

"What exactly is your research about? What are you looking for?"

"Clues, I guess," said Harold. "Clues that help me to understand more about the ancient culture of the people that lived here."

"Do these pillars also make sounds?"

"What?"

"Like Stonehenge. Remember? You told me that the Stonehenge pillars make ringing sounds when you knock them."

Harold smiled. "As a matter of fact they do. This is a very important part of my research. In fact the pillars here at Gobekli Tepe exhibit very similar archaeoacoustics to the pillars found at many other ancient megalithic sites around the world, including Stonehenge."

"Fascinating," said Tracy.

"Ah. There he is now," said Harold, looking up as a man in a pair of ripped jeans and a black polar-neck approached them. "Massimo!"

"Harold! Berat!" Massimo replied in a foreign accent that Tracy recognised as Italian.

Massimo swung his hand into Harold's with a loud clap, followed by a warm embrace. He turned to Berat and hugged him too. "Ciao," he said to Tracy with a slight dip of his head. He extended his hand in a greeting. "You must be Tracy. Pleased to make your acquaintance." A grin stretched right across his face.

Blood rushed to Tracy's face as she coyly shook Massimo's hand. It was warm to the touch. She opened her mouth and, of course, nothing came out. She felt like such an idiot.

"She is truly magnificent," said Massimo to Harold. "A specimen of exquisite beauty. She must take after her mother because you, I'm afraid, are a sight for sore eyes. Bellisima!"

This time, Tracy looked away in embarrassment. She thought that either her head was going to explode or just turn into a big, ripe tomato for the rest of the day.

"Hey, Massi. That's my daughter over there," cautioned Harold. "My little girl. If you lay one finger on her, I'll…"

"Professor Barnes," said Massimo. "I would never disrespect you like that!"

Harold clapped Massimo on the back. "Just kidding," he said with a chuckle. "Did you see his face Berat? It looked like he was going to shit his pants!"

"He-he. That would not have been good," said Berat. "I mean all the tourists would leave. Not good for business."

"Very funny, you two," said Massimo with a dejected look on his face.

Tracy giggled.

"Not you too!" exclaimed Massimo.

"Massimo is also a professor," said Harold to Tracy. "Professor Massimo Vago from the University of Milano."

"At your service, Madame," said Massimo curtsying graciously.

Tracy blushed once more. Massimo had a mop of dark brown, wavy, shoulder-length hair that looked like it hadn't been brushed in weeks. His face sported a few days' stubble. Tracy guessed his age at around thirty years. He had a twinkle in his eye and a mischievous grin that got Tracy breathing faster than usual. An image of Josh popped into her head, and she immediately felt a pang of guilt.

"Is she always this talkative?" enquired Massimo of Harold. He winked at Tracy. This time she managed to hold his gaze with a smile.

148

"Only when she is the centre of attention," he replied. "Massimo is the reason we are here in Turkey. You have something to show me?"

Massimo nodded. "Yes, yes! Of course. Come," he beckoned. "Follow me. Andiamo." Massimo led the small party across the wooden walkway, to the other side of the enclosure and towards a small structure with a sign outside that read, *Gobekli Tepe Site Office*. "Welcome to my office," he said, ushering them through the front door with a smile. The site office was a long, narrow building, about the size of a large shipping container. Three desks with PC's, two of them occupied, lined the left side of the building, with one long table on the right, covered in an assortment of stone ornaments and archaeological tools. A large machine that looked like a giant photocopier was positioned next to the table. At the other end of the office, stood a row of shelves reaching right up to the ceiling, filled with larger stone artefacts. Massimo led them past the two young women glued to their screens at their desks, and over to the other side of the office. Tracy shivered upon noticing several human skulls on one of the shelves. Broken stone statues and other unidentifiable artefacts covered the rest. Massimo picked up a small, red step-ladder leaning against the wall, opened it up, and placed it down in front of the shelves. He climbed up the ladder to retrieve a small, narrow, light-brown, wooden case from the second-highest shelf. "It's a first, Harold!" he said, as he stepped off the ladder, excitement in his voice. He gingerly handed the case over to Harold whose eyes lit up in anticipation.

"Good God," he whispered, carefully opening the case to reveal a long, narrow stone artefact nestled on a black, velvet inner lining inside. Tracy noticed her father's eyes well up with tears. He quickly blinked them away.

"What is it?" said Tracy.

Berat leaned over Harold's shoulder for a closer look. "Looks like some kind of stick," he said.

"You are correct, Mr. Berat," said Massimo. "It *is* a stick. It's the very first evidence of petrified wood that we have found on the site."

"Petrified wood?" said Tracy frowning. "You mean this was a piece of wood, now turned to stone?"

"Yes, yes!" said Massimo excitedly.

"But doesn't that take millions of years? Like a fossil?"

"It is true that most petrified wooden artefacts are millions of years old, but the petrification process can begin as early as 10,000 years. Remarkable," said Harold, carefully admiring the stone stick.

"So how old do think this is?" said Tracy.

"Oh, probably well over 12,000 years," said Massimo.

"What a find!" said Berat.

"But what is it exactly?" enquired Tracy.

Massimo took a deep breath. "Come and have a look at the scan results," he said, leading the trio to the front of the office. "You can put that down over there," he said gesturing to an open space on his desk. "Here," said Massimo, handing Harold a file.

Harold flipped through the documentation until he reached a page with several black and white, grainy images.

"The scan results," said Massimo.

"Are these from the Tescan?" said Harold, looking up from the file.

Massimo nodded. "It's a Vega 3," he said, pointing at the photocopier-looking machine.

Harold nodded, turning his attention back to the file.

"What's a Tescan?" said Tracy.

"This baby," said Massimo, walking over to the photocopier-thingy, "is a Tescan Vega 3, a state-of-the-art, scanning electron microscope. We used it to scan the artefact so that we could determine its properties. We found a series of small indentations across the piece, deliberately made and unevenly spaced. Our theory is that it is some sort of measuring instrument."

"Used in the construction of the temples," whispered

150

Harold in awe. He turned back to stare at the piece of petrified wood as if it was something otherworldly, something magical.

"Exactly," said Massimo. "We believe that the artefact was used by the builders as part of their construction process. Perhaps to measure the distances between the stone pillars or even their dimensions."

"What do you mean temples?" said Tracy. "There are more of them?"

"There are approximately 200 t-shaped pillars, making up a total of 15 temple structures spread out over this area," said Massimo. "The others are still buried and will take over 100 years to excavate unless we develop some kind of advanced excavating technique in the not too distant future."

"Wow!" Tracy said in awe.

"I have an idea," said Harold. "Where can we find a 3-D laser-printer?"

Massimo drew a sharp intake of breath. "You want to print the artefact!"

"Yes," said Harold. "But it will first require some graphic design work. Are these scans," he held up the file, "enough for us to replicate the artefact exactly as it was 12,000 years ago?"

"Hmmm." Massimo ran his hand through his long, unkempt hair. Tracy wondered how it didn't get stuck in the mass of twisted curls. "We will have to visit the Sanliurfa Museum. They have a 3D-printer and a graphic designer who will be able to assist us."

"Excellent!" said Harold. "Well? What are we waiting for? Let's go!"

20 ~ Copycat

Tracy marvelled at the museum in Urfa that appeared quite modern by Turkish standards. She gazed up at the three-storey building, adorned in light brown coloured tiles, designed to blend in with the arid surroundings.

"It was built in 2015," said Berat proudly, stopping to stand next to Tracy. "The original museum was built in 1969 and is less than half the size of this one." Berat continued towards the double-glass entrance doors, following Harold and Massimo who seemed to be trotting at quite a pace up ahead.

Tracy ran to catch up with the group.

Massimo signalled to security as they bypassed the turnstiles and entered via an administration office, into a large room filled with electronic equipment. Tracy noticed a variety of monitors and desktop computers, as well as a host of unfamiliar devices that hummed, whirred and vibrated with a life of their own.

"Professor!" A young man in a bright green sweater jumped up from his desk in alarm. "Buongiorno."

"Buongiorno, Phillippe," said Massimo. "This is Professor Harold Barnes, his daughter, Tracy and you know Berat, of course," said Massimo, introducing everyone. "This is Phillippe Dubois, graphic designer extraordinaire."

"My pleasure," said Phillippe.

"Please, sit down," said Massimo. "We require your assistance. Here," he said, handing Phillippe a flash drive. "It's a scan of an artefact we found at Gobekli Tepe."

Phillippe pushed the flash drive into the USB slot at the back of his Mac and opened the file. "What is it?" he inquired, staring at the 3D-rendered image on the screen.

"We believe it's a tool used by the builders of Gobekli Tepe to measure the distances between the t-shaped, stone pillars," said Massimo. "See those round indentations spaced unevenly apart? They must be holes. Can you clean it up for us? Remove all those rough, uneven bits?"

"Sure. Won't take me that long," replied Phillippe.

"Super. Also, can you work out the measurements?"

"Measurements?"

"Yes, between the holes, the length of the artefact, etcetera."

"Oh, okay, yes, of course." Phillippe used a track-pad to move his mouse pointer around the screen, working deftly to smooth out the image, removing all the obvious anomalies as a result of the calcification of the artefact as it slowly turned to stone, deep underground. Gradually, the image began to take shape as he continued to work on cleaning it up, section by section. He smoothed out the indentations, revealing perfectly rounded holes in their place and then set out to measure the distances between each hole in relation to the length of the artefact from end to end. Finally, he entered the calculations into a spreadsheet he had open in the corner of his screen.

Massimo moved closer to the screen to scrutinise the numbers, his eyes darting over the spreadsheet. "Harold. Come and look at this," he said, his voice a mere whisper.

Harold pulled out his reading glasses to get a closer look.

"Can you see it? Do you recognise the pattern?" Massimo pointed at the table of numbers and then at the image on the screen. "See this first hole and then the space between it and the next three? And see how these three holes curve around the

153

artefact?"

"Can it be?" Harold said in awe.

"Fibonacci," confirmed Massimo. "The holes have been deliberately placed around the artefact using the Golden Ratio."

"Oh my God," said Harold. "Do you know what this means?"

"Isn't Fibonacci the same as phi?" said Tracy.

Massimo nodded. "To create a Fibonacci spiral, you would draw circular arcs connecting the opposite corner of squares, followed by a grid, by multiplying the first square, and then consecutive squares by phi or 1.618."

"The architects of Gobekli Tepe knew the Golden Ratio. They used the Golden ratio," said Harold slowly. "This is ground-breaking news, Massimo!"

"This explains a lot," said Massimo. "The alignment of the t-shaped pillars and the distances between them. What do you think the holes on the artefact are for?"

"Maybe there's another piece that slots into each hole?" said Berat. "Perhaps we are missing another piece of the puzzle?"

"Why do you think the holes don't go all the way through?" said Tracy. "There's nothing on the opposite side to show that they do."

"The artefact could be hollow," suggested Harold. "Imagine its creator, carving it out of wood, hollowing out the stick, marking each hole, meticulously placing them apart from one another based on the Golden Ratio. I still cannot believe it, that these people living over 12,000 years ago had the mathematical knowledge of the Golden Ratio. It's just unfathomable."

"Well, it *is* evident in nature," said Massimo. "Always has been. Since before man was created. But yes, you are right. This is knowledge that must have been discovered and then somehow lost again."

"Rediscovered during the time of the Great Pyramids in Egypt," said Harold.

"Yes, of course!" said Massimo. "The Pyramids were built using the Golden Ratio. But that was about 7,000 years later."

"There, it is done," said Phillippe. "I hollowed out the entire thing, including the holes."

The graphical image on screen was completely smooth, free from any imperfections. Phillippe rotated it with his track-pad so that they could see it from every angle. It looked like a beautiful work of art, with the holes geometrically placed in a captivating pattern around its diameter.

"Can we print it now?" said Harold.

Massimo nodded to Phillippe, who stood up and made his way towards a machine behind them.

"Is this a 3-D printer?" said Tracy, following him. "How does it work?"

"Yep. It's quite simple, actually," said Phillippe. "It works just like any printer, except the cartridges, contain different types of printing plastic. Some printers also print in metal. This baby over here uses carbon fibre," he said proudly. "It's much stronger and lighter than anything else used in the industry."

"But how does the printer print in 3D?"

"Well, the printer needs to connect to a computer programme such as CAD." Massimo pointed to his screen. "The information is fed into the printer that begins printing the design one layer at a time from the bottom up."

"Must take some time," said Tracy.

"Depends on the size of the item to be printed."

"So how long do you think it will take to print the artefact?"

"Oh, about 45 minutes to an hour," he replied.

"Dad, did you hear that," said Tracy turning to her father. "It's going to take about an hour to print."

Harold looked at his watch. "Don't worry. We still have some time."

"Let's go to the cafe," said Massimo. "It's just past the entrance. They make great coffee."

◊ ◊ ◊

Tracy scanned through the menu. The Shepherd's Turkish

Salad looked good. It was made with chopped tomatoes, parsley, cucumber, onions, tossed with lemon, vinegar, and olive oil and seasoned with herbs. "Can I please have a Shepherd's Salad," she said to the waiter. "And some apple tea." She was starting to enjoy its mild, sweetly fragrant taste. She pulled out her phone to look at the time - 1.48pm, and then started counting backwards on her fingers. Twelve, eleven, ten, nine, eight, seven, six. That's seven hours. 6.48am. Lisa was probably still lying in bed.

Tracy: *Morning Lis. You awake?*

Within seconds, her phone vibrated in response. *Hey, girl. Wassup? How's Turkey? How's your hawt Dad?*

Tracy: *I told you to stop that?*

Lisa: *What?*

Tracy changed the subject. *Did you hear the latest about Mickey and Steph?* Michael Stopforth and Stephanie Crawford were two rising Hollywood stars with their own reality television show.

Lisa: *Yeah, can you believe it? They're getting married!*

Tracy: *Was bound to happen.*

Lisa: *Yeah but so soon!? Guaranteed they last a year, maybe two.*

Tracy: *You're probably right. Just like all the others.*

Lisa: *They're too young. Too immature. Too much pressure.*

Tracy: *I know. Hard to imagine being in their shoes. All those fans and paparazzi watching their every move.*

Lisa: *Must be horrible. But even so, I'd still kill to be Stephanie Crawford for a day at least!*

Tracy: *Did you see what she was wearing?*

Lisa: *In that announcement pic?*

Tracy: *Yeah. That black number. Sick. Definitely a red carpet designer. Probably Dior or Armani.*

Lisa: *I wish.*

Tracy: *You got the body, girl! It's hot AF.*

Lisa: *No way. I could never wear anything like that. My butt's too big for that dress.*

Tracy: *You talk so much shit, Lis. You have the hottest body in school. And you know it!*

Lisa: *Thanks! So, tell me about Turkey? Howsit going? Still no hot men besides your Dad?*

Tracy: *It's been so much fun. We went to this huge cathedral which was a mosque and is now a museum. Sounds a little confusing but it's really old and has been occupied by so many different people over the years. We also visited a palace of the Sultans where we saw this huge diamond. Today I visited a fortune-teller, and this place called Gobekli Tepe, one of my Dad's research projects.*

Lisa: *Wow! Sounds like you've been busy.*

Tracy: *Very. Trying to cram everything into a few days isn't easy. Right now, I'm sitting at a cafe in this museum in a little town called Urfa. I'll tell you more later. Gotta go, my food has arrived.*

Lisa: *Later bae. Love you.*

Tracy: *xxx*

Tracy pushed the phone into her pocket and began to tuck into her salad, savouring every tasty mouthful. Harold, Berat, and Massimo were in deep conversation, the excitement in their voices quite palpable in the museum's small cafe. Tracy began to think about the artefact, imagining what it could have been used for. A device used to measure the distance between the t-shaped pillars didn't quite seem right. *What were the holes for? Why were they spaced out using the Golden Ratio?* She wondered if by using her powers of divination, she could determine its use. She first had a sip of tea, enjoying the warm, fruity liquid as it warmed her throat, then took hold of her crystal in her hand, sat back into her chair and closed her eyes. She focused on her breathing and concentrated on the stone, allowing her mind to drift into a state of calm, tranquil thoughts. She pictured sailing on the Bosphorus, the wind in her hair and the setting sun on her face. The fortune teller's face appeared before her. She was speaking. Whispering. She could hear her voice in her ear like the wind in her hair.

You have the power of sight. It is a gift that you must treasure. It grows stronger every day. Use it wisely by helping others, and you will be helped in return.

She turned her attention to the artefact, picturing it in her mind, turning it over and over, trying to imagine what it was exactly. The fortune teller's whispering voice faded away into the whistling wind. The wind. It sounded different this time. Whistling. Ringing like a distant melody.

"Tracy. Tracy."

Tracy opened her eyes. The room seemed to be swaying like the ferry on the Bosphorus.

"You okay?" said her father.

She nodded, sitting up to have another sip of tea.

"Come, we're going back to check on the printing. It should almost be ready."

Tracy looked at the time. 2.28pm. She took another long sip of tea and stood up to follow the others out of the cafe.

◊ ◊ ◊

Phillippe was standing over the 3D printer as the group returned to the room. "Ah! Just in time," he said in his French accent. "It's almost done." The printer was making a high-pitched, whining sound.

Tracy walked over to have a look. Beneath the perspex cover, was the almost completed, printed artefact. It looked just like the design on Phillippe's Mac, right down to the silvery-grey colour. It was about a foot and a half in length, longer and narrower than Tracy imagined it to be. Tracy noticed the precisely carved holes across its surface. The melody of the wind played in her ears again, and then her heart stopped.

"I know what is," she whispered.

"What did you say?" said Harold.

"I said I know what the artefact is. It's a flute. I heard it. The wind. The melody in the wind."

Harold stared at the object inside the printer with eyes wider than Tracy had ever seen them.

"Could it be?" said Massimo.

"There," said Phillippe as the printer head returned to its starting position. "It's done." He opened the perspex cover and delicately lifted the finished artefact copy from the printer.

"Trace, I think you're right," said Harold, taking the 3D-printed, carbon-fibre piece from Phillippe. He examined it lengthwise, peering down its narrow, hollow shaft. He gripped it nimbly in his hands, covering several holes with his fingertips, pressed one end to his lips and blew. The sweetest sound poured forth. Harold dropped into Phillippe's chair in shock. His face was pale.

"Wow," whispered Berat, aghast.

Harold stared at the flute in his hands. "This... flute..." He turned to Phillippe. "Thank you, Phillippe. Thank you." He looked up at Massimo who just stood there, speechless.

Everyone was silent, save for the buzzing of the machines in the room. Tracy yearned to hear the sweet sound of the flute again. She stared at the carbon-fibre thing in her father's hands as if it were a magical wand from another dimension.

"Dad," she whispered. "Blow it again."

Harold raised the flute to his lips and blew again, this time moving his fingers randomly over the holes. He was no musician, and yet the sounds that came out were pure and clear as a singing bird at the break of dawn. He stared at the flute again, clearly overawed at the discovery.

"Phillippe," said Massimo, pulling out the wooden case containing the original artefact from his bag. "This is the original," he continued, opening up the case. "I need you to print me another copy, and then I'm going to place the original and the second printed copy in the Gobekli Tepe exhibit in the museum." He turned to the Professor, "Harold, swap the original artefact in the case with that printed copy you're holding. You're taking it home."

Massimo removed the original stone artefact from the case, and Harold placed the printed copy inside as instructed. Massimo closed the case and handed it over. "Thank you, Professor," he said, shaking Harold's hand warmly. "And thank you, Miss Barnes," he said to Tracy. "Without your insight, we would never have concluded that the artefact was indeed a flute."

Tracy blushed.

"I believe that you've a plane to catch," Massimo said with a smile. "Come, let me direct you to the exit. I'll remain behind to install this wonderful piece," he said, holding up the original artefact.

"Bye Phillippe," Tracy said, turning to the graphic designer.

"Au revoir," he replied, bowing his head. "Pleasure to make your acquaintance."

Tracy caught up with Berat and her father with Massimo leading the way.

"Thank you, all of you," said Massimo, as they reached the front of the museum. "This has been an enlightening experience. We're going to have to make a public announcement soon. I'll set up a meeting with the museum Director tomorrow."

"Sounds good," said Harold.

Berat's phone rang as soon as they climbed into the car.

"Hello," he answered. "Yes. We're leaving now. Their flight is at four. You what? No! Zehra, I said no. I promised that you could meet her. That's all. Yes, yes, I know." Berat shook his free hand in the air in agitation as he spoke. "Okay, okay, but just two nights. Yes. Just be ready. Bye." He pushed his phone into his pocket.

"Your daughter?" said Harold.

"Yes. I promised her that I would introduce her to Tracy. Now, she has made plans to fly back to Istanbul with you. She will stay at her cousin there." Berat shook his head. "You see what I mean? She has a mind of her own."

"Well, at least she calls you to ask," said Harold. "Could be worse."

"Ha-ha-ha!" Berat laughed in a deep baritone. "Ask? You think that was a request?" he said, pointing at his phone. "That was an order. She called me to tell me her plans because she needs a ride to the airport!" he said, grinding his teeth together and pulling his face into an angry sneer that made both Tracy

Richard Gradner - Acoustic Alchemy

and Harold laugh out loud.

I think I'm going to like this girl, thought Tracy to herself.

21 ~ Night Owl

Berat pulled up outside a modern-looking apartment block. Harold looked out the window. "New place?"

"Yes," replied Berat. "Moved in about three months back. It's a little smaller, but at least it's new, quite central and we have a view."

"Great!"

Berat honked his horn several times and then climbed out of the vehicle. "Wait here," he instructed and then turned to march towards the apartment block, disappearing inside. After a few moments he emerged, wheeling a large, red suitcase. A young girl with long, straight, black hair followed close behind. Zehra. Berat was shouting in Turkish and waving his free hand about excitedly in the air. Zehra shouted defiantly back at him as they approached the car. She wore a long, dark green dress with a red and gold shawl over her shoulders. She had dark, piercing eyes and an attractive face. Tracy watched as the two of them continued to argue while Berat loaded her case into the trunk. He slammed it shut with a bang. Tracy jumped.

Zehra opened the door, and the exasperated look on her face turned immediately into a charming smile when she saw Tracy sitting in the back. "Hello," she said warmly. "I'm Zehra.

Pleased to meet you." She extended her hand.

Tracy shook it. Her grip was strong. "Tracy. Tracy Barnes. Nice to meet you," she said, smiling broadly in return.

Zehra jumped into the car. "Sorry about that," she said, jerking her thumb over her shoulder. "My father drives me crazy. He's a mean old fart."

"Hey!" said Berat as he climbed into the car. "I heard that. Apologise."

Zehra folded her arms and pressed her lips together.

"Zehra!"

"Sorry, Papa," she snapped.

"Please. These are my guests. I will not tolerate your attitude, especially not here, not now."

"Hello, Zehra," said Harold, turning around in his seat.

"Hi, Professor Barnes," said Zehra. "Good to see you. It's been a while."

"It sure has. You have grown into a beautiful young woman."

"Why, thank you, Professor," said Zehra, dropping her head coyly.

"I believe you're joining us on our flight back to Istanbul."

"Yes! It's so exciting. I thought that it would be a good opportunity to show Tracy around town tonight if that's okay?"

Tracy gasped. "Wow! Really? Dad, can I? Please?"

"It *is* Saturday night," said Zehra. "There's this cool party by the river that I'm going to and…"

"Definitely not," said Berat firmly.

"But Papa!"

"Berat," said Harold. "It's okay."

"But…"

"I'm fine with it," said Harold. "Tracy is a big girl now and your daughter is a local. She knows her way around. I'm sure she'll take good care of Tracy, won't you, Zehra?" he said with a wink.

"Of course, Professor." Zehra turned to Tracy with a grin and winked. "I'll take great care of her."

Tracy smiled in return. She was looking forward to a great party. Her only concern was what she was going to wear.

◇ ◇ ◇

The flight back to Istanbul was uneventful. Tracy spent most of the short trip asleep on the plane, exhausted from the jet lag that had caught up with her.

Back at the Intercontinental Hotel, Tracy looked over her shoulder in the mirror. She thought her black, skinny, ripped jeans didn't make her look that skinny. She shrugged her shoulders. *Oh well. It's all that I have. It'll have to do.* She loved her brand new, navy-blue Tommy Hilfiger bomber jacket that she received as a gift from her uncle Jimmy and aunt Sarah for her birthday. They always spoilt her with really special presents. Last year, they gave her a beautiful, black leather handbag with a butterfly subtly embossed on either side that reminded her of the animals carved in relief into the t-shaped pillars at Gobekli Tepe. That got her thinking about the flute again. She looked at her phone. 7.48pm. Zehra planned to meet her in the hotel lobby at 8. She stepped into the bathroom to check her makeup. Her washed and blow-dried, dusty blond hair hung loosely across one side of her face and down, over her shoulders. She pouted her lips and blew a kiss into the mirror, admiring her profile and then snapped a selfie with her phone. *You look hot, girl. Let's do this,* she said assuredly to herself. She sent the photo to Lisa with the caption, *Hitting the town, bae. Don't wait up!*

Tracy's phone vibrated with Lisa's response. *OMG! You look so hot, Trace. Just like Steph! Sick jacket. I want one!*

Tracy: *Thanks.*

Lisa: *Where are you going? Hot date?*

Tracy: *This Turkish girl I met today is taking me to a party by the river.*

Lisa: *Sick! Who is she? How'd you meet her?*

Tracy: *It's the daughter of one of my Dad's friends. Her name is Zehra.*

Lisa: *Cool. Send me pics!*
Tracy: *K. Will do. Bye.*
Lisa: *Bye.*

Tracy had one last look in the mirror and then stepped out of her room. She knocked on her father's door. "Dad?"

Harold opened the door. "You look stunning, Trace. So beautiful."

Tracy blushed. "Thanks, Dad."

"You on your way?"

Tracy nodded.

"You have your phone?"

"Yes, Dad," she said, holding up her device.

"Okay. Good. Enjoy yourself and be safe. And please try not to come back too late."

Tracy gave her father a hug and a kiss. "Don't worry. I'll be fine."

She waved to her father and then made her way to the elevator that took her down to the lobby to meet Zehra who was waiting patiently at reception.

She wore long, black tights, a matching black top and high heels.

"Hi," said Zehra with a smile. "Ready to party? You look great. I like what you've done with your hair."

"Thanks. So do you."

Zehra winked. "Thanks. I've just called an Uber. Should be here any minute," she said as she made her way towards the exit.

Tracy climbed into the navy blue Toyota Corolla that pulled up outside. The back seats and the dashboard in front were covered in plush, brown fur and the car interior smelt of a mix between lavender and oranges. Turkish music was playing.

"Hello Zehra," said the driver, looking in his rear-view mirror at Tracy.

"Uh, no, that's Zehra," said Tracy, pointing.

"Oh, I'm sorry."

"No problem."

"We're going to Club Bosphorus," said Zehra.

"Yes. Okay," said the driver, checking the map on his phone.

"This place is great," said Zehra, excitement in her voice. "It's literally on the river."

"Sounds beautiful," said Tracy.

"Yes. You can look out across the water while you're dancing."

"Cool."

"I know the DJ. He organised me tickets."

"Free of charge?"

Zehra nodded.

"That's incredible."

"Yes. He said we could go behind the DJ box while he is playing."

"Ooh. I'm so excited!" Tracy rubbed her hands together in anticipation. She gazed out of the window as they drove through the traffic. "How long is the ride?"

"Oh, pretty quick. Another five minutes or so."

They soon pulled up outside the club. Tracy stepped out of the car and followed Zehra towards the venue. There was a short queue outside.

Zehra turned to Tracy. "It's still early. This queue eventually stretches around the block."

Zehra brazenly walked to the front of the line. Tracy followed. A young girl with a pink streak through her dark hair gave Zehra a look of disdain as they passed. Zehra held her head up high, ignoring her blatant glare. "Hi," she addressed the bouncer at the door. His shoulders were so broad in his black tuxedo that he easily blocked out the entire width of the entrance. "I'm on the list."

"Whose list?" said the bouncer in a deep, baritone.

"Tomi's."

The bouncer pulled a mini-tablet out of the inside of his jacket pocket and wiped his finger slowly up the screen. "Name?"

"Zehra Polat. Plus one."

The bouncer squinted his eyes as he scrolled through the

166

list. He stopped swiping, tapped the screen once and then pushed the tablet back into his jacket pocket. He glared at Zehra and Tracy and then stepped aside to let them pass. "Welcome to Club Bosphorus," he boomed. "Stamps," he pointed at a counter with a perspex screen that dropped down two-thirds of the way.

Zehra pushed her arm under the counter, and a lady with short-cropped peroxided hair on the other side pressed a round, rubber stamp into her wrist.

Then it was Tracy's turn. She pulled her arm out and looked at her wrist. There was nothing there. She turned back to the lady behind the counter and opened her mouth in consternation.

Zehra grabbed her arm and pulled her away. "Come silly. It's invisible," she said, showing Tracy the underside of her wrist.

"What do you mean? Why? What's the point?"

"It's only visible under ultra-violet light. Looks way better than a blob of messy ink that takes ages to come off."

"Oh." Tracy felt dumb for a moment, but the incident was soon forgotten as she followed Zehra up the stairs and into the club where she was greeted with an array of flashing green, red and yellow lights pulsing around the room. The club wasn't very full. Most of the people inside were gathered around the long bar to the left. There were only a handful of people on the dance-floor, twisting their bodies to a slow rendition of *Everybody Wants to Rule the World* by Tears for Fears.

"Let's get a drink!" Zehra shouted into Tracy's ear over the music. She pointed at the bar.

Tracy followed Zehra to the bar, which wasn't very crowded.

"Merhaba," said a young guy to Tracy.

"Um, hello," said Tracy.

"Oh, you English?" said the boy. He had straight, black hair and wore a black hat that looked like a beret.

Tracy nodded. "American."

"Ah, you have rosy cheeks and glowing eyes." He smiled, and Tracy noticed that most of his teeth were crooked.

She smiled in return, and her cheeks blushed. Now they truly were rosy. "Uh, okay," she said. *Glowing eyes?* She thought to herself. "Thank you."

"You also have lovely udders," he said, gazing at her breasts.

Tracy involuntarily lifted her arm and draped it across her chest. "I think you meant... actually I have no idea what you meant. That was just a little too weird."

Zehra turned around. "Here," she said, handing Tracy a glass of white wine. "You okay? Looks like you've seen a ghost." She turned towards the boy in the beret. He had a goofy grin on his face. "He bothering you?" She tilted her head in his direction.

"Uh, I'm not sure," said Tracy. "He said that I had lovely udders."

"Ha-ha-ha!" Zehra laughed. "Sapık lanet," she said to the boy. She turned back to Tracy. "Come, follow me." Zehra marched boldly across the dance floor towards the DJ. He looked up as the two girls approached and waved at Zehra. "Come," said Zehra, pulling Tracy by the hand.

"What did you say?" said Tracy. "To the boy."

"Oh, I just told him that he was a pervert and that he should go and bother someone else."

"Thanks!"

The girls walked around the speakers to the rear of the DJ box. Tracy stepped up and into the DJ booth. She waited while Zehra chatted to the DJ. Tracy expected him to be much older, but he looked quite young. He had long, dark hair that fell across the side of his face and a friendly smile. Zehra turned around and pointed at Tracy. The music was too loud to hear anything. She stepped forward to introduce herself.

The DJ cupped his hand close to Tracy's ear. "Hi, Tracy, I'm Tomi," he said. He stepped back and held out his hand. Tracy extended hers. He took hold of it and kissed it gently. Tracy was thankful that the dark club hid the crimson tide that flushed her face.

"He said we could stay here for as long as we want!" Zehra shouted.

Tracy nodded and gave her a thumbs-up.

Tomi winked at Tracy and then turned around to focus on his DJ'ing.

Tracy and Zehra put their wine glasses down and began to dance. Tracy looked out across the crowd of people that were slowly beginning to fill the club. She tapped Zehra on the shoulder to get her attention. "This is so cool!"

Zehra grinned and nodded.

Tomi mixed the track into another and Zehra stepped down from the DJ box. She signalled for Tracy to follow her to the other side of the dance floor. A metal railing separated them from the glass windows that stretched from floor to ceiling.

"Wow!" said Tracy as she gazed out the windows at the expanse of water that was the Bosphorus River. "This is so beautiful." She counted the twinkling lights from three boats as they sailed passed. In the distance, the city lights on the other side of the river sparkled like glittering diamonds.

"Yes, I know, hey?" said Zehra. "Best club in Istanbul. Shall we go and sit down?" Without waiting for Tracy's response, Zehra pulled her by the hand again, but this time, towards a booth near the bar. The seats were comfortable, and the music wasn't nearly as loud.

"So, do you have a boyfriend?" said Zehra, getting straight to the point.

"Yes," said Tracy. "His name's Josh."

"Hmm. I wanted to introduce you to someone I thought you might like. Show me a pic."

Tracy turned on her phone. The home screen photo was a pic of her and Josh at her birthday party.

"Ooh. He looks cute! How long you been dating?"

"Um, about three months. But we've known each other like forever. Is he here?" Tracy stuck her head out of the booth to look around the club.

"The guy I wanted you to meet? Not yet. He's coming with a friend. They should be here soon."

"Your boyfriend?"

"No, just a friend." Zehra smiled coyly.

"So you two have hooked up?"

"Kinda. We're just friends, I guess."

"You like him, don't you?" Tracy prompted.

"Maybe."

"Can I try something?"

"Sure."

"Give me your hand."

Zehra extended her right hand across the table.

Tracy took Zehra's hand in hers, grabbed hold of the crystal around her neck with her other hand and closed her eyes. The music in the club reverberated through her body like a beating drum, matching the throb-throb-throb of her heart in her chest as it pumped blood through her veins. In her mind's eye, she was on a ship, sailing across a tumultuous ocean, holding desperately onto the mast as she strained to see the distant shore. And then all of a sudden, the storm abated, and she found herself drifting serenely across a blood-soaked sky with not so much as a ripple in the water around her. Without warning, a mist rolled in, its watery tendrils brushing past her face like the tentacles from an octopus feeling its way across the rocks at low tide. The mist began to take shape, forming itself into indistinct patterns that Tracy glimpsed out of the corner of her eye. The patterns became clearer until she recognised faces that appeared and then disappeared again as the mist rolled in. The mist thickened until the faces that kept forming, retained their shapes for longer, becoming more recognisable as time wore on. The misty apparitions had mouths that began to move, slowly at first, but then faster. With this, came a sound; a strange hissing noise, that grew louder and more distinct. Tracy began to recognise words. Names. The faces in the mist were speaking to her, repeating names. *Their* names.

Tracy let go of Zehra's hand and opened her eyes. "Murat

and Hasad," she said.

Zehra quickly withdrew her hand and gave it a shake in the air. "Goosebumps! How did you know?" she said, flabbergasted. "My father put you up to this?" She stared at her hand and then at the crystal around Tracy's neck. "It has something to do with that," she said, pointing at the stone. "Doesn't it?"

"Kind of," said Tracy. "It enhances things."

"What do you mean?"

"I have a gift. I can see things. Things that are going to happen."

"You mean you're a fortune-teller?"

Madame Kezia's face flashed before her. Tracy smiled. "Kind of."

"So, those names just came to you while you were holding my hand?"

"Yeah."

"Incredible! How long have you had this… gift?"

"Not long. My grandmother gave me this crystal for my seventeenth birthday." She fingered the stone. "That's when it started, I guess. The more I practice, the easier it gets."

"I'd kill to have that kind of power," said Zehra. "You're so lucky. You could make some serious moolah, you know? Why don't you open up shop? Start a website or something? Sell your services? Could even lead to a TV show. You could become famous. A star!" Zehra waved her hands through the air for added effect.

"Oh, I dunno. I haven't thought about it much. It's all so new. I don't think my grandmother would approve if I commercialised it."

"I think you're making a big mistake. I mean, just think about all the people you could help, including yourself!"

"Yeah. I'm just not the type to draw attention to myself."

Zehra turned around. "Look," she pointed across the club.

Tracy followed Zehra's gaze. Two boys were walking towards them. Tracy immediately recognised their faces from her vision.

171

"Murat! Hasad!" said Zehra. "Good to see you. This is my friend, Tracy. She's visiting from America."

The boys sat down at the booth next to Zehra and Tracy.

"Hi," they said together.

"How long you in town?" said Hasad. He had very short, dark hair and unusually piercing blue eyes.

"Monday."

"This Monday? You mean the day after tomorrow?"

Tracy nodded.

"That's a pity," said Hasad. "There is so much to see and do in Istanbul."

"Well, I've already seen quite a bit. It's a beautiful city."

"You have beautiful eyes," said Murat.

Tracy looked down, embarrassed. "Thank you."

Murat's hair was also dark, except that it was longer than Hasad's. He wore glasses and had a moustache.

"Please get us some drinks," said Zehra, pointing at her empty glass. "Drink up," she instructed Tracy. "White wine," she said to Murat as he stood up from the booth. Hasad followed close behind.

"They seem nice," said Tracy.

"Hasad is okay. Murat can be a bit irritating," said Zehra. "But I guess you know that already." She grinned.

"Actually, no. This is all still pretty new to me. I could only work out their names. Nothing more. Maybe if I spent more time…"

"Hey, have you ever thought about helping the police catch criminals? Like that television series. What's it called again? Now, that would be cool."

Tracy scratched her head. "Well, I haven't really thought about it. Could be dangerous."

"Danger is my middle name! Come let's dance!" Zehra pulled Tracy up from her seat. The dance floor was beginning to fill up. Tracy closed her eyes as the lights flashed behind them. She smiled as she moved to the mesmerising music, her thoughts happy and carefree.

22 ~ Visions

It was 2.33am when Tracy finally returned to her hotel room. She was surprisingly wide awake. *My body clock must be totally screwed up with the adjustment in the time zone;* she thought to herself. She pulled off her clothes and climbed into the shower, closing her eyes as the hot water pulsed over her head and ran down her body, washing away the stale smell of smoke and alcohol. She looked down at the crystal around her neck and smiled. Granny Sybs' face smiled back at her. She climbed out of the shower, dried her body and then blow-dried her hair. It was still a little damp as she climbed into bed. She curled onto her left side and quickly fell into a deep, even sleep.

Tracy dreamed. She opened her eyes. She was lying in her bed at home. She sat up, pulled back her curtains and looked out of the window. The moon was partially obscured by some clouds in the sky. It was almost full, so it lit up the heavens like a powerful headlamp, glowing eerily behind the clouds, causing them to shine white and bright in its magical light. She opened her window and carefully climbed out and onto the slanted roof on all fours. She dropped to her knees and then pushed herself up to standing, steadying herself as her ten toes, bearing her full weight, gripped the roof tiles at a dangerous angle. She looked

173

towards the moon and extended her arms out to her sides. She looked down at her feet and pushed then up until she was balancing precariously on her tippy-toes. She wobbled a little, trying desperately to maintain her balance until she felt the weight gradually leave her feet and then slowly, gracefully, she lifted off the rooftop. She glided across her garden and over the very tops of the trees beyond, gradually climbing higher and higher into the air. The feeling of weightlessness was incredible. Her skin broke out in a hive of gooseflesh, and she couldn't contain the great, big smile on her face.

The clouds parted to reveal the moon in all its glory, a giant, glowing orb of magnificence. The moonlight shone down from the sky, illuminating the Earth with its silvery brilliance. Tracy was energised as she floated higher and higher into the sky, free as a bird with the wings of an angel. She gazed up and watched as the clouds moved across the sky. The light dimmed, the wind picked up and the clouds thickened like someone was stirring up a broth in the heavens above. Still, she drifted higher. Still, the wind picked up, pushing at her hair, buffeting her nightgown across her body like there were forces at work trying to disrobe her. She thrust both arms in front of her face and picked up speed, flying across the sky like a rocket, sensing the currents and manoeuvring through them like she had done this so many times before.

The clouds became even thicker and darker, spreading themselves lavishly across the moon's surface like a thick layer of soot, blotting out the moon's light altogether, plunging the night into deep, dreary darkness. Tracy looked up. There was a storm brewing. She had to outrun it. She had to fly away from the darkness that was building around her, expanding, growing with every breath that she took. The wind around her began to increase in intensity until it became harder to navigate, so she dived, flying towards the ground in an attempt to find protection from the elements. She approached a forest and flew amongst the trees, decelerating until she glided down between them, landing gently on the earth below, the soft sand pushing up between her toes as the weight returned to her body. The trees sang loudly as the wind tore relentlessly through them, whipping about her lithe frame and through her hair like a frenzied animal on the loose. She moved through the forest, following her instinct, that was guiding her to a destination unknown. She approached a dark smudge on the forest floor, a pit; the charcoaled remains of a fire. She stared at the charred coals and saw the flames as they were, burning bright, licking the wood as they twisted, crackling loudly, incessantly. She saw two figures, one, hunched against a tree, concealed beneath a dark robe. Unmoving. The other was a girl. Her arms extended up towards the night sky, her head thrown back, her long, matted hair hanging past her shoulders as she slowly, resolutely circled the fire.

Tracy tried to understand what she was seeing. The image of the girl flickered and quivered as she shimmied around the flames like an old movie projector was playing out the scene before her, frame by frame. Tracy glanced at the figure by the tree who now appeared to be rocking from side to side, to a mysterious ballad that only it could hear. The girl continued moving around the flames until she reached the opposite side of the fire and was facing Tracy. Tracy squinted, trying to make out the face of the girl through the flickering flames. She gasped. The girl was naked, save for streaks of mud across her body and bits of leaves and dirt clinging to her hair. She made out a stone tied around her neck, but it was unlike Tracy's. It was black and seemed to suck the light right out of the fire. Tracy looked down at the crystal around her own neck. Her eyes widened in awe. It was glowing; pulsing with a bright pink light. She closed her hand around the stone and looked up as the flames jumped higher into the sky. The girl snapped her head up and stared directly at Tracy, her eyes piercing right through the flames, boring deep into Tracy's head like a pair of hot pokers. Tracy was locked in her stare, like a startled deer in the headlights. Try as she might, she couldn't tear her gaze away. The girl opened her mouth, and a high-pitched wail escaped,

175

burning Tracy's ears with its voracity. Tracy clamped her hands over her ears to block out the piercing screech and at the same time, squeezed her eyes tightly shut.

The screaming stopped, and Tracy opened her eyes. It was dark. She sat up and rubbed her eyes, taking a few moments to realise where she was. The baby finger on her left hand burned. She flicked on the light, and the shadows jumped away in alarm. The side of her hand was dark red, caked thick with blood. She jumped out of bed, ran to the bathroom, flipped open the faucet and let the water wash over her hand. She watched as the water turned pink in colour. She lifted her hand and twisted it sideways so that she could find the injury. There was none. The burning pain was gone, and her skin was smooth where there should have been some kind of wound, otherwise how else could one explain the phenomenon? Had she imagined the blood? She looked into the sink. Traces of pink still lingered in the water around the drain. *No. It was real.* She looked into the mirror, and then the memory of the dream hit her like a tsunami. She reeled, rocking back, staggering away from the basin, finding the wall behind her to steady herself as the penetrating eyes from the girl by the fire caused fear and panic to bring bile up and into her throat. She grabbed the glass bottle of water by the sink and downed it all in one go. She wiped her mouth with the back of her hand and stared into the mirror again. She pinched her arm, hard, and blinked her eyes a few times, squeezing them shut for a few moments each time.

She climbed back into bed and looked at her phone. 4.55am. *Biff.* She punched her pillow, turned onto her side and dozed off into a dreamless sleep.

23 ~ Spin

"Trace. You're so quiet. You okay? How was your evening?"

Tracy slowly swirled her spoon through her cereal. She took a deep breath and sighed it out. "All good."

Harold raised his eyebrows. "Okay. What happened? This is not like you. You sure you're okay? What time did you get in?"

"Dad, I'm fine. Promise. Just jet-lagged."

"How was the party?"

"Nice. Zehra is cool. She introduced me to a couple of locals. We had fun."

"Great!" said Harold with a grin. "Listen. I've got some work to do today, so you're welcome to chill." He lifted his coffee to his lips and took a sip.

"Okay cool. Will be nice just to chill after all the missioning around. Oh yeah, that reminds me - Zehra wanted to take me out for lunch. Is that okay?"

"Sure, sure. I've nothing planned."

Tracy absentmindedly rubbed the side of her left hand. "Cool. Thanks." She pulled out her phone and started typing a message to her mother. *Hi Mom. Just having breakfast with Dad, so by the time you read this, I will probably be having lunch! Istanbul is great. It's been quite the adventure. I'll tell you all about it when I'm back. Dad's*

friend Berat introduced me to his daughter Zehra, and she took me out last
night. We had lots of fun. Love you X

"Dad."

"Uh-huh."

"Have you ever heard of dreams that become real?"

"No. What do you mean?"

"I mean if something happens to you in a dream, that it
affects you physically."

"You mean like if you fall and knock yourself in your
dream then wake up with a bruise?"

"Yeah. Something like that."

"No. It would more than likely happen the other way
around."

"What do you mean?" Tracy scratched her head.

"I mean that if you somehow fall out of bed and hit your
head while sleeping, this could manifest in your dream state
while you are sleeping. To be affected physically, you would need
to hit yourself in the real world to get a bruise. But," Harold
raised his finger, "there are some cultures that use the dream
world to inflict physical harm on others."

"Really?"

Harold nodded. "South American shamans, for example.
They travel into the spirit world with their patients to fight off
evil curses. They fight magic with magic and end up inflicting
physical harm in the process."

"Wow. How?" said Tracy.

"Well, they shoot enchanted arrows at the person who laid
the curse, causing them harm in the spiritual world. This
transfers to the physical body in the real world."

Tracy shivered. "That's creepy."

"Why do you ask? You have a bad dream?"

"Something like that," said Tracy, examining the side of her
hand. She spooned a mouthful of muesli into her mouth.

"Don't worry," said Harold, waving his hand dismissively
through the air. "I doubt very much that a shaman from the
Mapuche tribe is out to get you."

Tracy nodded as she swallowed her food. "Gotcha. It's just that the dream I had was so vivid."

"Hmm." Harold stroked his chin. "It may have something to do with your new powers."

Tracy laughed. "Dad, you make me sound like a superhero or something. I don't have *powers*."

"Well, you know what I mean. What I'm saying is, if it's really troubling you, maybe you should speak to your grandmother? Perhaps it has something to do with your gift."

"Yeah, maybe."

"Okay. Please excuse me. Gotta get to my work," said Harold standing up from the table. "See you later?"

Tracy nodded. "Sure, Dad. See you later." Tracy closed her eyes and thought back to the dream. Unlike the fleeting dreams that she normally had, this one was lucid. She remembered it like she was really there, at home, standing on the roof of her house. She remembered looking down and the feeling of giddiness that washed over her. She remembered the cool breeze that tickled her face and the weightlessness that caused her to rise up and into the night sky. She remembered the moon; its light illuminating the sky like a magnificent, glowing orb. She remembered the clouds and the strength of the wind that pushed her down and into the forest; the dark, dense forest. And then there was the fire and the figure hunched against a tree nearby, and the girl with the long, matted hair and naked frame covered in streaks of mud caked all over her body, shifting slowly, purposefully, around the flames.

Tracy opened her eyes and shivered. She didn't want to see those dark, piercing eyes ever again. She thrust another spoon of muesli into her mouth and gazed out of the hotel window at the river beyond, its tranquil waters soothing her anxiety somewhat. *He may have a point,* thought Tracy to herself. She made a mental note to give Granny Sybs a phone call a little later.

"Tracy!" shouted Zehra as she rolled down the window. "Come, get in."

Tracy held onto the seat in front of her as the taxi sped through the streets of Istanbul. "Shoo, he's in a hurry!"

Zehra looked at her watch. "Maybe it's cos I told him that I was late." She laughed and then muttered an instruction in Turkish to the driver. He glanced in his rear-view mirror at Zehra, nodded and then took his foot off the gas. The vehicle slowed down, and Tracy released her grip on the seat.

"That's better. Where we going exactly?"

"Surprise. You're gonna love it!" Zehra grinned.

With a squeal of brakes, the taxi ground to a halt, throwing Tracy and Zehra forward into the back of the front seats.

The taxi driver opened his window to shout profanity at a man crossing the street with his horse and cart.

"Özür dilerim," said the driver over his shoulder.

Tracy looked at Zehra and shrugged her shoulders.

"It means 'sorry'," explained Zehra with a grin.

Tracy looked out of the window and up at the sky. It was grey; covered in clouds. "Is it going to rain today?" Tracy turned to Zehra.

"I think so. But don't worry. Where we're going, it won't really matter," she said with a wink.`

The taxi continued on its way, winding through the streets of Istanbul, finally coming to a stop outside a stone-coloured building.

"Here we are. Teşekkür ederim," said Zehra to the driver.

Tracy climbed out of the car. A sign greeted them outside the building that read, *Museum Entrance.*

"We're going to a museum?"

"It's not just any museum," said Zehra. "It's the Galata Mevlevi. Every Sunday, inside the *semahane*, a religious ceremony takes place."

"What's the *semehane*?"

"Se-ma-ha-ne. It's a special hall inside the museum," said

Zehra. "Come, let's go. It's about to begin."

Tracy followed Zehra into the museum. They walked through a large room and turned left into a long corridor. A man in a black robe opened the white double doors at the end, and they stepped into a large, round room. An unusually high ceiling with a magnificently designed inlay drew Tracy's breath away. The outer ring of the hall was filled with people; other tourists, all seated and waiting in anticipation for something about to happen. Tracy sat down next to Zehra and gazed upon fifteen men seated on the wooden floor in front of them with their eyes closed. Some were gently swaying from side to side as if they were in a deep, hypnotic trance.

"What are they doing?" whispered Tracy.

"You'll see," responded Zehra.

The men were all identically dressed. They wore long, black cloaks, with unusually tall, tan-coloured hats that reminded Tracy of those black furry ones worn by the Queen's Guard outside Buckingham Palace in London. Tracy spotted even longer white undergarments that stuck out beneath their black robes. The incessant whispering in the room between all the people seated and watching, dissipated as the fifteen men began to chant. It was a haunting sound, enhanced by the acoustics of the circular hall and high, domed ceiling. Traditional Turkish music began to play. Tracy looked up. It sounded like live music coming from a clandestine room in the upper level of the hall. The men rose to their feet and, one by one, very slowly, began to march around the room, bowing to each other as they moved. After completing several revolutions, the men removed their black cloaks and handed them to an usher who quickly stowed them away. Their long, white undergarments dragged on the floor, hiding their shoes. The music continued to play as the men moved into a line. They closed their eyes and started chanting again, swaying their bodies to the rhythm of the melody. They began to step out of line until they were spaced evenly around the hall. And then, much to Tracy's amazement, they began to turn their bodies, picking up momentum so that

181

their undergarments began to lift up and off the floor, flaring around them like giant fans. They extended their arms either side of their bodies, right palm facing up and left palm down, allowing them to fly freely through the air as they spun. With eyes still closed, they dropped their heads to one side. It was a beautiful sight to behold, all fifteen men turning about in unison, spinning on their feet, twisting their bodies to the mesmerising beat of the music as it played.

Zehra cupped her hand to Tracy's ear. "They're Sufis," she explained. "They've been doing this for hundreds of years. It's called the dance of the Whirling Dervishes. It's a spiritual practice designed to bring them closer to God."

"I can just imagine," said Tracy. "All that turning must surely spin their heads into a trance."

"Exactly."

The Sufis continued to turn their bodies, stepping to the music, moving about the circular room in formation, twisting, spinning and chanting together. The dance lasted about thirty minutes until the men slowed their stepping and twisting, and their gowns drifted slowly back onto the floor in a pool about their feet. They returned to sit on the floor but this time in a circle, wrapping their arms around their neighbour's shoulders and swaying their upper bodies in a circular motion until the music finally faded.

"Wow! That was amazing!" said Tracy as they stepped out of the building.

"I'm glad you enjoyed it," said Zehra with a grin.

"So you say it's hundreds of years old?"

Zehra nodded. "This particular *semahane* has been around since the 1400s, I think. My father once told me that Rumi started it."

"Rumi, the mystic?"

"Yep. The story goes that he was walking through a market one day and overheard the hammering sound of a gold-beater. He closed his eyes and the hammering translated into words."

"Words?"

"Yes. The hammering sounded to his ears like the chanting love for God. Rumi was so overjoyed that he extended his arms and began to spin about in a circle and the Sama was born."

"The Sama?"

"The name of the dance that we saw today."

"Oh, wow. What an incredible story. So Rumi was clearly a Sufi."

"Correct. He was, in fact, a Sufi master!"

"Makes sense," said Tracy. "I love his poetry. It's so meaningful. Crazy to think it was written so many hundreds of years ago."

"Yes," agreed Zehra. "Don't know about you, but all that spinning has made me so hungry." Zehra tapped her phone. "The Uber will be here in two minutes."

Tracy felt a few drops on her arms. She looked up into the sky. The clouds were thick and heavy with rain. A cold wind brushed her face and tickled her neck like the long fingers of a ghostly apparition. She shivered, squeezed her arms to her sides and pulled her jacket snugly about her body as flashes of her nightmare came to the fore. The storm. The forest. The fire. That face.

"Tracy? You okay?"

"Huh?"

"You look a bit pale." Zehra frowned, concern in her voice.

"Oh. No. I'm fine." Tracy forced a smile. "Just a bit cold, you know?"

Zehra's phone beeped, signalling the arrival of the Uber. "Hey, here it is."

Tracy recognised the Hyundai symbol as a red car pulled up. A few more drops of rain landed on her arms and head.

"Just in time," said Zehra looking up at the ominous clouds.

Tracy looked out of the window as the rain began to fall. The harder it fell, the slower they seemed to progress. "Where we going?"

Zehra smiled. "Not far. It's a nice, traditional restaurant called Khorasani situated in Sultanahmet. Their speciality is kebab. It's the best in town."

By the time they reached the restaurant, the rain had turned into a mild drizzle. Zehra and Tracy were forced to walk the last block because the restaurant was in a pedestrian area, and the Uber could get no closer. Despite the rain, the streets were still busy and the restaurant even more so. A waiter led them to a reserved table by the window, and soon Tracy was tucking into the most succulent tasting meat that she had ever eaten.

24 ~ First Breath

"Gran, can you hear me?"

"Tracy, is that you? I was expecting your call."

Of course, you were. "Yes, Gran. It's me."

"How are you, my child?"

"I'm fine, thanks."

"You are far away. Far from here."

"Yes. Turkey. Istanbul. With Dad."

"Ah yes, of course, that explains it."

"What do you mean?"

Granny Sybs chuckled. "My vision. I saw you. You were in the old land. Close to the birthplace of your ancestors."

The hairs on Tracy's neck lifted. "What else did you see?"

"Hmm. Something that I haven't seen for a while. Something different."

"What do you mean?"

Syb's cleared her throat. "It wasn't very clear, but the energy pattern was unmistakable. I recognised it immediately. The familiarity of it."

Tracy held her breath in anticipation of what Granny Sybs was going to say next.

"My grandmother told me the story when I was your age.

185

She showed me things. I saw what she saw, and, for a brief moment, felt it too. When she was young, she encountered another Sybil."

"What do you mean, another Sybil? There are more of us?" questioned Tracy.

"Remember I told you that originally there were two Sybils? They were sisters."

"Yes. You said that one was evil. You said that she was banished."

"Correct. Her name was Sabbe," said Sybs, spitting the name into the phone.

"You mean she still lives?"

"Well, not exactly. But there's a chance that she also continued her lineage through the ages, just as we have."

"What happened to the other Sybil? The one that your grandmother saw."

"I have no idea. She just disappeared, but before she did, she threatened my grandmother. She warned her to heed the return of the Sabbe. She came to her in a powerful vision; a vision that was laced with a twisted, vile kind of energy. The same energy that I experienced last night in my dream. The same energy signature that my grandmother shared with me."

"Why did she share it with you?"

"It was a warning. She never explained why at the time, but now I know. She knew that this day would come. She knew that I would experience it again. She knew that I would encounter this energy, this foreign power once more."

"What does it all mean?"

"What did *you* see, my child? Tell me about your dream."

It was then that Tracy knew, without doubt, that she could never hide anything from her grandmother. "I was flying," said Tracy. It was as if her voice belonged to someone else as she spoke into the phone like it wasn't her own. "I flew high into the sky and over a forest, and then a storm forced me to the ground. I saw a figure sitting on the ground next to a tree, hunched over and concealed. A fire raged nearby, and a naked

186

girl danced around it. She was covered in dirt and leaves."

"Leaves," whispered her grandmother on the phone.

Tracy felt the hairs on her neck rise once again. "She stared at me with crazy eyes and screamed."

Silence; there was no response from Sybs.

"Granny Sybs? Hello? You there?"

"Yes, my child. I'm still here. I'm sorry. I was just thinking. This is portentous news. Deeply concerning. I must prepare you. I must equip you with the tools to guard you, to protect you. When are you home?"

"Um, we'll be back on Tuesday."

"Good, so I will see you then."

"You mean you're coming to Milwaukee?"

"I *can* drive, you know. I'm not an old dinosaur in a wheelchair. Not yet, in any event." Sybs chuckled. "Are you still wearing the crystal?"

Tracy fingered the stone around her neck. She looked down at it. "Yes. Haven't taken it off, not even when I'm sleeping."

"Good. If you ever feel uneasy or scared, hold the crystal in your hand and think of me. Just picture my face. Okay?"

"Yes, Gran," said Tracy. "I'll be fine. See you on Tuesday. Bye."

Tracy stared at her phone. A million thoughts raced through her head. The girl in her dream. Her ear-piercing scream. That crazy look in her eyes. She pushed her thumb and forefinger into her eye-sockets in an attempt to squeeze out the disturbing memories.

25 ~ Going Home

Tracy still couldn't get over the size of the airport terminal. She gazed around in awe at the height of the ceiling and the row upon row of check-in desks representing so many different airlines. The hundreds of people walking across the concourse reminded her of an ant colony, deep underground, robotically going about their business as if they were programmed to do so by their queen.

"Trace!"

Tracy jumped.

"You okay?" said Harold, concern mirroring his voice.

"Yeah. Sorry, just lost in thought there for a moment."

"Come, we're going to be late," he beckoned.

"Sure." Tracy jogged to catch up with her father, her backpack bouncing up and down as she ran.

Harold hoisted their bags onto the luggage conveyor and checked onto the flight.

"Thanks, Dad. That was the best birthday present," said Tracy, giving her father a hug and a kiss on the cheek.

"My pleasure, poppit. I'm glad you enjoyed it. Please let Mom know we've checked in and the flight is on time."

"Sure," said Tracy, tapping a message into her phone. "Have

you got the flute?" she said, looking up at her father.

"Safe and sound," said Harold, patting his bag.

"Can I look at it again?" said Tracy.

"Sure. As soon as we're through security. Come, let's go," he said, jerking his thumb in the direction of the departure lounge.

◊ ◊ ◊

Tracy placed the narrow, wooden case on her lap and lifted the lid. She stared wide-eyed at the flute nestled inside like a kid in a candy store.

"Well? Aren't you going to take it out?" said Harold.

Tracy placed her hand over the flute and closed her eyes. The back of her skull tingled as a sense of trepidation washed over her. She lifted the flute out of the case. It felt surprisingly light, yet quite strong. She was still amazed that it had been laser-printed. She lifted it to her eye and stared down the shaft. Perfectly aligned. Straight as a ruler.

"Why don't you blow into it?"

"Here?" said Tracy looking around the lounge. A young Asian girl and her mother sat three chairs down. The girl was glued to her tablet. An old couple was sitting two rows in front of them, engaged in conversation. Several other travellers casually strolling by, stared into the retail outlets lining the walkway.

"Sure," said Harold. "Just a quick one. No one will notice."

Tracy stared at the carbon-fibre instrument in her hands. She glanced around again, hesitantly and then brought the instrument to her lips. She placed her fingers loosely over some of the holes and blew gently into the shaft. The beautiful sound that came out seemed to emanate from all around her like it was in stereo. It had that same sweet quality as the first time she heard it, but there was a slight difference, a vibration that lightly tickled her ears, bringing a smile to her face. She quickly looked

189

around. Her father was right. No one had taken any notice. She blew into the flute again but this time for a little longer, playing her fingers randomly over the holes. For a moment, Tracy thought that her mind was playing tricks on her. She noticed a shimmer, hovering in the air just above the flute, as if the notes that she played came to life, their energy dancing through the air in front of her like a flutter of fairies. She looked towards the terminal windows, expecting to see shards of sunlight slicing through the lounge, explaining the phenomenon, but there were none. She examined the flute again in her hands. It was truly a magical thing. Something so old brought back to life. She tried to imagine the sheer inspiration and unbridled talent required to design such a thing so many thousands of years ago. The question was, who taught the creator of this flute? Who taught him, or her, and so many others, how to design and craft such a thing of beauty? And aligned to the Golden Ratio! What inspired these people to design the megalithic stone monuments of Gobekli Tepe? Why? So many unanswered questions.

Tracy stared at the silver flute in her hands. She knew that it was the key. A key. A key to unlocking some of those questions. Perhaps it was her ability to see beyond what others saw, perhaps it was pure intuition. Either way, she knew deep down inside that the flute was a piece of a puzzle that, once unlocked, would open the way to a deeper understanding of the ancient history of these people, their culture and something more; something otherworldly. She could just feel it. She could almost see the answers like the scribblings on the leaves, indecipherable at the moment, not ready to reveal their meaning just yet, but soon, very soon.

26 ~ What's in a Name?

The rose-scented incense masked the smell of stale smoke and sweat in the shop. The high-pitched buzzing sound could have been mistaken for electric hair clippers, but it came from a tattoo machine, wielded by Johnny B Ink, a master at his craft. He sat on his leather-bound stool, hunched over a shirtless man, carefully tracing out a large motif of a wolf in what looked like the very last unmarked space available on his back. Johnny wore cream-coloured, rubber-latex gloves and a pair of denim dungarees. A mash-up of images covered his body, each one telling a fascinating story all of its own. An Indian Chief blew smoke into the face of a young, topless girl on horseback. A large, fire-breathing dragon wrapped its claws around his right shoulder, its tail twisting across his back, disappearing beneath blue denim. A dozen stars floating in a sea of black wound down his arm like a laurel wreath, and a beautifully designed red, yellow and green mandala was emblazoned across his chest like a beacon of fiery energy.

Johnny inked most of the gang members in Chicago. They came to him because he was the best, but also because he was safe. He never gossiped about his clients and only accepted hard, cold cash as payment. Miguel Hernandez had been

191

coming to Johnny for years. He hailed from the older generation, who traditionally inked themselves from a young age as a commitment to the gang and its culture. Nowadays, though, the youngsters who were recruited were encouraged not to ink at all for fear of being identified by the authorities. Just recently, there had been a spate of arrests by the NDA, just for having gang-related tattoos. But Miguel didn't care. It was too late for him. He had been marked for too long. They all knew who he was, and he knew almost all of them. Besides, he had contacts in the prisons and across the border who would do all they could to release him if he was ever detained. He was a valuable asset. He knew a lot. Too much, some would say. He was feared as a result; feared by his fellow gang members; feared by the authorities. He had learnt from a young age, that his life was ruled by fear. If you were feared, then you had power, and if you had power, then nothing could stop you.

Miguel clearly remembered getting his first tattoo. He was very afraid. He remembered the screaming but not the pain. He didn't remember the pain. He was just ten years old when two older men held him down, while a third inked the underside of his right arm with the initials M.S. That was when his life changed. He became someone. He was no longer an orphan on the streets. He no longer had to beg for food or money. He was part of a family now. He was baptised. He was a member of MS-13, for Life.

MS-13 stood for Mara Salvatrucha, the most notorious gang in the United States; some would even say the world. And the all-powerful number thirteen represented the position of the letter M in the alphabet. It was also the magic number that was used during part of the gang's induction process. With his arm, still red and raw from his first indelible tattoo, Miguel was thrown to the ground and then kicked and beaten by fellow gang members for thirteen seconds straight.

Thirteen seconds.

Thirteen seconds sounds relatively quick, but it felt instead like thirteen agonising minutes of pain and torture. The result was three cracked ribs and dozens of heavy bruises all over his body. But it was worth it. It was worth the pain and suffering that he had to endure afterwards. It was worth every cent.

MS-13 started in Los Angeles in the early 80s and spread quickly to other parts of the US, Canada, and Mexico. The Chicago division had been around for almost twenty years, and, with the recent arrest and indictment of Anthony "Siniestro" Martinez for a triple murder, Miguel had automatically inherited his territory, making him the most powerful and revered gangster in the area.

"Devo," said Johnny. Devo was the nickname Miguel gave Johnny to call him by. He didn't know him by any other name, and if he *had* heard it, he chose never to listen. "Whatever happened to your cousin?"

Miguel shifted his body forward slightly on the table until he felt more comfortable. "He was shot and killed. 'El Lobo.' That's what we used to call him. The Wolf."

Johnny smiled. The tattoo made more sense now. "You know, Devo, you're running out of space over here."

"There's always more space, Johnny. That's why I pay you - so that you can find the emptiness and colour it in; so that you can fill the voids in my life. You da man, Johnny B. You da man." Miguel closed his eyes, focusing on all the good memories, tearing his mind away from the excruciating pain as the needle pierced his skin again, and again, inking it like a tapestry.

Johnny cocked his head in response to the sound of the buzzer. Faith would get it. She was up front. Faith had been with Johnny for a long time. He had taken her in after she was badly abused by her boyfriend one night. Devo and his boys sorted him out. They broke both his legs and messed up his face with a baseball bat. That was about seven years ago.

Faith was an addict. Heroin.

It was a tough battle, but Johnny endured, and so did she. He saw something inside of her. Something beautiful. It was a will to live, to survive, and he felt that it was his duty to save her, to help her fight the demons. Three years. Three years and seven days. That's how long she had been clean. She still kept count on a calendar hanging in the office upfront. They celebrated just a week ago. Johnny took her for dinner to La Fiasco, a great Italian place downtown. She looked beautiful. Radiant. He was so proud. He loved her. But not like that. More like a father would a daughter. He just wanted to protect her, to keep her safe. She smiled, and his heart moved.

Faith pushed the black button on the wall alongside the reception desk and the security gate released with a buzz and a click. She pulled her long, black hair away from her face to reveal a nose and matching lip ring. Faith was into piercings. She had them all over her body. She loved the way they made her feel when her clothes rubbed over them as she moved. "Yeah? How can we help you?" she said to the girl that stepped into the shop.

She had long, dark hair just like Faith's, except that it was matted. Not braided like dreadlocks, but matted, like it had never been brushed. It looked as if it had been hastily tied up, pulled back into a ponytail to reveal a face covered in tattoos. Faith blinked in the fluorescent light of the shop as the girl approached her. She had a strikingly beautiful face with big, dark eyes and prominent features, but the markings on her face weren't like regular tattoos at all. Faith hadn't seen anything like it before. Both of her cheeks were covered in what looked like scars. She imagined a creature tearing its claws across her face, cutting into her skin, leaving behind a bloodied mess, like that scene from the movie Carrie, when her face was completely covered in blood. Faith shivered.

The girl whispered something indistinct.

"Excuse me?" said Faith leaning forward. "I didn't hear you."

"Miguel," said the girl, this time a little louder.

"Sorry, we don't have anyone here by that name. It's just me and Johnny B today. Are you sure you're in the right place?"

The girl just stood there, staring at Faith with cold, hard

eyes.

"Did you hear me? I said there's no one here by that name."

The girl looked past Faith and then raised her hand, pointing at the inter-leading door behind her.

Faith turned, following the girl's extended finger. "That's where we ink," she said. "Like I said, there's no Miguel here. Look, do you want a tattoo?"

"Miguel," said the girl once more. This time she sounded insistent.

"Okay, listen. Just wait here. I'm gonna call Johnny."

Johnny looked up as Faith stepped into the room.

"Customer?" he said. "Tell him I'm going to be a while still. At least three hours."

"It's a girl. I think she's confused."

"What do you mean?"

"She's looking for a Miguel. I told her that there's no one here by that name, but she keeps repeating the name like she's lost or something. She's a bit freaky if you ask me."

Miguel lifted his head. "What's her name?"

"I don't know. She didn't say."

"Must be Maria," said Miguel. "Long, dark hair?"

Faith nodded. "It's matted. A bit of a mess, actually."

Miguel frowned. "Matted? You mean, braided?"

"No. Matted. Full of knots."

Miguel frowned. "That's not like Maria. She has thick, straight hair."

"Get her name and number and tell her to come back later," said Johnny. "Either way, she's not going to…" Johnny looked past Faith, a surprised look on his face. "Can I help you?"

Faith turned around. "Hey, you can't be in here. I told you that there's no Miguel here."

"Faith," said Miguel pushing himself up to a seating position on the table. "It's all right."

"But Devo," said Faith.

"It's all right." Miguel waved his hand through the air in dismissal. "Let me speak to her."

Faith opened her mouth and then closed it again.

"Who are you?" said Miguel. "How do you know me? What do you want?"

"El Lobo," she whispered.

Miguel turned to Johnny and frowned.

Johnny shrugged his shoulders.

"You knew El Lobo?"

The girl shook her head slowly from side to side.

"I saw the Wolf fall," she said. Her voice was soft, distant. "I am there."

"What are you talking about?" said Miguel. "You are making no sense. You are here, girl. What is your name?"

"Sabine," she whispered.

"Sabine," repeated Miguel. "If you do not start talking sense, and quickly, I am going to gut you like a rabbit and feed you to the dogs." The sharp, metallic clicking sound of Miguel's switchblade cut through the air.

"Devo, take it easy," said Johnny.

Miguel raised his index finger to his lips. "Shh. Let the girl speak."

Sabine smiled. "We will dance," she said in a whisper. "And I will show you things. I will show you where to go. I will show you how."

"What the hell has this bitch been smoking?" said Faith. "She's definitely high."

"Tell me about the Wolf," said Miguel. "What do you mean, you saw him fall?"

"I watched him die."

"You saw who killed El Lobo?"

"Devo…" said Johnny. He had a bad feeling about this. He looked about the shop and pictured himself and Faith cleaning up the girl's bloodied remains.

"Wait." Miguel raised his hand. "I wanna hear what this little bitch has to say. I asked you if you saw who killed El Lobo?"

Sabine smiled again and nodded. "I saw. I am there."

196

"You mean you *were* there?"

"Yes."

"Can you identify him? The killer."

"Yes."

"Who sent you?" said Miguel sliding off the table. He walked over to Sabine and lifted the knife to her throat. "Tell me, or I'll finish you."

Sabine looked into Miguel's eyes, and he glared back at her menacingly. Then his head felt funny, and he forgot why he was angry for a moment. Her eyes. They were so dark. So deep. Miguel blinked and shook his head to clear it. He stared at the markings on her face. It seemed as if they were alive, moving, shifting like worms. Big, fat worms. Caterpillars. He imagined how she got them. Perhaps with a blade. Perhaps with a machete, his weapon of choice.

"He is called Flaco."

"What? Who is this Flaco?" said Miguel, pushing his blade against Sabine's throat. "The one who sent you?"

"No. He is the killer."

"Flaco. Flaco," repeated Miguel. "Now where have I heard that name?" He turned to look at Johnny, who shrugged his shoulders and turned his hands palm-side up. Miguel turned back to Sabine. He couldn't understand how she just stood there with such a calm demeanour. Emotionless. He imagined that she was smirking behind that deadpan, scarred, striking face of hers. He lowered his blade. "Who is this Flaco? Huh? Tell me," he said with menacing tone to his voice.

"Sanchez," Sabine whispered.

"José 'Flaco' Sanchez?!" Miguel was livid. "Are you sure?"

Sabine nodded imperceptibly.

"Do you know what you are saying, girl? Sanchez is dead. He has been dead for two years. Killed in El Salvador. Everybody knows that."

Sabine shook her head. "He lives. In the shadows."

"Puta Madre!" Miguel threw his blade across the room. It spun through the air and landed with a thud, embedded in the

197

wall on the far side of the room. "If what you are saying is a lie, then you will die. Do you hear me, bitch?" Miguel waved his finger in Sabine's face. She still didn't flinch, which only enraged him more. "Haaaaaaaa!" He screamed. He spun around. "I gotta get to the bottom of this," he said to Johnny. "You're gonna have to finish this another time, esé. Entender?" he said, stabbing his thumb at the unfinished tattoo on his back.

"Sure thing, Devo," said Johnny, pulling off his latex gloves. "Whenever you're ready. Let me just wipe down…"

"No time for that," spat Miguel, pulling his vest over his head. Speckled patches of blood began to seep into the back of his vest. "You," he pointed at Sabine, "are coming with me." He walked over to the wall and pried his switchblade out. "I'll be back," he said, as he marched out of the room without looking back.

Sabine turned to follow him just as the speakers suspended in the shop blared out a verse of Hells Bells by AC/DC:

I won't take no prisoners, won't spare no lives
Nobody's putting up a fight
I got my bell, I'm gonna take you to hell
I'm gonna get you; Satan get you
Hell's bells
Yeah, hell's bells
You got me ringing hell's bells
My temperature's high, hell's bells

27 ~ Home

Tracy stepped out of the shuttle to find Granny Sybs and her mother waiting with open arms and great big smiles on their faces.

"Welcome home," said Camilla. "How was it?"

"So much fun," said Tracy, kissing and then hugging her mother affectionately. "But it's good to be home. I'm exhausted."

"Hello, Trace."

"Gran. So good to see you again so soon," she said, also giving her grandmother a kiss followed by a warm embrace. "How was the drive?"

"Oh, uneventful, but I knew that before I left."

"Ha-ha. I'm sure you did. Where's Dyl?" Tracy asked her mother.

"Still at school. He should be back soon."

Tracy slapped the palm of her hand onto her forehead. "Totally forgot. I've so lost track of time. It's Tuesday, right?"

"Uh-huh," acknowledged her mother, looking past Tracy at Harold as he pulled the bags out of the shuttle. "Why don't you go and help your father?"

"Oh, sure. Sorry Dad!" she shouted, skipping over to

Harold. "Here, let me help you with that," she said, grabbing hold of her suitcase.

"Hello hun," said Harold, pushing Camilla's dusty blond hair aside and giving her a peck on the lips.

"Hello. You two have fun?"

Harold turned to look at Tracy with a smile. "We sure did. Come, let's go inside and we'll tell you all about it."

◊ ◊ ◊

"And we went to a club," said Tracy.

"All on your own?"

"Mom, she's 21. We met these two guys - friends of hers. Don't worry, nothing happened. We just danced and had fun. Then the next day she took me to this old museum where these men called Sufis wearing dresses, spun around in circles."

"Men in dresses?" Dylan exclaimed. "You are so weird, Sis. I wouldn't go there if you paid me."

"They've been doing it for like thousands of years. It's very spiritual and so beautiful."

"Whatever floats your boat."

"Dylan. Don't be rude," said Camilla.

"What? Am I the only one around here that thinks that men spinning around in dresses is weird? What's with you people?"

"It's a cultural thing," said Tracy. "You'll never understand it."

"Yeah, right. Cultural. It's just plain weird," said Dylan shaking his head.

"So, you going to show us?" said Camilla, quickly changing the subject. "The flute."

"Yes, yes, of course," said Harold, retrieving the long, narrow, light brown, wooden case and placing it on the table. "Open it, Trace."

Tracy flipped open the latch and lifted the lid to reveal the long, silvery-grey flute nestled inside.

"Wow," whispered Camilla, peering at the instrument.

200

"Incredible."

"Doesn't look like anything special," said Dylan with a shrug of his shoulders.

"Well, it's not the original," said Harold. "As I explained earlier, this is a laser-printed replica."

"I still don't see what the big deal is," said Dylan flatly.

"Dyl, the original is over 12,000 years old," said Tracy. "It's the first time that anything like this has been found. The fact that an artefact like this was discovered at Goblekli Tepe is crazy. But the fact that it was designed using the Fibonacci sequence defies logic."

"She's right," confirmed Harold. "The flute is an anomaly. There is still so much out there that we don't even know."

"Like why men in dresses spin around together?"

"Very funny, Dylan," said Tracy.

"You know that you're never gonna live this one down. I mean, who goes to watch men dance together? But even worse than that, they're wearing dresses. I mean, come on!"

"Dylan," said Camilla sternly, "that's enough. Leave your sister alone."

"Here Dyl, this is for you." Harold threw him a red plastic packet.

"Cool! What is it?"

"A dress," said Tracy with a giggle.

"Hey!"

"Well, you asked for it."

"It's a fez," said Harold. "A Turkish hat."

"Oh, cool." Dylan stuck his tongue out at Tracy, and she returned the gesture. He pulled out the red fez and placed it on his head. "So aren't you gonna play the flute?" said Dylan, turning to his sister.

Tracy looked at her father for affirmation. He smiled and nodded. Tracy lifted the flute out of the case. She was still amazed at how light it felt in her hand. She brought it to her lips and took a deep breath. She placed her hands gently over the holes, closed her eyes, and blew into the shaft. The beautiful

201

sound of the flute filled the room, resonating at a delightful frequency that tickled her ears.

"Wow," exclaimed Camilla.

"It's beautiful," said Granny Sybs. "Gentle, yet strong, just like you, Trace."

Tracy blushed. "Thank you."

"May I?" Granny Sybs held out her hand.

"Sure."

Sybs examined the flute. "It's as light as a feather," she remarked. "And you say that it's a printed replica of the original?"

"Yep," Harold nodded.

"Fascinating," Sybs whispered. "Technology," she said, shaking her head in disbelief. "What next?" Sybs closed her eyes. "There is something. Something else," she continued. "I can't put my finger on it, but this flute... it's more than what you think it is."

"What do you mean, Ma?" said Camilla.

Sybs opened her eyes. "It's a thing of value that will become sought-after. It must be kept safe. Hidden." She looked at Harold, her eyes turning to slits. "You are its custodian. You must not announce its discovery."

Harold's brow furrowed. "Now *that's* going to be rather challenging. I don't really see..."

"No, you don't," interjected Sybs. "That's *my* job. Trust me, Harold. The outcome doesn't look all that positive if you get my drift?"

"But I don't see how a simple flute..."

"It's not just a simple flute, and you know that. It's more. Much more." Sybs looked at Tracy. "You're very much part of this too, Trace. Remember when I said I wanted to see you?"

Tracy nodded.

"About your dream?"

Tracy nodded again. She could feel the apprehension building up inside of her.

"She's part of this too."

"The girl?"

Sybs nodded.

"What girl?" said Harold quizzically.

"Yes, what girl?" said Camilla.

"Tracy had a dream," Sybs began to explain. She squeezed Tracy's hand. "You tell them."

Tracy took a deep breath and looked around at her family. "It was our last night in Istanbul. I dreamt that I was flying." She closed her eyes. "It began as this incredible experience flying through the sky, but then there was a storm that forced me to take cover in the forest below." Tracy shivered before continuing. "That's when I saw her - the girl. She was dancing around a fire. Naked." Tracy opened her eyes to witness the enthralled expressions on her parents' faces, but also because she felt a pang of fear; a sense of foreboding. She didn't want to see that face again, especially in the dark recesses of her mind.

"Who was she?" whispered Camilla. "Did you recognise her?"

Tracy shook her head. "No, but she was scary. She stared at me and screamed in a high-pitched wail that tore right through me."

"Hooo," said Dylan. "So scary." He waved his hands around for effect. "It's only a dream, guys. What's the big deal?"

"The big deal is, this girl is real," said Sybs.

"What do you mean, real?" said Dylan. "Tracy just told us that it was all a dream. There's no Freddy out to get us!"

"This girl is just like Tracy and me," said Sybs. "She comes from a long lineage of powerful seers." She turned to Tracy. "That other figure that you said you saw in your dream - the one that was sitting by the tree."

Tracy nodded.

"Did you get to see a face."

Tracy shook her head. "No. Who do you think it was?"

"Her grandmother," said Sybs, absentmindedly scratching her head.

"You mean…?"

"Yes. She is a descendant of Sabbe, ancient twin sister of Sambethe, the first Sybil."

"I'm confused," said Dylan. "What and who are you talking about? Sabbe, Sambethe. Who are these people? What do you mean they're real? How can they be if Tracy has only seen them in a dream?"

Sybs took hold of Dylan's hand and squeezed it reassuringly. "Sometimes, dreams are manifestations of the mind, a collection of mixed memories and experiences, but often they can be real projections or thoughts of others."

Dylan's brow creased.

"I know it's hard to believe, but your sister experienced this kind of dream. She shares something with me. A kind of ability or awareness that allows her to have dreams of real events, with real people, even if she hasn't seen them before."

"You mean you have them too?"

"Sometimes. It's hard to tell them apart - the regular dreams from real events or visions."

"So they're more like visions?" said Dylan.

Sybs nodded. "Correct."

"So you mean to say that you can see into people's minds like Professor X?"

"Who?"

"Professor X from the X-Men! Come on, Gran. Don't tell me you've never heard of Professor X. The bald guy in the wheelchair."

Sybs chuckled. "The only bald guy in a wheelchair that I know of is Timothy Roland. But he's long gone, bless his soul."

"Huh? Okay, never mind then," said Dylan.

"I cannot see into people's minds, Dylan," said Sybs. "The only person who can do that is that guy from Marvel comics who runs a school for mutants. I think his name is Charlie or something."

"Gran, you have got to be kidding me. We're both talking about the same dude. That's him. Professor Charles Xavier and Professor X are one and the same."

204

Sybs chuckled again. "Oh, silly me. Is *that* his name?"

"So if you can't see into people's minds, what can you do, besides have dreams of real people and events?" said Dylan.

"I can sometimes see what's going to happen."

"Wow. That's so cool. So you can see into the future?"

Sybs nodded. "And your sister too."

"How come? What about me? Do I have any special powers?"

"Unfortunately it's a gift that is only passed down from grandmother to granddaughter."

"Oh. Okay. So you reckon that there's another grandmother and granddaughter with the same powers? The ones that Tracy saw in her dream?" said Dylan.

Sybs looked at Tracy. "I'm afraid so."

"Any idea where they are now?" said Camilla.

Sybs shook her head. "Hard to say, but wherever they are, they are up to no good. Trace, if you happen to dream about them again, I want you to conceal yourself."

"What? How?" said Tracy, confused. "You mean I can do stuff inside a dream?"

Sybs smiled. "You'd be quite surprised at what you can do."

"Okay, but how do I hide inside a dream?"

"You focus on your environment and blend in. Like a chameleon. You become inconspicuous."

"But how? How do I do that?"

"Practice. Next time you go to sleep, you will dream. Inside your dream, close your eyes and focus. Focus on your breathing. Deep, belly breaths in and out."

Tracy smiled. Granny Sybs reminded her of Denise, her yoga teacher during Shavasana at the end of class.

"When you become one with your breath, you will find it easier to connect to the substance of your dream and become a spectator, rather than a participant. This is the practice of present awareness. To be in the moment and have complete control over what's going on around you. The more you practice this, the easier it will become to have control over who sees you inside your dreams."

"Does she know about us?" said Tracy.

"You mean the girl? More than likely."

"What do they want?"

"Nothing good, I'm afraid," said Sybs. "Their mission is to spread fear. It somehow fuels their powers, and if they are working together as I suspect, you will need more than just common sense to outwit them."

"This sounds serious," said Harold. "How can we help protect Tracy?"

"There's not that much you can do, I'm afraid," said Sybs. "There's no immediate threat, so all we can do is take precautionary measures. I will need to get involved."

"You can stay over for a while," said Camilla. "We'd love you to."

"Yes, please Gran," said Tracy. "Will you?"

Sybs smiled. "I already have my bag packed. It's in the car."

"Dyl, please fetch Granny Sybs' bag, will you?" said Camilla.

Dylan pulled a face. "Why me? Why always me?"

"Because you're the strongest in the family," said Harold.

"Blah, blah. That reverse psychology doesn't work on me," he said as he walked out the door. "I'm only going because I feel like exercising," he shouted over his shoulder.

Sybs, Camilla, Harold, and Tracy all broke out into fits of laughter.

28 ~ Pillars

The stone towered above her, a giant, t-shaped pillar embedded in the ground like a statue, casting its shadow over her like a cloak of protection from the harsh sun that beat down from above. She stared at the relief that had been carved into its surface and traced its outline with her eyes. It was a lizard. It looked so familiar. She had seen it before.

It moved; the tail. It flicked from side to side.

The eyes. They blinked.

The tongue. It darted in and out of the mouth of the creature, testing, tasting the air.

She turned to look at the other stone pillars. The carvings upon them also appeared to be moving, shifting over the surface of the pillars as if they had somehow been magically brought to life.

Tracy noticed other people between the pillars. Some were on their knees with their eyes closed, rocking gently from side to side. Others were looking up into the sky together, pointing at some kind of celestial object that only they could see. All of these people wore similar garb - crudely made, long, leather tunics with sheepskin boots and loosely-fitted pants.

Conceal yourself.

That voice. It was Granny Sybs. She closed her eyes and remembered what her grandmother told her - to hide inside her dream, to blend in like a chameleon. *Become a spectator, not a participant.* Tracy focused on her breathing; deep belly breaths in and out. She moved between the people inside her dream, and they were oblivious to her as if she was just a spectator looking in. She could hear them talking. It was a strange dialect, a guttural tongue, completely foreign to her.

And then she heard it. The sound. The beautiful sound. She tilted her head in its direction. It came from just beyond the next pillar. She hurried through the maze of megalithic monuments, twisting around the giant stones until she came upon a sight that was impossible to fathom. There were three people with their backs to Tracy. Two of them stood resolutely beside the third who was blowing into a flute. They faced an impossibly large block of stone that seemed to be floating in thin air. Tracy stared in wonder as the flute player maintained a high-pitched note, directed at the megalith. She stepped past the trio to look more closely at the ten-ton boulder as it hovered inexplicably just inches from the ground. Could it be the flute, she wondered? Could this pied-piper be playing a magical melody that caused the stone to become temporarily weightless?

She turned around to look at the musician and gasped. It was like looking into the mirror. It was her face; Tracy's face. Tracy looked down at her hands. They were clammy. Her heart raced. She rubbed her eyes and gazed at this other Tracy in awe. Her eyes were closed in concentration as she blew into the flute. The other two people were males. The one on the left of her doppelganger brought another flute to his lips and began to blow, matching the same note that came from the girl's flute. The giant rock appeared to wobble slightly and then steadied as the girl dropped the flute from her lips to take a breath. The third man stepped forward, gingerly placed both palms onto the megalith and began to push. The stone moved as if it were a giant balloon filled with helium, floating lightly in the air. The girl brought her flute up to her lips again and began to blow, this time giving the man a chance to take a breath. The two flute players stepped slowly forward, just behind the third member, following him, as he pushed the floating megalith away from Tracy.

Tracy stood with her feet rooted into the ground like the t-shaped pillars all around her, unable to move or even flinch her body, in complete and utter shock from what she had just witnessed. All she could do was stare incredulously at the three strangers and the giant rock as they gradually disappeared into the distance.

What did I just see? The flute, the sound, the frequency; causing the giant stone to float in the air.

Tracy opened her eyes. Her room was dark and quiet. The dream was so vivid, so clear in her mind, that she felt as if she was really there in that place. That place filled with t-shaped pillars and strange people in strange attire and an even stranger language. She has stepped back in her dream to a time of an ancient Gobekli Tepe, thousands of years ago.

Tracy pulled the covers up to her chin and closed her eyes. A thousand questions raced through her mind. *Was my dream real or something conjured up by my mind? Do I have the power to see into the past as well as the future?* She thought about the other Tracy. That must have been a trick of her mind. *Were the other people real?* She imagined the sound that came from the flute. Not when *she* blew it, but when her lookalike did, inside her dream. That steady, high-pitched note. Pure magic. That's what it was. Pure magic. A musical instrument designed around the Golden Ratio, able to produce a note at the right frequency, a frequency that could disrupt the physical properties of matter, causing it to become weightless.

It was then that it just clicked into place, like a puzzle piece in one of those thousand-piece puzzles that was so difficult to complete. It was a deep-rooted, gut-wrenching feeling that whatever Tracy saw in her dream, *was* real. There was no doubt in her mind. It was a vision. A vision of the past of what once was. It was a vision that was revealed to her so that she could apply it in this time, this place, right here, right now. Could it be Sambethe showing her the way, revealing to her clues about the past so that she could unravel the future? Whatever it was, she felt it. Energy. Karma. Destiny. Fate. It was hard to put it into words, but the feeling of just knowing that what she felt was the construct of all things past, present, and future. She knew that her gift gave her access to these experiences, like a golden ticket, where she could catch glimpses of the workings of the universe and the events that shaped it into being.

29 ~ Scheming

The old, nondescript warehouse in Ford Heights looked deserted. The streetlight on the other side of the road cast a wan, yellow light across the side of the building. An ominous wind pushed a tin can against the gutter with a clatter. Miguel banged the side of his fist on the corrugated metal door. It had been painted blood-red in colour in an attempt to cover some graffiti, the outlines of which could still be seen underneath. Miguel scanned his surroundings with slitted eyes and waited. He glanced at Sabine, standing resolutely behind him. She wore a dark cowl that had been pulled over her head, so he couldn't see her face in the dim light but imagined her piercing eyes boring into the back of his head like a pair of lasers. He turned to face the building and shivered.

"Ola," said a voice from behind the door. "Who is this?"

"Pinto," said Miguel. "It's me, Miguel. Open up."

The scraping sound of a bolt being released, followed by a clang as it shot to one side, reverberated through the metal door.

"Miguel! Good to see you," said Pinto. "Come," he beckoned. "I see you have a friend," he continued, looking at Sabine curiously. "Ola senorita," he said with a mischievous grin. "Does she speak?" Pinto tried to peer beneath the cowl.

"Only when she wants to," said Miguel. "Her name is Sabine. She is here to help us track someone down."

Pinto seemed satisfied with Miguel's retort because he quickly stepped back to allow them inside. He slammed the door shut behind them, bolting it once more. Darkness enveloped them like a blanket. Pinto flicked on a flashlight. His face lit up. It was free of tattoos. Only his arms were covered in markings that identified him as a member of MS13. "Follow me," he instructed, as the light cut through the darkness. He led them into another room at the back of the warehouse. A fluorescent light illuminated the space filled with several men. At the rear of the room was a locked cage, guarded by a burly looking fellow with a red bandanna tied across his forehead and a black eye-patch over his left eye. A heavily tattooed man sat smoking at a desk. Signs and markings covered his face, just like Miguel. One of the old guard. Miguel eyed the bottle of half-empty Jack on the table as the man looked up.

"Miguel!" The tattooed man stood up. His wooden chair scraped backwards across the floor with a screech. He placed his hand on the desk to steady himself and barred his teeth in a half-drunken sneer.

"Jules," Miguel nodded.

"Who's the bitch?" Julian pointed at Sabine. "Lemme see her face," he leaned forward.

"Don't," Miguel raised his hand. "She's with me. She's here to find a killer."

Julian roared with laughter. "Miguel has a puta! Hey Miguel, when we gonna take a turn?" Julian waved his arm about and laughed even harder. The other men laughed with him. "Because we're all killers!" he roared.

Miguel charged forward, and in an instant had his switchblade pressed against Julian's throat. "Don't tempt me, Jules," he hissed through clenched teeth. He could taste the Jack on Julian's breath, he was so close. "I'm in no mood for your bullshit, esé."

"Hey, calm down bro," said Julian, raising both hands into

the air in supplication. "I was just kidding." He glanced at Sabine behind Miguel, who had dropped the cowl from her head, exposing her face. "What the…?"

Sabine was staring at Julian with her cold, hard eyes.

"Her eyes," he whispered. "Why she staring at me? And what's wrong with her face?"

Miguel stepped away from Julian. He flicked his switchblade through the air, *click, click, clack*, before thrusting it back into his pocket. "She knows who killed El Lobo."

"What? El Lobo?" said Julian. He jerked his head at Sabine. "She's looking at me like I did it. I'll take her out, right here, right now." Julian shrugged his shoulders and raised his fists to either side of his face.

"Jules. Stand down," said Miguel. "It's not you."

"Then tell her to stop staring at me. I don't like it."

Miguel turned around to find Sabine pulling her cowl over her head again. "Okay, listen. Her name is Sabine. She says she was there when El Lobo was killed. She saw the killer."

"Who was it?" said Pinto.

"Flaco. José 'Flaco' Sanchez."

Julian roared with laughter again. "A ghost. You mean to say he was killed by a ghost? Flaco has been dead two years already. Everybody knows that."

Miguel turned to Sabine. "It's time," he said. "Time to prove that what you are saying is true."

Sabine stood by resolutely. There was complete silence in the room aside from the high-pitched buzzing sound coming from the fluorescent tube suspended in the ceiling. She pulled back the cowl from her head once again and gazed around the room, making sure that she made eye contact with everyone present. "Trece Diablos," she rasped. "There will be much bloodshed. You must wait until the moon is hidden before the next job."

"What?! She knows," said Julian, aghast. "What have you told her, Miguel?" he demanded sternly.

"Nothing. I swear it."

213

"Then *how* can she know? We are the only ones who have spoken of the plan, and you are the only one of us that has been with this bitch." Julian spat vehemently onto the floor.

"What does she mean, 'wait until the moon is hidden?'" said Pinto.

"I think she means that we must wait until there is no moon, right?" Miguel looked at Sabine.

Sabine nodded. "Otherwise, you will all die."

Julian spat on the floor again. "I'm not listening to some strange bitch walk in here and tell me what to do!"

"Little Anna," whispered Sabine.

"What?" said Julian. "What did you say?"

"Little Anna. She is tired. It has been a long day toiling with her mother in the fields. The days are hot, and they are tired."

Julian's eyes widened. He looked around the room in shock. "How did you...?"

Sabine stared at Julian. Her eyes seemed to bore into his soul.

"She's a witch," blurted Julian, pointing at Sabine. "Keep her away from me."

"Who is Anna?" said Miguel.

Julian raked his hand nervously through his hair. His face was pale. "She... No. How can she know?" He looked imploringly at Miguel. "Not even you know," he whispered in disbelief. "I've told no one." Julian shook his head in disbelief. "She's my daughter," he said in a wavering voice. "She lives with her momma in El Salvador. The last time I saw her was over ten years ago. She was just a baby..." Julian stared at Sabine again. "Are they okay?"

There was an uncomfortable silence in the room. Sabine closed her eyes. "They are doing fine," she said. "Mariana works hard so that she can provide for her daughter."

"Mariana," Julian whispered again. He closed his eyes and smiled, remembering those carefree days in El Salvador. "Mariana." He enjoyed the sound of her name on his lips. It had been so long. So very long. He was happy to know that they

214

were okay. He looked at Miguel. "Okay," he nodded. "She can be trusted, but keep her away from me." He shook his finger in her direction. "She gives me the creeps."

"So what we gonna do about the operation, boss?" said Matias, a scrawny looking character with a large skull and crossbones tattoo on his left shoulder. He looked over a pair of Wayfarers that balanced on the tip of his nose and chewed gum with his mouth wide open as he spoke.

"We'll wait, just as she says," replied Miguel. "Why don't you check the phases of the moon?"

"What?" said Matias.

"The moon, dumb-ass," said Julian. "It changes shape, or haven't you noticed?"

"Oh, that," he said. "Didn't know what you meant."

Julian shook his head from side to side. "Give me that," he said, yanking the phone out of Matias's hands. "Okay, so tomorrow is the 21st, right?" He tapped on the screen. "Right, here we go. The next new moon is on Sunday."

"New moon?" said Matias scratching his head.

"It's called a new moon when there's no moon in the sky," said Julian.

Matias glanced up at the ceiling as if he could see right through the roof. "So that's what she means when it's hidden." Matias grinned. "So we make our move on Sunday?"

"Finally Matias gets it," said Julian with a sneer.

"Yes. We move on Sunday," said Miguel.

"What about Flaco," said Julian. "You really think he's alive? How's it possible?"

Miguel looked at Sabine. "She says that she was there. She saw him. I believe her."

Julian nodded. "So, what are we waiting for? Let's go and get him. That murderous pig!" Julian spat on the floor again. Where is he?"

Miguel looked to Sabine again.

"Not far," she said. "He will be in Chicago tomorrow night. He will be at *Forest Bar* in Forest Heights."

215

"You sure?" said Miguel.

"I'm never wrong," said Sabine. "Never." Her eyes bored into Miguel's. He looked away.

"Miguel," said Julian. "I just have one question."

Miguel raised his eyebrows.

"What's in it for her? I mean, why is she telling us all this shit? What does she get out of it?"

A smile began to creep across Sabine's face. "I need their eyes."

"What the fuck? What is she talking about, Miguel?" Julian's eyes widened.

"Whose eyes?" said Miguel.

"The ones who are killed," Sabine whispered. "The ones that you kill." She pointed around the room. "The eyes of the ones that each of you kill." She lowered her arm. Her wicked grin remained, etched onto her face like an oil painting.

"Oh, shit," said Matias. "Oh, shit."

30 ~ Suspended

She closed her eyes. The dream was still so vivid inside her head that it felt like a real memory. She imagined the sun baking down on her head and the high-pitched sound of the flute in her ears.

The flute.

Tracy opened her eyes and glanced at the wooden case that lay nestled in her lap. She sat alone in the lounge. The first vestiges of soft, morning light created an ambient glow, and her ears pricked to the faint shrill of the birds outside. She looked at her phone. 5.18am. She hadn't been able to sleep since she had woken from the powerful dream. Her mind was racing. She looked at the case again and carefully pried it open. Her hand trembled with trepidation as she lifted the flute out of the case. She still couldn't get over how light it was in her hands. So light, yet so strong. She searched the room. The television. The vase. The magazines. Something small. Smaller. The remote. Okay. She took a deep breath and stared at the black television remote sitting on the coffee table in front of her. She traced its outline, followed its curved edges, rolled her eyes over the tiny buttons and then slowly, painstakingly brought the flute to her mouth. She was still holding her breath as the flute touched her lips.

217

Her fingers found the holes on their own, guided there by pure instinct. She closed her eyes again and pictured the remote in her mind's eye; a blueprint taking shape until it filled her head. She let out her breath, pushing it into the instrument with just enough force to bring it to life. She shifted her fingers over the holes of the flute until she found the identical, high-pitched note that she heard being played in her dream and opened her eyes to stare intently at the remote once again.

Now that she had found the right note, Tracy took another deep breath and blew into the flute with a little more gusto. The sound seemed to fill the room, pouring into every single corner, into every single crevice. She blinked her eyes. The remote shimmered in front of her. It seemed to blur like she was looking at it through a thin veil of water inside a glass. She blinked again, and her vision cleared. She could now make out every detail on the remote. Even the tiny symbols beneath the buttons jumped out at her as if they had been magnified a thousand times over. And then her brain was telling her something that didn't make any sense. She creased her brow as if to ask herself, *well that can't be happening now, can it?* The remote was no longer on the table. It hovered just inches above it, suspended on thin air. Tracy imagined she could see the energy of the high-pitched notes that came out of the flute wrap around the remote, caressing it like it was floating in a stream, bobbing about in the water with a will of its own. Her brain registered that the impossible was happening and she let go of the flute in complete shock. It fell into her lap together with the remote that clattered loudly onto the table, now without the magical sounds from the flute to support it in limbo.

Tracy's ears tingled with the residue of the high-pitched, enchanting notes that came from the flute and filled the room. The enormity of what just happened overwhelmed her so much that she began to hyperventilate, breathing a series of quick, sharp breaths in and out of her mouth. Her heart thumped in her chest, and the blood pulsed loudly inside her ears. She pushed her fingers into her eye sockets, rubbing her watering eyes and then took the deepest breath that she could muster, letting it out with a great big sigh. She carefully replaced the flute inside the case and closed it with a click. She picked up the remote, gave it a shake, and then examined it closely. It was real, all right. What just happened was real. She wasn't dreaming this time. She slapped the remote against her thigh. It stung. She pressed the power button, and the television sprang to life. She stared at the screen, watching a lone deer grazing in silence. It lifted its head, cocking its ears in response to a distant sound. It turned it's head towards the camera, towards her, as if to say, *was that you? Was that you making that sound? Was it?* Tracy felt a shiver run up her spine. She quickly changed channels, creeped-out by the way that the deer looked at her, its round, innocent, glassy eyes peering deep inside her head, searching for the answers to its prying questions.

"Trace. Trace?"

Tracy looked up from the screen. It was her mother.

"You all right?"

Tracy just stared blankly across the room.

Camilla rubbed her eyes and yawned. "You could say good morning at least. How long you been up?"

"Huh? Oh. Sorry, Mom. Morning."

"What you watching?" Camilla peered around at the television. "I'm sure I heard some music."

Tracy stared at the case lying next to her. She imagined that it moved. "Sorry," she said. "It's on mute now."

"Oh, Okay." Camilla walked into the kitchen and switched on the kettle. "Tea?"

"Sure, Mom. Thanks." Tracy took a deep breath. Her heart was still beating faster than usual.

"Back to school today."

"I know. Don't remind me." Tracy stared at the case again. She was going to have to tell them. She closed her eyes and pictured them laughing. She pictured Dylan dancing around the house, mocking her. No. She would have to show them. Just the thought of it made her feel anxious. She looked up as her mother approached. "Thanks, Mom," she said carefully taking the hot mug of tea from her. She brought it up to her lips, and the rising steam caressed her forehead with its invisible touch.

Camilla sat down beside her. She looked at the case. "Fascinating, isn't it? Such an old thing restored to its former glory. Amazing, the technology today."

Tracy nodded. "Yeah. It was the first time I've seen a 3D printer in action."

Camilla opened the case. The flute stared back at them.

"How long did it take? To print."

"About an hour or so. There was this Frenchman. Phillippe was his name. He was a graphic designer at the museum. He used a graphic design programme to replicate the original artefact and then print it."

"So the original is at the museum?"

"Yes. On display there. "

"Clever."

"It was Dad's idea."

"What?"

"To make a copy of the flute and print it."

"He's not just a pretty face, your father."

Both Camilla and Tracy laughed out loud together.

"You know, that I have not seen you smile or laugh since you've been back," said Camilla. "What's on your mind? I know that something is not right." She tapped her temple with her finger. "Mother's intuition."

Tracy laughed. It was a nervous laugh. "I know, Mom. Love you." She lent across to kiss her mother on the cheek. She sat back into the couch and sighed heavily. "You're right, of course. There is something heavy on my mind, and I promise to tell you. I will show, you but I need Dad here. And Granny Sybs."

"What about Dylan?"

"Well, of course, Dylan. He won't want to miss this."

"Well, speak of the devil," said Camilla as Harold stepped into the room.

"What's with all the commotion?" said Harold.

"Is Gran awake?" said Tracy.

"Not sure. Shall I check? What's wrong?" Harold creased his forehead in concern.

"Nothing, dear," said Camilla. "Tracy just has something to tell…" She looked at Tracy and smiled. "I mean, show us."

"Okay." Harold disappeared into the back of the house.

"Dylan! You up?" Camilla called. There was no answer. "Dylan!"

"What?!" shouted Dylan from his room.

"Please come to the lounge. Tracy has something important to show us."

Granny Sybs arrived with Harold in tow. She looked at Tracy and smiled. "Good morning, all."

"Morning," said Tracy and Camilla together.

"I hope we didn't wake you, Gran," said Tracy, looking at the time. It was 6.35am.

"No, don't worry. I've been up since six. Besides, I had a feeling that today was the day." She winked at Tracy.

"What day?" said Dylan walking into the room yawning.

"Mom, I lied," said Tracy.

"What do you mean?"

"The music you heard this morning. It didn't come from the TV. It came from the flute."

"Why didn't you want me to know?"

"Well… I guess I was in shock," said Tracy.

Camilla looked confused.

"What do you mean, Trace?" said Harold, concern in his voice. "You okay?"

Tracy nodded. "I'm fine." She looked around the room. Her stomach grumbled in anticipation of what was to come. She ignored it by turning her focus to opening the case once again. "I have something really important to show you all," she said looking around at her family. She turned to her grandmother who smiled warmly in return. "I had a dream last night. I dreamt that I was back at Gobekli Tepe. I was with all these people.

"What's Gobekitep?" said Dylan.

"Gobekli Tepe," corrected Harold.

"Whatever."

"It's one of the places that Dad took me to," said Tracy. "An ancient temple in Turkey. Anyway, in my dream, I saw these people. They wore strange clothing and one of them was blowing a flute, a single high-pitched note. She looked exactly like me and the flute looked just like this one." She tapped the case sitting next to her on the couch.

"Wooo," said Dylan, waving his hands through the air and rolling his eyes. "That's spooky."

Tracy ignored her brother's retort. "The weirdest part was, a giant rock, a megalith, was hovering just above the ground. It was just floating there. And then this man pushed it, and it moved as if it weighed next to nothing. Another man blew on another flute, giving the woman time to take a breath, so as not to disrupt the sound. I soon realised that the impossible was true. The power of the flute and the sound that poured out of it, caused this huge rock to easily float above the ground. Like magic."

"Okay, I'm outta here," said Dylan, turning to leave the room.

"Dylan Barnes," said Camilla. "Will you stop being so rude and let your sister finish?"

"But I thought she was finished. I gotta get ready for school."

"Just wait one more minute," said Camilla imploringly.

Tracy opened the case and took out the flute.

Granny Sybs took in a short, sharp breath.

"Okay, just keep your eyes on the remote," said Tracy, pointing at the TV remote on the table. She carefully placed her fingers over the holes on the flute. She took a deep breath, brought the flute up to her lips, closed her eyes, and began to blow. She pictured the remote in her mind's eye. She focused on its shape and form, tracing its outline as the perfect note rang strong and true, echoing through the room as before. She opened her eyes and watched as the black television remote wobbled and then lifted off the table.

Camilla gasped, and Sybs clapped her hands together in excitement. Harold's eyes widened like saucers, and Dylan's mouth dropped open in awe. Tracy ran out of breath, and the remote dropped back onto the table with a clatter. Everyone stared at the remote as it spun around a couple of times before coming to rest.

Dylan began to applaud. "Well done. Neat trick." He dropped to his knees and looked under the table. "Okay. How'd you do it? What's the secret?" he waved his hand over the remote and squinted up at the ceiling. "A piece of thread? A magnet? Mirrors? Come on, Trace, you can tell me."

Tracy shook her head slowly from side to side. "It's the flute," she whispered, holding up the instrument.

"Can't be," said Dylan. "How's that even possible?" He turned to his father.

"It kind of makes sense," said Sybs. "It explains how those huge pillars were possibly moved and put into place. Perhaps it's the same technology that was used to build the pyramids!"

"Tracy," said Harold. "I don't know what to say. This is just incredible. Look," he said extending his hand, palm down. "It's shaking! My brain is struggling to make sense of what my eyes just saw."

"Let me see that," said Dylan taking the flute from Tracy. He held it up and stared down its shaft, looking for some evidence that would explain what he just witnessed. He blew into the flute, and a flat, out-of-key noise came out the other end. "How does it work, exactly?"

"I have a feeling that it's more than just blowing the flute," said Sybs.

"What do you mean, Gran?" said Dylan frowning.

"I think that for the magic to work, it needs someone with a kind of magic of her own," she replied, winking at Tracy.

"Oh, here we go again," said Dylan rolling his eyes. "Tracy's magic powers."

"There is definitely some kind of symbiosis going on," said Sybs. "I could feel it. Tracy definitely had a mental connection to the remote as she began to blow into the flute. Am I right, Trace?"

"Now that you mention it, I guess so," said Tracy. "I had to concentrate quite hard on the object, tracing its shape in my mind. And then when I started blowing into the flute, it was like the single note that came out, was alive, like a snake, that began to wrap itself around the remote, lifting it off the table."

"Fascinating," whispered Harold in awe. "It was probably a pretty rare occurrence, to find someone who had your abilities back then, which explains why this supposed skill has been lost over time. I'm still finding this hard to digest. Do you know what this means?"

"That Tracy's going to be famous?" said Dylan.

Camilla laughed.

"What? I'm serious. She should enter America's got talent."

"Dyl," said Harold. "Great idea, but I think this is more important than just a magic show. Granny Sybs is right. This discovery could explain a helluva lot that we have up until now, just theorised. What if we could harness this power for flight? Space travel? The possibilities are endless. Anti-gravity technology has been the stuff of science fiction up until now."

"Wow," said Dylan. "You're right. We're *all* going to be famous."

Everyone began to laugh out loud. Even Dylan joined in.

31 ~ Tests

"Good morning, sleepy-head," said Harold, poking his head around the door. "You up?"

"Dad, it's a Saturday," said Tracy, peeking out from beneath the covers. "I'm allowed to sleep in."

"Yeah, I know, but we have places to go, things to do, remember?" Harold chimed, while tapping the case he carried under his arm. A wide grin spread across his face, and his eyes sparkled with the excitement of a child on his way to the theme park.

And then Tracy remembered. She promised her Dad she would accompany him to his lab so that they could run some tests with the flute. She took a deep breath. "Okay, gimme five minutes. I'm getting up."

"Cool. I've made you some tea."

"Thanks, Dad." She turned over in her bed and closed her eyes. Memories of those strange-looking people in her dream played over inside her head like an old television documentary on National Geographic. The girl playing the flute turned to face her, and this time, it was the girl from the forest. Her face was blood-streaked. She opened her mouth to scream. Tracy quickly rolled over and opened her eyes. A chill ran down her spine along with the faint echo of the scream in her ears.

She climbed out of bed and jumped into a quick shower. The cleansing water washed away the vivid memories, clearing her head, wiping it clean. She stepped out of the shower, coming to stand in front of the mirror as she dried herself off. The steam from the shower fogged up the mirror for a few moments. She peered at her reflection that gradually came into view as the steam evaporated. She stuck out her tongue, scrunched her nose and tilted her head to one side. Her long, wet hair stuck to her face like glue. She towel-dried her hair and then blow-dried it, brushing it out in long, even strokes.

She pulled on a pair of jeans and a green top covered in tiny red flowers that she loved and then checked her phone. She had twelve WhatsApp notifications. Eleven from Lisa and one from Josh. She opened Josh's message first.

Hey, bae. You free tonight? Let's go to Sensual Shakes?

Tracy closed Josh's message and opened up Lisa's eleven messages.

Morning Miss jet-setter. How's the jetlag?

Call me when you up.

Wake uuuuuuuup!

You won't believe it but that bitch Veronica Lipman is dating Griffin Balfour! He's such a dork. I saw them kissing under the grandstand during phys-ed yesterday. Forgot to tell you. They deserve each other. Cow

Why you ignoring me? Can't believe you're still sleeping! I'm going to the mall. Have to buy a dress for Shelley's party next week. Please come with me to the mall? What are you wearing? Helooooooo

Okay. I'm officially getting pissed. Why aren't you talking to me? Whyyyyyy?

Wanna do something tonight? Let's get some pizza and hang out. Keen?

Are you with Josh? Is that it? If you've dumped me for Josh, then I'm really going to get mad

It's not that fun talking to myself here. Earth to Tracy. Please respond!

The next message was a series of random emoji's, followed

by a GIF of a man running around in circles. Tracy grinned. Crazy chick.

Tracy began typing out a response to Lisa. *I'm up. Was in the shower. Soz can't join you, have to go with my Dad to the lab this morning. Send me pics of some dresses, and I'll help you choose. Maybe let's go for lunch? Chat later.*

Tracy didn't know what to say to Josh about later that evening. She wanted to spend time with him but didn't feel for Lisa's wrath. She preferred to meet with Lisa face-to-face to discuss her intentions. She didn't want to keep Josh hanging either but felt that she had to clear the air with Lisa first. WhatsApp could be so impersonal. Sometimes she wished that it had never been invented. She took a deep breath and typed out a message to Josh.

Hey, handsome. On my way to the lab with my Dad. Will let you know a bit later. Can't wait to see you xxx

She pushed her phone into her jeans pocket, smeared on some lip gloss and bounced down the stairs. Both her parents were in the kitchen.

Harold handed her a hot mug of tea. "Here you go, my angel," he said with a warm smile.

"Thanks, Dad," she replied, gingerly sipping the tea. It was just perfect. Not too hot. Not too cold.

"Morning, my baby," said Camilla. She cradled a pink mug in her hands. Tracy could smell the coffee aroma as it steamed out of her mother's cup. "You sleep all right? Any more scary dreams?"

"Morning." Tracy smiled warmly. "Thankfully, no. No more scary dreams." She rolled her eyes.

Camilla walked over to Tracy and gave her a one-armed, consoling hug. "Great. You ready for your little outing?"

Tracy looked over at her father and nodded. "Ready as I'll ever be!"

Harold beamed. Tracy didn't think she had ever seen her father this excited before. He looked like one of those toy marionettes with a permanent grin on its face.

◊ ◊ ◊

The ride to the lab was uneventful. Tracy gazed out of the window as George Michael's *Faith* played in the car. She looked up and squinted into the sky. A drizzle fell from the grey, gloomy clouds, and the roads seemed busier than usual.

The melancholic morning seemed to have no effect on her father, who didn't stop talking all the way to the lab. "Oh well, here we are," he said, pulling into a parking bay with his name printed neatly on a board in black letters. **PROF H.W. BARNES.** "Come on, let's go," he said to Tracy, who was gazing dreamily out of the window at the board.

Tracy stepped out of the car. She had to walk quickly to catch up to her father, who was striding towards the laboratory building with an urgency in his step. The Lab was a long, narrow, white building covered in hexagonal shapes. It looked like a giant beehive from outer space. It was built by Jeremy Lipshitz, a famous Chicago-based architect whose designs often made it into all the coolest magazines. The Lab was featured in Wallpaper Magazine soon after its construction about five years ago, as part of a fashion shoot for some famous Italian clothing brand. Probably Versace or something. Tracy couldn't quite remember, but what she did remember quite vividly, was the model in the shoot. She wore a shiny, short, white miniskirt, a matching white wig, and white lipstick. To top it off, she had a pair of those spooky, white contact lenses that made her look like a possessed demon-alien from another dimension, standing in front of her beehive spaceship, ready to subjugate the planet and steal all the flowers to make white, milky, space-honey, so that she could feed her evil race of space-aliens. Tracy laughed to herself at her vivid imagination.

Harold pressed his index finger into a biometric fingerprint reader suspended on the wall next to the front door and stared into the screen above it for just a moment. *Welcome, Doctor Barnes*, said a voice. It sounded electronic to Tracy, but she wasn't sure. These days it was difficult to tell the difference. The double-biometric security protocol had only recently been installed after a break-in to the lab about three months back. Even though nothing seemed to be missing after the incident, Harold and his team ramped up the security by installing additional biometric fingerprint readers on several doors inside the lab that led to sensitive information.

"Morning Prof," said Marjorie, as Harold and Tracy entered the building. Marjorie May was the Lab's secretary. Tracy had known her for years.

"Morning, Marj," said Harold.

"Tracy. Nice to see you," said Marjorie. Her great big smile pushed her plump cheeks against her eyes, turning them into slits so that she looked like a Chinese doll with a permanent grin on her face. "You grow more beautiful every day!"

Tracy dropped her head and blushed. "Thanks Marj. Nice to see you too. Hope you're well."

"Just dandy," replied Marjorie cajolingly.

Tracy followed her father as he led them down the passage and past several closed doors. They approached a door with a plaque attached in bold, black letters that read, **PROFESSOR HAROLD W. BARNES**. Harold pressed his finger against the biometric reader and opened the door. The office was a mess as usual. Piles of papers and books were stacked precariously on Harold's desk, leaving barely enough space for him to work. There was a musty smell in the air as if no one had stepped foot into the office in months. Tracy gazed around the room. A distressed leather couch lay beneath an abstract piece of art that hung askew on the wall. Tracy tilted her head, trying to make sense of the painting that looked like an alien landscape with triangular-shaped clouds floating above an orange lake. Tracy thought she saw something move in the lake; a ripple that was there and then gone in an instant. She blinked her eyes a couple of times and then dropped down onto the couch with a sigh, spreading herself across it with bent legs, her head resting against one cushioned side.

Harold pulled open the drawers in his desk and began rummaging through them.

"What you looking for, Dad?" enquired Tracy, pulling out her phone to scroll through Instagram.

"A spare lanyard," he replied. His voice sounded muffled as he crouched behind his desk. "You'll need one for the lab."

"Oh, okay." Tracy giggled. One of her classmates had posted a video of Mrs. Perkins in class. She was wearing a ridiculous, bright yellow dress, cut with a cleavage so low, you could practically see her navel. Her boobs looked like they were going to fall out. She walked over to Paul Williams, grabbed him by the ear and led him straight out of the class. The door closed behind her, and the entire class erupted. Scrunched up pieces of paper flew through the air and one of her classmates (she couldn't make out who in the video) began to draw pictures all over the board.

"Ah, here it is," said Harold, producing the spare lanyard. "Come, let's go." Harold led Tracy out of his office and down the hall until they reached a set of double doors at the very end with a small, square, white perspex sign affixed to them that read, **LABORATORY. STAFF ONLY BEYOND THIS POINT**. Harold pressed his finger into another biometric reader and opened the door. Tracy expected the whooshing sound of compressed air to escape, along with a puff of smoke for added effect, but there was nothing more than a subtle click. Tracy and her father stepped through and into a small space with a low ceiling and a series of white panels on the walls. The purplish glow from a hidden light source filled the room. Tracy imagined that she had stepped into a spaceship.

"Hold your breath and close your eyes," cautioned Harold.

Tracy did as she was told, sucking in her breath and holding it tightly.

The finest mist began to spray all over them. It tickled Tracy's face and the back of her neck. Just when she thought that she couldn't hold her breath any longer, the spraying stopped. A beeping sounded, and Tracy opened her eyes.

Harold opened a door on the other side and beckoned Tracy through and into the laboratory.

"Was that some kind of disinfectant spray?"

"Sure was," Harold nodded. "That's the sterilisation room. The spray you felt is a standard disinfectant, and the purple light is an intense UV energy field that disinfects in a matter of seconds."

"Oh, wow," said Tracy, aghast. "Pretty cool." She rubbed her arms and turned her palms face-up. "I'm all squeaky clean now."

Harold smiled. "Come. Let's go and say hi to Shirley."

Shirley Sandhoven was one of Tracy's father's associates, responsible for the day to day running of the lab. She was sitting alone on an aluminium stool, hunched over a microscope, as Harold and Tracy approached.

"Morning, Shirley," said Harold.

Shirley looked up from the microscope, rubbed her eyes, and picked up a pair of tortoiseshell spectacles. She pushed them over her nose and turned to Harold. "Morning, Harry. And who have we here? Tracy! It's been a while. You're looking well. Oh, yes, happy birthday! Can't believe you're seventeen already."

Tracy grinned. "Hi, Shirley. Thanks. Yeah, neither can I. It's kinda surreal."

"Surreal? You wanna see surreal? Just take a look through here," said Shirley, pointing at the microscope. She pushed her feet into the ground and rolled away from the desk so that Tracy could get up close.

Tracy pressed her eyes over the lenses. "Oh, wow! That's amazing. What are those little blue things?"

"Those are synaptic vesicles."

"English, please."

Shirley smiled. "What you are looking at is a synapse, the origin of every thought and feeling."

"Wow."

"The synaptic vesicles run through the synapse.

Neurotransmitter molecules run through these vesicles. But enough about this stuff. Is that it?" said Shirley excitedly, pointing at the case tucked neatly under Harold's arm.

"Yep. This is the artefact," said Harold, tapping the case. "Well, a digitally printed copy." He opened the lid, and Shirley drew in a sharp breath.

"Can I… touch it?" she said, gingerly extending her hand out towards the flute as if it was alive.

"Of course," said Harold, lifting the silver instrument out of its protective case. It sparkled in the light. "Here you go," he said, placing the flute in Shirley's outstretched hand.

"It's so light," she said, lifting it up and down. She raised it to her left eye and peered down its shaft. "Remarkable. So precise. And the holes…" She twisted the flute around in her hands, silently counting the perfectly round indentations. "So this is what you meant by Fibonacci."

Harold nodded.

"Unreal," whispered Shirley in awe. "It's just so surreal. The Golden Ratio." She shook her head slowly from side to side, gradually taking in the magnitude of the discovery.

"May I?" she said, lifting the flute to her lips.

"Sure," replied Harold. He glanced at Tracy and winked.

Shirley gently placed three of her fingers over the holes, took a deep breath, and blew softly into the instrument. The flute produced a crisp, clear note. She took another breath and blew harder this time.

Tracy closed her eyes. The sound was pleasant, yet it felt to her as if something was lacking, missing. She waited in anticipation for the vibration; a tingling sensation that tickled her lips and then travelled up her fingers and into her arms when she blew into the flute, but it didn't come. The magic was absent. The flute was just a simple instrument in Shirley's hands. Nothing more, nothing less.

Shirley lowered the flute from her lips. "Beautiful, Harry. It sounds so beautiful. Amazing. Great work!" She turned the flute over in her hands once more, marvelling at its design.

"Thanks," said Harold with a smile. "But it's Tracy that's the real star in this movie," he said ruffling her hair. "If it weren't for her, the flute would still be just a stick with holes."

"What do you mean?" said Shirley creasing her brow in confusion.

"She's the one that was first to identify the artefact as a flute when we all believed it to be a measuring device of some kind. But what I'm about to show you is even more unbelievable," said Harold. "Set up the video camera in the boardroom and you'll see."

Shirley obediently hopped off her stool, handed Harold back the flute and skipped over to the boardroom with the others in tow. Harold flicked on the lights. The fluorescent tubes popped to life. Harold pulled out his mobile phone and looked at Tracy. "Will this do? It's about the same size as the remote. Maybe a bit heavier."

Tracy shrugged her shoulders. "Guess so. I've only tried this twice, remember?"

"Okay. Let's do this!" said Harold, rubbing his hands together in anticipation. He placed his phone in the centre of the table.

"What are we doing, actually?" said Shirley, obviously still quite confused. She tilted her head, creased her brow, and stared at Harold's phone on the table.

"Just set up the camera and tell me when it's running," said Harold. "You'll soon see." Harold handed Tracy the flute. "Stand over there," he instructed Tracy.

Tracy went to stand on the other side of the room.

"Do you think you're close enough to the phone?"

Tracy nodded.

"Okay. The camera is up and running," said Shirley.

"Great! Come and stand over here," he said to Shirley. He looked at Tracy and smiled. "When you're ready."

Tracy closed her eyes. The flute was so smooth in her hands. She gently stroked its surface, rubbing the tips of her fingers over the holes, picturing the Fibonacci spiral in her mind's eye. She opened her eyes and stared at the mobile phone on the table, tracing the rectangular outline until its silhouette burned into her vision like a glowing beacon of light. She lifted the flute to her lips, took a deep breath, and exhaled into the instrument. The sound that emanated was so pure, so clear. Shirley gasped. Tracy adjusted the pitch slightly, and the long and steady note felt like a lotus flower, rising from the mud and opening to the light inside her head. The energy, the magic was almost palpable this time. It became an extension of her senses, almost like a brand new appendage that only she could sense and feel. She directed it towards the object on the table, stroking it, caressing it, lifting it up, higher and higher.

Shirley's mouth dropped as she watched Harold's phone miraculously rise off the table and hover in mid-air. The melodic sound coming out of the flute permeated every crevice in the boardroom, reverberating in and out of every nook and cranny. Tracy allowed the phone to gradually lower back down onto the table as her breath began to run out. It touched down gently like a drone coming in to land. The silence that followed still echoed with the captivating tone that came from the flute.

Shirley glanced at the camera, checking to see that the red recording light was blinking. "If I hadn't have seen it with my own eyes then I wouldn't have believed it," she said, clearly in shock at what had just transpired. "This is beyond incredible, Harry. Simply astounding." She looked at Tracy and the flute in her hands. "Why... how...?" She was at a loss for words.

"I'm not sure if it's an inherent skill," said Harold, "but Tracy seems to have the ability to use the sound produced by the flute to reverse the force of gravity around solid objects, thereby causing them to levitate."

"I have so many questions," said Shirley. She placed her hands either side of her head. "Too many!"

Harold smiled. "I know. It's quite overwhelming. This changes everything."

"Acoustic levitation," said Shirley. "That's what it's called. I've heard of experiments in controlled, scientific environments where specific frequencies are produced in order to levitate tiny droplets of fluid. But this! This is revolutionary. And the fact that this phenomenon was produced via the replica of an artefact over 12,000 years old is simply mind-boggling. Talk about advanced pre-civilisations in history!"

Harold smiled. "I knew you'd find this fascinating."

"We have to run more tests," said Shirley. Her voice trembled in excitement. "Is there a limit to the mass of the object?" She turned to Tracy.

Tracy's eyes widened. She shrugged her shoulders. "Um… I don't know. This is only the third time that I've done it."

"And? How did it compare to the first two?"

"Well," said Tracy staring stoically into the top right corner of the room. "It was kinda different."

"How?"

Tracy thought carefully for a moment about what she felt before she articulated her experience. "I think that this time, I had more control over the sound, which gave me more control over the object being lifted than before."

Shirley smiled. "Good, good. So the whole process felt easier?"

"I guess so, yes."

"There's just one thing that I don't understand," continued Shirley. "Harry, you mentioned that Tracy can reverse the force of gravity, yet when I blew into the flute, I experienced no such capability. Is this something I need to learn?"

"That is a good question," replied Harold. "I may be wrong, but I think that this ability has something to do with a gift that she recently acquired." Harold winked at his daughter.

"A gift? What kind of gift? Can I see it?"

"You just did."

"Whatever do you mean? Harry, stop playing games with me. I'm serious." Shirley pressed her hands against her hips in earnest.

"Tracy inherited it from her grandmother. I guess you can call it a personality trait; a genetic disposition."

235

"I still have no idea what you are talking about."

"She has the ability to predict the future."

"You mean like a psychic? Really?" said Shirley in amazement.

"Yep. And I think that this ability has something to do with how she's able to manipulate the frequency produced by the flute to lift objects."

"Hmm." Shirley rubbed her chin, deep in thought. "A possible explanation, but highly speculative. Where's the scientific proof?"

"Out the window," said Harold.

"Excuse me?"

"Shirley. Do you believe what you saw?"

Shirley nodded.

"I saw you checking the camera. It was hard for you to understand that what you saw was in fact real. I'm still trying to wrap my head around this, believe me. My scientific mind demands proof that this... this instrument is able to produce a sound frequency that disrupts the very matter of an object, causing it to become weightless. Yet here we are. Documented proof on camera that it just happened. Right before our very eyes. Yes, I agree, we need to do further testing, but this experiment clearly explains the mysteries associated with all the ancient megalithic stone structures and how these tons of rock and granite were transported from remote locations and set in place to create the structures we find today. I mean just look at the pyramids. This could easily explain how these hundreds of thousands of giant stone blocks were moved into place. What fascinates me more is how this technological mystery was mastered by people living on Earth over 12,000 years ago. Where and how did they acquire this knowledge? How did they pass it onto the Egyptians and other cultures such as the Myans, etcetera? And how did this powerful skill become lost in the annals of time?"

"This is much bigger than all of us, Harry." Shirley's voice was but a whisper. "I mean, just think of the possibilities - anti-gravity technology. We won't need powerful rockets or planes to launch us into the sky. The force of gravity has been mastered. A new age is upon us."

Harold nodded silently. "Right now, let's keep this between ourselves until we can figure out what steps to take next. I don't want this falling into the wrong hands."

"You mean the military," said Shirley flatly.

"Exactly. Tracy that goes for you too. Especially for you. It's for your own safety, okay?"

"Sure, Dad, I understand. Nothing we have discussed leaves this room."

"Atta girl. Now hand me the flute. Let me put it away for safekeeping."

Tracy handed her father the silver instrument. Just as she placed it in his hand, a sharp, shooting pain shot into her head. She dropped to her haunches, squeezed her eyes shut and winced.

"Trace, you okay?" said Harold quickly stepping over to Tracy in alarm.

Tracy slowly straightened up. Tears streamed from her eyes. She rubbed them dry with the back of her sleeve. "I'll be fine. I saw her."

"Who? Where?" Harold looked around instinctively.

"The girl from my dream. She was in my head. I think she knows we have the flute."

32 ~ Lights out

The whites of his knuckles appeared to glow in the light of the streetlamp outside as Miguel gripped the hard vinyl, textured, black steering wheel of the 1976 Chevy Chavelle Laguna. He looked into the rearview mirror and could just make out Sabine's hypnotic eyes in the darkness as she stared back at him eerily. He looked quickly away.

"How much longer must we wait?" said Julian.

"We go when she tells us to," said Miguel.

Julian looked furtively out of the window at the passersby. He turned his face up to the sky above, looking in vain for the moon.

"Is Pinto in position?" said Miguel.

"Yeah. He's ready and waiting at the back."

"Good."

"Now," said Sabine. "The time is now."

"Okay, let's do this," said Miguel. He turned to Sabine. "You just wait here. We won't be long."

Sabine just stared at Miguel as if she hadn't heard him.

Miguel stepped out of the vehicle. The crisp night air stung his face for a moment. He closed his eyes and took an icy breath. He looked around, surveying the scene before brushing

238

his hand across the back of his jacket, checking to feel the hard shape of the concealed handgun pressed into the small of his back and tucked into his jeans.

Forest Bar was diagonally across from the Yankee Stadium. The neon sign of the stadium glowed brightly against its towering walls. Miguel pushed open the door and stepped into the bar with Julian at his side. Their heavily tattooed features raised a few eyebrows from some of the patrons at the bar, but they quickly turned back to their beers and conversations, as the two newcomers made their way inside. Julian cocked his head towards the back of the establishment, indicating a vacant table beneath a gloomy lampshade.

Miguel scrutinised every person as he made his way towards the table but found no resemblance to the infamous José "Flaco" Sanchez. He was beginning to regret not bringing Sabine inside. On second thought, her queer-looking demeanour would have raised more attention than he would have liked. Miguel wondered if Flaco had somehow disguised himself since he last encountered him. That murderer. That murderous pig. Coward. Hiding all these years. He never doubted Sabine's powers of divination. She was special. A secret weapon. *His* secret weapon. He grinned.

"Evening, gents," said the waiter, as Miguel and Julian settled into their seats. "What will it be this evening?"

"Two beers," said Miguel.

"We have 24 beers on tap," said the waiter.

Miguel frowned. "Just bring me a couple of Coronas, esé."

"Sure thing," said the waiter. He was gone before Miguel looked up again.

"What is it with people these days," said Miguel. "Why do they have to make things so damn complicated? How does he expect me to choose from between 24 beers? Fucking idiot."

"Do you see him?" said Julian looking around.

"Flaco? No."

"Where do you think he is? I mean, do you think this bitch even knows what she's talking about?"

239

"Yes. He's here. Somewhere," said Miguel softly.

"Why doesn't one of us go and stand by the restroom. He's bound to go in there at some point."

"Too conspicuous."

"But you agree that we take him out there, right?"

Miguel nodded. "Yeah. The restroom. That's how it's gonna go down. When we spot him, and only then, we keep an eye on him until he decides to go. I'll follow him inside and you follow exactly one minute after, comprende?"

Julian nodded.

"As soon as you step inside, hold the door closed. That's when I'll make my move. It's gonna happen real quick, so stay alert."

"Here you go, gents," said the waiter returning with two Coronas. He placed them down on the table. "Enjoy."

"Gracias," said Julian, lifting the ice-cold bottle to his lips. "Hmm. Tastes great."

The waiter smiled. "Can I get you two anything else?"

"Just move," said Miguel. "You're blocking the screen."

"Oh, sorry," said the waiter jumping out of the way. He disappeared again in a hurry.

Miguel wasn't really watching the football game. He was more interested in the patrons, of course. Most of them had their backs to him, so Flaco could be anywhere.

"Pssst," Julian nudged Miguel and tilted his head in the direction of a figure walking towards the bar.

Miguel looked up. It was him. Flaco. He could tell just by the way he moved. It was something in his gait, something that triggered a distant memory, an intuitive feeling that confirmed his suspicions almost immediately. He was walking towards the bar, *from* the restroom. "Shit."

"What? Oh." Julian clicked. "He's just been. We're too late. What we gonna do, boss? It's gonna be ages before he goes again. *If* he goes again."

Miguel took a long sip of his beer. He wiped his mouth with the back of his sleeve and stared at Flaco, thinking, contemplating, scheming. "I have an idea," he said.

"What?"

Miguel signalled for the waiter.

"Yes, my good, sir," said the waiter.

"What is your name?"

"Um, Patrick," said the waiter with a nervous smile.

"Patrick," said Miguel pressing a crumpled up 20 Dollar bill into his hand. "I need you to do me a favour."

Patrick glanced down at the note. "Yes, yes, sure. How can I be of assistance," he said, a hint of trepidation in his voice. He cleared his throat with a cough.

"See that man over there by the bar?"

Patrick began to turn around.

"Don't look now," hissed Miguel. "He's wearing a black leather jacket, glasses and has a moustache. If you turn around, he's sitting to the right with his back to the restroom."

Patrick nodded.

"I want you to go over to him and tell him that one of the patrons in the bar saw him drop something on the floor in the restroom as he was leaving. Just point towards the restroom. Don't look in our direction. Okay? Got it?"

"Uh, yes, sure." Patrick looked a little bewildered.

"Just follow my instructions. Simple. Comprende?"

Patrick nodded again like the obedient servant he was trained to be.

"Okay. You can go now." Miguel ushered Patrick away. He watched him turn around and make a zigzag towards the bar, towards Flaco. Good, less conspicuous. Patrick approached Flaco from the other side so that he would turn to his right without drawing attention towards Miguel and Julian. Miguel watched as Flaco stood up from his chair to look in the direction of the restroom. He pushed his hands into his pockets and then scratched his head. He turned back and looked around the bar. Miguel and Julian looked down at their beers. When they looked up again, Flaco was halfway to the restroom.

"It worked!" Julian jumped in his chair with excitement.

Miguel stood up from the table. "One minute, okay?"

Julian nodded. "One minute."

Miguel made his way towards the restroom, making sure that Flaco was inside before he increased his pace. He pushed open the hinged door, keeping his head low as he stepped inside. Flaco was looking under the basin, oblivious to Miguel flanking the door. Flaco walked towards one of the cubicles. Miguel quickly scanned the room. There were three urinals and three cubicles, two of which appeared to be vacant, while the third looked like it was occupied - the door was closed. Miguel watched as Flaco stuck his head inside the first two cubicles and then prodded the door of the third. It let out a creak as it swung wide open. There was no one inside. Miguel made his move. In one swift motion, he bounded towards the cubicle, whipped out his switchblade and gave Flaco a shove, pushing him inside. Flaco flew forward with the force of the push, hit his shins against the toilet bowl, and fell forward, connecting his forehead on the cistern with a bang and a grunt. Instinctively, he pushed his hands out in front of him to stop himself from falling onto the floor, but Miguel was already on top of him, thrusting the switchblade in a series of short, sharp stabs into his back and side. He could feel the blade tear into flesh like a hot poker, the gush of warm blood exploding onto and over his fist with every strike. Flaco gasped for breath, trying desperately to turn around inside the small cubicle. He reached his left arm out behind him, grasping at thin air in an attempt to grab onto his attacker. Miguel stepped back for a moment and watched as Flaco flailed his arm around like a bird with one wing, flapping it around in a vain attempt to fly. Miguel reached back for his gun and then faltered, not wanting to attract any undue attention with the sound of a shot. Damn. He wished he had a silencer like they always had in the movies.

"Finish him."

Miguel turned. It was Julian. Miguel looked back at Flaco, who was making a concerted effort to stand up. He held a gun in his right hand. Miguel reacted instinctively. He thrust the switchblade up and into Flaco's neck before he had time to raise his weapon for a shot. Flaco opened his mouth. His eyes bulged as he dropped the gun into the toilet bowl with a splash. Miguel could see the tip of his blade protruding into Flaco's mouth as blood gushed inside, quickly filling up before pouring out together with a final wheeze of breath. Miguel spat onto the floor. "Puta!" He yanked his blade out in a downward thrust and Flaco dropped to the floor in a lifeless heap.

"Miguel," said Julian.

"What is it?" replied Miguel, turning around. Miguel's eyes widened. It was Sabine. "I thought I told you to stay put." She just stood there, arms folded, hoodie half-concealing her face. "Okay, I know. You want the eyes." Miguel dropped to his haunches, carefully pushed the switchblade into Flaco's left eye socket and pulled it around the perimeter, cutting through tissue and membrane. He twisted the blade, prying the eyeball from its socket. A gush of blood mixed with fluid oozed out as he popped the eyeball into his other hand. He slowly stood up, dropping the eye into Sabine's outstretched hand before turning back to remove the other one. Miguel wiped his hands on his jeans after he was done, closed the blade, and pushed it into his pocket. He pulled the cubicle door closed from the inside, locked it, proceeded to climb onto the toilet bowl and then over and into the middle cubicle, effectively sealing Flaco inside. He walked over to the washbasin and began to wash his blood and gore-soaked hands.

Miguel looked into the mirror, staring back at his reflection in earnest. He shifted his gaze to watch Sabine's reflection as she held the pair of eyeballs in her hand, scrutinising them intently. The bitter taste of bile burned his throat when she popped them, one at a time, into her mouth. He turned around, wide-eyed, as Sabine closed her eyes and began to shake like she was having an epileptic fit.

"What's happening?" said Julian, aghast.

Sabine dropped to her knees and placed her hands on the floor for support. The convulsions subsided. She hung her head, her long, dark hair hanging down over her face like a mop.

"Sabine? You all right?" Miguel bent down, extending his hand out towards her, his voice quavering.

Sabine threw her head back and glared up at Miguel. He jerked his hand back and jumped up in alarm, his eyes as wide as hubcaps. Sabine's face was contorted, and her eyes glowed red like the embers of a smouldering fire. They stared right through Miguel. He could feel them bore deep inside his soul, ripping through his head like a pair of hot pokers, tearing through his defences, his memories, his thoughts. And that smile; that wicked grin - it looked as if it was permanently carved into her face to thwart him, to taunt his conscience after the fatal stabbing in the cubicle.

With effort, Miguel tore his gaze away. He looked at Julian, who had backed up into the corner of the restroom, his face pale with dread.

33 ~ Clues

"Red," said Trudeau.

"Huh?" Doctor Isaac Lloyton looked up from eating his chicken salad. A piece of lettuce was unknowingly plastered to his lower lip as his mouth dropped open.

"Her hair. Mrs. Landman. Her hair was red."

"Oh. Oh yes. Natural?"

"Think so."

"Well, then, that definitely rules her out," said Isaac, returning to his meal.

Trudeau pulled up a chair and sat down in front of his Greek pasta salad and a can of Coke. Several black olives poked up through the pasta ribbons. His stomach rumbled. He looked around the canteen. Jeff Mills was sitting across from Melody Hugo on the other side of the room. Trudeau glanced up at the television that was broadcasting an advert for peanut butter and took a sip of his Coke. "Doc."

"Hmm?" replied Isaac, his mouth full of food.

"Thought I'd let you know that we found the car."

"Oh, really?"

"Yup. It was found abandoned in Ford Heights."

"Ford Heights as in Chicago?"

245

"Yeah, I know, right. She drove it all the way there and then just dumped it."

"You sure it's the vehicle?"

Trudeau nodded. "Registered to the late Mark Landman."

"Have you notified his wife?"

"Not yet," said Trudeau shaking his head. "We're still running tests."

"Forensics?"

Trudeau nodded. "We found a blood-soaked cloth and more hair samples."

"Black?"

Trudeau nodded. "Uh-huh." He looked up at the television once more, picking up snippets from the news anchor.

"They are known as the most notorious gang in the U.S., spreading terror to gain respect in the streets. The letters MS stand for Mara Salvatrucha, and the number thirteen represents the letter M, the thirteenth letter in the alphabet. Part of their initiation includes a thirteen-second beating by several gang members. Their members have been linked to violent stabbings, shootings, and rapes all over the country and are very difficult to eliminate because there are dozens of autonomous groups with no centralised chain of command. Their motto is *mata, viola, controla* - kill, rape, control, and many of them carry out these despicable acts in the name of the devil. This latest incident is believed to be the work of MS13 because the victim's eyes were gouged out as part of some sort of satanic ritual. We cross now to Malcolm Grossman, our reporter on the scene in Chicago. Malcolm."

The scene changed to a man holding a microphone in front of yellow police barrier-tape. "Thank you, Penelope. Another gruesome, senseless killing by MS13, an international criminal gang that originated in Los Angeles, California, in the eighties. MS13 is predominantly made up of immigrants from El Salvador, whose members are characterised by specific tattoos covering the entire body, including the face and neck. Anyone with any further information about this incident should please contact Detective Phil Fickson of the Chicago P.D."

Trudeau dropped his fork, pushed his chair back, and immediately stood up. "Doc. Gotta go."

Doctor Isaac Lloyton pushed his wire-framed spectacles up the bridge of his nose and rose from his chair. "This time, I'm joining you," he said determinedly. "Let me just get my bag. I'll meet you at the car."

◊ ◊ ◊

Trudeau deliberately approached the uniformed officer standing with his arms folded in front of the yellow barrier tape outside *Forest Bar* in the Bronx. The flashing red and blue lights from the police car parked nearby blinded him momentarily. "Trudeau, Lloyton," he gestured to Isaac, "FBI." He flashed his ID badge at the officer.

"FBI? What you guys doing here? This is our gig."

"Not any longer, pal. We'll take it from here."

"I'm not even gonna ask."

Trudeau stared at the officer's badge. "Smith? Yeah, well don't, cos the answers are above your pay grade."

"You fellas are all the same, you know," said officer Smith icily. "Throwing your weight around like you own the city. Well, let me tell you that if it weren't for us, you guys wouldn't be here. Who do you think calls the cops? Yeah, that's right. *We* are the ones that get the call, not you pencil-pushers. You don't wanna get your hands dirty. You'd rather leave us to do all the dirty work and then you just magically appear like this and take all the credit."

"Someone has to clean up your mess, that's all," said Trudeau.

"Look, pal, I don't have the energy to waste on you lot. At least now I can get to watch the game. So, I guess I'll just say thanks for cleaning up the so-called mess we made and be on my way. If that's okay with you, Agent Trudeau, sir?" he said, with enough sarcasm to melt a block of cheese.

Trudeau forced a smile. "Aye, aye, Captain," he saluted the officer who stepped aside, allowing Trudeau and Isaac to duck beneath the barrier tape and into the venue.

Forest Bar was deserted, save for a few police officers who were milling around. Trudeau and Llotson made their way over to the restroom. The body of the victim had just been lifted onto a stretcher and a police officer wearing a pair of tight, blue rubber-latex gloves, was securing the deceased by way of two black, nylon straps to prevent the body from falling off. He looked up at Trudeau with a frown as he leaned over the body.

"Oh, sorry," said Trudeau flashing his badge. "We've just taken over this case. I'm Trudeau. This is Lloyton."

"Fernandez," said the officer introducing himself. "Chicago P.D." Officer Fernandez was around 5'9 with dark, wavy hair and a round, jovial face, covered in pockmarks. He watched as Trudeau studied the victim's face and the gaping holes that once contained eyes.

"Time of death?"

Fernandez cleared his throat. "About three hours ago."

"And he was found in there?" Trudeau pointed at the cubicle behind Fernandez.

"Yeah. It was locked from the inside."

"Interesting. You ID the body?" Trudeau noticed the tattoos all over the victim's body. Even his mutilated face, caked in dried blood was heavily marked.

"José Sanchez. MS13 gang member. Very dangerous. I'm guessing that's why you guys are here?"

Isaac nodded. "Yeah. MS13. High priority."

"President's orders?"

"Something like that."

"I heard Sanchez was killed a few years back," said Fernandez matter-of-factly.

Isaac scrutinised the corpse. "Well, obviously not," he said. "He was probably in hiding from whoever finally killed him."

"But why the eyes?"

"That's what we're here to find out," said Isaac flatly.

"Devil killing. That's what they're saying anyway," said Fernandez. "It's those sick MS13 bastards. They believe in all that shit. Just look at this." Fernandez pulled back the victim's shirt. Crudely carved into the flesh across his chest was a gruesome design. Dried blood had already formed thick, dark scabs along the edges of where the skin had been cut. Two, long jagged lines had been sliced from the centre of Sanchez's chest, up at an angle, across each nipple, towards each shoulder. The two lines were joined at the bottom by another short wavy line. "It's supposed to represent a fist with the index and pinkie fingers sticking up like the horns of the devil."

"You find the eyes?" said Trudeau.

"Nope," said Fernandez, pulling the victim's shirt back down over his chest. "Probably hanging from the dashboard of whoever took him out." Fernandez chuckled.

Trudeau wasn't one for humour right now. He just stared at Fernandez grimly, who quickly shut his mouth. Trudeau walked over to the cubicle and took a look inside. The door had been pried open. The lock was all twisted and broken. There was a big pool of dark-red blood on the floor and smeared all over the wall.

"Was he shot or stabbed?" enquired Isaac.

"Stabbed. Multiple times. Lower side of the body and then it looks like a final blow up into the throat." He made an upward, thrusting movement with his hand.

"Bastards." Trudeau spat into the cubicle. "Witnesses?"

"We have some statements," said Fernandez handing Trudeau his notepad. "They all say the same thing. Two heavily tattooed men came into the bar, sat down, and ordered a couple of beers. Then they went to the restroom. Together."

"Any detail on the tattoos?" said Isaac.

Fernandez shook his head. "Nope. Just that they had them on their faces."

Isaac looked at Trudeau. "That does narrow it down a bit," he said, stroking his chin. "The youngsters don't brand themselves much anymore, let alone their faces."

Trudeau nodded. "Old guard. Sanchez was in his late 50's. My guess these two were roughly the same age. Oh, we'll find them, all right," he said confidently.

Isaac shook Fernandez's hand. "Thanks, Fernandez. You've been very helpful."

"No problem."

"Anything else you can tell us?" said Trudeau.

"Just the girl," he replied.

"What girl?"

"The one with the long, dark hair. Look at my notes," Fernandez said, pointing at his notebook. "The witnesses said she came into the bar afterwards. They noticed her because… because she looked, well, different."

Isaac stared at Trudeau. "What do you mean, different?" he turned to Fernandez.

"Like she didn't quite belong inside the bar. They said she wore a black hoodie and had unusual markings on her face."

"Tattoos?" said Isaac.

"Well, no, not tattoos. Markings. The one guy said it looked like her face was scarred. Apparently she walked straight to the restroom and then left with the other two a short while later."

"Could it be?" said Isaac to Trudeau.

"You find any evidence?" said Trudeau. "The murder weapon, maybe?"

Fernandez shook his head. "Nothing. Nadda. The victim wasn't even carrying ID. If it wasn't for his tattoos, we wouldn't have been able to ID him."

"Can I borrow that for a moment?" Trudeau pointed at Fernandez's black, standard-issue flashlight clipped onto his belt.

"Sure, here you go," he said, handing Trudeau the flashlight.

Trudeau flicked it on, shining it into the cubicle.

"We've scoured the area," said Fernandez. "As I said, there's nothing."

Trudeau ignored Fernandez. He backed out of the cubicle and bent over, carefully scrutinising the restroom floor. He closed his eyes for a brief moment, focused his thoughts, slowed down his breathing. This is why he was here. This is why he was an Agent. He was trained for this. He smiled. This is why he enjoyed his job. It was the little things. It was the little things that made him smile. It was the little things that made his heart swell with pride, with reverence for who he was and what he represented. An agent for the Federal Bureau of Investigation. Investigation. That's what it was all about. Investigate the facts and find the answers. Find the truth, and it will set you free. He swept the flashlight slowly and deliberately across the floor as if it was a metal detector and he was straining to listen for the slightest hint of treasure. And there it was - a single strand of long, black hair. It gleamed for a moment in the bright light of the flashlight. Trudeau bent down and picked it up off the floor. He held it out at arm's length, shining the flashlight onto it so that everyone could see.

"You reckon it's hers?" said Fernandez, curiously.

"Oh, most definitely," said Trudeau confidently. "It's hers all right. And I'm sure there's more to be found." Trudeau held out his hand. "Think about it. This is the men's restroom. Why would a long, black hair, clearly longer than most men's hair, be found in here?"

Isaac pulled out a small, transparent plastic bag and Trudeau dropped the strand of hair inside. Isaac sealed the bag and pushed it into his pocket.

"Good point," said Fernandez scratching his head.

"Here you go," said Trudeau handing Fernandez back his notebook. "Thank you for your assistance."

"No problem. Hope you catch those thugs," said Fernandez. "Who's the girl, anyway?"

"If it's who we think it is, she's our mystery girl, the one we have been tracking for a while now," said Trudeau. "Here's my card. Call me if anything else comes up, will you? Anything."

"Sure thing. I'm taking the body to the morgue. The autopsy will probably be done first thing tomorrow morning."

"I'll be there," said Lloyton.

251

"Oh, did I tell you that he's a doctor?" said Trudeau, jabbing his thumb in Isaac's direction.

"No," replied Fernandez. "Good to know."

"Yeah. Forensic specialist. The best in the business."

"Great!" said Fernandez. "You fellas have yourselves a good evening." Fernandez nodded at Trudeau and Lloyton as he backed out of the restroom, pulling the stretcher along with him.

"Well, that was interesting," said Lloyton.

"Yeah. The girl. Very interesting. Let me know when you've analysed that strand of hair. I'm sure it's a match."

"I wish we knew who she was and what her motives are. And her connection to MS13."

"Isaac, your guess is as good as mine. All I know is, if it is the same girl, then we have a really interesting case on our hands. A really interesting case."

◊ ◊ ◊

The FBI Laboratory, located at the Marine Corps Base Quantico, in Quantico, Virginia, is one of the largest and most impressive crime labs in the world. The forensic experts at the lab, work tirelessly, assisting the FBI to solve all sorts of cases involving the analysis of DNA, bullet casings and cartridges, documents, signatures, drugs, and alcohol. Agent Trudeau followed Doctor Lloyton as he led them through the state-of-the-art facility, stopping momentarily to gaze into a room filled with a team of investigators examining the bomb fragments gathered from a recent incident in Washington DC where, fortunately, no one was injured.

"Here we are," said Isaac, unlocking a door with a sign that read, *Lab H445*. Trudeau stepped into the laboratory behind Isaac, who flicked a switch on the wall. The ceiling came to life, illuminating the room in LED light. Loyton walked over to an electron scanning microscope in the far corner of the room. He removed the hair sample from the plastic bag and secured it onto a specimen holder using a small swab of conductive adhesive. He powered up the microscope. It purred like a restless cat. He placed the sample inside the machine and tapped the touch-sensitive control panel, configuring it for a detailed scan. Lloyton stared at the digital display, transfixed by the flickering shapes like a baby watching a mobile.

Isaac pushed his head forward, squinting his eyes behind his spectacles to read the results, as the machine completed its scan. "It's her. The hair belongs to the girl. The same girl that was at the first murder scene. I recognise the signature."

"You sure?" said Trudeau.

"One hundred percent." Isaac nodded.

Trudeau scratched his head. "What the hell is going on? I mean, just think about it, Isaac. What is her motive? What does she want? She kills a car salesman, takes off in his car, drives to the coast, hooks up with MS13 gangsters, and then joins them on another killing spree."

Lloyton shrugged his shoulders. "What's even more perplexing, is what would MS13 gangsters want with a crazy antique dealer?"

"Maybe that's it," said Trudeau, shaking his index finger in the air. "Maybe you've hit the nail on the head, Isaac. Maybe she's paying them to find her some kind of rare antique piece, an artefact of sorts? Something really old. Like that ring or that obsidian blade. We need the results of that autopsy. We need to check if the same blade was used to kill Sanchez. I'm going back to the office to find out all I can about José Sanchez. The answers are there, Isaac. We just have to look a little bit deeper to find them." Trudeau rubbed his hands together and grinned. He loved a good investigation.

34 ~ Shake

"I'm not really supposed to say anything," said Tracy, wondering how they got onto the topic. She tried to think of something else to say to change the subject.

Josh was persistent. "What do you mean? Why won't you tell me?"

"Just because, okay?"

"That's not an acceptable answer." He was pushing her. "I thought that we were in an honest, open relationship. If you won't tell me, how am I supposed to trust you with anything else?"

His guilt trip was starting to work. It was beginning to erode her defences. "Okay, if I tell you, will you promise not to tell anyone?"

"Your secret's safe with me. Promise. Pinky swear." Josh thrust his pinky finger at Tracy. His mischievous grin brought a smile to Tracy's face.

"Okay. All right, I'll tell you." Tracy hooked her little finger around Josh's. She decided to tell him the truth, but not all of it. "It's a flute."

"A flute?"

Tracy nodded. "But it's no ordinary flute."

"What do you mean?"

"It's over 10,000 years old."

"Oh, wow. Does it still work? I mean, can you still play music with it?"

"Well, the original is still in Urfa, Turkey. In a museum over there."

"What's the point of that? You went all the way to Turkey to check out this ancient flute and left it there? Oh, wait, you said the original. Is there a copy?"

Tracy nodded excitedly. "Yes! You got it. We made a copy."

"How?"

"This guy at the museum printed a scanned copy out of carbon-fibre using a 3D printer in under an hour. It was incredible."

"But what's so important about this flute that you couldn't tell me?"

Tracy was waiting for this question. She was certain that Josh would be satisfied with the answer. "Because we discovered that the holes drilled into the flute were purposefully spaced out according to the Fibonacci sequence."

"Fibonacci? Name rings a bell."

"Yes. He was an Italian mathematician who lived around the twelfth century. He developed this sequence of numbers, where each number is a sum of the two that come before it. So, one plus one is two. Two plus the one before it is three. Three plus the two before it is five. Five plus the three before it is eight, and so on."

"Ah, yes. So what is the significance of the holes and how they are spaced on the flute?"

"Think about it. The flute is over 10,000 years old…" Tracy let this fact simmer.

Josh's eyes widened in realisation. "Fibonacci lived much later."

Tracy grinned. "Much, much later. The artefact is believed to be over 12,000 years old. That's 6,000 years older than the Pyramids!"

"Crazy."

"Yeah, I know, right? Just think about it. Fibonacci's discovery was preceded by thousands and thousands of years!"

"How can you be so certain? Maybe the flute isn't as old as you think?" Josh shrugged his shoulders.

"Trust me, it is. The original turned to stone."

"What do you mean?"

"The original flute was made out of wood, but the one we found had petrified. Petrified wood takes at least 10,000 years to turn into stone."

"Unless Medusa had a look at it. Then it would be instant, right?"

Tracy laughed. "Yeah, sure. The Medusa flute. That's what I'm gonna call it from now on."

"Ha-ha-ha!" Josh laughed. "So, this is the classified information that you didn't want to tell me about? A flute?"

"Josh, I'm serious. My dad is busy studying the artefact in his lab as we speak. He is trying to understand how people that lived so long ago, understood a modern-day mathematical sequence of numbers and applied them to something like a flute."

"Aliens. Must be aliens."

"You sound like my brother."

"Well, he's probably right. Either that or time travel was involved. Maybe someone from the past travelled to the future, studied Fibonacci's sequence, and then travelled back to the past and applied it there?" Josh was on a roll. "But why? Why would someone do that? Why would someone use the Fibonacci sequence to design a flute?"

It was time. Tracy knew that she had to change the conversation before it led down the path of no return. "That's what we're trying to find out. That's why it's top secret, and no one is supposed to know. You get it now?"

Josh nodded. "Yeah, sure. I get it. Like I said, your secret is safe with me."

"Here you go," said the waiter, placing two cocktail glasses down on the table.

"Thanks," said Josh with a smile.

The waiter nodded. "Enjoy!"

Tracy studied her glass. She had ordered the milkshake of the month. It was called Perfect Love. It was a vanilla and black current, ice cream-flavoured drink, served in a tall glass. A big fat dollop of cream bulged over the rim, and a single, bright red cherry perched precariously on top, its stalk sticking up like an antenna, sending warning signals into the cholesterol cosmos. She brushed aside the alarm bells, closed her eyes, and sucked on the wide, paper straw. The mix of fruity flavours awakened her taste buds, and the thick, ice-creamy texture slid down her throat like a sleigh on a slope of softly fallen snow. She smiled. It was pure heaven.

"How's that?" said Josh.

"Wow!" replied Tracy. "It's incredible. Here, you try." She pushed her glass over to Josh.

"Hmmm. Oh my goodness," he remarked. "That's really good. Here, try some of mine."

Josh's milkshake was served in the same, tall glass and was light brown with swirls of darker brown, like marble. Tracy took a sip. "Ooh. That's nice. Definitely tastes like its namesake, Chocolate Dream. Yummy." Tracy took another sip of her shake. She gazed about the establishment. *Sensual Shakes* was Milwaukee's most popular milkshake bar. It was really busy this evening, yet she felt rather isolated with Josh inside their red, padded cubicle. She gazed into his bright, blue eyes. He was so handsome. Despite the cold ice cream in her mouth, she could feel the blood rush to her cheeks. She gazed awkwardly down into her milkshake, searching for some place to hide. She looked up again, this time in reaction to Josh's gentle squeeze of her hand. He was leaning across the table, just inches away from her face. She moved forward, and their lips met, gently touching for a brief kiss. She pulled quickly away and looked around, abashed.

"Don't worry," said Josh. "No one's watching us. We're safe

here in our little spot." He squeezed her hand reassuringly.

Tracy smiled. Her cheeks turned crimson again, but this time she didn't care. She gazed directly into Josh's eyes, losing herself to his charm. She sat there, staring at him for what seemed like an eternity. Josh was right. They were alone in their cubicle as it raced across the universe like an interstellar craft, cut off from the world around them as they sucked on their delicious shakes, and simply enjoyed each other's company.

"I was just wondering…" said Josh.

"Yeah?"

"That flute…"

Oh boy, here we go again.

"You didn't exactly answer my question earlier. I asked what the significance of the holes was and why they were spaced out according to the Fibonacci sequence. Does it make a different sound when you blow into it?"

"Kinda."

"What's that supposed to mean? Kinda. Hang on, so you *have* blown it?"

Tracy nodded. "Yep."

"And?"

"And, it sounds like a flute, but with slightly different tones, I guess. As I said, my dad is still studying it and the significance of the Fibonacci sequence. It's his specialty."

"Oh yeah, that's right, he's a professor of music."

"Something like that." Tracy took another sip of her shake. "Thanks for this. It's great."

"My pleasure," said Josh with a smile. He slid off his seat and stood up.

"Where you going?"

Josh crossed over to Tracy's side of the table and sat down next to her. "Move up."

"Wait. What are you doing? Josh!" Tracy eased over the red, padded seat of the cubicle, sliding her milkshake along with her across the table.

"Don't worry. Like I said no one's looking. It's just you and me." Josh pushed himself up close next to Tracy, moving his arm around her shoulders into a comforting embrace.

Tracy twisted her body so that she could face Josh, his musky aroma causing her to swoon as he pressed his hard, muscled body against hers. She felt light-headed with excitement as her heart began to pump furiously inside her chest. She smiled and dropped her head sheepishly. She felt Josh's finger gently lift her chin until she was staring into his eyes. He was so close she could feel his breath on her face. It was short and fast. Tracy licked her lips. She could feel them trembling beneath her tongue. She closed her eyes just as their lips touched. She pictured her and Josh in a passionate embrace at her birthday party amidst the whistling from her friends, and the thump of the bass from the music Dylan was playing in the garage. She gently thrust her tongue against Dylan's as her face grew hot with the passion of the kiss. Her head swam with emotion as she frolicked in its waves, tumbling through them like a dolphin at play. She let herself go, and something inside her stirred. She embraced the feeling and smiled deeply. Wow. Just wow.

35 ~ Don't Look

Marjorie May lived alone in a modest apartment, in North 61st Street, just fifteen minutes from Milwaukee High. She had lived there for the past seven years, ever since she landed her job as a receptionist at the Lab, working for Professor Harold William Barnes. She remembered that day. She was so full of nerves that she forgot her bifocals in the car. But Professor Barnes put her immediately at ease. He was such a nice man. So friendly and relaxed. And intelligent. And handsome. So very handsome. She glanced at the picture of him and his family on his desk. They looked so happy. She was happy and happier still when she learnt that she was going to work for him.

Marj stood in her kitchen, preparing dinner, as she did most nights, except Wednesdays and Saturdays when she spoilt herself by ordering takeouts or spending time with the girls at the bowling alley. She loved bowling. It was so much fun. Seven years. She sighed. It had flown by so quickly. She wiped the tears away from her eyes with the back of her hand. Cutting onions always made her cry. Onion tears. She enjoyed crying, especially when she watched an emotional movie. It made her heart tingle with a mix of emotions that brought her a sense of contentedness. Yes. Content. She felt content. And complete.

Satisfied. Ready to take on something new. She smiled as the onion tears rolled down her plump, rosy cheeks once more. She squinted through them at a blurry shape that moved quickly past her.

"Garfield? Garfield. Here boy."

Garfield was Marjorie's cat, named after the original cat from Jim Davis' comic strip. He was an orange tabby, not quite as fat as the animated Garfield, but with the same distinctive swirling patterns on his coat.

"Is that you?" Marj wiped the back of her hand across her face again and looked around the kitchen for her cat. "Garfield. Where'd you go now, boy?" She walked towards the kitchen door and then jumped a step backward in surprise. "Hello. Who are you? Who let you in?" Marjorie still had the pairing knife in her hand. She raised it instinctively, defensively.

The girl stared at the knife. She had long, matted black hair and her face… Marjorie's eyes widened. Scars covered her face. Marjorie took another step back. "Who… who are you? What do you want?" Marjorie stuttered. Tiny droplets of sweat began to break out across her forehead and at the nape of her neck. "Why won't you answer me?" Marjorie's voice grew high pitched and then wavered. "I'll… I'll call the police!"

What happened next, took place very quickly, although Marjorie would have told you that it seemed to happen in slow motion. The girl moved. She stepped towards Marjorie, reached for her hand, the one that was holding the knife, and twisted it. Marjorie felt a shooting pain in her wrist. She thought that she was going to drop the knife, but the girl squeezed her hand while twisting it. She squeezed it hard, so hard, that it felt like it was being crushed beneath a press. Marjorie looked at her hand, mouth agape, as the knife, now turned towards her, moved closer and closer towards her body. Dangerously close. Her hand was beyond her control, as if her muscles refused to comply, or just couldn't, because the force of the energy behind the twisting and pushing of her hand was just too much for her to bear. She watched, mesmerised, as the knife punctured her

261

clothing and continued to press through and into her chest. It was as if she was watching it all happen to someone else; it was such an inconceivable event.

The same warm feeling she felt inside her heart when she watched those emotional movies, washed over her in a wave. She smiled as tears rolled from her eyes; real tears this time, not those fake onion tears. No way. These were real. She cried because the warmth inside her heart seemed to continue to spread all over her body, and it felt so lovely. She closed her tear-stained eyes. She felt content again, at peace but this time she knew it was final. The end.

Marjorie dropped to her knees with a thud on the kitchen floor and keeled over onto her side. She wheezed out one final breath before coming to rest on her back, her sightless eyes staring up at the ceiling, her blood-soaked mouth twisted into a strange, eerie-looking grin.

Sabine tilted her head to one side so that she could study the lifeless face of Marjorie May as she lay motionless on the kitchen floor. She was particularly interested in her eyes. Those big, brown eyes that stared up at the ceiling without blinking. She licked her lips in anticipation. A pool of dark, red blood that resembled cranberry syrup began to gradually form around Marjorie's body, oozing out of the wound in her chest like hot lava from a volcanic fissure. Sabine removed the obsidian blade from beneath her black leather trench-coat. She held it up to the light and twirled it around in her hand, admiring its smooth, shiny surface. She dropped to her knees next to Marjorie, taking hold of her pudgy right hand in her own. She gripped Marjorie's index finger and pulled it up like a lever while pushing the rest of her hand down and into the floor.

Crunch!

The sound made by the obsidian blade as it sliced Marjorie's finger right off her hand. Like a carrot. Sabine wiped the bottom of the bloodied finger on Marjorie's floral green dress, leaving behind long, red, paint-like daubs. She rose to her feet and moved over to the kitchen drawers, rummaging around until she found what she was looking for - a transparent sealable plastic bag. She dropped the amputated digit inside the bag, placed it on the counter-top and then went back to work, gouging out Marjorie's eyes with her sharp blade of ancient origin. She pulled open the bag, dropped one of the eyeballs inside, and popped the other one straight into her mouth, throwing back her head to swallow it whole. She placed her hands on the kitchen counter to steady her body as it writhed around with a life of its own, curiously absorbing the metaphysical energy of the eye as it went down her throat.

◊ ◊ ◊

The dozens of tiny spotlights installed around the beehive-like structure at night, made it look even more like a foreign spacecraft that plonked itself down on Earth for all to see, as a solitary figure with long, matted hair, furtively approached the biometric security system outside the front door to the Lab. She reached into her jacket and retrieved a transparent plastic bag, streaked with dried blood on the inside. She turned it upside down, spilling its contents into her hand. She pressed the index finger into the fingerprint reader and held the eyeball up to the screen.

There was a beeping sound, followed by a digital, robotic voice. "Eye scan not detected. Please try again."

She scrutinised the blood-smeared eyeball, wiped it gently across her leather jacket and then held it up to the digital screen once again.

"Welcome Marjorie May," said the voice, and the doors to the lab slid open.

Sabine stepped inside and closed her eyes for a moment, revisiting a scene in her mind's eye. She walked down a passage on the left-hand side of the lab, making her way, without hesitation, to Professor Harold Barnes' office. She used Marjorie's finger on the reader outside to gain access and went straight to the filing cabinet in the far corner of the room. She pulled open the third drawer and withdrew a long, narrow, wooden case from inside. She placed it down on Harold's desk, flipped the latch, and lifted the lid. She grinned wickedly upon discovering the shiny instrument inside. The flute seemed to shimmer in the wan light, in anticipation of what its new beneficiary was planning to do with it. Sabine snapped the lid shut and made her way out of the lab, tossing Marjorie's finger into the trash on the way out. She reached into the bag and popped Marjorie's other eyeball into her mouth and then ducked into some bushes, disappearing into the night.

36 ~ All is Not Lost

Agent Wesley Trudeau carefully scrutinised the video footage.

"There. See?" said the controller, a bald, middle-aged man with a bushy, Tom Selleck moustache. He pointed at the screen.

The video was fuzzy and quite dark, but Trudeau could definitely make out a girl with long hair, pop something into her mouth and then throw her head back as if to swallow it.

"What do you think that was?"

Trudeau squeezed his eyes to slits and frowned, scrutinising every aspect of the scene. "I have no idea. Probably some kind of anti-psychotic or something."

"Can't make out her face, but see this shot from outside?" The controller pointed at a second screen. "She had to have used the deceased's eye and finger to get inside. That security is tight. See how she's pressing the fingerprint reader and holding something up to the screen at the same time?"

"Yeah," said Trudeau. "Makes sense. We found the finger in the trash by reception. Quite ironic. The victim was the receptionist at the lab."

"What about the eyes?"

"No trace."

"This is a weird one. What did you say she stole?"

"Some kind of artefact."

"That's it?"

"Yeah. As far as we know," said Trudeau. "The Lab Professor is coming in for questioning this afternoon when I hope to find out more."

"As I said, weird," said the controller. "Must have been a valuable artefact for this girl to have killed someone just to get access to the Lab."

"Yeah, really valuable." Trudeau pondered over all the evidence and the chain of events that led up to this point. Each new incident threw the case into a different direction. The latest homicide was no different. The only thing that tied them all together was the eyeballs gouged out of each murder victim; the eyeballs that were nowhere to be found.

◊ ◊ ◊

"Professor Harold William Barnes," said Trudeau, slowly enunciating every syllable, rolling the words around in his mouth as if peanut butter laced his gums. He paced deliberately around his office, walking behind Harold as he sat calmly in a black, standard-issue office chair.

"That'd be me," said Harold, cheerfully.

"Princeton. Hmmm. Cum Laude. Impressive." Trudeau raised his eyebrows for effect, even though it wasn't the first time he was reading Barnes' file. "It says here that you've been running the Laboratory for, um, five years?"

"Five years and three months to be precise."

"And this is the second robbery in that time?"

"Yes." Harold looked up at Trudeau. "I had a state of the art security system installed. How on Earth did they manage to get inside?"

"She."

"What?"

"Never-mind," said Trudeau shaking his head, "I'll get to

that, but first you need to know that a murder has also been committed."

"What?" Harold jumped in his seat. "Who? When?"

"Just before the break-in. Her name was Marjorie. Marjorie May."

Harold's mouth dropped. "Marjorie? Oh, dear God. Why? What? What was she doing there in the middle of the night? Are you sure? Marjorie?" Harold was clearly shaken.

"She was murdered in her apartment. The killer cut off her finger and gouged out her eyeballs to get inside the Lab."

"Oh my God," whispered Harold. He shook his head in disbelief. "I cannot believe what you are telling me."

"I'm afraid it's true, sir," said Trudeau gravely.

"Do you know who it was?"

"We have an idea."

"What does that mean? You know who it was and have people out there trying to find them? Bastards!" Harold spat. "Fucking bastards."

"Not exactly," said Trudeau. "Firstly, we know that it was a female."

"What? The killer? A female? And the others?"

"There weren't any others. She acted alone."

"Shit." Harold ran his hands through his hair. He took a deep breath and sighed it out. "What the hell is going on?"

"I was hoping you'd tell me that, Professor," Said Trudeau, dropping into his chair and folding his arms. "Tell me about the artefact. It seems that it's the key to all of this…" he waved his arm about the room, "mess."

"It wasn't even the original," said Harold. "It was a digitally printed replica."

"So where is the original artefact? Hmm?"

"Turkey. Urfa. In a museum there."

"What is it exactly?"

"A flute. A very old flute."

"How old? What's it worth?"

"That's the thing. The replica isn't really worth much."

"What about the original?"

"Priceless. It's a one-of-a-kind."

"I see." Trudeau scribbled some notes down into the file. "So, in your opinion, Professor, do you think that the murderer-thief believed that the artefact she was after was the original?"

Harold scratched his beard thoughtfully. "I guess so. Makes sense. I mean, why go to all the trouble of... of killing someone just to get access to a worthless digital copy?"

"You sure there was nothing else? Nothing else that she could have taken?"

"As far as I know, nothing else has been reported missing," said Harold. "I still can't believe Marjorie. Oh, Marj." Harold hung his head. "Poor Marj."

"Professor."

Harold lifted his head.

"I'd like your assistance, please."

"Sure. Anything."

"Can you get hold of the museum in Turkey and ask them to safeguard the original artefact? I'm going to send my people over there in case the suspect decides to pay the museum a visit."

"Yes, yes, of course," nodded Harold. "Anything to help, Agent Trudeau."

"Oh, and you didn't tell me how old the original flute was."

"About 12,000 years."

"12,000 years? Wow, that *is* old."

"Yes. It's the oldest musical instrument ever found. Older by about 8,000 years."

"Remarkable. Now I understand why you said that it's priceless. Nothing quite like it. Here," said Trudeau thrusting his card in Harold's direction. "Call me if anything comes up."

Harold took the card. "Thanks. I will. Does Marjorie's family know?"

"Someone has been in touch with them. Yes. But they don't know about the connection to the robbery. Please keep this between us for now, all right?"

"Yes. Sure. Of course."

Trudeau stood up from his seat. "Thank you, Professor, for your time," he said, extending his hand.

Harold stood up and shook it. Agent Trudeau's grip was hard and strong. "Thank you. Will you let me know if and when you catch the thief? I'd really like my flute returned."

"Oh, we sure will, Professor. We sure will," said Trudeau with a reassuring grin that reminded Harold of Bobby Blackthorn, his old anthropology teacher at Princeton, who took some kind of egregious pleasure in loading him with more homework than anyone else in the class.

◊ ◊ ◊

"Massi, listen to me," said Harold with urgency in his voice. "I said I need another copy. As soon as possible. Like immediately."

"But Professor, the museum is closed at the moment. It's after 8pm here." Massimo sounded like he was in the next room; his voice was so clear.

"Okay, then tomorrow. First thing tomorrow morning. I need you to go there, to the museum, and speak to that Phillippe guy. Whatshisname?"

"Dubois."

"Yes, the Frenchman. Tell him to print me another digital copy of the flute and then you need to convince him that he needs to get rid of the file. He needs to hide it off-site."

"You mean the print file? Of the flute?"

"Exactly. There's been a robbery here. Someone stole the replica. It's actually quite a big case because there's been a murder as well."

"Holy shit," said Massimo on the other end of the phone. "Who was murdered?"

Harold took a deep breath. "It's a long story, Massi. Just get me another copy of the flute, okay? And one more thing."

"Yes?"

269

"The original artefact. It needs to be hidden too."

"Why?"

"Trust me, Massi. Just hide it. The thief, the one that stole my copy, could be going to Urfa to try and retrieve it."

"Seriously?!"

"Yeah. I'm serious. Now get cracking!"

"Yessir! Leave it to me. I'll DHL you the copy as soon as it's ready."

"Good man." Harold ended the call and sighed. He gazed out of his office window, lost deep in thought. He picked up the card lying on his desk, turned it over, and scanned the print. *Agent Wesley Trudeau. Federal Bureau of Investigation. Richmond office.* He wasn't about to involve Tracy in all of this by telling Trudeau what she could do with the flute. *The video.* He'd better hide it. He picked up the phone and punched in 085. "Shirley, you free? Good. Please pop into my office. Thanks."

A few moments later, there was a knock at the door. "Hi, Harry. How did it go? Do they know who it was that took the flute?" said Shirley as she stepped into the office.

"Yes. They seem to know. But it gets worse."

"What do you mean?"

"There's been a murder."

"What?"

"Yes. Marj."

"What do you mean? Marjorie? Our Marj?"

Harold nodded solemnly.

"Oh, my God. Harry. I've been trying to get hold of her all morning when she didn't come to work. It's not like her not to call in…" Tears welled up in Shirley's eyes. I can't believe… Marj. Poor Marj." Her voice cracked.

Harold sighed heavily. "Yeah, I know. It's terrible. Tragic."

There was an uncomfortable silence in the room.

"Please. Sit down," Harold gestured. "It seems that there is more to this story than meets the eye."

Shirley gasped. "You mean they know about Tracy and the flute?"

"Yes. I mean, no." Harold quickly shook his head. "I mean, I think they're hiding something."

"What *do* you actually mean?" Shirley shook her head and frowned. "What did you tell them?"

"Well, that's it, you see. I don't want Tracy involved in this. So I never told them about her. I never told them what happened in the lab."

Shirley nodded imperceptibly.

"She hasn't done anything anyway. I mean, this investigation is about a murder and a robbery."

"Sure," said Shirley.

"Which is why we need to hide that video and *you* need to forget what happened in there." Harold pointed towards the laboratory. "Speak nothing of it. To anyone. Tracy's abilities have nothing to do with this. Agreed?"

"Yes, yes, of course. Do they have any idea who did it? The FBI?"

"I think they do, but like I said, I don't think they're telling me everything. Just what I need to know."

"Typical."

"Yes. Which is why our information is also on a need to know basis. The FBI doesn't need to know about this. So if you happen to get a call from this guy," Harold pushed Trudeau's card across the desk, "or anyone else from the FBI, please don't even think about saying anything about Tracy and what went down in the lab. Please."

Shirley picked up the card. "Agent Wesley Trudeau. What's he like?"

"He reminds me of that guy from The Matrix. What's his name?"

"Neo."

"No. The bad guy. The agent."

"Oh. Agent Smith. Hugo Weaving."

"Yeah. Him. Trudeau's got this buzz cut. And his eyes. They're blue, but that piercing blue that can see right through you. I think I kept my cool, but it felt like he knew there was stuff I wasn't telling him."

"It's their training," said Shirley. "They know how to get stuff out of you like they're tapped into the matrix." She grinned.

"Very funny. Should I take the blue pill or the red pill?"

"Depends how far down the rabbit hole you'd like to go today, Professor."

"I've ordered another one," said Harold. "Another flute."

"What?" Shirley's mouth dropped. "You mean another digital copy? From Urfa?"

Harold nodded. "Just spoke to Massimo. He's going to ship it over as soon as it's ready. Should receive it in a couple of days."

"You think that's a good idea? What you gonna tell the FBI?"

"Need to know, remember?"

"Okay, but if they're also on a need to know, like if there's stuff that they aren't telling you, then maybe they know why the flute was stolen? And anyway, how the fuck did the robbers get inside? I mean the new security. The biometric scanner. Do you think it was an inside job?"

Ghastly visions of Marjorie's sightless face flashed before Harold's eyes. "Maybe," he said. "I mean, no. It wasn't an inside job."

"How can you be so sure?"

"Because, like I said, I think the FBI know who it was. This guy," Harold pointed at the card in Shirley's hands, "told me that they knew it was a female."

"The robber or the killer?"

"Both. They are saying that she killed Marjorie and then broke into the lab."

"But why kill Marj? I don't get it."

Harold sighed again. "Please. Please don't repeat this." He gazed into Shirley's tear-stained eyes. "They told me Marj was killed so that the killer could use her finger and her eye to bypass security."

Shirley's face dropped. Her eyes welled up with tears. "I think I'm gonna be sick," she whispered. She buried her face in her hands.

"Sorry, but that's the truth. That's what they told me."

Shirley wiped her eyes on her sleeve. "Who the fuck kills someone just to steal a flute. And it's not even the original!"

"I know. That's why this is so messed up. Now you understand why I don't want Tracy to be a part of this. Let the FBI do their thing and catch the killer, and then we can, carry on with our lives. I have this feeling that this girl has killed before. Think about it. Why else would the FBI be involved? This is a high-level operation, and I think they're onto her."

"Please God they catch her. Crazy bitch!"

"Just be careful. I don't want you getting hurt," said Harold. "Lock your doors and stay alert. Call me if anything strange happens, like if this guy calls you or you find anything else missing, okay?"

"Sure, Harry. Of course. Don't worry, I'm fine, just shook up is all." Shirley stood up to leave.

Harold stared out of his window, lost deep in his thoughts once more.

37 ~ Double Up

"Something quite disturbing has happened," said Sybs, as she sat down on the cream-coloured two-seater couch in Tracy's room. Her face was gaunt.

Tracy looked at her grandmother with wide eyes. "I felt it too. I thought about telling you but then didn't because I thought you'd think me to be crazy."

"What? Don't be silly, my child. What exactly did you feel?"

Tracy took a deep breath. "A deep sadness. A kind of heartache. What does it mean?"

Sybs sighed. "Come over here. Sit next to me." She gently patted the couch.

Tracy sat down next to Sybs, who took both of her hands in hers. They were soft and warm to the touch. She squeezed Tracy's hands and gazed into her eyes. Tracy became lost in their greenness. She imagined she was floating through a forest with tall, green trees reaching high up into the sky.

"Remember when you called me from Turkey?" said Sybs softly.

Tracy nodded.

"And I told you that I had an omen?"

Tracy nodded again.

274

"She is here."

"The girl from my dream? Where?"

"She came for the flute."

"What do you mean?" Tracy's brow furrowed. "The flute?"

"Yes. She has it now."

"You mean she stole it?"

Sybs nodded. "She knows what it can do."

"But how? How is this possible? You mean she is here? In Milwaukee? She broke into the lab?"

"Yes. And that's not all. She murdered someone."

"Holy crap. Are you sure? Who?"

Sybs let go of Tracy's hand and rubbed her temples with her thumb and forefinger. "It's not that clear who it was, but I'm certain that she killed someone. Brutally. And the eyes…"

The silence that followed was oppressive. "What are we going to do Gran?" Tracy's voice sounded hollow.

"When I received this disturbing vision, I decided to do some investigating of my own. I called on my power to divine the future." Sybs sighed heavily.

"What did you see?"

Sybs closed her eyes. "It is dark. Very dark. But the sky is bright with stars. So bright." The corners of Sybs' mouth turned up into a smile. "So beautiful. I cannot see the moon. Where is the moon?" Her eyes flashed open. "That's it! It's a new moon," she blurted excitedly.

"Huh?" Tracy looked perplexed.

"In my vision, there was no moon in the sky. Quick. Check the lunar calendar on the internet."

Tracy tapped away on her iPhone. "Hmm. Sunday. Sunday is the next new moon." She looked up at her grandmother, expectantly.

Sybs placed her hands on Tracy's shoulders. "Tracy. Listen to me. I want you to take a deep breath. I'm going to need your help. I can deal with the girl, but I fear that she is not going to be alone."

"Her grandmother," Tracy whispered.

Sybs nodded. "Yes."

"But how will we find them?"

"You leave that to me. In the meantime, we have a few days to regroup; to plan this out. I'm going to have to give you a crash course." Sybs smiled reassuringly.

"I think I'm more upset about the flute," said Tracy hanging her head.

Sybs gently lifted Tracy's head with her forefinger beneath her chin. "Listen to me, my child. The flute is just an instrument that can be replaced. What is more important is this." She placed the palm of her hand over Tracy's heart. "This is something that they can and will never steal. You are a direct descendant of Sambethe, the first oracle. You carry deep within you powerful energy; a special gift that you will learn to cultivate and use to protect those that you hold dear. This is your destiny." Sybs' voice was a mere whisper, yet it was infused with a clarity of purpose that raised Tracy's spirit, making her ears prick as she listened to her grandmother. "Come, let's sit together. I will be your guide."

Sybs grabbed two cushions from Tracy's bed and threw them onto the floor. She sat down on the edge of one cushion and indicated for Tracy to join her on the other one, facing her, cross-legged. As soon as Tracy was comfortable, Sybs shifted a little closer until their knees were touching. She gazed into Tracy's face again and turned her lips up into a smile. Her cheeks expanded, and her green eyes sparkled. Tracy returned the smile, and her face flushed with warmth as she breathed in her grandmother's familiar, comforting scent.

"Chin up, chest out," instructed Sybs.

Tracy thrust her shoulders back and pushed her chest out. Her head lifted up and back automatically.

"That's it. Now breathe. It's all about the breath. But close your mouth, like this." Sybs sucked the air in through her nose. "And imagine that it's flowing deep inside of you, past your lungs and into your tummy so that it expands like this. Sybs tapped her lower abdomen that had swelled with her in-breath.

276

"Hold it for a second and then breathe out." She pushed the air out of her nose. "But remember - keep your mouth closed. Always. Okay? Got it?"

Tracy nodded. "I can do that," she said. "It's the same as in yoga. Deep belly breathing." She remembered Denise's voice in class, repeating the instruction.

Expand your belly as you breathe in. Now suck in just a little more air. Hold it and breathe out…

"Yes! Of course! Exactly," said Sybs with a grin. "Great, so the first lesson is already complete. This is going much quicker than I expected. Now, place your palms over mine and close your eyes." Sybs raised her hands, and Tracy placed her palms over her grandmother's and closed her eyes as she instructed her to do. "Now breathe with me, in and out. We need to synchronise our breathing until it becomes one. In, out, in, out, in, out."

Tracy closed her eyes and breathed in unison with her grandmother until it felt as if the very room around them was expanding and contracting like a giant inflatable balloon with every in and out-breath.

"Don't let your thoughts linger," continued Sybs. "Focus on the breath. Imagine that it's a silver thread that enters into the crown of your head and spirals down, inside your body, into your very being, expanding it with silvery light, filling it up until it's full, before letting it out again. Picture the flow of energy as it fills you, expanding and blossoming like a flower in bloom."

Tracy listened to her grandmother, imagining the silver energy flow inside of her like a flower blooming. It morphed into a river, a churning body of water, travelling deep into her belly and then through her entire body, filling it up and charging it with life force energy. And then she sensed a deeper presence, another energy, a warmth that she could not quite explain. It held her, gently, guiding her as she breathed, while the flow of energy coursed through her. She smiled deeply, knowingly. Tracy felt a sense of comfort as their breathing merged into one strong and steady flow. Tracy's palms began to tingle. The tingling spread throughout her body until it felt as though she was lifting, weightless, off the ground.

Focus on the breath.

With her eyes still closed, Tracy began to see shapes; shapes that gradually began to form into recognisable images. Silhouettes became clearer, yet still retained a dull, grey hue that seemed to permeate this almost familiar landscape. It was as if she was lucid dreaming, floating through a spiritual realm, filled with ethereal creatures in an alternate universe. She squeezed her eyes tight and the murky shapes dissolved away, leaving behind a void, nothingness.

Focus on the breath.

She pictured the silvery light enter her body once more and envelop her entire being. The mist lifted, and the shapes returned, this time, more vivid than before. They floated past her; ghosts in limbo, taking shape and then disappearing again into the grey.

A voice broke through the gloom. It was warm, comforting. *Come. Come with me.*

She looked up, and it was Sybs, a spiritual manifestation in this place, this place of shadows and wraiths. She held out her hand, and Tracy reached forward to take it. She looked down in alarm at her own fuzzy, ghost-like arm and then Sybs whisked her, quickly, away from the mist, away from the clouds of melancholy that threatened to engulf her into their density. They flew together, up towards the stars that twinkled in the sky like fairy lights. Tracy looked down and saw what looked like a giant body of water; an ocean, that stretched as far as the eye could see. A shape began to emerge ahead of them, growing larger and larger as they glided forward towards it on a current of ethereal energy.

Tracy blinked. The shape before them looked familiar as it solidified into a dark, grey mass. Of course! The mountain! It was the same mountain that she dreamt about in the car on her way to Chicago to meet her grandmother. The same mountain that sang to her in that enchanting voice that Sybs told her

278

belonged to Sambethe, the first Sybil. Tracy looked up into the night sky. The moon was just a crescent; a slither in the cape of darkness. Its wan light barely lit up the mountain as she approached with Sybs, gliding down to land gracefully on its barren surface. This time, there was no voice, no familiar singing that welcomed them as they arrived. Instead, the cold, stark sound of silence greeted Tracy and Sybs like a solitary soldier, standing guard at the gates of purgatory.

Tracy turned to her grandmother standing next to her and opened her mouth to speak, but there were no words. She was mute. She tried again in vain, opening her mouth and straining against what felt like an invisible wall that silenced her vocal cords like she was trying to talk underwater. Sybs raised a finger to her lips and smiled. She sat down on the ground and signalled for Tracy to join her, just as they had done in her room back home. Tracy complied, sitting down cross-legged once more, her knees pressed against her grandmother's, their palms touching. She closed her eyes.

Focus on the breath.

This time she heard Sybs' voice inside her head.

Focus on the breath, and you will find your voice.

Tracy breathed. She breathed in, picturing the air like a silver ribbon, twisting deep, down into her abdomen, filling her being with its pure, magical light. She recognised Sybs' voice, a gentle, tingling sensation that vibrated inside her ears as she allowed her breath to release. She took a long, deep breath again and sighed it out, this time engaging her own vocal cords, joining Sybs in a bee-like humming sound that tickled her nostrils. Instinctively, she wrinkled her nose, wriggling it from left to right. She breathed in and out again, each time humming louder than before. Tracy smiled as the invisible wall of silence melted away with each powerful hum. She had found her voice, and it was stronger than ever before.

Something lightly brushed her arm. Something soft. Like a feather. She opened her eyes. Leaves. Leaves drifted down from the sky, hundreds of them, floating down ever so gently and onto the ground around them as Tracy and Sybs sat together on the mountain top. The leaves glowed, pulsing with a light of their own. Tracy studied them carefully and noticed that the glowing light came from hundreds of tiny letters magically etched onto each leaf in what looked like luminous ink.

"What do they say?" said Tracy, surprised to find that her voice had returned.

"I don't know," said Sybs shrugging her shoulders. She smiled warmly. "Do not worry, my child, they will reveal their secrets. In good time. In good time." Sybs nodded her head.

Tracy stared at a leaf that had come to settle gently in her lap. She slowly released her palms from pressing against her gran's and picked up the leaf. The letters pulsed in soft, green light. They were meaningless to her. Little squiggles scratched curiously into the leaf. Little squiggles. She lifted the leaf to scrutinise the writing more intently, and that's when they moved. The letters moved! Tracy rubbed her eyes. She watched as the letters rearranged themselves, twisting and turning on the leaf like a clew of grubby worms. One word. The letters shifted and then settled to spell one word.

Sabine.

Tracy mouthed the name silently to herself.

"Sabine," she whispered. "It's a name."

"Her name," said Sybs. "The name of the girl. The one that murdered. The one that stole."

"The flute," Tracy gasped.

Sybs nodded.

Tracy watched as the worms began to move once again. They rearranged themselves, settling to form a pair of letters and numbers.

"MS13. What does it mean?"

Sybs shrugged her shoulders. "No idea. An abbreviation maybe?"

"Coordinates?" said Tracy. "Look, it's changing again."

"UBSCHI," said Sybs, spelling out the letters this time.

Tracy looked at her grandmother and frowned. "Huh?

Sabine. MS13. UBSCHI. What's the connection?"

"Not sure," replied Sybs.

Just then, an icy-cold wind lashed the mountain top, ruffling Tracy's hair and scattering the leaves around them. Tracy studied the leaves, only to find that the glowing letters had faded. She looked up into the night sky. The stars were gone, replaced by dark, grey clouds that seemed to have appeared out of nowhere. The wind grew in intensity until Tracy had to squint against tears that began to form in the corners of her eyes.

"It's time," said Sybs, her voice straining against the powerful wind. "Time to go." She lifted Tracy's hands and pushed her palms into them. "Close your eyes. We must return."

Tracy closed her eyes, and within moments, she felt the wind lift her with ease, just like one of the leaves on the mountain top. A tingling sensation returned to her body, starting with her hands, running into her shoulders, down the back of her neck and into her waist. The wind subsided as quickly as it had come. Tracy opened her eyes and found herself back where she started, sitting opposite Sybs, safely inside her room in Milwaukee.

38 ~ Logic

"It's a gang," said Tracy. "MS13." She pointed at her laptop screen. "Look."

Sybs squinted through her spectacles in an attempt to read the small text on the screen. "Mara Salvatrucha," she said, slowly enunciating the Spanish words. "Drug trafficking, prostitution, murder. Oh my goodness, the list is long!"

"I know, right? It says here that they are the meanest gang in America. Their members come mostly from El Salvador. And they have loads of tattoos. I think I've seen a documentary about them on TV. I remember now. It was filmed mostly inside a prison. They interviewed this one dude. Tattoos covered his face. He said he was serving a life sentence with no parole. They said he killed seven people. It's really quite sad." Tracy hung her head.

"Yes. Very sad. Unfortunately, things like these are beyond our control," said Sybs.

"Are they?" Tracy looked up, enthusiastically. "If we can predict the future, surely we can change it? Surely we can prevent murders and things like these from ever happening?!"

Sybs smiled. "It's a little more complicated than that, my child."

"How so?" Tracy frowned.

"Have you heard of the Butterfly Effect?"

"Wasn't that a movie?"

Sybs nodded and then smiled. "Yes, I believe there was a movie made with that name. It's part of Chaos Theory - things like the weather and the stock market, that are beyond our control. The Butterfly Effect is one of the principles of Chaos Theory. It means that everything around us is connected. If a butterfly flaps its wings in Milwaukee at just the right time, a tornado will whip itself up in Texas. So, a small change in a condition results in a drastic change to the result. This is why one needs to be very careful when deciding to change the future because the result of this change could be worse than the original event."

"But what could be worse than murder?"

"Even more murder. You have to weigh up all the possible results of your actions when you decide to change the future."

"How? How do you weigh up the options? There must be so many!"

"My grandmother, your great-great-grandmother, taught me patience. She always said that patience is a virtue and that it must be upheld at all costs when manipulating a future event so that the outcome remains good and pure."

"What does that really mean? Patience is a virtue."

Sybs smiled again. "It means that it is a noble cause to learn the art of patience and apply it successfully. It means that one should appreciate the natural order of things and allow them to happen in their own time, instead of forcing things to take place at the wrong time which often leads to despair, frustration, and resentment."

"But it kind of sounds like we must sit back and do nothing. What help is that?"

"Not nothing. Changes can and must be made. They must just be effected subtly and in the right time."

"Okay, so learning the art of patience will teach you what changes to make and when to make them?"

"Exactly. You got it." Sybs winked at Tracy.

"Can you teach me? Please, Gran."

"Of course. This is part of the crash course I was telling you about."

This time it was Tracy's turn to smile. "I'm curious. If you know that by changing a future event, you have the power to avoid something bad, how long do you have to wait before making that change to ensure that it's the right one to make and at the right time? How patient do you have to be?"

"Ah." Sybs rubbed her hands together. "That's the crux of it, isn't it?" She chuckled. "I remember once, I was about your age, maybe a little older. I was with my brother, your uncle Harvey. We were getting ice cream at the ice cream parlour in town when I had a vision of him covered in blood. I panicked. I told him that I was feeling ill and had to leave immediately."

"What happened?" Tracy gasped.

"There was a bus crash. Twelve people were killed."

"But you saved uncle Harvey's life!"

"Perhaps. It's just that the bus crashed three blocks from where we were."

"I don't understand," said Tracy.

"Had we not left when we did, the bus would have probably crashed into the ice cream parlour, injuring Harvey, but in my vision, there was no way of knowing who else was injured or even killed. The blood all over Harvey could also have belonged to someone else. What I'm trying to say is, that maybe, if I hadn't panicked and left the ice cream parlour when I did, I could have saved those twelve lives."

"But you could never have known that," remarked Tracy.

"Oh, but perhaps I could have," said Sybs. "What I'm trying to teach you is not to panic and make quick decisions based on a single flash of the future."

"So then what are you supposed to do?"

"You need to take stock of the situation and look at all the scenarios. Put things in context before deciding on a course of action as a result of a future, preordained event."

"What do you mean? How?"

"A vision is usually the ripple effect of a powerful event in the future. Imagine throwing a stone into a lake. What happens?"

"There's a splash."

"Correct. And then what?"

"Um… ripples?"

"Yes! The splash is the big event. The ripples represent the aftershock of the big event. The physical ripples fade away *after* the main event."

"But that doesn't really make sense." Tracy scratched her head. "If the ripples from an event fade away after an event, into our future, how do you anticipate the energy of an event *before* it happens?"

Sybs smiled. "That's the lesson right there, Tracy."

Tracy frowned, totally confused.

"For every action, there is an opposite reaction. So, for every physical ripple that moves away from the main event, there is a spiritual ripple moving towards it long before it even happens."

"Ah! Now I understand," said Tracy, excitement building in her voice. "So the visions that we see are the spiritual ripples moving towards the big event."

Sybs smiled. Her green eyes twinkled. "Such a clever girl!"

Tracy grinned from ear to ear. "Okay, I get it! Now, where were we?"

"Well, we know that the girl's name is Sabine," said Sybs, pulling on her pinkie finger. "And we know about MS13, this dangerous street gang." She pulled on her ring finger. "What was that last word?"

"UBSCHI. If you can call it a word."

"Hmmm. You're right. It must be an abbreviation. I thought maybe UBS Bank in Chicago?" said Sybs.

"But what does that mean? What is the significance?"

"Think about it. Sabine. MS13, UBSCHI. Maybe Sabine and the MS13 gangsters plan to rob UBS Bank in Chicago?"

"Oh, my Lord. How do we stop them?"

"Remember what I said?"

"Take stock and look at every scenario?"

"Correct! Let's think about what else we know."

"We know that this is going to take place at the time of the new moon this Sunday."

"Correct," said Sybs.

"Do we go to the police?"

Sybs shook her head. "We have no evidence. They will think we're crazy. Trust me; I've been down this road before," she said, gazing out the window and recalling a distant memory.

"But how are we going to stop them?"

"We must be very careful. Remember, Sabine can also predict the future. And she might be with her grandmother."

"Maybe we should tell Dad. Does he know about the break-in? The flute?"

Sybs nodded solemnly. "He had a meeting with the FBI today."

"No. I don't believe it. The FBI? What have they got to do with this?"

"Not sure. I think you better ask your father."

"If the FBI is involved, then maybe we can turn to them? Maybe they know more than the police? Maybe they'll believe us?"

"You may have a point there, Trace. Come, let's find your father," said Sybs pushing herself up to stand. "Maybe he can point us in the right direction. Ooh. I'm not as young as I used to be," she said, as she stretched her legs. "These achy bones are stiff."

"It's just past four," said Tracy checking the time on her phone. "Shit."

"What is it?"

"I have like a gazillion messages from Lisa."

"Your friend, Lisa?"

Tracy nodded. "Uh-huh."

Sybs smiled. "What a lovely girl."

286

"Yeah, well, she's gonna kill me. I promised her I'd see her, but with all this stuff going on, I totally forgot."

"Just tell her that I'm visiting and you've been preoccupied. It's the truth."

"Yeah, guess so, but she's still gonna want to see me, and we need to speak to Dad."

"Why don't you call your father and find out what time he'll be home? Then you can tell Lisa that you'll see her later tonight."

"That's exactly what I'm doing," she said, pressing her father's number on speed dial.

Harold answered after three rings. "Tracy, what a pleasant surprise!"

"Hi, Dad. What time will you be home today?"

"In ten minutes. I'm just pulling off the interstate."

Harold's voice sounded tinny. Tracy pictured him on speaker-phone in his car. "Cool. You're early."

"Yeah, been a rough day to say the least. Everything okay?"

"Yeah. All good. Just have something to chat to you about. See you soon. Bye." Tracy killed the call. "He's almost home," she said to Sybs.

"Perfect, now you can arrange to meet Lisa with plenty time to spare."

"Thanks, Gran," said Tracy, hugging her grandmother.

"I'll see you downstairs," said Sybs, leaving the room.

Tracy flopped down on her bed and began typing a message into her phone.

Hey. Sorry Lis. Been super busy with my gran who's come to visit. Haven't even looked at my phone.

Lisa replied, almost immediately. *Granny Sybs! Oh, I love her! How is she? Please kiss her from me.*

Sure x

Sorry about all the messaging. I was worried about you. Where've you been?

Tracy thought about all the crazy things that had been going on. *Oh, here and there,* she responded.

I wanna hear all about it. Like tonight. Okay?
Yeah, cool. What time? Where?
Why don't we go to the mall. Like 8pm?
Okay. Sounds good. See you then. Love you.
Love you x

Tracy put her phone down on her bedside table and closed her eyes. She felt completely exhausted after the day's ordeal. Maybe she could have a ten-minute, power nap.

39 ~ The Plan

Tracy rolled over and looked at her phone. 6.43pm. *SHIT! It's been almost two hours! Why didn't Granny Sybs wake me? Or Dad?* She sat up and rubbed her eyes. Her stomach grumbled. She stretched her arms high above her head and yawned. A wave of anxiety washed over her. *I'm almost out of time. Dammit! I still have to get dressed, grab a bite to eat, speak to Dad, and get to the mall by 8pm.*

"Hello, sleepy head," said Camilla as Tracy walked into the kitchen. "Why so grumpy?"

"I overslept. Why didn't you wake me?"

"You looked so peaceful up there," said Harold. "We didn't want to disturb you."

"Hi, Dad."

"Hi, my angel. Now, what was it that you wanted to chat with me about?"

"Where's Gran?" said Tracy, looking around.

"She's reading, I think," said Camilla.

"Gran!"

"Please don't shout," said Camilla. "Why don't you go and talk to her like a normal human being."

"Sorry. It's just I need her here to speak to Dad with me.

289

And it's kinda urgent."

"What's this all about?" said Harold.

"The flute," said Sybs stepping into the kitchen.

"What do you mean?" said Harold, a look of confusion on his face.

Sybs smiled. "I know. I know what happened."

Harold sighed. "Of course you do." He turned to Tracy. "And now I have to contend with you too. As if one wasn't enough. Okay, so how much do you know?"

"We know that the flute was stolen," said Tracy.

"What?" said Camilla flabbergasted. "What do you mean? From the lab? Harold?"

"She's right. There was a robbery."

"And a murder," said Sybs.

Camilla's face turned the colour of the kitchen countertop. "What do you mean a murder? Who? Who was murdered?"

"My receptionist. Marjorie May," said Harold bleakly.

"Marj? No. Really?" said Camilla. "Shame. She was such a lovely lady. So sweet. How tragic." Tears began to well up in her eyes.

"I'm afraid so," said Harold.

"Marjorie!?" said Tracy in shock. She looked at her Gran. "You didn't tell me it was Marj."

"Do they know who it was?" said Camilla. "Have they caught him?"

"Her," corrected Harold. "Apparently, it was a woman."

"Wait," said Harold pointing at Tracy and then Sybs. "You two… you two know who she is, don't you?"

Tracy looked at her grandmother and shrugged her shoulders.

"Yes. We know," said Sybs, folding her arms.

Harold absentmindedly fingered Agent Wesley Trudeau's card in his pocket.

"And we know that you were questioned by the FBI," continued Sybs flatly.

Harold jerked his hand out of his pocket as if he received a powerful electric shock.

Camilla sat bolt upright. "The FBI?! Harold! Why didn't you tell me?"

"I... uh... I was going to," stuttered Harold. "I mean they only just questioned me this afternoon."

"What did they want?" said Camilla.

"It was an agent. I went to his office in Richmond. Trudeau was his name. He wanted to know about the flute."

Tracy looked at her father; alarm etched across her face.

Harold shook his head. "He doesn't know what it can do, Trace. Don't worry. They are after the killer and wanted to understand why the flute was so valuable. I told him the original was old and priceless, but this copy is far from that. When he discovered that the original was in Turkey, he said he'd be sending some of his guys there in case the suspect suddenly arrived looking for it. That's when I decided to call Massimo to get him to print another copy."

"Another copy?" said Tracy.

"Yep. The FBI doesn't know it yet, and hopefully, they never will, but the museum in Urfa are printing another copy of the flute, and then Massimo will ship it here, to the house. It all doesn't add up though," said Harold shaking his head. "The stolen flute isn't even the original. It's not worth much. Unless..." His eyes lit up. "Of course. She knows. The girl who stole it knows of its power!" He looked at Sybs. "How? How can she know? The flute hasn't left my possession since I brought it back from Turkey." Harold scratched his head.

Sybs pulled back a chair and sat down at the table. "Tracy. Please, come sit down," she said, dragging the chair next to her back a few inches.

"Harold," said Sybs. "You know my story. Our story."

Harold licked his lips. "You mean... yes, yes. Your powers and where they came from and all that."

"There's another part of the story that I've never told you." Sybs looked at Camilla. "Camilla knows." Sybs turned to Tracy and squeezed her hand. "As you know, we are descendants of

Sambethe, the first Sybil, a great oracle that lived thousands of years ago. She used her powers of divination for good. She believed in helping people find the truth. She believed that everyone that crossed her path deserved to be guided towards their true destinies immediately, instead of after having lived through many lives. She made it her life mission to help others realise their dreams by showing them what they were capable of. What I've never told you is that she had a twin sister with the same power of prophecy. Her name was Sabbe. The difference was that she was bad. Evil."

"What happened to her?" said Harold.

"She was tried for her wicked crimes and banished, never to be seen again. I have reason to believe that the killer, the thief that stole the flute, is a direct descendant of this evil twin. And I also believe that she has inherited the same power that Tracy and I share, which makes her a dangerous adversary."

"What does she want with the flute?" said Camilla.

"Nothing good, I'm afraid," replied Sybs, shaking her head.

"Does she know how to... use it?" said Harold.

"We have to assume that she does, I'm afraid," said Sybs.

"Well, can't you stop her or something?" said Camilla.

"We can only try. And that's not all. It seems that she may be working with a street gang called MS13."

"Harold," said Camilla, "I think you should call the FBI. Agent whatshisname."

"Trudeau," said Harold.

"Yes. This is far too dangerous for Sybs, and I'm definitely not letting Tracy go out there," she pointed at the window, "and risk her life with this killer out on the loose. And who knows what this gang is capable of."

"No. Not the FBI," said Sybs. "They'll never understand."

"What about the police then?"

"Even worse."

"Mom," said Tracy. "I know that you're worried, but Granny Sybs and I know what we are doing. We have a plan."

"Does this plan of yours involve confronting this girl, this murderer?"

"Camilla," said Sybs. "You have my word that Tracy will be safe. I'll make sure of it. I promise. Our plan is just to find her and observe; to watch her from a distance. To learn of her motives and gather information so that we are well equipped to stop her when she decides to cause trouble. Then we will call the FBI to step in."

Camilla sighed. "Mom. Why are you always so stubborn?"

Sybs smiled. "I know you're concerned. I would be too, but there's nothing to worry about. We will be fine."

"Do you know where she is or what she plans to do?" said Harold.

"I'm not certain where she is, but I know that she plans to do something on Sunday. Something big. Something important."

"This Sunday?" said Camilla. "In two days?"

Sybs nodded. "Yes. This Sunday."

"I'm coming with you," said Harold emphatically.

Tracy opened her mouth. "But…"

"There's no debate," snapped Harold. "If I cannot join you, then no one is going."

"What about the FBI?" said Camilla.

"Sybs is right," said Harold. "No point bringing them in until we have some hard evidence. Okay, now what's the plan?" he said, loudly smacking the table with both of his hands.

40 ~ Bestie

"You're late," said Lisa, as Tracy approached. She was standing outside a beautiful shop-front, filled with colourful shoes of all shapes and sizes with her hands on her hips and a scowl on her face. She reminded Tracy of her math teacher, Mrs. Daversham when she was upset.

"Sorry. Traffic and all."

"Yeah. And all. Come here, my beautiful friend," said Lisa, throwing her arms around Tracy and hugging her tightly, her scowl quickly turning into a big grin. "I want to hear all about it, okay?"

"What?" said Tracy, genuinely confused for a moment. "Oh, you mean my trip?"

"Duh! No, your diet. I want to know how you keep so skinny all the time. I mean just look at you!"

Tracy blushed.

"*Obviously* your trip. But I'm not joking about your diet. I need to know what you eat, girl. I feel like I'm having an ongoing battle with my fat self. It's like she's deep inside me; another person fighting to get out. All the time. It's sooo damn draining."

"Here," said Tracy handing Lisa a small, brown bag. "This is for you. All the way from Turkey."

"Oh, my goodness, you shouldn't have," said Lisa taking the bag. "What is it?"

"Open it, silly."

"Okay." Lisa opened the bag and stuck her hand inside. She pulled out a brightly coloured green and yellow scarf. "Oh, wow, Trace. It's beautiful." She pressed the scarf into her face. "Hmmm. I don't think I've ever felt anything so soft!"

"It's cashmere," said Tracy. "Real cashmere."

"Amazing! Thank you. Thank you. You're the best!" she squealed, giving Tracy a peck on the cheek.

"What's in the bag?" said Tracy, pointing at the big, brown bag Lisa was holding.

"It's a dress I found for Shelley's party."

"Oh, I'm sorry."

"Whatever for?"

"I said I'd help you find one."

"Yeah, well, I got here early, and you were late, so I had time to kill, I guess. And the shops are closing soon, anyway."

"Can I see?"

"Sure. Here," said Lisa, pulling the dress out of the bag. It was pastel orange in colour. "Doesn't look like much, I know, but when it's on…"

"I'm sure it's stunning. Love the colour."

"Thanks," said Lisa with a smile. "Come, let's go grab some coffee at that café near the entrance."

"Java Café?"

"That's it!"

◊ ◊ ◊

"I'll have a Macchiato," said Lisa, flashing a smile at the waiter. "Please make sure it's extra hot, okay?"

"Very well, Madam. And for you, Miss?" said the waiter, turning to Tracy.

"Um… I'll have a Flat White, please."

"Very good," said the waiter. "Will that be all?"

"Yes, thanks," said Lisa.

The waiter nodded and turned to leave.

Lisa grabbed hold of Tracy's hand and squeezed it excitedly. "Right. Now, talk to me. How was that party? The one you were going to the day I spoke to you when you were sailing on the river with your Dad. You were going to send me pics, remember?"

"It was okay. Sorry didn't send you anything. I only have one of me and that girl I told you about, Zehra."

"Okay? What do you mean okay?"

"Well, it was fun, I guess. Zehra is really cool."

"She introduce you to some guys?"

"Yes."

"I knew it!" said Lisa clapping her hands together and giggling hysterically. She quickly looked around the café. "Don't worry. What happens in Turkey stays in Turkey."

"Lisa! Stop it! Nothing happened, okay?"

"Hey, no need to be so touchy," said Lisa, winking at Tracy.

"Yes, I met these two guy friends of Zehra's, but they were definitely not my type, and besides, I'm with Josh."

"Okay, okay. So how was the rest of the trip?"

"So, so amazing! It's such a beautiful city. There's all this ancient architecture everywhere. You'd love it. There's this huge bazaar filled with literally hundreds and hundreds of traders, selling everything from pots and pans to a huge variety of food. It's where I bought your scarf."

"Oh, wow! cool."

"Then my Dad took me to this amazing site just outside Istanbul called Gobekli Tepe. It's the oldest temple in the world."

"Oh, wow," said Tracy, a dreamy look in her eyes. "I wish I was there with your Dad. He's such a hunk."

"Lisa! It's enough! What's wrong with you? Ewwww."

Lisa giggled again. "I can't help it. Okay, okay. Calm down. I was only teasing. I love watching your face every time I talk about him."

"I'm starting to doubt that," said Tracy. "Have you spoken to Paul again?" she continued, trying to steer the conversation away from her father.

"Not since I refused his invitation to go to the prom with him."

"Well, who are you gonna go with then?"

"Ahh, I dunno. Don't worry; I'll find someone."

"Yeah, but the idea is for someone to find you. Someone needs to ask you."

"Listen, bae. It's the 21st century. Us girls have the power now, you know? I can ask whoever I want."

"So, who's it gonna be? Have you decided?" said Tracy.

"Hmm." Lisa looked past Tracy. "Danny."

"Danny Gordon? No way!"

Lisa grinned. "Yes, way. Have you seen his dimples?"

"But he's…"

"What? A nerd? He's just a late bloomer. Behind those glasses and long, shaggy hair, there's a jock just waiting to get out."

"And you know this because?"

"I saw him in the boys' changing rooms."

"Lisa!"

"What? I was just walking past when the door opened, and Julian Reynolds stepped out. Danny was standing behind him with just his towel wrapped around his waist. His hair was wet, his glasses were off and his chest. Well let's just say, I didn't recognise him at first, he looked so… fit."

"How do you know he hasn't asked someone already?"

"Come on, Trace. This is Danny Gordon we're talking about. Danny Gordon."

"Yeah, I guess you're right."

"There are gonna be some conditions though."

"What do you mean?"

"He's gonna have to get a haircut and contacts."

"Seriously? You're gonna tell him that?"

"For sure! If he's going to the prom with me, the one and only Lisa Fitzgerald, then he's gonna have to clean up his act. He's gonna thank me afterwards, you know. After I'm finished with him, he'll be hot property, baby! Tsssss," she said through clenched teeth, as she licked her finger and touched Tracy on her arm for effect.

Tracy shook her head. "You're crazy, Lis. But that's why I love you."

Lisa grinned. "Lisa Fitzgerald. Making the world a better place, one nerd at a time."

"Flat White?" said the waiter, arriving with their coffees.

Tracy raised her finger. "Here."

"And the Macchiato," he said, placing the cups down gingerly on the table.

"Thanks," said Lisa.

"Anything else I can get you, young ladies?"

"We're good," said Lisa.

The waiter nodded. "Enjoy," he said, before turning to leave.

"You know, come to think of it," said Tracy, "he's got quite a dry sense of humour."

"Danny? Really? I haven't heard him talk much."

"Yeah. I overheard him in the canteen last week chatting to Paul."

"Ehh." Lisa turned her mouth upside down. "I hope he told Paul where to get off."

"Well, actually, yeah, he did in a way. It was quite funny now that I think about it. Paul was struggling with the vending machine. You know, the new one that dispenses plasters and medical supplies and stuff?"

"Oh yeah."

"He was kicking it and cursing, you know as he does."

Lisa smirked.

"So, Danny comes along and says, 'hey dude, stop making so much noise.'"

"So, Paul replies, 'what's it to you, Gordo?' in this really sarcastic tone."

"And then Danny says, 'you're gonna wake the sleeping pills!'"

"Ha-ha! Hilarious! What did Paul say?"

"He was so pissed. He zapped Danny and just cursed some more."

"Prick," said Lisa disdainfully. "He's just rude. Plain rude, that Paul Williams. He got what he deserved. I wish I were a fly on that wall."

"Yeah, you shoulda seen his face. He was so mad."

"You see?" said Lisa. "Just wait. Danny is an unpolished gem. When I'm done with him, his looks won't be the only thing that'll be polished."

"Lisa!"

"What? I'm gonna need some sort of reciprocation for my efforts. I have needs too, you know. Besides, I'm sure he's never been with anyone. I mean, someone has to teach him the ropes!"

"You're just so wicked."

"Well, you know what they say," said Lisa. "Girls they wanna have fu-un," she hummed the Cyndi Lauper tune. Tracy joined in. "They just wanna, they just wanna-a-a, girls just wanna have fu-un."

Tracy laughed with Lisa so hard that tears began to stream out of her eyes.

41 ~ Going In

"Pinto," rasped Julian. "What are you doing? You high?"

"No, boss," replied Pinto, shaking his head. "I was just looking for the moon."

"You idiot! There *is* no moon. That's why we're doing this tonight, remember?"

"Yes, I know, just checking."

"Listen, if you fuck this up, I will personally gouge your eyes out and give them to that... that bitch." He jerked his thumb behind him and then glanced over his shoulder, half-expecting a pair of dark eyes to be boring into his soul.

"I won't, boss. Where is she anyway? I thought she was supposed to be here."

Julian coughed loudly, spat into the gutter and then squinted into the darkness of the street. "I have no fucking idea. I'm sure she's with Miguel. That bitch follows him around like she's his puta."

"She gives me the creeps," said Pinto.

"Where's that other clown?"

Pinto glanced at his phone and then looked down the street. "Five minutes. He said he just picked up Miguel."

"No mention of the puta?"

"Nope."

"Maybe we'll get lucky," said Julian.

"Yeah, maybe she crawled back into the hole from where she came."

The shadows jumped at the other end of the street, charging towards Julian and Pinto like a mob of angry monsters on the loose. Julian shielded his eyes from the twin beams of light that pierced the darkness as a vehicle approached them at high speed. It slowed down at the last moment, coming to a stop with a squeal of rubber on tarmac. It was a white delivery van, with the name *Bluebay Electrical* emblazoned down the side and a bright, blue lightning bolt positioned just above it. The side door slid open and Miguel stepped out. Both Pinto and Julian's faces dropped when a second figure came into view right behind him. Sabine. She was wearing tight, black leather pants and a matching jacket. Julian felt a wave of relief wash over him when he realised that her prying eyes were hidden from view beneath a black baseball cap pulled firmly down over her scarred face. The driver's door opened, and the unmistakably scrawny frame of Matias stepped out of the car.

"You said eight-thirty," snapped Julian.

"Ask your friend over there why we're late," said Miguel tipping his head in Matias' direction.

"Sorry, boss," said Matias. "Had to make a quick drop and my boy let me waiting, you feel me?"

"I don't give a flying fuck what you and your boy get up to, but when it cuts into *my* time, then I get pissed. You feel *me?*" said Julian. "This is a serious job. If you can't play by the rules, then get the fuck outta here. We're a team, and I need to know if you're in or not."

"Sure, boss," said Matias. "I'm in. Won't happen again."

Julian gritted his teeth. A guttural growl escaped his mouth. "Better not, otherwise you're finished here." He made a slitting motion with his hand across his neck.

"Julian," said Miguel. "As welcoming as ever."

"Stay outta this, Miguel. I take care of my own. Boy needs

to learn the rules."

"Agreed," Miguel nodded. "But we're here to do a job, so let's get to it," he said glancing up into the night sky. "Time waits for no man. Right. Let's all recap," he continued. "Gather round."

Matias, Pinto, and Julian moved in as Miguel pulled a small, black notebook from his jacket pocket and opened it on the bonnet of the van. Sabine seemed to slink backwards, away from the gangsters as if the darkness itself began to swallow her up into its folds of shadow and gloom.

Miguel flipped to a schematic in his notebook with yellow highlighted areas. He pointed at the page. "The goods entrance on the side of the building is where we enter. My man Pedro will meet us here and let us in."

"How much time do we have?" said Julian.

"Twenty minutes."

"Seems too long," remarked Pinto.

"We need this time to get in, do the job and then get out of the building," said Miguel. "We just gotta take it nice 'n slow, so as not to raise any alarm bells."

"Did Matias get the lifter?" said Pinto.

"Yeah," said Miguel. "It's in the van. We'll drop you into position two blocks from the building. Wait for my signal before you cut the power. The switchover is only about ten seconds, so we have to time this well."

"Okay," said Pinto. "Will you send me a text?"

"No, you idiot, I have these," said Miguel, unclipping a two-way radio from the belt at his waist. "The others are in the van. Matias, you're gonna wait inside the vehicle while Julian and I head inside the building."

"Yes, boss," said Matias.

"Okay. Julian," said Miguel. "Seventeenth floor. Right. Fourth door on the left. Got it?"

"Yep," Julian nodded. "What about security?"

"If we stick to the story, we'll be fine."

"What about her?" said Julian, jerking his thumb in Sabine's direction.

"Don't worry about her. She'll be right behind us."

The back of Julian's head tingled. "But I don't see the point…"

"I trust her, Julian," said Miguel cutting him off. "She's coming with us. Let's just leave it at that, okay?"

"Okay, okay. Sure. Whatever you say." Sarcasm laced his last words like hot sauce.

Miguel ignored him. "Right. Your overalls are in the van. Let's do this!"

◊ ◊ ◊

The van door slid open, and Pinto jumped out. He glanced furtively up and down the street before turning around to receive a yellow, trolley-like contraption from Julian, consisting of a long pole with a pair of handles on top and two small wheels beneath, intersecting a shorter pole with a large, round magnet suspended on the end. Pinto rolled the contraption over to the manhole cover nearby. He raised the pole so that the magnet on the shorter end lowered, dropping onto the cover with a loud clang. He then proceeded to push the handle down with the force of his weight behind it. With a loud scraping of metal against metal, the cover reluctantly lifted to reveal a large gaping hole in the middle of the street. Pinto rolled the manhole cover lifter, with the manhole cover dangling precariously beneath it, over to one side, collected four waist-high orange cones from the van and slammed the door shut. With a screech of its tyres, the van sped off into the night. Pinto spaced the cones evenly around the hole, zipped up the front of his overall and proceeded to climb backwards into the manhole, making his way gradually down the rusty metal rungs until he completely disappeared.

Matias rolled down his window. "Evening," he said with a smile to the security guard, a burly looking character with a big, black, bristling moustache. One more jam doughnut and his navy blue shirt looked like it would burst open, it was under so much strain.

Miguel leaned over Matias. "Pedro, it's me, Miguel."

"Ah, Miguel didn't see you there. Drive on through," he said, pressing the button on his remote to open the red and white striped security boom. "Park in bay F11."

"Yes sir," said Matias, bringing his hand to his forehead in a firm salute.

Julian, Miguel, followed by Sabine, stepped out of the vehicle. They all wore the same black overalls with the *Bluebay Electrical* logo and bright blue lightning bolt stitched onto the right-hand side pocket. Sabine still wore her baseball cap, pulled tightly over her face.

Miguel walked over to Pedro, handed him a white envelope, and embraced him warmly. "Just a small token of our appreciation. You'll get the rest after the job as planned."

"Thanks, Miguel," said Pedro. "Much appreciated." He removed his UBS-branded cap and tipped his head in Sabine's direction. "Ma'am"

Sabine just surveyed him with her cold, hard eyes, before spinning around to follow Miguel and Julian towards the elevator.

◊ ◊ ◊

The elevator doors shuddered. *Ping!*

Julian stuck his head out, twisting it from right to left. "Clear. Let's go," he said, stepping out of the elevator. Miguel and Sabine followed.

"This way," said Julian, turning right. A strip of LED lights lit up the corridor from below. Julian counted the doors as he walked. "Here we are. Door number four." A sign on the door read, **JONATHAN MULLER, BANK MANAGER.** He pulled on the handle. "Locked."

Miguel held up a key-card that was hanging around his neck on a lanyard.

"Where'd you get that?" said Julian.

"Pedro," Miguel said with a grin. He pushed the card into the electronic slot over the door handle, opened the door and stepped inside the dark office. He flicked on the light switch and the room lit up to reveal a large mahogany desk in the centre. Julian and Sabine followed close behind.

"Where is it?" said Julian, scanning the room.

"Search the desk," said Miguel, "I'll check the cupboards."

"There," said Sabine, pointing at a filing cabinet in the corner of the room.

Miguel stepped over to the filing cabinet and pulled open the first drawer.

"At the bottom," said Sabine.

Miguel pushed the top drawer closed and pulled open the bottom one as instructed. "There are just a bunch of files." He pulled on the hanging files. "Nothing else... wait." Miguel reached behind the files and retrieved what he was looking for. He held it up for Julian and Sabine to see. It was a round, black, and silver device about the size of an apple. There was a keypad and a small digital screen on one side.

"So that's it," said Julian. He rubbed his hands together in anticipation.

"Don't get too excited," said Miguel. "We still have to get inside."

"I know, but so far, so good, right?"

"Yeah," said Miguel. He looked at Sabine. "I told you we should trust her. See?"

"How does it work?" said Julian.

"It fits onto the vault on this side." He flipped the device over. "It's magnetic."

"Oh, okay. And then you just punch in a number, and the vault opens?"

Miguel smiled. "Something like that," he said. "When the

correct combination is punched in, the device emits a high-frequency signal that sends a verification code to the bank's mainframe."

"And then?"

"Well, the mainframe needs to verify the code."

"And I guess you've got that covered."

"I hope so."

"What do you mean, you hope so?"

"Don't worry, Jules. It's all under control."

Julian looked at Sabine. She was staring at him again, making him feel uncomfortable. He turned back to Miguel. "How the hell do you know all of this shit?" said Julian.

Miguel smiled. "Months and months of planning. And patience. Lot's of patience."

42 ~ Stakeout

"This is Trudeau."

"Hi, yes, Agent Trudeau?"

"Yes. Speaking. Who is this?"

"Um. It's Professor Harold Barnes."

"Prof, I'm glad you called. I was just thinking about you. What have you got for me?"

"Well, I do have something that I thought you should know."

"Yes?"

"I think I've found your girl."

"What? The murderer? Where? How?"

"Let's just say; I was tipped off."

"Where is she?" Trudeau's voice was insistent.

"UBS Bank, Chicago. Upper Wacker Drive."

"Right now?"

"Yes. Right now. Bring backup."

"Okay. Fortunately, we're not too far away. See you soon."

"Happy now?" said Tracy.

Harold nodded, placing his mobile onto the magnetic holder. He looked out of the car window and shifted in his seat. "We're out of our depth here. Your mother was right. This is becoming too dangerous. You sure she's here?"

"When have I ever been wrong, Harold?" said Sybs.

"Yes, but we don't have any evidence. I'm surprised Trudeau even bought my story."

"She's here, all right," said Sybs, squeezing Tracy's hand.

"Gran's right, Dad. I can sense her too. It's like that feeling you get when you arrive home from work, and you just know Mom's around. There's the smell of food coming from the kitchen. You hear her humming. You close your eyes and smell her scent. There's no mistaking it."

"Great. So, when Trudeau gets here and asks me where she is and how I know she's here, I'll just say my daughter closed her eyes and sensed her. What's her name anyway? You know, don't you?"

"Sabine," said Sybs.

"Sabine," Harold said her name slowly.

"We have to get closer," said Sybs. "She's inside."

"It's dark outside," said Harold. "We're in the city of Chicago, in the middle of the night. How the hell are we going to get inside a heavily guarded bank that's all locked up."

"I didn't say that we have to go inside the building, just that we need to get closer."

"Okay, okay, I'll drive closer," said Harold turning the key and starting the engine. "But we're not getting out, all right? Whatever's going on is not good. Not good at all."

Harold pulled out of the parking lot and made his way towards the UBS buildings a few blocks away.

"There. Look," said Tracy, pointing at the side of the building. A street light illuminated the silhouette of a security guard standing just outside a parking entrance. "Pull in over there," said Tracy, indicating an open bay diagonally across from the entrance.

Harold reversed into the bay and switched off the car. "Do you think he's seen us?"

"Don't think so," said Sybs. "Look, he's busy on his phone."

"Okay," said Harold. "So we'll just wait here for Trudeau. I still have no idea what I'm going to tell him. Maybe we should question the guard? Ask him if he's seen anything."

Tracy looked out of her window and up at the building. It was about twenty floors high. She noticed the lights burning in a few of the offices.

"He knows nothing," said Sybs.

"How can you be so sure?" said Harold.

"Just look at him. If there was anything suspicious going on, why would he just be standing there playing with his phone?"

"I guess you're right but then how can you be so sure the girl is here?"

Sybs glared at Harold as if he had just insulted her.

"Okay, okay. It's just hard to believe that she's here when everything just seems so quiet."

"Maybe the guard is in on it," said Tracy.

Harold squinted out of his window. The guard was walking up and down the street now. "Could be… Okay. I'm going to talk to him," said Harold, opening his door. "You two stay here."

"I thought you said we weren't getting out of the car?"

"Well, I changed my mind."

"Be careful, Dad," said Tracy. "He could be dangerous."

Harold leaned across his seat and kissed Tracy on her forehead. "I'll be fine. If anything out of the ordinary happens, call this number, okay?" said Harold, handing Tracy Trudeau's card. He climbed out of the car and crossed the street.

Tracy watched her father from the safety of the car. A pang of anxiety caused her neck hairs to rise. *He's going to be okay,* she told herself, absentmindedly squeezing the pink crystal around her neck.

Harold cleared his throat, and Pedro looked up. "Good evening," said Harold with a smile.

"Good evening sir," said Pedro in a thick Mexican accent. He tipped his hat in Harold's direction. "Can I help you?"

"Um, well, I'm kind of looking for someone."

Pedro looked up and down the street.

"Who exactly are you looking for, senôr?" he said, his thick, black moustache moving like a lazy caterpillar as he spoke.

"A girl."

"A girl?"

"Yes. Have you seen a girl pass by here recently? Her name is Sabine. She may have been with others."

"Others?"

"Yes. Suspicious characters. From a street gang."

The guard pushed his phone into his pocket and folded his arms. His voice took on a different tone. Harold thought that it sounded more guarded, almost defensive. "No, senôr. I haven't seen anyone that fits your description, sorry." He looked up and down the street again. "Street gang members don't really frequent these parts."

"Is there anyone inside?" said Harold pointing at the entrance to the parking garage.

"There are always staff members working late here," said Pedro.

"Oh, okay," said Harold peering past Pedro.

He moved to stand in front of Harold. "I already told you that there is no one around here that matches your description," said Pedro, glaring at him.

"Sure. Well, if you happen to see a girl…"

"She your daughter?" Pedro's eyebrows lifted.

"No. She's… wanted."

"You mean by the cops?"

"Something like that. She's dangerous."

Pedro snorted. "Ha. A girl? Unlikely."

"Yeah, well, if you happen to see her or anyone that fits her description, I'll be in that car over there," Harold pointed.

"He's pointing at us," said Tracy as she watched her father. "Why? Is he crazy? I'm telling you something's not right."

"Relax, my child," said Sybs. "I'm sure your father has everything under control. Look, here he comes."

Harold opened the door and climbed back into the car.

310

"Well?" said Tracy. "What'd he say? And why were you showing him where we parked?"

"Because I want him to know that we're watching him. I don't trust him."

"Told you!" said Tracy. "I told you that he was in on it. Am I right?"

"Not sure," said Harold. "But I don't want to take any chances. He seems guarded. I definitely caught his attention as soon as I mentioned Sabine and the street gang."

"Now what?" said Tracy.

"We wait."

Tracy folded her arms and gritted her teeth.

"What?" said Harold. "You were the one who said that we were just going to observe. What else do you want me to do? I can't exactly karate-chop the guard, run inside and grab whoever you think might be in there. I'm not Superman, you know."

"I never said that," grumbled Tracy.

"Come on, you two," said Sybs. "There's no need for bickering. Let's just wait for the FBI to arrive and then they can take it from there."

"At least there's someone that has some sense inside of them," pipped Harold.

Tracy glared at her father.

"Here," said Harold, handing Tracy a teal-blue metallic flask.

"What's that?"

"Coffee. We're on a stake-out, so I thought this would be appropriate. We have to stay alert, you know." Harold grinned, pouring some coffee into the cup.

"Thanks," said Tracy taking the cup from her father. The coffee wasn't quite hot enough, but it still tasted good. Her father was right. Tracy immediately felt the caffeine go to work, making her feel more alert. The warm liquid also soothed the tight, anxious feeling in her tummy. She stared out of her window at the guard as he paced up and down the street. He stopped and turned to stare at the car for a moment. Tracy slid

down, into her seat, ducking to one side. She closed her eyes
and saw the girl before her. Sabine. She was standing around a
fire. Her dream. It was a memory of her dream, the one she had
when she was in Istanbul. But something was different. Was it
the fire? The flames seemed to be frozen in time. In fact
everything seemed to be frozen except for the girl. Sabine. She
turned towards Tracy, slowly, very slowly, like one of those slow-
motion scenes in a movie when, in the heat of the action, all the
sounds become muted, and the characters glide slowly along,
frame by frame. The dark crystal around her neck seemed to be
calling Tracy, pulling her in like a magnet, an unexplained force.
Sabine was staring at her now. She opened her mouth and
spoke. "Tr-a-ceeee…" she hissed.

Tracy opened her eyes and gasped for air as if she was
underwater. A cold shiver coursed through her body. "She
knows," she whispered.

"What my child?" said Sybs, placing a hand on her shoulder.
"What is it?"

"My name. She knows my name." Tracy's face was ashen.

43 ~ Cracked

To a casual observer watching the monitors in the security office, the trio that stepped out of the elevator appeared to be routine electrical maintenance staff in their branded blue overalls. The man at the rear glanced momentarily at the security camera and then followed the other two as they crossed over to the basement elevator on the opposite side of the lobby. The girl in the centre wore a black peak cap that hid her face, and the one in front seemed to know exactly where he was going. He touched a card hanging from a lanyard around his neck, to the digital panel beside the elevator and the doors opened. The trio stepped inside and disappeared from view. Another camera installed in the top right corner of the elevator picked them up as they made their way down four floors to the basement level beneath the parking garage. The elevator shook slightly as it came to a halt at the bottom. The doors opened, and they stepped out into a small area surrounded by thick, stainless steel bars that reminded Miguel of his prison cell at Lincoln Correctional Facility. He squeezed his eyes shut and shook off an apprehensive shiver in an effort to erase the memory, before boldly stepping forward and into his destiny.

Julian pointed at the small, black security camera in the

corner of the ceiling. "There's a camera," he whispered.

Miguel nodded. "Pedro has it under control. It's playing back a recording of an empty room."

"Good," said Julian. "What about these bars?" said Julian. "Is this where we call Pinto to cut the power?"

"No. Not yet," said Miguel.

"Then how we getting through? I don't see no digital panel. In fact, I don't see no door or nothing. It's like this area is completely sealed off."

"Just wait and see," said Miguel with a grin. He turned to Sabine. "It's all yours," he said, extending his hand. "Jules. Step back. Let her pass."

Julian moved aside to let Sabine through. He frowned, unsure what was going on. He glared at Miguel who raised his finger to his lips and then also took a step backwards to give Sabine some room.

Sabine stepped forward, dropped to one knee, and shrugged off her black, nylon backpack. She pulled back the silver zipper and carefully withdrew a long, wooden box. She placed it on the ground and lifted the lid. The light reflected off a shiny long, silver object inside.

"What the fuck?" said Julian.

"Shhh." Miguel silenced him.

Sabine carefully lifted the flute out of the box and held it up high. She brought it down close to her left eye, peered down the shaft for a moment and smiled, apparently satisfied with her appraisal. She stood up, placed her fingers meticulously over some of the oddly placed holes, and then lifted the flute to her lips. She took a deep breath and blew into the mouthpiece. The single sound that she produced sounded so pure and strong that Julian gasped and held his breath until Sabine ran out of breath. She adjusted her fingers over the holes, closed her eyes, took another deep breath, and blew into the flute once more. The pitch was different; higher, sharper.

Miguel was forced to squint his eyes because the sound seemed to mess with his vision, making everything go fuzzy like it was vibrating very fast. He turned towards a soft scraping sound that came from the stainless steel bars around them. Julian's face dropped in awe. Several bars were moving, sliding sideways into one another to reveal a rectangular opening. Sabine stopped her blowing, and the doorway remained open. She placed the flute back into the box, pushed it into her backpack, and then retrieved Miguel's black and silver device in its stead.

"Thank you," said Miguel, taking the electronic keypad from Sabine. "Well," he said to Julian, "don't just stand there, dummy. Let's go!" He stepped through the doorway, and Julian followed. Sabine came last. "*Now* we call Pinto," said Miguel pulling out his receiver. "Ola, Pinto. You there?"

There were a few seconds of static on the two-way, followed by Pinto's voice. "Yeah, Boss. Ready when you are."

"Okay,' said Miguel. "Just gimme a minute." He stepped over to the vault and placed the electronic device onto the stainless steel exterior. It sucked magnetically onto the door with a loud *clang*.

"Hey," said Julian, furtively looking around. "Not so loud!"

"Don't worry," said Miguel reassuringly. "No one can hear us down here." He lifted the receiver. "Okay, Pinto. Hit it. Now!"

Moments later, the lights went out. Miguel already had his LED torch switched on. He shone it onto the electronic keypad, quickly punched in a code and then hit enter. Seconds later, the lights came back on, and there was another loud scraping sound, this time from inside the vault.

"Okay, let's give it a go," said Miguel, pointing at the circular handle protruding from the vault.

Julian stepped forward, took hold of the handle on one side, while Miguel gripped the other side. Julian pushed, and Miguel pulled. Miguel grunted. Nothing happened.

"Come on, put your back into it!" shouted Julian, bending his knees and moving in closer to gain more leverage.

"You sure we're pulling and pushing in the right direction?"

enquired Miguel.

"Yes. One hundred percent sure. I watched the video about a dozen times. It's definitely anti-clockwise."

Miguel stepped closer, pulling even harder this time. Julian pushed. And then the handle turned, slowly at first and then more quickly, spinning in an anti-clockwise direction, much to Julian's satisfaction.

"Yesssss!" Julian punched the air with his fist. He grinned at Miguel. "It's open!"

Together, they pulled on the round handle, and the two-foot-wide thick vault door slowly swung open.

"This is it," said Miguel. "We've hit the big time." He grinned at Julian.

"Yeah, baby!" Julian cried, pulling out three compressed duffel bags from his backpack.

"Only hundreds," said Miguel. "We fill them with hundreds. Nothing else," he instructed.

"How much fits into one of these?" said Julian pointing at the bags.

"Well over two million."

Julian counted on his fingers. "Six million?! Hoooo! That's…" He looked at Sabine. "What about her? What's her share?"

Miguel looked at Sabine. "There's five of us, bro. Don't forget Pinto and Matias. She gets a mil," he said, jerking his thumb in Sabine's direction. "So do the others, and then there's still Pedro. He'll end up with 500k."

"That leaves three for us, right?"

"Ha! So, you're not just a pretty face."

"Fuck you, Miguel."

"No. Fuck you. Now, come on, let's fill these bags and get the hell out of here," said Miguel, looking at his watch. "We don't have much time. Let's move!" Miguel grabbed the bags and stepped inside the safe. Julian followed while Sabine remained standing outside, idly surveying the two tattooed gangsters like she had all the time in the world.

44 ~ Chase

Rap, Rap, Rap!

Harold pressed the window button. "Agent Trudeau!"

"Prof," said Trudeau, tipping his *New York Nicks* baseball cap in Harold's direction. He peered inside the car. "Who have we here?"

"Um. This is my mother in law, Sybs and my daughter Tracy." Harold looked passed Trudeau. "Are you alone?"

"My partner is in the car back there," said Trudeau. He looked up and down the street. "Isn't it a bit dangerous for your family to be here with you?"

"They're fine," said Harold. "They've been, um, helping me."

Trudeau quickly cut to the chase. "So, where is she? Where's the girl?"

"I believe she's in there," said Harold, pointing at the bank building.

Trudeau turned around, placed his hands on his hips, and surveyed the UBS building. "So, you were tipped off, eh?" he said, turning to Harold again. He raised his eyebrows in Sybs' and Tracy's direction.

"I spoke to the guard over there," said Harold pointing. "I

don't trust him."

"How do you really know that she's in there?"

"Just speak to the guard. He definitely knows something. He was acting really guarded. Excuse the pun."

"Professor Barnes," said Trudeau. "I need a little more to go on than a hunch. If you're wasting my time…"

"Listen," said Harold. "You told me to call you if I knew something. Well, this is it. That… that killer, that crazy girl who killed my secretary and stole the artefact from my office, is in there doing something bad, and if you aren't going to do anything about it, I will." Harold pulled the door lever and pushed the door open.

Trudeau, resting his hands on the window, pushed back, slamming the car door shut. "Relax, Prof," he said. "I got this. Sit tight. I'll be back." He turned away from Harold and walked towards the bank. "I'll be back," said Tracy in the deepest voice she could muster, mimicking Arnold Schwarzenegger.

Harold and Sybs burst into laughter.

"Evening," said Trudeau as he approached Pedro. He extended his right hand. "Agent Wesley Trudeau. FBI."

Pedro took a step backwards. "Hello. Pedro Sanchez. How can I help you?" he said, looking up and down the street.

Trudeau smiled. He was trained to read people, and this guy was nervous. Very nervous. "May I ask you some questions, sir?" Trudeau watched Pedro pull his right earlobe and swallow hard.

Pedro nodded. "Yes. Yes, of course."

Trudeau noticed that Pedro's forehead was covered in perspiration. "How long have you been working for UBS, Mr. Sanchez. Pedro. Can I call you Pedro?" said Trudeau with a smile.

Pedro nodded again. "Seven years. I've been working here seven years." He folded his arms.

"And tell me, Pedro," continued Trudeau. "Have you noticed anything unusual here this evening?"

Pedro pushed his forehead into a frown. He looked really

318

confused. "What do you mean unusual? There's just been the usual stuff, you know?" he shrugged his shoulders.

"Okay," said Trudeau, stroking his chin. "So you must have quite an important job here, Pedro. Am I right?"

Pedro shifted his weight from left to right and smiled. "I'd like to think so," he said.

"You are the one who knows exactly who goes in and out of this building, right?"

Pedro nodded. "Yes, yes. Well, only during my shift. Another guard takes over at 6am."

"So, you do the night shift."

"Uh-huh." Pedro nodded again. "8pm to 6am."

"Wow. 10 hours. That's a long time to be standing out here," remarked Trudeau, glancing at his watch. "So, in the last two hours of your shift, you haven't seen anything unusual. No unusual deliveries? No unusual people coming in or out through this entrance?" Trudeau stepped past Pedro and peered inside the garage.

Just then, there was a screech of tyres, and the burning smell of rubber permeated the air. A white delivery van bolted out of the parking garage, smashing the red and white security boom to pieces, nearly knocking over both Trudeau and Pedro in the process. Trudeau jumped back in alarm, landing with his back on the sidewalk in a huff. Pedro was also forced to dive out of the way, landing safely on top of a bush on the sidewalk. The van bounced into the road, turned hard right with another squeal of tyres and sped off at high speed. Trudeau pulled himself up and ran back to his car to give chase.

"Dad! Look!" shouted Tracy. "It's them! Come on! Let's go!" she nudged her father in the ribs with her elbow.

Harold instinctively started the car and pulled out of the parking bay. He looked out of his window and saw Agent Trudeau and his partner pull out on the other side of the road in a dark blue Chevy Impala. He allowed them to shoot ahead and then floored the pedal to catch up. "Do you really think that this is a good idea?" he said.

"No," replied Sybs. "But at least we got the FBI in front of us!" She grinned. "This is getting so exciting," she continued, rubbing her hands together.

"I'm sure you think so," said Harold. "Am I supposed to feel reassured? You've obviously seen how this is going to end."

"Not quite," said Sybs. "There is always more than one possible ending."

"Can we please choose the one that ends where the FBI catch the killer, and we all go home safe and sound?"

"Harold, you know that it's not that simple," said Sybs.

"Look out!" shouted Tracy, and Harold swerved to avoid a motorbike. "Dad, please keep your eyes on the road. Gran, stop distracting him."

"I'm okay," said Harold, swerving again. He floored the pedal again to catch up to Trudeau just ahead of them. "Can you still see the van?"

Tracy stuck her head out of the window. "Yes! There it is! Come on, Dad, don't lose them!" she shouted into the wind and then pulled herself back into the car, gripping the dashboard to keep herself from being flung around as Harold wove between the traffic, the car's wheels squealing in protest.

Harold gripped the wheel in earnest. "Sybs, please strap yourself in!" he shouted with a glare in his rear-view mirror. He was not impressed.

Sybs sat in the middle of the back seat, holding onto the sides of the two front seats, with a huge grin stretched across her face. "Okay, okay, Harold. No need to get your knickers in a knot," she said, sitting back into the seat and pulling on her safety belt. "There. Happy now?"

Harold glanced in the mirror again but chose not to respond. He turned his focus back to the road ahead of them as they raced through the city.

Tracy looked out of the window. She saw a sign with an arrow. *Jersey City*. They were heading south. Then she saw another sign. *Hoboken*. South. Yes, definitely south. Tracy looked ahead. The FBI car had gained some distance between them.

320

She could barely read the plate now. "Dad! We're going to lose them," she said in a panic.

"Calm down. We're not going to lose them," said Harold. "Your mother is going to kill me," he mumbled under his breath. He pressed his foot on the pedal, and the car sped up.

Tracy looked at the dashboard. The speedometer was pushing just over 100 miles per hour. Fortunately, there wasn't too much traffic at this time of night.

"Hold on!" shouted Harold as they sped over a hill. Tracy's stomach dropped as the car left the ground, came crashing down onto the road in an eruption of sparks and screeching rubber, and then ploughed on, into the night.

"I can't see it anymore. The truck," said Tracy, her head out of the window. "Wait. There," she pointed. "There it is. It's turning right." She held onto the dashboard again as Harold pulled the wheel hard to the right. The tyres screeched in consternation.

"Come on, Dad. You can do it," said Tracy reassuringly.

"What's that?" said Sybs from the back. She was pointing at something flying through the sky.

"A trash can?" said Harold in awe.

The black FBI vehicle swerved to avoid the trash can as it fell from above, exploding into a mess of rubbish when it hit the ground.

"It looked like someone threw it at them," said Tracy. "But from where?" She stuck her head out of the window again.

Harold reached over with one hand, gripped Tracy by the back of her top and pulled her into the car. "I don't want you doing that," he said. "It's too dangerous."

"Sorry, Dad," said Tracy.

"Look out!" shouted Sybs. Another trash can hit the ground right next to them. Harold swerved.

"What the hell is going on?" said Harold. "Where are these trash cans coming from?"

"From the side of the road," said Sybs gazing out of the window.

Tracy and Sybs watched as another trash can lifted up and into the air. It floated uncannily for a moment in the air and then came crashing down. This time, there was a direct hit onto the roof of Trudeau's car. Harold swerved again as the trash can smashed onto the ground just ahead of them.

"The flute," said Sybs. "She's using the flute."

Tracy strained her ears and thought she heard the distinct sound of the magical instrument. "Are you sure, Gran?"

"Oh, I'm sure, all right. Just a sure as flowers bloom in the springtime. You saw that trash can. There's nothing that can lift a metal trash can off the side of the road during a high-speed car chase and then fling it down onto the ground again with force, other than the flute. She is definitely using it. And she has mastered its power. We must stop her."

"I'm doing the best that I can," said Harold. The gap between them and Trudeau had narrowed. "But these flying trash cans are making it very difficult to navigate."

This time, Harold, Sybs, and Tracy watched as two trash cans came crashing down right in front of Trudeau's car, causing him to swerve to the left. One of the trash cans connected with the right corner of the car. The vehicle lifted up and then rolled several times across the road, before coming to rest upside down, in the middle of the street.

Harold hit the brakes, swerved hard right and came to rest just a few yards away from Trudeau's car. The wheels of Trudeau's car were still spinning, as Harold stepped out of his vehicle. Sybs and Tracy followed. Harold ran over to the driver's side of the vehicle and tried to open the buckled door, but to no avail. He dropped to his knees and peered inside. "Trudeau. You okay?" Harold heard a click and a thud, followed by a grunt, as Trudeau released his safety belt and dropped onto the roof of his car.

"*Cough*. Yeah. I'm fine," said Trudeau, sliding head-first out of the car window.

Harold helped him to his feet. He had small gashes across his forehead and left cheekbone.

"What about your partner?"

"I think he's okay. Smith!" he shouted as he looked inside the bashed up vehicle.

"Yeah?" came a voice.

"You all right?"

"Yeah. Think so. Just need help getting out of this safety belt. It's stuck."

"Hold on," said Trudeau, pulling a small blade out from inside his left sock. He proceeded to climb back inside the vehicle, and soon he was helping Smith out again. Trudeau dusted off his suit and rolled his left shoulder around with a grimace. "Bastards!" he spat, looking in the direction of the vehicle they were chasing.

"Did you get a good look at the registration?" said Harold.

"Yeah," said Trudeau. "Stolen. As suspected. Don't worry, we called it in and alerted the cops."

"So they should catch them?"

"As long as they stay on the road, yes. But, chances are, they'll dump the truck and switch vehicles." Trudeau turned to his partner who was sitting on the sidewalk, rubbing his right knee. "Smith, you sure you're all right?"

Agent Javier Smith had short-cropped, wavy, sandy-coloured hair. His black, pin-striped suit jacket was torn on one side, and he was missing a shoe. "Twisted or something," he replied. "Hurts like hell."

"Here," said Trudeau throwing his partner a small, white container that rattled as he caught it out of the air. "Take two of those. That'll sort you out for a bit. Let me get your shoe."

"I'll get it," said Tracy already climbing into the vehicle.

"Thanks," said Smith, popping two tablets into his mouth as instructed.

Trudeau narrowed his eyes as he gazed in the direction that the truck went. "Take us back," he said.

"Excuse me?" said Harold.

"Back to the bank. Take us back to the bank."

"Oh, yeah, sure," said Harold, as Trudeau went to help his

partner to his feet.

"I need to find out what they were doing there. And I need to find that security guard. He and I have lots to talk about," continued Trudeau, escorting a limping Javier Smith towards Harold's car. Sybs opened the back door as Trudeau helped his partner inside. He returned to stand in front of Harold. "Looks like they had help," he said. He tilted his head to one side as he surveyed his smashed up vehicle. "From your position, did you get a good look at who was throwing those trash cans at us? Must have been other MS13 gang members," he mused. "Uncanny how quickly they got into position. Just goes to show how strong their network really is."

Harold opened his mouth and then shut it again.

"No?" said Trudeau.

"Sorry, was concentrating on the road."

"What about you two?" said Trudeau turning to Sybs and Tracy.

They both shook their heads.

"What was strange," said Trudeau, "was how the trash cans behaved like targeted missiles. Like they were being controlled. Strange as fucking hell." He scratched his head, puzzled at the anomaly.

45 ~ Switch

"I think we lost them," said Matias, looking into his rear-view mirror. He pulled the van around the next bend and slowed down to fifty. "Did you see that? Holy shit! Did you see what she did? Those... those trash cans. They were flying around behind us!" Matias stared at Sabine in the mirror with wide eyes like she was an alien from another dimension. He watched her carefully pack the flute back inside the wooden box and then push it inside her backpack. He looked around at the others for reassurance, but they all sat silently looking the other way.

"We need to ditch this van," said Miguel. "Like now."

"Mat," said Julian. "How far we from the drop off?"

"Two blocks," replied Matias, turning left. "Almost there."

"Don't worry, Miguel, it's all under control," said Julian reassuringly.

"Who was that behind us, anyway?" said Matias. "The pigs?"

"Must have been," replied Julian.

"You think Pedro maybe tipped us off?" said Matias.

"That was him standing outside talking to that dude in the baseball cap," said Matias. "That's why I floored it through the barrier. He looked like a cop."

"Yeah, Julian's right," said Matias. "Must have been the cops. Otherwise, why would they give chase?"

"That fuckin' Pedro Sanchez," said Julian. "I knew he couldn't be trusted."

"No," said Miguel shaking his head. "Pedro and I go way back. There's no way it was him. He would never double-cross me. He would never risk losing his family over this."

"Well then, what's your theory?" said Julian, folding his arms. "How could they have known we were there? I mean, we only just changed the plan. We only just changed the day we were going to do this because she told us to." He jerked his thumb in Sabine's direction. "If it weren't for her, we would have done this job on another night, when there wouldn't have been any cops lurking around."

Miguel turned to Sabine. She sat at the back with her black peak pulled down over her face, eyes closed. "Or it could have been worse," said Miguel. "They could have been waiting for us when we arrived. I think that by changing our plans, we made it. We pulled it off. I think we have Sabine to thank for that. Matias is right. She got rid of our tail with that magic flute. I dunno how she did it, but this girl's got the shit. She's our secret weapon. And I think she knows. I think she knows who tipped us off. Sabine?"

All eyes were on the girl with scars on her face. Sabine lifted her head and opened her eyes.

"Do you know who told the cops about the job?" said Miguel. "Huh? Do you?"

Sabine nodded.

Matias whistled. "Hoo. This bitch has the power, man. She's like the MS13 witch. Where'd you find her, Miguel?"

"Tracy," whispered Sabine.

"What?" exclaimed Julian. "Who?"

"She said Tracy," said Matias over his shoulder. "Even I heard her from here."

"I know, dumbass," said Julian. "I was just asking her *who*

Tracy was. Will you shut up and drive like you're supposed to?"

"Fuck you," said Matias. "And your momma."

"Hey!" shouted Julian. "If you mention my momma again, bro, I'm gonna knife you. In your sleep!"

"Shut the fuck up!" said Miguel. "Both of youse. You sound like a bunch of fucking kids."

"It was him," said Julian. "*He* mentioned my momma. Nobody talks about my momma and gets away with it."

"Okay, just drop it now," said Miguel. "We have far more important shit to deal with." He turned to Sabine. "Who is this, Tracy? Where is she? Why did she tip us off."

Sabine smiled. "She can see."

"Huh?" said Julian, his forehead creased in confusion. "So she's not blind? What the fuck does she mean?" he said, looking around.

"It's figurative," said Miguel. "I think she's saying that this Tracy can see the future. She can see what's going to happen, much like Sabine can."

"Fuck," said Julian. "Just our luck. There's another one. Another messed up bitch that can see into the future. Why'd Sabine even come to us?" said Julian. "I mean, what's really in it for her?"

Miguel turned to Sabine. She had closed her eyes again and dropped her head. "She brought us Flaco, man. José Flaco Sanchez. A gringo we all thought was dead. And then she saved us tonight, man. And all she wants is eyes. The eyes of her victims. You've seen what happens. They give her some sort of power. Energy."

The silence that followed was palpable. All eyes were on Sabine. Even Matias was staring into the rear-view mirror. He pulled into a parking garage, next to a mustard-coloured, 2002 Dodge Ram and turned off the motor. Everyone climbed out of the van and began transferring the three duffel bags into the back of the Dodge. Sabine stood by and watched with cold, hard eyes.

"I'll drive," said Miguel. "Sabine will sit upfront with me."

Matias tossed Miguel the keys. A look of relief washed over his face as he climbed into the back seat of the pickup along with Julian.

"Hope Pinto got out okay," said Matias.

"Yeah, he did. He'll catch up with us later," said Miguel, waving his hand through the air.

Miguel started the pickup, looked left, then right and slowly began to make his way out of the parking garage.

46 ~ Free Ride

Tracy sat in the back between Granny Sybs and Agent Smith, and Trudeau sat in front with Harold.

"Thank you for lifting us," said Trudeau. He twisted around in his seat. His piercing blue eyes caught Tracy's. She looked away. "Smith, you holding up okay?"

"Fine," said Smith between clenched teeth. "I'll be fine."

"Good, good," said Trudeau. He flashed a toothy grin at Tracy. "You sure you never saw anything back there?"

Tracy shook her head. "We were too busy dodging those flying trash cans. One almost hit us."

"Yeah, I know. *We* weren't so lucky." He turned to face the front. "Prof. I don't believe that you've told me who tipped you off. About the girl. How did you know that she was inside UBS Bank? You mentioned the guard, Sanchez. Did you know him from before? Did he call you?"

"No. I only met him for the first time tonight."

"Okay, but your story still doesn't add up. Who told you to go to the bank? I'm just trying to piece this all together."

Harold glanced at Tracy in his rear-view mirror. "I got an anonymous call." He lied.

"Hmm," said Trudeau. "Male or female?"

329

"Definitely male," said Harold. "He just said, 'if you want to find the killer, she's inside UBS Bank, Chicago'; that's it."

"So then the three of you just drove on down here?"

"Yeah. That's when I called you."

Trudeau turned to gaze out of the window, silently contemplating the facts, and then his phone rang. "Trudeau," he answered. "Yes. I'm on my way there now. Yes. Yes, I know. Okay. Yes, sir." He turned to Harold. "The bank has been robbed."

"What?" exclaimed Harold. "UBS Bank? Bastards!"

"Was probably an inside job. That guard. Sanchez." Trudeau twisted to face Smith. "Get me everything on Pedro Sanchez. Security guard, UBS Bank, Chicago."

Javier nodded and then proceeded to call the FBI office in Richmond.

"If you're right and he's involved, I doubt he's still there," said Harold.

"Don't worry, we'll find him. We'll catch him, and he'll talk," said Trudeau confidently.

The familiar sight of blue and red flashing lights brought a pang of unease to Tracy's gut as they approached the bank. Harold drove as close as he could before pulling over on the side of the road.

"Thanks for the ride," said Trudeau.

"No problem," said Harold.

"Now you folks get on back home where it's safe. I don't want to see any more of this vigilante stuff going on. Especially from you, Professor. We'll take it from here; this is our job."

"Yes, sir," said Harold.

"And if you get any more tip-offs, call me, okay?"

"Very well."

Trudeau climbed out of the car and then opened the back door to assist his partner out.

"Good evening, ladies," said Smith with a forced smile.

"Bye," said Tracy and Sybs together.

Tracy watched the two agents, one with his arm around the

other, slowly make their way towards one of the police cars. "Dad," she said, leaning forward in her seat. "He gives me the creeps."

"Who? Trudeau?"

Tracy nodded.

"They're all the same, those agents. It's part of their manifesto at the FBI. Cold, hard, emotionless Feds. Okay, where to now?" Harold raised his eyebrows as he spoke.

"Trudeau told us to go home," said Tracy.

Harold glanced at his wristwatch. "Wow! It's after eleven! Where did the time go?"

"Time flies when you're having fun," said Sybs cheerfully. Her mouth turned up into a grin, and her eyes sparkled.

"Fun!? You call this… this… fun?" exclaimed Harold, waving his hands animatedly around. "We could have been killed and you're telling me that it was fun."

"Calm down, Harold," said Sybs. "I would never put you and Tracy in mortal danger. You'll always be safe with me." She smiled.

"So you knew what was going to happen all along?"

"It's a bit more complicated than that. Let's just say that I knew no harm was going to befall us tonight."

"Right. And you're never wrong," said Harold, tight-lipped.

"Well, so far, I've never been wrong," said Sybs.

"Ha! Well, that's reassuring. You're saying that you have never been wrong *yet*, but that there is a chance that you *could* be at some point in time?"

"Perhaps," Sybs mused.

Harold shook his head. "I guess I'll never truly understand you, Sybs. And what about you, Miss Barnes? Hmm?"

"What? What did I do?" said Tracy perplexed.

"Ah, forget it," said Harold, grumpily as he started the car. "It's late, I'm tired, and we still have a long drive ahead of us."

Tracy stared out of the window. "I wonder if they'll find them?"

"I think they will," said Harold. "Once they get hold of that security guard, Sanchez, it should be a piece of cake. Despite his cold, hard demeanour, I think Trudeau is good at his job." He pushed the car into gear and pulled away from the crime scene.

47 ~ Ripples

Tracy was exhausted. She could barely keep her eyes open as she brushed her teeth. She stared hard into the mirror. Her eyes burned. She squeezed them shut in a futile attempt at flushing the sleep away. She flopped onto her bed with a welcome sigh and fell asleep within a couple of moments.

At first, there was just a haze, but it gradually lifted to reveal a gravel path beneath her feet. It was faint and narrow like it hadn't been used for a while, but Tracy could still make it out as it curved across a mountainous terrain like a snake, disappearing for a moment and then materialising again as she rounded the next hill. She looked up. The haze never fully cleared. Instead, it hung, suspended from above like a mass of grey, glowing, goo, threatening to descend again and conceal her within its clammy essence. She looked down at her feet. She was wearing her favourite tan leather boots - perfect for hiking. The *crunch-crunch* of loose stones beneath them, gave her a sense of self-confidence as she strode purposefully towards her destination. She smiled because she knew where she was going. With every step, it became abundantly clearer to her. With every step, the haze seemed to lift higher as if it sensed her growing enlightenment, that came with quickness of breath and a growing urgency to arrive.

Tracy looked down at her wrist. She was still wearing the Nazar Boncuk beaded bracelet that she received from Madame Kezia in Istanbul. The little blue-eyed bead stared back at her. She could almost feel the invisible aura of protection that it cast around her, warding off the mist as it threatened to engulf her in its sticky clutches. She huffed and puffed as the path rose steeply. She looked up and saw a tree. Succulent looking black berries adorned it in clusters. She moved in closer and smiled when she recognised them. Mulberries. Her heart was pumping both from the exertion of the climb but also with excitement. She had arrived. She looked past the tree, and there it was in all its glory, just as she knew it would be - Gobekli Tepe, the ancient megalithic temple just outside Urfa. She had stepped back in time once more. She knew this because Gobekli Tepe was a solid structure. The standing stones were whole, not broken and in disrepair as she had seen them during her visit to Turkey with her father. And there were those people again, dressed in long, leather tunics and sheepskin boots, all making their way towards the stone structure. A pang of anxiety briefly washed over her as she recalled her last visit to this place when she saw her doppelganger, a spitting image of herself, deep inside the temple structure. She glanced at her amulet and marched on, dispelling her negative thoughts, concentrating instead on what she came here to find.

She reached the entrance to the temple and gazed up, marvelling at the massive stone pillars in front of her. She watched several people make their way inside, and she followed, eventually reaching the centre, where at least fifty of them had gathered. Tracy watched as they all began to take a seat on the cold, hard floor in silence and closed their eyes. The flickering light from several sconces burning on the walls cast eerie shadows across the faces of the people around her as if the spirits inside the temple had been brought to life. Tracy found an open spot and sat down. She watched the people begin to move in their seated positions, slowly rolling their hips around in a clockwise direction, controlled like marionettes on strings from above. She closed her eyes and was surprised to discover that even through closed lids, she could still make out the silhouettes of the people around her and their swaying, circular movements. She placed her hands on her knees for support and joined them, rolling her body around, completely in unison with the group.

A deep, humming sound emanated from the people around her, building in strength as everyone joined in. It was like the pranayama chant of Om in her yoga class, resonating with such power that Tracy's earlobes tickled with the vibration of sound through the air. The humming continued as the group swayed their bodies round and round. She became part of the collective as she moved with those gathered inside the ancient monument, guided by instinct, fuelled by intuition. And then she heard another sound and her soul stirred, bringing tears to her eyes. The flute; a sound so pure and unsullied. It was the treble to the humming bass, the sweet honey to the bitter lemon. It was so magical, so enchanting, that Tracy's heart ached with elation. She took a deep breath and hummed it out, merging her voice with the others as the sound of the flute lifted her spirit and set her free.

Time seemed to stand still as she continued to breathe deeply in and hum out. In, out, in, out, in, out, until her breath merged with the group as one continuous energy flow, guided by the sound of the flute.

The flute. *What was its purpose?*

She pondered this thought, and then it struck her like a wave. The power of the flute went beyond the ability to lift physical objects. This dream was a lesson, a learning experience. Tracy opened her eyes and found that she was no longer seated inside the temple. Instead, she was astral travelling across space and time in a corridor of magnificent light along with the group of fifty souls around her. Despite the daunting experience, she felt safe and protected, but most of all, she felt happy, free, and connected; connected to the people around her, the universe, and all life within it. Life. It was a celebration; a celebration of life. This self-realisation resonated with her, strengthening her resolve, changing something deep inside her. She was enlightened, evolved, and ever so grateful that she cried. The tears flowed from her eyes like a river that began in her belly. They poured out of her, blinding her until she could not see. They washed through her, cleansing, rinsing, purifying, and she basked in their revitalising waters like a mermaid in the deep, blue sea.

The flute changed pitch. It began to make a strange, repeated sound like it was stuck on one note. The tunnel of light began to flicker, and sparkle like one of those sparklers on a cake, and the humming sound from the fifty souls around Tracy faded altogether. The back of her head ached terribly. She closed her eyes, rubbed them with the palms of her hands, and then opened them to the sound of her phone alarm going off next to her bed. She reached over and shut it off. The pain in her head persisted, as if she had just banged it against something. It throbbed from her neck, down and into her upper back. She took a deep breath, sighed it out, and then realised that her face was wet. She slowly sat up and found that her pyjama top was wet too. She pinched the skin between the bridge of her nose and squeezed her eyes shut once more. And then it all came rushing back to her like a torrent. Gobleki Tepe, the humming, the flute, the flight through space and time.

And the tears.

Tracy pulled her top up over her head and wiped her face with it. She wriggled off her bed, made her way to the bathroom, and splashed cold water over her face. The throbbing in the back of her head faded somewhat. She noticed a half-full bottle of drinking water on the edge of the basin. She unscrewed the lid and downed the entire contents in one gulp. She craved more; she was so thirsty. She stared into the mirror. Her eyes were red, and her cheeks looked swollen like she had been partying all night long.

What the hell just happened? She thought to herself as she gripped the basin. *Was that real? It sure felt like it. I mean, just look at me!* She wiped her hair away from her face. She needed to have a shower. She felt dirty, soiled.

Tracy closed her eyes as the water ran down over her face. She could still see Gobekli Tepe and the people inside it, humming and swaying in unison. She could even smell the smoke from the burning sconces on the wall. The memory triggered a shiver through her body and the hairs on her arms lifted despite the warm water from the shower washing down over her body. She was there. It wasn't just a dream. Somehow, part of her went back in time. Part of her sat with those people inside the ancient temple. Part of her joined them on a spiritual journey through space, and it changed her. A veil had been lifted. She could see. She could *truly* see. Through time. Her gift had truly manifested itself, and she embraced it whole-heartedly.

48 ~ Delivery

"Dad! It's for you!" Dylan shouted from downstairs.

Tracy looked out of her bedroom window and down onto a man in a yellow and red peak cap and matching jacket. She looked across the garden and spotted a DHL delivery van parked outside. *The flute!* She pulled on her jeans, threw on a vest, and bolted downstairs to find her father standing at the front door.

"Here you go, sir," said the delivery man. "Please sign here."

"Do you have a pen for me, please?" said Harold.

Tracy peered over his shoulder.

"Just use your finger," said the man. "It's digital."

"Oh. Okay," said Harold tracing his index finger over the screen on the handheld device. "Amazing, isn't it Trace?" He said, turning to Tracy.

The man handed Harold a long, narrow parcel in yellow plastic wrapping. "Here you go."

"Thank you," said Harold, closing the door.

"Is it?..." said Tracy.

"The flute?" said Harold. "Yes, well, I hope so," he said, handing Tracy the package.

Tracy stared at the parcel.

338

"Well, go on, then. What are you waiting for? Open it."

Tracy ran into the kitchen, placed the yellow parcel down on the counter, grabbed a knife, and cut open the plastic wrapping to reveal a box beneath. She lifted the flaps and looked inside. Styrofoam chips filled the box. She pushed her hand into the chips and pulled out a long, narrow object wrapped securely in bubble wrap. She used the knife to cut through the bubble wrap and pulled the flute free. "Wow. It looks exactly like the other one; an exact replica."

"Here, let me see," said Harold. He lifted the flute to his eye and gazed down its shaft. "Hmm. Yes. Perfect!" He handed the flute back to Tracy, pulled out his phone, and began to record a voice note. "Berat! Thank you, my friend. The flute has just arrived. All intact. Will be in touch. Take care."

Tracy lifted the flute to her lips, deftly placed her fingers over the holes and blew. The sound was magical.

"Wow," said Harold. "Somehow it sounds even better than the other one. Is this even possible, or have you just had more practice?"

Tracy smiled. "Kinda sounds the same to me. I think I'm just getting used to it. Pity we don't have that box," she said despondently.

"I think I have something," said Harold. "In the garage. Wait here." He stepped outside.

Tracy turned the flute over in her hands. It felt different. Lighter maybe? She wasn't sure. Maybe her Dad was right. Maybe it was a better version than the first one that was printed. No. Impossible. It was printed off of the same design, on the same printer.

Harold returned. "Here you go," he said, placing a black velvet bag on the kitchen counter. "It should fit in there."

"Cool," said Tracy. "Where'd you get it?"

"Oh, I've had it a while. Got it from a convention I went to in Cancun a few years ago."

"What was inside it?"

"This," said Harold, holding up a circular hand drum.

"Cool."

"It's called an ocean drum. Listen." Harold held the drum in his hands like a tray and then slowly twisted it back and forth. The thousands of tiny metallic beads inside shifted across the bottom of the drum, producing the sound of waves breaking on a beach.

"Amazing," Tracy exclaimed. "It sounds just like the real thing!"

"Hey, maybe we can start a band, you and I."

"Ha-ha, very funny, Dad."

"We'll call it Ocean Mist, and we'll have a neat trick."

"What's that?"

"During the performance, you'll make everyone lift out of their seats!"

"Dad! You're so silly!"

Harold broke out into fits of laughter.

Tracy joined in. It felt good to laugh. It felt good when the muscles in her cheeks began to ache. She examined the flute once more. It felt so light in her hands. Such a simple instrument, yet imbued with such power, such finesse. "Dad."

"Yep."

"Have you ever wondered where the idea came from?"

"Huh?"

"The flute." She held up the instrument. "Where the idea came from to design this thing. It's… it's just so advanced for its time. I mean even today, this is something so… foreign. Do you think Dylan's right?"

"What do you mean?"

"Aliens. Remember when he suggested that those ringing rocks came from aliens? Do you think aliens visited the people living so many thousands of years ago and gave them the technology to design this?"

Harold sighed. "It's a very interesting question, Trace. As a professor of science, everything that I believe, is based on physical facts and proof. Theories need to be proven scientifically for me to accept anything as the truth. In this case, we have this phenomenal instrument - hard evidence that something advanced existed a long, long time ago; something that even today is hard to believe, let alone understand. So yes, one could believe that it was advanced sentient beings that brought this technology to Earth. However, in my mind, this is still a theory because I don't have proof of the actual aliens themselves. There are hundreds of stories about artefacts like this one that people have attributed to aliens that have all been debunked over the years. These are often referred to as out-of-place artefacts. Have you heard of the Antikythera Mechanism?"

Tracy shook her head.

"It was an ancient Greek device that was used to calculate the movement of planets in our solar system. It's a remarkable artefact because one was found that is over 2,000 years old. It's dubbed the oldest computer ever found; an analogue computer, but a computer nonetheless. You know, come to think of it, just like the flute, they constructed a modern working model!"

"Wow! Really?"

"Yeah. Then there's the Baghdad Battery, a device also over 2,000 years old, that is believed to represent the first battery. There's the Iron Pillar of Delhi, the wrought iron, rust-free pillar that was constructed hundreds of years before the Indians had the means capable of doing so. And there are plenty more. Even The Pyramids are believed by some to be the work of aliens."

"I guess we can now add the flute to the list."

"We sure can, but, as I said, despite all of these out-of-place artefacts, there's still zero evidence to suggest that aliens were involved in their construction. In the case of the flute, like so many other things that today we find hard to explain, the ancients must have had knowledge that was passed down to them in some shape or form that has been lost over the ages. I mean, just look at this," said Harold pointing at the flute. "The Golden Ratio, built into a musical instrument over 12,000 years ago." Harold shook his head. "I still find it very hard to digest.

It goes against everything I have learnt over the years as a professor of the sciences."

"But isn't this just the kind of thing that you look forward to discovering? Isn't this what makes it all worthwhile?"

Harold smiled. "Come here, pumpkin," he said, pulling Tracy into a warm embrace. He kissed her on the head. "You're one hundred percent correct. This *is* what makes it all worth it. All the countless hours of research, experiments, and searching for answers, and here we are. Sometimes the answers we find are unexpected. Sometimes they're difficult to explain and even harder to accept, but when we do find them, there's that eureka moment that tops everything. That discovery that makes all the blood, sweat, and tears worthwhile."

"There's more to the flute," whispered Tracy.

"What do you mean?" said Harold frowning.

"I mean, it's more powerful than you think. I had this dream last night."

"Yes?"

"I was back at Gobekli Tepe. But it was thousands of years ago. The stones, they were whole."

"Really? Wow."

"Yeah. I was with all these people. We... how do I explain?" Tracy closed her eyes. "Someone was playing the flute. It lifted us; not our bodies, but our spirits. The sound of the flute lifted us up and into space. I was flying through the galaxy, amidst the stars. It was beautiful." Tracy was whispering again.

"Wow. Amazing, Trace." Harold was in awe.

Tracy opened her eyes. "Yeah. Was incredible. That's why I asked you the question - if it maybe came from aliens. It felt so... alien. Like nothing I've ever experienced before."

"Hmm. Harold stroked his beard. Interesting. Very interesting. I see your point. Did you hear anything else? I mean, besides the flute. Anyone speaking to you or anything like that?"

Tracy shook her head. "No, not really."

"I wonder..."

"What?"

"I mentioned the ancients."

"Yes?"

"It's believed by many that there were ancient civilisations. Civilisations that existed tens of thousands of years ago, long before the Egyptians, the Incas and the Myans."

"You mean, like Atlantis?"

"Exactly. There's no real proof, just hints of it. Myths, legends, passed down over the millenia; unexplained megalithic constructions like Gobekli Tepe that defy existence. And then there's this," he said, pointing at the flute. "A powerful artefact with the ability to move objects through the air; to overcome the force of gravity. And perhaps even bend the fabric of space and time as you have just experienced in your dream. I believe that it represents real proof that these ancient civilisations existed; that they had access to knowledge that has been lost over the ages. Powerful knowledge that could change everything we know about everything! In the wrong hands..."

"Sabine..."

"Yes. She has the other flute. She's still out there."

"She must be stopped."

"How?" said Harold. "How do we even find her?"

"Granny Sybs. She'll know."

"I've got to get to the Lab," said Harold. "Please call me after you've spoken to her. Promise?"

"Promise."

Harold hugged Tracy affectionately and left the house.

49 ~ Lesson

"Morning, Gran," said Tracy. "You okay?"

Sybs smiled. She was sitting up in bed as Tracy walked into her room. "Yes, I'm fine. Just a little tired. This body aint so young no more."

"Look," said Tracy holding up the flute. "It arrived!"

"Oh, wow, let me see," said Sybs taking the flute from Tracy.

"Just as light as the other one. How does it sound?"

"Listen," said Tracy, taking the flute back from her grandmother and bringing it up to her lips. Her fingers were already delicately placed over several holes. She took a deep breath, closed her eyes, and blew into the instrument. The sound was as beautiful as ever.

Sybs gasped. "Is it my imagination, or does it sound even better than before?"

"Ha-ha-ha!" laughed Tracy. "That's exactly what Dad said!"

Sybs smiled. "Great minds think alike."

"Gran."

"Yes, dear."

"I had another dream."

Sybs smiled. Her eyes glistened.

344

"You know, don't you?"

Sybs nodded. The smile never left her face. "It usually takes place a few weeks later."

"Wait," said Tracy, wrinkling her brow. "Are we talking about the same thing here?"

"Well, I'm not sure what you dreamed about exactly, but what I do know is that you experienced something profound. The final step in your journey to becoming an oracle. You have finally come fully into your abilities." Sybs continued to smile.

"But how? How did you know?"

"Oh, your aura," said Sybs simply. "It's on fire."

Tracy looked at her arms and then flipped her hands back to front several times. "I do kinda feel like there's this buzzing in my ears and like I've got loads of energy. I thought it was my imagination playing tricks on me."

"Oh, that's it, all right," said Sybs. "There's no mistaking it. It's called the *flux*."

"The flux?"

Sybs nodded. "I remember when I got it like it was just yesterday. It was similar to the feeling I had when I first came into my powers but different."

"Yes!" Tracy exclaimed. "Exactly. I remember at my birthday party. I was awake but dreaming at the same time."

"Lucid dreaming."

"Yes. I flew through space. I saw some crazy stuff. I never really knew what it meant until now."

"So, what happened this time?"

Tracy took a deep breath. "I was back at Gobekli Tepe. And when I say back, I mean way back, like thousands of years ago. It was so real like a proper memory. I could even smell the dampness in the air. Someone was playing a flute. It sounded just like this one, except that there was a melody; a tune that kept repeating itself, again and again. And then before I knew it, I was flying through space again except that this time, I was aware of all these people around me. And then I cried. It was so weird though because I felt very happy at the same time."

345

"Tears of joy!"

"Yes! Exactly! I felt connected to everything."

"The flux." Sybs squeezed Tracy's hand and smiled.

"And free. I felt so free."

"May all beings be happy and free," said Sybs.

"I've heard Denise say that before. Where does it come from?"

"Denise?"

"My yoga teacher."

"Oh. Makes sense."

"How so?"

"It's a Sanskrit mantra that's thousands upon thousands of years old."

"Wow. Really?"

"It's a mantra that was passed down from the Ancients themselves."

"Who are the Ancients?"

"Ancient deities. Immortals. Lokah samastah sukhino bhavantu. That's the Sanskrit translation. In English, it means, may all beings everywhere be happy and free, and may the thoughts, words, and actions of my own life contribute in some way to that happiness and to that freedom for all. The Ancients created this mantra to raise the vibrational frequency of the universe. They chanted it all the time so that they could constantly remove themselves from their egos and practice love for others; so that they could become part of the universe and act as a positive force on behalf of all creation. The Ancients used sound in the form of mantras to invoke the building blocks of creation."

"Fascinating."

"It's similar to the saying, do unto others as you would have them do unto you, but much more impactful. This is what you experienced. The flux brings it on."

"How long does it last, this flux?"

"Oh, a couple of days."

"And then, what happens next?"

"Then you are fully aware. You become fully awake to your gift of prophecy."

"What about the flute?"

"What about it?"

"I mean, in my dream, it was the flute that lifted me up and into space with all those people. If it weren't for the flute, I wouldn't have this flux thing."

Sybs smiled again. "The flux is not dependent on anything. It happens, no matter what."

"Okay. So let's say that you're right. Then how do you explain the dream that I had? All those people. The flute. Flying through space. What does it all mean?"

"It appears that the flute and the sounds it produces have opened up a rift in time, transporting your spiritual essence to a place that once was. Also, there's the matter of Sabine. You have dreamt about her too." Sybs' voice sounded grave.

Tracy shivered.

"I've underestimated her. She has mastered the power of the flute. It seems the only way to stop her is to fight fire with fire."

"What do you mean?"

"I'm going to have to help you master its power too. It's the only way."

Tracy looked at the silver stick in her hand. It was so shiny. "But how? How am I going to fight her? She's much stronger me. You saw what she did with those trash cans!"

"Yes, but things are a lot different now. You are in flux. You can overcome her if you tried."

"Okay. So how do we start? What must I do?"

"Let's sit down on the floor together," said Sybs. "Here," she continued, throwing Tracy a cushion from her bed. "Sit on this. It's much more comfortable."

Tracy followed Sybs' instructions. She folded her legs, sat down on the cushion and dropped the flute into her lap.

"Okay, now place your hands on your knees, close your eyes, and relax. That's it." Sybs sat down opposite Tracy, their

347

knees just touching again. "Right. You know what to do. Remember?"

Tracy closed her eyes and remembered. She focused on breathing deep into her belly. Slowly in, slowly out. She listened to the sound of Sybs' voice. It was so soothing, so peaceful.

"Breathe. Just breathe. Focus your intention on your breathing."

Sybs was right. This time, things *did* feel different. Tracy was more aware, more in control of her surroundings. This time, she stepped into the spiritual realm with Sybs right by her side. There was no gloomy, grey landscape filled with wraiths and spirits. Instead, she drifted on a current of warm air, traversing its path as if she had done so countless times, happy and free.

The flute. It was Sybs' voice inside her head.

What must I do?

Blow into it.

But it's not here, in this place.

Oh, but it is. Everything that exists in physicality also exists here. You just have to manifest it.

How?

You're sitting in my bedroom, and the flute is in your lap, right?

Yes?

You need to reach back into the physical world and take hold of the instrument. Then it will appear here.

Tracy projected her intention back into the physical world. It felt weird, like having half of her body submerged inside a swimming pool and the other half completely dry outside. She reached down and took hold of the flute. Then she consciously moved away from the physical and back into the weightless environment where Granny Sybs was waiting. Much to her surprise, she took the flute with her, just as Granny Sybs has said.

Well done. Now, lift it to your lips and blow.

Tracy blew into the flute, gently at first, but then harder. Tracy noticed that the spiritual world was just like the vacuum of space, devoid of any sound, which is why she couldn't hear her grandmother speak except inside her head, so she was surprised when the sound of the flute ripped through the fabric of the world she was in with such alacrity.

How? Tracy questioned.

The universe is filled with music. It's made out of music. Celestial music. So when you hear the flute, it's connecting with the universe in song. Everything in the universe is music.

How so?

Everything in the physical world is matter vibrating at a particular frequency. So, it stands to reason that every single object has a unique frequency or song. Match the frequency of an object, and you control its properties.

But what about here, in the spiritual realm? There are no physical objects. There is no matter. What then is the point of playing the flute? Tracy was beginning to get frustrated. Why did her grandmother bring her here if the flute had no power over physical objects or things?

Ah, but you're wrong, said Sybs as if she was reading Tracy's thoughts. *Remember what I said about everything in physicality existing here, in this place?*

Tracy nodded, yet she was still confused by her grandmother's contradiction. How could physical things also exist in the spiritual?

There is a balance in all things, Tracy. Disturb that balance, and there is an imbalance. Instability. Chaos. Find the frequency of the object or thing that you are trying to affect, connect with it, and you take control. You take control of that object, that physical thing. In the real world, when you find and connect with the frequency of a physical object, you can to take control of it and move it. But when you connect to the frequency of an object in this world, the spiritual, you can change its very properties.

Tracy was silent for a moment. Silent with her thoughts as she gradually took in what Sybs was elucidating to her.

That means...

You have the power to destroy things; reduce them to piles of ash.

Tracy's mind raced.

But... what about... living things?

Living beings, much like animated objects, are far more complicated, Sybs explained. *They're made up of multiple frequencies. Very hard to scan and even harder to connect with.*

So that's what it's called? Scanning an object?

Correct, said Sybs. *You're learning quickly. I'm impressed. That's the first step. Okay, enough for now. It's time to return to the physical world.*

Tracy closed her eyes and focused on her breathing once more. She was surprised at herself for the ease at which she navigated into and through the astral realm. Maybe it was because Sybs was with her, guiding her, facilitating the process, and yet her instincts deep down inside told her that it was because she had evolved, become enlightened somehow, just as her grandmother had said. Tracy opened her eyes and found herself back in the bedroom, staring deep into her grandmother's radiant face. In her dreamlike state, she half-expected Sybs' voice to come to her again inside her head, even though she knew it was impossible.

"How are you feeling?" Sybs eventually whispered.

"Fine."

"Good. Now for the second lesson." Sybs stood up, went over to her dresser, and returned with her hairbrush. She handed it to Tracy, who looked at it askance.

"I don't need…"

"It's not for your hair," said Sybs interrupting her in mid-sentence. "I want you to examine it. Study its shape and form. Hold it close and then further away. This is your second lesson."

"But I don't understand."

"Just do as I say. You will understand soon enough."

Tracy did as her grandmother instructed. She stared at the brush, slowly turning it over in her hands. Shiny, black plastic with a black, rubber handle. She felt the grooves in the rubber and ran her hands over the dozens of bristles protruding from a deep-red, rubbery cushion, with tiny, round tips on the ends, that reminded her of one of those wiry head massager thingy's. She brought the brush up close to her face and looked at the

350

strands of her grandmother's hair caught between the bristles. She held the brush at arm's length and took in the size, shape, and weight of the brush, before looking expectantly up at her grandmother.

"Good, good. Now place the brush down on the floor but don't lose focus with it. Keep on looking at it. That's it. Now, what do you see? Look beyond the brush. Take your time."

Tracy's eyes were beginning to burn as she stared at the brush. She tried not to blink. And then she thought that it moved like it was vibrating. She blinked. She saw an outline; a blue outline. It glowed. No. It pulsed. "I see something," she whispered. "Something blue." She blinked again, but the colour remained, and it still pulsed and shifted beyond the shape of the brush.

"That's it," whispered Sybs excitedly. "You can see it; the energy. The frequency of the brush. Does it pulse with a life of its own?"

Tracy nodded, still silently staring at the brush. Her eyes were beginning to water. "Like it's breathing. Like it's alive."

"Everything on this planet pulses with a unique frequency. Study each thing long enough, and you will see it; an aura that is alive with energy. Without realising it, when you play the flute and focus on an object, you can connect to the frequency of that object and raise it off the ground, defying the laws of gravity. Now that you know how to recognise the frequency of objects, you can connect to almost anything and move it."

"Even heavy objects? That's impossible."

Sybs smiled. "I'm sure you've heard that the word impossible, spells, I'm possible, right? When you say impossible, you are really saying that anything is possible."

"Funny, Gran. No, really, how do you expect me to lift anything bigger and heavier than this brush?"

"If you were listening, then you would understand that it's got nothing to do with the weight or size of an object, but rather the frequency at which it's vibrating. Now, turn your attention to this chair," said Sybs, pointing at the chair pushed into her dresser. She walked over to the chair, pulled it out, and turned it around to face Tracy. "Study it. Go on, get up, and take a good look at it," she urged her.

The wooden chair was painted white and had a soft, lime-green coloured seat with tiny white flowers stitched into it. Tracy ran her hands over the frame, from the front all the way over to the back. She took note of all the tiny scratches and uneven sections. She scrutinised the paintwork and examined the stitching in the fabric. She took a step backward and surveyed it from afar. "Okay. I'm done."

"Can you see its energy?"

"Not yet." Tracy stood still and stared at the chair for a few moments. "There. I see it now," she said as a faint blue aura shimmered at the edge of her peripheral vision.

"Good. Now, pick up the flute." Sybs pointed at the instrument lying on the floor.

Tracy picked up the flute.

"Keep looking at the chair while you blow into the flute. You will need to match the note that you play with the frequency of the chair."

"But how will I know when I do?"

"Oh, you'll know," said Sybs with a grin. "You'll know."

Tracy blew into the flute, all the while staring at the chair. And then she watched, as Sybs took a seat on the chair and folded her arms across her lap. Tracy moved her fingers deftly over the holes, changing key. She blinked. The blue aura of the chair vibrated faster like the snow on a television out of tune. She maintained this key, blowing even harder into the flute. Then she heard a buzzing in her ears like there were hundreds of bees around her head. She focused on the chair like she did on the remote control, and it magically began to lift up into the air. Tracy was so shocked that she lost focus and stopped blowing, and the chair dropped to the ground with a thud. Sybs held onto the sides of the chair as it rocked once from left to right before coming to a standstill.

"I did it!" squealed Tracy. "I really did it!" She dropped the flute and ran over to hug her grandmother.

"I knew you would get it right," said Sybs. "Well done!" she beamed. "Now, you must practise because practice makes perfect."

Tracy picked up the flute again in awe, slowly shaking her head in disbelief. "It's incredible that something this tiny has the power to do that," she said, pointing at the chair.

"I told you it's not about the size or weight."

"Yes, I know, it's about the frequency at which the object is vibrating. But it still feels unbelievable. Can we try it again?"

Sybs laughed. "Yes, of course, my dear, but I'm afraid I've had enough of being lifted into the air. Why not try it on my bed?"

Tracy looked at the bed and then back at Sybs with wide eyes. Sybs just shrugged her shoulders and smiled. Tracy turned back to focus her attention on the bed. She slowly traced its outline, walking around the other side and bending down to gaze beneath it, before returning to stand in front of it. She stared at the bed long and hard, closed her eyes to slits and brought the flute up to her mouth. She took the deepest breath she could muster and let it go, pushing it into the narrow, shiny, carbon-fibre instrument and the most beautiful, long, high-pitched tone came forth. The bed responded almost immediately, like an obedient dog to its master's voice. It made a scraping noise on the floor and then gradually lifted into the air. It kept rising until it was at least three feet in the air. Tracy eventually ran out of breath, and the sound from the flute began to fade. The bed slowly lowered back down and then dropped the last few inches, landing on the floor with a bang.

"Well done, Trace," said Sybs proudly.

"Thanks, Gran. This is incredible. Thank you, thank you, thank you!"

"But I didn't do anything," said Sybs. "It was all you." She winked at Tracy.

Richard Gradner - Acoustic Alchemy

50 ~ Pain

Tracy couldn't sleep. She tossed and turned in her bed. Her mind raced. All the images in her head were outlined in cobalt blue. She rolled onto her back and stared up at the ceiling. She touched the crystal around her neck and closed her eyes. The images gradually began to fade until she found herself floating through a grey, insipid wilderness, devoid of any colour. It was as if someone had edited the scene, selected the black and white contrast option in her photo library, and then hit save, changing the properties of the environment forever. She looked down but couldn't see her feet. They were concealed by a thick, low-hanging mist that swirled around her ankles like the steam that poured out of a block of dry ice as it melted directly into gas from its solid state.

Something caught Tracy's eye as she looked ahead. Something shiny. Something red. Colour. Colour had returned to this place. Tracy moved towards it, intrigued by the anomaly. It moved, so she followed it. She looked down at her arms. They were bleached white. Colourless. Her clothes. Colourless. Everything was without colour like it had been washed away, except for the red glowing thingy. It continued to move, so she followed it. The funny thing was, she could never get any closer.

354

The more she tried to reach it, the further away it moved. When she moved, it moved, as if it was anticipating her advancements. She concentrated harder, attempting to move faster towards it and then it just disappeared, winking out of existence. She continued to move towards where she last saw it and then she was falling, sliding down some sort of imaginary slope, into the mist that was now thick in front of her face as she fell. There was no gravity in this place, so technically she wasn't really falling and yet she knew she was going down. Definitely not up. Down.

The grey gloom gradually became darker, until Tracy could see no more than a few yards in front of her. The mist appeared to have cleared, and the red light had returned, the only beacon in this barren wasteland. She trudged on, following the moving target as it led her forward. *Forward*. She told herself. *At least I'm moving forward*. The light disappeared again and she found herself in complete darkness. She turned around, straining to see something, anything, but to no avail. And then it returned - the red light. But this time, it was moving towards her. It created an aura, a glow that lit up what looked like a silhouette beneath it. Tracy froze. The light was making a bee-line directly towards her, and as it came closer, Tracy could now clearly make out someone beneath it. A figure, concealed by a cowl, a hoodie pulled over his head. Or her head.

The figure stopped about ten feet away. The red light was coming from the end of a long staff held in the character's right hand. It cast an eerie red glow that was quickly engulfed by the thick, clammy mist. Tracy strained her eyes to see who was beneath the hood but to no avail.

"Hello?" Her voice sounded muffled, as the mist quickly consumed it like a hungry beast. "Who are you? What do you want?"

"Traceeee," rasped the figure.

Tracy gulped in fear. She had heard that voice before. Her dream. Her vision. By the fire. Tracy was still frozen, unable to move a muscle. Her eyes widened as the character slowly lifted

355

her head. The hoodie dropped back to reveal a striking face with scarred cheeks and piercing eyes. "Sabine," Tracy whispered.

"Yesss. My Sisssterrr." Her snake-like, rasping reminded Tracy of Bagheera, the infamous snake from *The Jungle Book*. "Come with me. Join usss."

Tracy was starting to shiver. She crossed her arms, wrapping them tightly across her chest. She couldn't speak.

"Your powers are strong. Together we can rule. Together we can be stronger than anything. Stronger than anyone. Come. Join usss." She raised her hand.

Tracy could make out the smirk on Sabine's face through the thick, hazy mist. She still couldn't speak but managed to move her head from side to side in refusal.

Sabine lowered her arm and within the beat of a heart was standing inches away from Tracy. "Lasst chance," she hissed. The glow from the staff cast them both in red, mesmerising light.

Tracy opened her mouth. "No," she whispered. "Never."

Sabine placed her hand over Tracy's face, and she reeled. A flood of macabre images flooded her head. Grotesque flashes of blood and gore, ghastly visions of death and destruction, fire and carnage. She was witness to an Armageddon that was to come, an end of days that brought with it Hell on Earth.

"Noooooo!" Tracy bellowed with all her might, and watched, as the power of her scream blasted the fires of Hell into smouldering embers like the shock-wave following a tremendous explosion.

Sabine snapped her hand away from Tracy's face. "Yesss." She grinned. "You *do* have the power." She brought her staff down, touching the fiery red light to Tracy's left shoulder and a jolt of scalding pain shot down her arm, causing her to drop down onto her knees in agony. "Aaaaaah!" she yelled, grabbing the end of the staff with her right hand to push it away. The pain shot down her other arm as soon as she touched the rod. She buckled even more. The pain was unbearable. It coursed through her body like an electric current. She felt as if she was

356

being roasted alive. Her breathing became ragged, and her lungs burned with every breath she drew into her ravaged body. There was no end in sight to this terrifying torture that Tracy realised was gradually sucking the very life out of her. Her vision began to blur, and the bright, red light began to fade. She closed her eyes and let go, succumbing to the pain, giving in to the forces that threatened to crush her very soul from existence.

◊ ◊ ◊

The pain was just a dull ache, a visceral sensation, completely devoid of any shape or form. She couldn't feel her body. It was as if she had left it somewhere and journeyed to this place of emptiness, this place of nothingness. Nothing. Just her detached thoughts, floating in a sea of nihility. Even her feelings were numb. She felt nothing, could see nothing; she *was* nothing. There was nowhere to go, nowhere to be but here in this place where she was safe from the torture. Safe from the pain.

Pain.

It was such a foreign thing. Just another feeling that she couldn't experience any longer. She drifted. Alone. Free. But was she free? She knew not what it was like to feel freedom. Freedom was just another feeling that she didn't have, that she couldn't experience because all feeling was gone. If she was not free, then was she confined? Confined to this place? Trapped for all eternity?

Something tugged at her mind, a flicker, a thought. A familiarity. A voice. She pushed it away, disregarded its pull and moved deeper into the void. But it wouldn't go away. It was persistent, like a mosquito. Buzzing. Irritating. She turned to face it and opened her eyes but she could not see. The voice became more coherent.

Lokah.

This time she heard it.

Lokah samastah… Lokah samastah sukhino bhavantu…

357

The words triggered a memory, a distant memory. Let all beings be happy and free. The words came again and again, repeated, over and over, buzzing louder and more persistent in her ears.

Lokah samastah sukhino bhavantu. Lokah samastah sukhino bhavantu. Lokah samastah sukhino bhavantu.

She tried to open her eyes again, and a slither of light broke through the heavy veil of her eyelids, piercing her eyeballs like a knife, causing her intense pain.

Pain.

She could feel it again. She welcomed the pain and then regretted it straight after. The pain was excruciating. It pulsed from her left shoulder down her arm like it was on fire. She still couldn't move, and when she tried to, the pain increased in magnitude until it felt as if she was going to return to the void, the empty place. The place where she could feel nothing. The place where she was alone. The place where she was pain-free.

"Tracy. Tracy."

She recognised the voice. It was her grandmother, Granny Sybs. She opened her mouth to speak, and all that came out was a croaking sound. Her throat burned, and her eyes watered.

"Shhh my child, shhh. Close your eyes. Rest now," she said reassuringly.

Tracy felt her grandmother's soft fingers slide down over her face, gently pulling her eyelids closed, wiping away her tears.

"Will she be okay?" said Camilla, deep concern in her voice.

"In time," replied Sybs. "I've given her some meds for the pain. She needs rest."

"What… how did this happen?" said Camilla, clearly distraught.

"It… it's hard to explain," said Sybs. "She has been… attacked in her sleep, in her dreams. I take full responsibility."

"It's these new powers that she has inherited, isn't it?"

Sybs sighed. "I'm afraid so. But if I hadn't prepared her as I did, things could have been a lot worse."

"Worse? Worse than this? Just look at her. She looks half

dead!"

"Shhh," said Sybs placing her finger across her lips. "Come, let's go and speak downstairs."

"Will she be all right here, all alone?"

"Yes, yes, of course," said Sybs reassuringly. "She is under my protection now. As I said, it's my fault. I should have been more vigilant. Come," she said, beckoning to Camilla.

Camilla leaned over Tracy. "Oh, my child," she said woefully, while gently squeezing her hand, before turning to follow Sybs out of the room.

The pain became a dull ache as the medicine began to release inside Tracy's body. Her ragged breathing became more regular as she drifted off into a deep and peaceful sleep.

◊ ◊ ◊

Camilla sat with her elbows on the table and her hands over her face. She dropped her head and ran her fingers through her dusty blond hair. "Will it heal?"

"You mean the mark?" said Sybs.

"Yes. What is it? Where did it come from?"

Sybs sighed. "It's complicated."

"Humour me. She's my daughter, Mom. Stop hiding all this shit from me. I know I don't share what you and Tracy have in terms of your… your… ugh, whatever you call it," she said waving her hand flippantly through the air. "But I have a right to know what's going on, dammit!"

"Okay, okay, Cammy. Calm down. Take a deep breath. Let me explain. Look at me."

Camilla lifted her chin.

"I said, take a deep breath."

Camilla drew in a breath and sighed heavily.

"Yes. That's it. Okay. So, the girl Sabine…"

Camilla opened her mouth to speak, but Sybs raised her hand to silence her.

"Yes, the same girl who killed Marjorie and stole the flute.

359

She came after Tracy."

Camilla opened her mouth once more, but Sybs raised her hand to silence her yet again. "Let me finish. Right. So, as I was saying, it was Sabine. She tracked Tracy down and hurt her."

"But how? The alarm was on, and the house was locked."

"This is where it gets complicated," explained Sybs. "Bear with me. I've been teaching Tracy about her newfound gift and how to use it. A lot of our visions come to us in our dreams. Well, they're more than just dreams - they're part of the spiritual realm, and it's also where we're able to experience conscious awareness. It's hard to explain, but just know that it's where intuition is born."

"Intuition? You mean like deja vu?"

"Hmm. Same but different. Deja vu is the feeling you get when you think you've seen or experienced something before. Intuition is that feeling you have in your gut when you know something without having proof."

"Ah. I see."

"Most people experience deja vu from time to time. Tracy and I experience intuition. *All* the time. We know things before they happen. When we travel to the spiritual realm, we experience the source of the intuition. Its origin. Intuition is far more powerful there as a result, which means that our visions are stronger, clearer. Because we can connect to intuition in this way, we are more vulnerable there."

"I don't think I follow you," said Camilla creasing her brow.

"Most people subconsciously travel into the spiritual realm when they dream. This means that they have no control there and don't remember much either. Tracy and I can consciously step into this domain. It's similar to diving into the ocean or going for a spacewalk. You travel to another environment where you still have control over your actions. But it's dangerous. If you run out of oxygen underwater, you'll drown. If your space-suit gets punctured, the vacuum of space will cause asphyxiation. In the spiritual realm, because we have full control and awareness of our spiritual bodies, they are vulnerable and

360

can be hurt. If our spiritual bodies are hurt, our physical bodies also suffer. This is what happened to Tracy."

"So are you saying that this Sabine also has your abilities and that she attacked Tracy while she was dreaming?"

"Yes. Exactly. That red mark on her collarbone is a burn that she experienced while she was asleep. Sabine came to her while she was in the spiritual realm and attacked her, burning her deeply. This destructive energy coursed through her body like a very powerful virus, almost killing her. She was brave. She fought back."

"How do you know?"

Sybs smiled. "Intuition."

"Do spiritual wounds heal quicker than physical ones?"

"Good question. Yes. She should be okay within 24 hours. She'll be very weak, but the red mark will fade. She is young and will regenerate her internal fire quite quickly. She is also in flux, which helps a lot."

"Flux?"

Sybs grinned. "Another story for another day."

51 ~ Healing

"I came as soon as I heard," said Lisa as she sat on the edge of the bed. "You look like shit."

Tracy managed a smile. "Thanks for the encouragement," she said. Her throat was still very sore, so all she could muster was a whisper.

"No, I'm serious Trace, your eyes are red, your skin is all puffy. Is it contagious?"

Tracy shook her head.

"Good, cos I have a date tonight, and the last thing I need is to get sick."

"A date? You didn't tell me. With who? Danny? Danny Gordon?"

Lisa smirked.

"No. You didn't."

Lisa nodded. "Ha-ha! I did, I did!" she yelped, bouncing up and down on the bed. "I asked him out on a date! Oops, sorry," she said apologetically, as she saw Tracy grit her teeth, pull a pain-face and grip the sheet with clenched fists.

"It's okay. It's just my shoulder. It's pretty sore, and the bouncing doesn't really help. Sorry."

"Hey, *I'm* sorry, bae. What kind of sickness is this anyway? I mean, why your shoulder?"

"It's some kind of body virus that's caused my shoulder to become inflamed," whispered Tracy. "Look," she said, pulling her top down.

"Ow! That looks nasty," said Lisa, eyeing the big, red welt.

"It's already much better than it was. Granny Sybs has been applying some of her special magic ointment. She said it would be better soon."

"Amazing. I think I need some too."

"What for? You all right?"

"It's just for backup."

"What do you mean?"

"Well, I'm taking my Dad's car tonight, and he doesn't know. The ointment might come in handy if I don't return the car in one piece."

Tracy closed her eyes for a moment. "You'll be fine," she whispered. "You'll take care of the car and bring it back just fine."

"What, are you some kind of guru now?"

Tracy opened her eyes and winked.

"Yeah, whatever. I'd rather be prepared, just in case. Oh, wait, I brought you something," Lisa rummaged in her purse. "Here," she said, throwing Tracy a small, rectangular box, wrapped in purple foil with a matching purple bow tied neatly around it.

Tracy tore it open. "Vosges Truffles! My fave. Thanks, Lis."

"Oh, no worries. It's an assorted mix. Enjoy."

"You're the best."

Lisa grinned.

"Hey, you still haven't told me where you're taking Danny."

"I told him just because I asked him out, doesn't mean I get to choose where we go. I'm leaving that to him."

"Clever. So, is it a surprise?"

"No. He said he wants to take me to the movies, to see that new movie with that girl from Fifty Shades, you know, Melanie Griffith's daughter? It's called Love Bite."

"Dakota Johnson. Hooo. I've heard it's pretty steamy."

"I dunno why but I'm really pretty nervous."

"You? *The* Lisa Fitzgerald? Nervous? Come on. Are you blushing? I don't believe it."

"It must be that image of him wrapped in his towel that's just got me, you know?"

"Um… no, not really." This time it was Tracy's turn to grin.

"It's like there's this other side of him that I don't even know. It feels more like a blind date."

"Lis. Believe me, when I say, I'm sure he's shitting bricks. He probably hasn't even dated before. It's Danny Gordon. Gordo, for fuck's sake. The geek at school with the glasses."

"Thanks, Trace for trying to make me feel better, but I saw him half-naked. I promise you, even you would have done a double-take."

"You'll be fine, Lis. You're one of the most confident girls I know."

"It might look like it, but most of the time, inside, I'm a mess."

"Well, like you always tell me, the best accessory a girl can own is confidence. You gotta own it girl."

Lisa laughed out loud, and Tracy did her best to laugh with her, despite the fire in her throat.

"Now, that's funny," said Lisa. "Tracy Barnes giving *me* dating advice."

"Well, sometimes there comes a time when even *you* need to listen to what you preach. Puts things in perspective, right?"

Lisa sighed. "Sure thing." She smiled. "Love you, bae," she said, giving Tracy a hug, careful not to touch her shoulder. "Gotta go. Getting my hair done at four."

"Thanks, Lis for popping in."

"You take good care of yourself, all right? Call me if you need anything," said Lisa, shaking her finger in the air.

"I'll be fine," whispered Tracy. "Good luck for tonight. Let me know how it goes."

"Mwah!" She blew Tracy a kiss and bounced out the door.

52 ~ Memories

Tracy slept for the rest of the afternoon and right through the night. She woke just after 5am the next morning with a rumbling stomach. She was famished. She climbed out of bed, went straight to the kitchen, and poured herself a glass of ice-cold milk. She drank it down in one gulp. "Aaahhhhhhhh" she breathed out loudly and then wiped her mouth with the back of her hand. It tasted so good. She stepped into the bathroom and looked at herself in the mirror. Her cheeks were rosy red, and her eyes sparkled. She was feeling much, much better. She pulled down her top and scrutinised her shoulder. The red mark had faded to dark pink. She prodded it softly. It was still tender but so much better than before. She smiled at herself in the mirror. "Tracy Barnes, you are looking sooo much better," she pipped. She winked at herself and then strode confidently back to her room.

Tracy's heart skipped a beat when she was surprised to find Granny Sybs sitting quietly on the cream-coloured couch in her room. "Gran! You frightened me."

Sybs chuckled. "Me? Frighten you?"

"Oh, you know what I mean. I never expected to see you here. What are you doing in my room so early?"

"I knew you were up, so I wanted to see how you were doing. You're looking much better!"

"I feel much better, thanks. That ointment you put on my shoulder worked wonders. Look!" said Tracy, showing her grandmother the faded pink mark.

"Hmmm," she mused, examining the wound. "Yes. Looks much better. Good. Come, sit," said Sybs, shifting up on the couch.

Tracy pulled her top back over her shoulder and sat down. "Gran."

"Yes, dear."

"How are we going to stop Sabine?"

Sybs sighed. "With my help."

"I remember everything."

Sybs looked expectedly at Tracy. "Tell me."

"It was Sabine"

"I know."

"She spoke to me. She said, 'join us.' Did she mean her and her grandmother?"

Sybs nodded. "Yes. Did you see her too?"

"No," replied Tracy, shaking her head. "Just Sabine. I was dreaming, yet it felt so real."

"Lucid dreaming. It wasn't your dream; it was hers. She came looking for you."

"Why?"

"She recognises your power. Together, the two of you will be a formidable force. That's why she tried to convert you."

"I fought back."

"I know."

"But she was too strong. She had this... this long staff with red energy. It burned," said Tracy, inadvertently touching her shoulder. She closed her eyes and shivered, recollecting the disturbing images she witnessed. "She showed me things. She put her hand on my face, and I saw... the future?"

"A possible future," corrected Sybs.

"There was fire and death and destruction. It was horrible.

Everything was dead or dying and burning. I could sense that she was happy, but like really ecstatic, in a crazy mad kind of way."

Sybs squeezed Tracy's hand.

"And then when I fought back when I screamed 'no,' she burned me with that thing, and then I think I must have passed out because everything went quiet all around me."

"It's okay, my child," said Sybs reassuringly. "I'm sorry I should have been there. I could have stopped her."

"It's all right, Gran. I'm okay now," said Tracy with a smile. "Thanks to you."

Sybs returned the smile.

"Where do you think she is?"

"Oh, we'll find her. Now that I know she's near, we'll find her just like she found you. This old bag still has a few tricks up her sleeve," said Sybs with a grin. She looked at her watch. "5.30. Go and get some more rest. You'll need your strength."

"When will we find her?"

"Soon, my dear, soon. I've got some work to do," said Sybs, winking at Tracy. She stood up, straightened out her nightgown and made her way back to her bedroom.

Tracy climbed back into bed, turned onto her side, pulled her duvet over her shoulder, closed her eyes, and quickly drifted off to sleep.

◊ ◊ ◊

Sybs closed her bedroom door, took a cushion from her bed, and placed it on the floor in the centre of her room. She sat down on the cushion and crossed her legs, pulling left over right into a half-lotus position. She reached inside her nightgown and pulled out a stone from around her neck. It was similar in size and shape to Tracy's amethyst, except that it was clear. She carefully removed the crystal from around her neck and held it up to the light. It sparkled, catching the light and reflecting it in a rainbow of colours like a twinkling star. She closed her eyes and remembered the moment that she received it from her grandmother so many moons ago.

"I have something special for you, dearest," said her grandmother, handing Sybs a black velvet bag.

"What is it?" said Sybs.

"Take a look."

Sybs pulled open the drawstring and reached inside. She even remembered the feeling she got when she first touched the cold, hard stone. An electric current shot through her fingers and she yanked her hand out instinctively. "Yikes! What is that?"

Her grandmother smiled. "Try again."

"But it's gonna give me another shock."

"Try again," insisted her grandmother.

Sybs reluctantly pushed her hand back into the bag. She sucked in a breath, bracing herself for the electric current once more, but instead, her hand closed over the crystal inside with no ill effects whatsoever.

"How come it's fine now?"

"Sometimes it happens, but just once," said her grandmother. "It's a defence mechanism. After that, the stone knows you. You know the stone."

"The stone knows me. Ha. You're kidding, aren't you? How does a stone have a conscience? It's just a stone."

Sybs' grandmother smiled. "Oh, it's much more than that. It's a powerful talisman passed down through many generations of seers. Deep within it is an incarnation of a divine being. One day, you will pass it on. One day when you die."

Sybs drew in a short, sharp breath. "Are you going to die Nanna?"

"Not yet," she smiled. "This crystal is yours, and I still have mine, see?" she said, removing a pink amethyst from beneath her top. I will give this one to you and then one day you will pass it on to your granddaughter."

"It's so pretty," said Sybs, admiring the pink stone.

"Here, let me put yours on," said her grandmother attaching the leather cord around Sybs' neck.

Sybs looked down at the crystal resting on her chest.

"It's quartz, a very powerful healing energy amplifier, and the ultimate balancing stone."

"Balancing? What do you mean?" said Sybs.

"When you focus your intention on the crystal, it balances your mood, your chakra, and even your immune system when you are sick."

"Wow," said Sybs in awe as she gazed down at the stone resting benignly against her chest.

"Another amazing quality that quartz crystals have is their ability to protect their users from negative energy," said her grandmother. "When it rests against your chest between the heart and solar plexus chakras, as you are wearing it now, it will keep your aura perfectly clear. Remember that. It will stand you in good stead to be aware of your crystal's power of protection."

Sybs opened her eyes and gazed around her bedroom. A slither of light shone out of the left side of the curtain, illuminating the room in a soft, warm glow. She shifted on her cushion, pushing herself up to stand and then pulled the curtain open slightly to really let the sunshine in. She returned to sit down on her cushion, facing the window to allow the sun to bask directly onto her face. She crossed her legs the other way around and then fastened the crystal around her neck. She took hold of the crystal in both hands and silently repeated her intention into the crystal. She cleared her throat and then began to repeat the same intention verbally. "Guide me safely through the spirit realm, protect me from the negative forces of energy that thwart to harm me, and allow me to return unharmed." She repeated this mantra seven times in total and then sat in silence for a few moments, allowing her intention to sync with the crystal, until it was programmed like the RAM inside a computer, ready to be accessed with the power of a single thought.

53 ~ Pedro

"What we got Trudeau?" said Chief Williams, leaning over Trudeau's desk.

Trudeau turned his screen around to face the Chief. "Pedro Sanchez. Security guard at UBS Bank, Chicago."

"Was he there during the robbery?"

"He was on his shift outside the bank. But I have reason to believe that he played a part."

"Inside job then," said the Chief. "Where's your evidence?"

"I spoke with Sanchez at the crime scene."

"When was this?"

Trudeau coughed. "Um, while the crime was being committed."

"You what?!" Chief Williams banged both fists on the desk. "What the hell are you saying, Trudeau?"

"I received a tip-off that the suspect in the recent killings was inside the building, so I went over to chat to the guard outside to see if he knew anything. I had no idea that there was a robbery in progress. It's in my report."

"I don't care about your fucking report, Trudeau, I care about results, and this isn't one of them. What makes you think that this Sanchez is anything more than a UBS security guard?

Where is he now?"

"That's what we're busy trying to find out, Sir. We gave chase when the perps came flying out of the building. When we returned to the bank, Sanchez was nowhere to be found. He was also unusually anxious while I was questioning him. More like shitting bricks."

"Sure sounds like our man!"

"Yes, Sir."

"Let me know when you find him," said the Chief turning to leave the office. "Oh, and Trudeau, don't fuck this one up," he growled, thrusting his middle finger into the air on the way out.

◊ ◊ ◊

Trudeau tightened the straps on his FBI-issue flak jacket and stepped out of the silver Chrysler. Agent Leonie Brorson, a seasoned field agent from the Bureau, climbed out the other side and followed Trudeau as he made his way towards the five-storey apartment block in Harwood Heights, Chicago. Brorson was 35 years old with dark brown hair and matching brown eyes. She wore a navy blue, NY-branded baseball cap. A ponytail stuck out the back of her cap, swaying from side to side as she walked. Brorson was fit, thanks to her intense training regime at *Powerup*, a local CrossFit gym in her neighbourhood. She was proud to be currently placed second on the gym's fitness challenge board, next to Mel Jefferson, a girl ten years her junior who had just entered *Ninja Warrior* for the third time. Brorson's muscular arms bulged against her cotton shirt as she walked. She touched her firearm reassuringly at her waist as she made her way up the stairs to the building's entrance.

Sanchez was proving to be quite elusive as expected. His registered address in the Bronx turned up empty, but Trudeau's latest intel led him here, to his half-brother Emilio's apartment. Emilio went by a different last name, so it took Trudeau a little longer to confirm the connection. Trudeau smiled. He could smell his prize. It was close now. He had never told anyone before, but Trudeau staunchly believed in fate. He believed that there was a higher power that controlled everything. He believed that because he took the time to focus his intention on his belief, things that happened around him were meant to be. He believed that his acceptance of things this way gave him a sixth sense of what was to come; a kind of intuition. That's what he felt now. It was a euphoric feeling of anxiety mixed with triumph, and it made him feel really good.

Trudeau pressed the silver buzzer to apartment 402. He held it down for four long seconds, took a step back, and looked up the front of the building. He already knew that 402 was the second apartment, just left out the elevator. He saw the flash of a face in one of the windows and then proceeded to push all the buttons on the door panel. He waited no longer than a few seconds before the glass-framed door buzzed open, allowing both him and Brorson to enter the building. Trudeau turned to Brorson and then pointed at the elevator. He took the stairs, bounding up the steps two at a time. By the time he reached the fourth floor, he was out of breath. He pushed open the landing door just as Brorson stepped out of the elevator.

Brorson looked at Trudeau. "The roof," she said, pointing up. Trudeau pulled open the fire-escape door and ran up the steps with Brorson in tow. He pulled out his Glock 19M just as he reached the top floor, cocked his weapon with a click and held it with both hands outstretched in front of him. The rooftop door was slightly ajar. Trudeau pressed his index finger to his lips and carefully pushed the door open. He crouched down and slowly shuffled outside and onto the roof.

"Sanchez!" Trudeau called. "FBI. There's nowhere to go. Give it up!"

"What do you want?!" Sanchez shouted in return.

"We just want to talk!"

"Bullshit!"

Trudeau edged further out onto the roof and then ran to hide behind the lift shaft. Brorson was hot on his heels. Sanchez fired a shot that ricocheted across the rooftop.

"We have Maria!" shouted Trudeau. "And little Catalina. Drop your weapon and come out with your hands in the air so that we can talk!"

Silence.

"Cover me," whispered Trudeau to Brorson as he stepped out from behind the lift shaft. He knew that Sanchez would never risk his family over this. "I'm coming out," he said. He placed his Glock on the floor next to him and raised his hands in the air. "I've dropped my weapon. Sanchez! Come out now, and this will all be over. If you cooperate, everything will be fine. That's my promise to you."

Silence. Trudeau waited for a few agonising minutes, and then Sanchez stepped out with his hands in the air. "You gotta promise to let my family go," he said.

"I promise," replied Trudeau. "They are in custody. Safe and sound. Just come with us and everything will be all right. Okay?"

"Okay," said Sanchez hanging his head.

Brorson stepped out, cuffed Sanchez and marched him towards the stairs. "Good job, Trudeau," she said.

Trudeau picked up his Glock and winked at Brorson. "Not too bad yourself," he remarked.

◊ ◊ ◊

"I want to see them," said Pedro looking up at Trudeau from the square, shiny stainless steel table inside the interrogation room. He shifted his feet, and the chain around his ankles rattled on the cold cement floor.

Trudeau stood on the other side of the table, with his foot on the empty chair and his elbow resting on his knee. He carefully examined the fingernails of his left hand. "All you need to do is tell me what I need to know first," he said.

"They'll kill them."

"Who will kill whom?"

373

"My family. They'll find my family. They'll kill them. It's all I have." Tears welled up in Pedro's eyes.

"They are safe and sound with us. No one is going to kill them."

"You don't know them. They're monsters. Killers."

"You're talking about MS13, aren't you?"

Pedro was silent.

"I need names. Who are they? Where do they live?"

Silence.

"If you don't talk, I'll let your wife and daughter go. Who's gonna protect them then? Who's gonna protect them when MS13 knows that you ratted them out?"

"What do you mean? I'm not saying nothin'," he spat on the floor.

"Yeah, but what do you think they'll do when we let the word out that we have you in custody?"

Pedro looked up at Trudeau. "No. You wouldn't. My family. They'll kill them."

"Maybe."

"How did you find them?" said Pedro looking up at Trudeau.

"We intercepted them on the way to Mexico. Did you think they'd be safer there? Come on, Mr. Sanchez," said Trudeau, his words dripping with sarcasm. "You know that MS13 are everywhere. That was a risky thing you did, sending your wife and child away. Sweet Catalina."

The tears began to roll down Pedro's face. "I was just trying to protect them," he mumbled.

"If you tell us what we need to know, we will place all of you in our witness protection programme."

"They'll still find us."

"No, they won't, Mr. Sanchez. We have thousands of people in the programme, some just like you and your family, and they're all safe and sound. You'll get new identities, and we'll move you far away from here. You'll get a new job, a new name, a new home. All you have to do is talk, Mr. Sanchez. Just tell me what I need to know." Trudeau folded his arms and smiled.

Pedro wiped his face with the back of his sleeve and stared at his reflection in the two-way mirror, while Chief Williams and Agent Brorson watched intently from the observation room on the other side.

"He's gonna crack," said Brorson.

"Looks like it," said the Chief.

"Okay. I'll talk," said Sanchez.

"Excellent," said Trudeau, opening a file lying on the desk. "I'm going to show you some pictures. All that I want you to do is confirm if you recognise anyone in them and what their roles were in the robbery, okay?"

Pedro nodded.

Trudeau opened the file and spun it around to face Sanchez. "Here's the first one. Take your time."

Pedro shook his head. "Don't know him."

"You sure? Marco Rodriguez."

Pedro shook his head again. "No. Never seen him before."

Trudeau flipped the page. "How about him?" he said, pointing at the next picture. It was another mugshot of a man in a white vest. Markings covered both of his arms.

Pedro nodded. "I recognise him. Pinto. His name is Pinto."

"Was he involved in the robbery?"

Pedro closed his eyes, trying to remember. "I never saw him there that night. No."

"Okay," said Trudeau, turning the page. "How about this one? He goes by the name of…" Trudeau stepped around the table, tilting his head to one side so that he could read the small, printed letters on the page. "Julian Domingo Martinez."

Pedro nodded.

"What? I can't hear you."

"Yeah, he's one of them."

"He was there that night? The night of the robbery?"

Pedro nodded again. He looked up at Trudeau with fear in his eyes.

Trudeau looked at the profile photo. Martinez looked to be

in his 50's. Heavily tattooed markings covered his face and body. "Hmmm. It says here that he has served a total of sixteen years of his life incarcerated across four different prisons. It also says he has several known associates, in particular, this man," he continued, flipping through the file until he reached what he was looking for. He stepped back to observe the reaction on Sanchez's face.

Sanchez baulked, just as Trudeau expected he would. He gripped the table with both hands, clearly exhibiting angst and fear.

"He was there too, right?"

Pedro sat frozen in his chair, staring at the mugshot of the man in front of him.

"Miguel 'The Scorpion' Hernandez. Do you know why he is called The Scorpion? Eh, Sanchez, do you?"

Pedro folded his arms. "I'm sure you're going to tell me, senór."

"It's because those who double-cross him, feel the wrath of his sting. But don't worry Mr. Sanchez, as I said, you will be under our protection."

Pedro placed both hands over his face. "Puta madre," he mumbled beneath them.

"Was he there, Mr. Sanchez? Was he at the bank that night, the night of the robbery?"

Pedro lowered his hands. They were wet. With tears.

"Did he threaten you, Mr. Sanchez? Did Hernandez threaten to harm your family?"

"He didn't have to, said Pedro. You don't understand, senór. This is MS13. They take no prisoners." Sanchez looked dejected, broken.

"Have you been in contact with any of these men since the robbery?"

Pedro shook his head. "No."

"But what about your share, Mr. Sanchez? As an accomplice to the robbery?"

Pedro looked up at Trudeau.

"That's right, Mr. Sanchez. We can put you away for a very long time. As an accomplice to the robbery, we can put you away for years unless you give us more information. That's the deal on the table, Mr. Sanchez. A deal so that you can save yourself. Do it for your family. It's your last chance. What do you know about a girl? A girl with long, black hair and scars across her cheeks."

"I don't know who you're talking about," said Pedro shaking his head.

"Come on, Mr. Sanchez. Think. You saw the team that came into the bank that night. Was there a girl with them?"

Pedro gasped. "Yes! Yes!" he cried. "A girl. Yes, now I remember," he said, slapping himself on the side of the head. "She wore a black hoodie. I remember her face - the scars. Looked like her cheeks had been sliced. And her eyes..."

"What about her eyes?"

"They looked right through me. She gave me the creeps."

"That's our girl. What else can you tell me?"

"That's it. That's all I know. I just gave them access. That's all."

"Now tell me, Mr. Sanchez. When were you planning on getting your share?"

"Midnight tomorrow," said Pedro quietly.

"Excellent, Mr. Sanchez. That wasn't too bad, now was it? Just one more question and then we're all done," said Trudeau with the biggest grin across his face. He was enjoying this. "Where exactly is the planned pickup?"

54 ~ Prophecy

Sybs gazed down at the crystal around her neck. The sunlight streamed into the room, filling the crystal with the sparkling colours of the rainbow until she was dazzled by its brilliance. She could almost hear the powerful energy buried deep inside the stone vibrate to sing a sweet song of praise. She smiled and closed her eyes, and then they began to dance behind her eyelids to the crystal's enchanting melody.

Sybs relaxed, allowing all sensation to dissipate like an evaporating mist. She was so familiar with the transition that it had become second nature. All that she was conscious of now was her breath. In and out, in and out, until that in itself became one with the cosmos, the heartbeat of the universe, all life and existence.

All physical sensation had left her. It was a distant memory, so very distant. There was just her spiritual body now, floating, rising up and into the place between places. She saw what she needed to see. Her foresight responded to her intention, and her intention was where she needed to go, so she went there, traversing the spirit realm with purpose. She had learnt over the years, to harness her powers and find what she was looking for in this place, this place of shadows and spirits. It was easy to lose your way here, to wander about aimlessly, with no direction or intent. Sybs had lost her way, many times, but through countless experiences, she had learnt how to overcome this vulnerability, this malady. She had found her purpose and made it part of her intention.

This time was no different, as Sybs began to unlock the power of her intention by tapping into her crystal. Much like the energy stored inside a battery cell, her intention, charged with pure sunlight, shone forth, radiating from the crystal against her chest in a powerful beam of light, first enveloping her like a sheath, before blasting off into the darkness. She followed the energy of her intention, knowing full well that it would lead her directly to her destination, the location of Sabine and her grandmother, her archrival.

Sybs' light shone across the spirit realm like a beacon, and she rode it expertly, like a wave-rider on a board of pure energy. Her spirit senses reined her in as she approached a dark, grey column of smoke, spiralling up into the darkness above. She had reached her destination.

Sybs Miller. We have been waiting.

Show yourself, said Sybs.

The column of smoke shifted, gradually transforming into a humanoid shape. The smoke finally faded to reveal a woman with long, grey, wispy hair and deep furrows all over her face. She smiled, baring just a few crooked teeth.

Who are you? What do you want with us?

You know who I am. The old woman smiled her crooked smile. *I am the descendant of the great Sabbe. My name is Selene.*

The Titan goddess of the moon.

You know your history.

You haven't answered my question, said Sybs. *What do you want with us?*

Selene turned her back on Sybs and raised her arms into the air. Smoke poured from her fingers like they were on fire. The smoke coalesced to form another humanoid shape and then lifted to reveal a girl with long, black hair.

You must be Sabine, said Sybs.

Yes. My granddaughter. Together we have come to take revenge.

For what?

For the banishment of almighty Sabbe. We have come to fulfil the prophecy.

What prophecy?

The one made by Sabbe after she was banished thousands of years ago. The prophecy of the Armageddon. We are the harbingers of the apocalypse. We are here to bring chaos and destruction to this world.

I will not let you, said Sybs.

You cannot stop us. We will crush you right here, right now.

Both Selene and Sabine raised their hands into the air, and smoke poured forth in thick, heavy plumes. It began to cover them, forming one long, thick column that thickened and darkened. Flashes of lightning arced through the smoke and then it twisted, bending over until it faced Sybs like a giant worm golem, brought to life with dark, sinister magic. Sybs didn't budge. She simply placed her right hand on her chest and closed her eyes. The smoke worm continued curving up and over, until it poured down right over Sybs, engulfing her into itself like a hungry snake devouring its prey.

55 ~ Feds

"Can you hear me?" said Trudeau into a small microphone. He eyed the monitor.

"Yeah. Loud and clear," replied Sanchez.

"Great. Now, just do as I say, and everything will be okay."

"This is crazy," said Brorson from the front seat of the surveillance van. "Why a school?"

"A school is a great place for a pickup. All those kids provide the perfect cover. Those MS13 gangsters know that if Sanchez has been marked, there's less risk for them being shot at with all the children around."

"Okay. Makes sense."

"They're probably inside the school already."

"Sanchez," said Trudeau, speaking into the mic again. "Where are you?" A phone rang. "Is that yours?"

"Yes," replied Sanchez.

"Answer it."

"Hello," said Sanchez.

"Can you see the yellow school bus outside the school?" said a voice with a Spanish accent.

"Yes," replied Sanchez.

"Climb onto it."

"Okay. I'm on my way," said Sanchez.

"Who was it?" Trudeau enquired.

"Miguel," Sanchez answered. "You heard what he said?"

"Yes," replied Trudeau. "Listen to me carefully," he continued. "I want you to follow Miguel's instructions. He mustn't suspect a thing. When you climb on the bus, I want you to look around and then give me a number. That number will be the number of school kids on the bus."

"Okay."

"And then as soon as you've made the pickup, let me know."

"Okay. I'm walking towards the bus now."

"Murillo!" Trudeau called to the driver upfront.

"Yessir!"

"See that yellow school bus standing in front of the school?"

"Yeah."

"Follow it as soon as it moves, but keep your distance."

"Understood, sir."

Trudeau watched Sanchez step onto the school bus.

"Five," reported Sanchez, indicating the number of school children on board. The bus pulled slowly away from the school, and the FBI surveillance van followed at least 500 yards behind it. The bus dipped over the hill and disappeared from view. The surveillance van approached the hill and then came to a stop.

"Shit," said Brorson, looking out of the window.

"What?" said Trudeau, standing up to peer out of the front window and into a parking lot filled with cars and several yellow buses.

"Which one is it?" said Trudeau. "I count five yellow buses." He sat down in front of the mic once more. "Sanchez. Which bus are you on?"

There was no reply. Trudeau turned up the volume. All that he could hear over the speakers was the drone of the Cummins diesel school bus engine.

"Sanchez!"

"Get up," came a voice through the monitor that sounded

like Hernandez. "We're moving."

"Murillo, let's get down there!" shouted Trudeau pointing at the parking area. "He's changing buses. Brorson, keep your eyes peeled. Can you see him?"

Brorson was sitting forward in her seat, staring intently at the five yellow buses. "Shit. They're all slowly making their way out of the other side of the parking area. I don't have eyes on him."

"Is there another way around the parking area?" said Trudeau, getting agitated.

"Don't think so, sir," replied Murillo. "We're on the only road in and out, and even if there were, it would take us much longer."

"Damn!" Trudeau slammed his fist down on the counter with a bang.

"Sanchez, I know you can hear me," said Trudeau into the mic. "We know that you're changing buses. Don't worry; we'll keep tracking you on your phone. Just keep calm. Everything will be all right."

By the time that Murillo made his way through the traffic and into the parking area, only two buses remained.

"The other three buses must be on the highway by now," said Brorson. "You have a fix on his location?"

"Just give me a moment," replied Trudeau, waiting for the GPS locator to update Sanchez's position. "There! Looks like he's heading south. Murillo, let's go."

Murillo eventually made it out of the parking lot and drove south on the 94 towards Lincoln Village, following the signal from Sanchez's phone.

"Looks like it stopped," said Trudeau.

"What do you mean?" said Brorson.

"The signal. It stopped. Not moving."

"Check the map. Where is he?"

"I am," said Trudeau. "Gimme a moment. Riley Elementary. The bus has stopped at Riley Elementary, 2447, 4th Street."

"Murillo," said Brorson. "You heard him. Floor it."

"Sanchez," said Trudeau into the mic. "We're right behind you."

Murillo took the next off-ramp, turned right, and then left into 4th Street. He slowed down as they approached the school. There was a single yellow bus parked right outside. He pulled over about fifty yards away. Brorson and Trudeau pulled out their revolvers and jumped out of the van, crouching low as they made their way cautiously towards the bus. On initial inspection, it appeared that the bus was empty, but Trudeau wasn't taking any chances. He was just pleased to be wearing his flak jacket.

Trudeau signalled to Brorson to go around to the driver's side, while he approached the bus from the passenger side. He rapped his gun against the glass folding doors. After a few moments, they opened with a squeal. Trudeau raised his weapon and stepped inside. The driver, an Indian man, wearing a dark green beret, jumped up in fright.

"FBI," said Trudeau flashing his badge.

"Whatchoo want?" said the driver. He turned, wide-eyed to stare at Brorson outside his door. "Dez no one on board. Are you crazy or what, waving your guns around on a school bus?!"

"We're looking for a man," said Trudeau. "Two men, actually. One is Mexican. Big guy. The other one has lots of tattoos, all over his body, his face…"

"Yes, yes, the one with tattoos climb on the bus when I stop at Hayes School. Then this big guy with moustache after. I tell them no, no misters, this is school bus, for children. The tattoo one tell me, 'just shut up and drive' so I drive down into Hayes parking lot and they get out."

Trudeau strode down the aisle, checking the seats either side as he walked. And there it was, Sanchez's mobile phone, lying wedged between two seats about halfway in. The folding doors swung open, and Trudeau stepped off the bus. "Brorson! Let's go!" he yelled, running towards the black surveillance van. "Wrong bus!"

Trudeau jumped into the van and grabbed the mic. "Sanchez. If you can hear me, say something, dammit!"

There was nothing but static in response.

"Murillo, get us outta here," barked Trudeau. "We're out of range. Get us back onto the freeway."

Brorson jumped back into the van and Murillo stepped on the gas, swinging the van around in a circle, taking them back the way they came.

"Sanchez! Speak to me," said Trudeau in earnest.

Still nothing.

"Sanchez!"

A crackling sound broke through the static. Trudeau made out a single word. "Lincoln."

"Lincoln," repeated Trudeau. "Did you hear that?" he said to Brorson. Trudeau searched the list of schools in the area. "Lincoln Avenue Elementary School. That's gotta be it!" he cried. "Murillo, take us to 1784 Lincoln Avenue and pronto!"

"Yessir!"

Brorson punched the address into the GPS navigation system. "Seven miles," she said over her shoulder. "We'll be there soon."

◊ ◊ ◊

The black FBI surveillance van arrived at Lincoln Avenue Elementary and pulled over just a short distance from the front gate. Trudeau and Brorson climbed out and entered the premises. They walked casually, keeping their weapons concealed this time, so as not to attract any wanton attention.

"There," whispered Brorson, pointing at a yellow bus in the school parking area.

"Easy, now, Brorson," said Trudeau. "We don't know what we're dealing with here. Keep an eye out for any kids in the area."

"Yeah, I will," said Brorson, looking about uneasily.

Trudeau and Brorson approached the bus together.

"That's far enough!" came a voice from inside. The doors flapped open, and a large figure came tumbling down the steps with a series of grunts, landing on the Earth with a loud thud. It was Sanchez. There was blood everywhere. It ran down the steps like a river. He was choking. He managed to lift his head in an attempt to draw in some air, but all this did was expose a long, red gash across his throat that just pumped out more blood until he dropped his head into the dirt with a scrunch, spraying up a fountain of blood in the process. The bus started up, and the folding doors shut with a clap.

"Come, let's go," said Trudeau, turning to run back the way they had come.

Brorson followed Trudeau as he sprinted towards the school gates. By the time they reached the entrance, the yellow bus was speeding past them, smoke pouring from its tyres, screeching rubber on tarmac, as it swung left out of the gates.

Murillo was ready and waiting in the van for Trudeau and Brorson. They jumped in, and soon they were giving chase down Lincoln Avenue.

"Hello, is that Saint Joseph?" said Brorson into her phone. "Yes. This is agent Brorson of the FBI. Please send an ambulance immediately to Lincoln Avenue Memorial School. There's been a murder."

"All units," said Trudeau into his two-way radio. "This is agent Wesley Trudeau of the FBI Richmond office. We are in pursuit of a renegade Blue Bird, yellow bus, license plate, ZV20345, heading East on Lincoln Avenue. Be warned, the suspect on board is Miguel Hernandez, the notorious MS13 gang member. He is armed and extremely dangerous. Exercise extreme caution, do not engage. I repeat, do not engage." Trudeau held onto his seat as Murillo navigated the van through the traffic at high speed.

The two-way crackled to life in response. "Suspect ditched the bus and is now travelling east on Old Orchard in a silver Dodge. We have units closing in on him now."

"Shit," said Trudeau. "He must have connected with other

gang members. Murillo, how far to Old Orchard?"

"About five minutes, sir," he replied, as he weaved the van nimbly through the traffic.

"We have forced the suspect to turn into Memorial Park Cemetery," said a voice on the two-way. "We have them cornered. I repeat, we have them cornered."

◊ ◊ ◊

The blue and red flashing lights of a Chicago PD vehicle greeted the black FBI van as it pulled up outside the cemetery entrance. A red-headed officer in uniform approached Murillo.

"FBI," said Murillo, flashing his badge at the officer.

Murillo proceeded to enter the cemetery. Trudeau looked out the window as they drove slowly inside. He counted six flag poles next to a water fountain at the entrance. The quiet, tree-lined entrance road belied the critical situation inside.

"Suspect is behind the chapel," came the two-way. "We're closing in."

Murillo approached the chapel, a prominent, square-shaped building with a dome-shaped roof, constructed out of large, grey stone blocks. A terra-cotta-coloured, brick-paved path surrounded the building, along with several wintergreens, several feet high. Four Chicago PD police vehicles were positioned outside in a semi-circle. Murillo parked the van just behind them.

Trudeau pulled his FBI badge over his head and loaded his Glock. He stepped out of the van and approached a police officer holding a megaphone. "You in charge?" he said to the officer.

"Yeah. Davids. Vice," said the officer extending his hand.

"Trudeau. FBI," said Trudeau, shaking Davids' hand. "Where are they?"

"Inside the chapel," said Davids, turning to gaze in the direction of the grey building.

"How many?"

"Three. I heard the APB. Miguel Hernandez. MS13."

"Yeah."

"You guys been after them a while?"

"Yeah, guess we have, but now they have nowhere to go."

Davids lifted the megaphone to his mouth. He pressed the lever, and it crackled. "Hernandez," his voice echoed loudly. "We have you surrounded. There's nowhere to go. Come out with your hands in the air."

There was no response from inside the chapel. Trudeau jumped as the side mirror of Davids' police vehicle exploded into a million fragments.

"Get down!" shouted Trudeau dropping to the ground behind Davids' car.

"Shot's fired!" yelled Davids. "Shots fired!" he repeated as he dropped down next to Trudeau.

Several more shots ricocheted off the car.

The other police officers returned fire, aiming at the stained-glass windows near the top of the chapel, from where the shots originated.

Brorson and Murillo appeared, crouching down next to Trudeau.

Brorson held up her Colt M4 Carbine assault rifle. "This baby's gonna do some damage," she said with conviction.

"Here," said Murillo, handing Trudeau a shiny, black Remington MK870P, fitted with a Trijicon reflex sight and a Speedfeed stock. "Time to kick some ass."

Trudeau holstered the Glock under his armpit and took the Remington from Murillo. "Thanks."

Brorson aimed and fired at the chapel. More stained-glass windows shattered.

"Get ready to cover me. I'm going in," said Trudeau, raising his Remington.

"I'm coming with you," said Brorson. "Stay here," she said, turning to Murillo. "Cover us."

"Let's go!" said Trudeau, dashing for the chapel. Brorson

followed close behind, while Murillo opened fire, spraying the chapel with bullets.

Trudeau and Brorson reached the base of the chapel unscathed. Brorson gave Murillo the thumbs-up. Trudeau edged towards the entrance of the chapel, making sure he was pressed up against the wall to avoid being seen by Hernandez and his troop. Brorson followed close behind.

"Careful," whispered Brorson. "One of them might be guarding the door."

Trudeau nodded in acknowledgement. He reached up and twisted the doorknob. It was locked from the inside as he suspected it would be. He turned to Brorson and made a circling motion in the air with his index finger. Brorson followed Trudeau as he made his way around the chapel, stopping beneath a small square window that was slightly ajar. As quietly as he was able, Trudeau reached inside the window, released the latch, and pulled the window open as far as it would go. He then proceeded to climb through the window, and into a toilet cubicle. He helped Brorson inside and then opened the toilet door just a crack to peer into the chapel itself. From his position, it looked completely deserted. He pushed the door open some more and stuck his head out. He looked towards the rear of the building where he noticed an alcove leading to a set of stairs.

Trudeau raised his Remington and stepped out of the toilet. Keeping his back to the wall, Trudeau edged his way towards the alcove. Brorson followed silently behind him, all the while gazing up towards the balcony that framed the perimeter of the first floor. More shots were fired from outside, followed by a barrage of bullets from upstairs in retaliation, giving Trudeau and Brorson an opportunity to make their way quickly upstairs without being heard. They reached the landing. Trudeau looked at Brorson and pointed left. He went right. The two FBI agents slowly made their way around the perimeter walkway towards the front of the chapel. Trudeau tightened his grip on the assault rifle and moved forward with purpose. The walkway began to widen until they reached a single door to the room where Hernandez and his associates were stationed. Trudeau gave the door a mighty kick and burst into the room, opening fire with Brorson at his side. One of the assailants was standing at the window. Trudeau gunned him down before he could even return fire. Another man, with tattoos all over his face, dived-rolled through a doorway dividing the room in two. Trudeau and Brorson moved quickly to either side of the open door. Brorson glanced over at the bloodied corpse lying against the window frame behind her.

"Hernandez!" Trudeau shouted. "Give it up. It's over!"

"Go to hell!" shouted Miguel. A spray of bullets exploded through the open door between Trudeau and Brorson.

"Puta!" came another voice and the second hail of bullets tore into the door frame like a swarm of angry wasps.

"This time, there's nowhere to go, Hernandez," said Trudeau. "Both of you. It's Martinez, isn't it? Julian Domingo Martinez."

Silence.

"Oh, yes, I know you. I know both of you. My name's Trudeau. Agent Wesley Trudeau from the FBI. And with me is Agent Leonie Brorson. We don't want to hurt you. We just want you to drop your weapons and come on out. Don't make this harder on yourselves than it already is."

"Ha! You know nothing about hard. Nothing!" shouted Miguel, opening fire again.

"We've got all day Hernandez, and you have only so many bullets. How do you think this is gonna end? Huh?" Trudeau heard what sounded like furniture being moved around inside the room. He looked across at Brorson and frowned.

Brorson raised her eyebrows and shrugged her shoulders. Then she clicked her fingers and pulled a pair of silver-reflective Rayban Aviators out of her pocket. She pulled open one of the arms and held the glasses out in front of her, angling the lenses so that she could see inside the room. Her eyes widened when she realised what Hernandez and Martinez were doing. She flipped her glasses into the palm of her hand and dropped them back into her pocket. Then she looked at Trudeau and made a thrusting motion with her index and middle fingers up into the air.

Trudeau looked up at the ceiling and shrugged his shoulders.

Brorson frowned, pointed heatedly in the direction of the other room and then up at the ceiling again.

Trudeau finally got it. He nodded his head and grinned. He stuck his head around the corner, and his assumption was confirmed. Martinez was standing on a table in the far corner of the room, hoisting Hernandez up into a small, square opening in the roof. Trudeau dropped back, turned to Brorson, stuck three fingers into the air and counted silently down to one, before charging into the room with Brorson by his side, opening fire, blasting Martinez's legs as they dangled from the ceiling. Martinez dropped like a stone, crashing onto the table beneath him with a roar and then rolled off the other side and onto the floor with a thud. The blood-soaked table fell with him, dropping onto its side, effectively shielding him from further attack.

Both Trudeau and Brorson opened a full magazine each into the table, shredding the wood into a million tiny splinters that flew up into the air like a blizzard. The dust settled, leaving the table looking like a porcupine's back. Both agents quickly changed magazines. At the same time, Martinez swung his weapon over the wrecked table and fired randomly across the room in an arc, hoping to find a target. He got lucky. Brorson was the unlucky one. A stray bullet punctured her left bicep, throwing her completely off balance. She dropped to her knees, raised the M4 in her other hand and opened fire again, this time blasting through the table and into Martinez's skull, pulverising it into a bloodied mess.

"Brorson!" yelled Trudeau, rushing over to his partner. "You all right? Here, let me get that," he said, ripping off her sleeve and tying it securely around her arm to quell the bleeding.

She winced. "I'll be okay. You gotta get to Hernandez," she said, pointing at the gaping hole in the ceiling. She crawled over to the corner of the room. "Climb on my back," she said, looking up at Trudeau expectantly.

"You sure?"

"Come on! It's the only way. You've gotta get up there after him," said Brorson. "I'm a big girl," she winked. "I can handle you."

Trudeau placed his Remington down on the floor, climbed up onto Brorson's back and then slowly stood up, wobbling as he reached up to grab hold of the edge of the hole in the ceiling. He fumbled around until he found a firm grip on a pair of wooden beams either side of the opening and then gradually hoisted himself up and into the roof. It was dark inside the ceiling, save for a small shaft of light coming from an opening to the outside about fifty yards away. There were only about three feet of space, so Trudeau was forced to crawl on his hands and knees over the wooden beams until he reached his destination. He looked up to find a trapdoor. He slowly stood up, sticking the top of his head out of the opening, just enough to peek outside. Trudeau followed the curve of the roof as it rose away from him. Hernandez was nowhere in sight. He climbed out and onto the roof, pulled out his Glock and proceeded to make his way up and over the top of the dome, keeping his eyes peeled for the slightest movement.

As Trudeau reached the roof summit, he spotted Hernandez on the far side of the building where the dome ended and met a rectangular shaped section. "Hernandez!"

Miguel spun around to face Trudeau and opened fire.

Trudeau felt a sharp stab of pain as a bullet hit him in the chest. The force of the impact sent him tumbling down the side of the roof. He rolled over several times before coming to lie on his back with stars in his eyes and the wind knocked out of him. He had lost his gun. He looked down at his chest. His chest was on fire, but he was all right. The flak jacket had saved him. He caught his breath, slowly rolled over and crawled around the base of the circular roof towards the rear of the chapel where he reached a ladder, about ten feet high, leading up to the section of the roof where Hernandez had gone. He began to climb up the ladder, slowly making his way to the top.

A sixth sense that tingled in Trudeau's peripheral vision alerted him to something swinging towards the side of his head that caused him to duck instinctively. Hernandez's gun clanged loudly against the ladder, sending a vibration into both of Trudeau's hands. Trudeau used the missed opportunity to pull himself quickly up and over the ladder, jumping down on top of Hernandez, crushing him with all of his weight. He grabbed hold of the barrel of Hernandez's gun and threw it to one side. Miguel punched Trudeau in the solar plexus and pushed him away, twisting over to reach for his weapon just a few yards away. Trudeau frantically grabbed at Hernandez's legs pulling himself over the gang leader's back. Hernandez twisted around again, swinging his fists wildly from side to side. Trudeau lifted his left arm to block the blows and then retaliated, punching Hernandez in the face. Hernandez twisted away like a worm, pulling himself onto his feet. Trudeau jumped up and kicked Hernandez's weapon across the rooftop. Hernandez wiped away the blood from the side of his mouth with the back of his hand and raised his fists.

"Come esé. Come. Let's fight," said Miguel, staring down Trudeau with clenched teeth.

"Where's the girl, Hernandez?" said Trudeau.

"What?"

"The girl. The one with the scars on her face."

"Fuck you," he sneered. "I'm not telling you nothing!"

"Oh, but you will, Hernandez, you will," said Trudeau with a grin.

Miguel lunged forward with a jab. Trudeau hopped back and then forward again with a counter. Miguel slapped it out of the way and then jabbed again, this time connecting Trudeau on his cheekbone, leaving behind a tender, red welt. Trudeau's head snapped back with the force of the blow. He shook his head to clear it and then moved in, kicking Miguel against the side of his leg, followed by a left hook to his ribs. Miguel buckled, winded by the blow. Trudeau finished off with an uppercut to the jaw, sending Miguel staggering backwards a couple of steps. Trudeau took the opportunity to run up to Miguel with a right hook, but he brought his left arm up to block the blow and front-kicked Trudeau in his stomach. Trudeau retaliated with a volley of punches. Miguel blocked most of them, save for one that got through that connected him above the left eye. The fight continued across the rooftop, blow for blow until both opponents' faces were bloodied and bruised.

"That all you got?" said Miguel, glaring at Trudeau through one eye; the other one was quickly swelling shut. He pulled a small, sharp knife from his belt and waved it menacingly through the air.

Trudeau wiped his bloodied nose with his sleeve and swung another left hook at Miguel. He jumped deftly to one side, slashing his blade across Trudeau's arm, tearing into his flesh. Trudeau dropped to his left knee, visibly shaken from the attack. Blood soaked his arm. He knew his energy would wane quickly now, so he turned around to face Miguel, who was preparing to launch another attack with his vicious knife. Trudeau grabbed Miguel's wrist with his hand as he brought it overhead to stab Trudeau from above. The two of them grappled with the knife until Trudeau brought his knee up into Miguel's chest with a short but hard blow, winding him enough to twist the blade down in an arc and into the side of his neck. Miguel's eyes bulged in horror at his predicament. He yanked the blade from his neck and blood began to pulse out in great big spurts, instantly draining all colour from his face. He opened and closed his mouth, trying desperately to breathe as the blood pumped inside like an open faucet. He grabbed his throat with both hands, dropped to his knees and keeled over, landing flat on his face.

56 ~ The Docks

Tracy opened her eyes and sat up. "Granny Sybs?" There was no one in her room, yet she imagined that her grandmother was standing right there, next to her bed. She swung her legs off the edge of the bed and stood up. She felt so much better. The throbbing in her arm was gone, and her head didn't have that heavy feeling any longer. She looked at her phone. 6.18pm. She had been sleeping all afternoon.

"Tracy?"

Tracy turned to find Sybs at her door. "I just imagined that you were right here. What's wrong? You look worried."

"I am. Come, we need to go. How are you feeling?"

"Much better!" She beamed. "Where are we going?"

"For a drive. We don't have time. I'll explain in the car."

"Okay, but I think we need to tell Mom and Dad first," said Tracy, hurriedly pulling on a pair of jeans.

"You get dressed while I let them know," said Sybs, disappearing before Tracy could even respond.

Tracy slipped into her sneakers and tied the laces. She ran over to her bathroom and hurriedly brushed her hair, wincing when the brush caught in her knots. While she was brushing her teeth, she had a powerful epiphany. She knew that she would need the flute, so she dashed back into her room, grabbed the black velvet bag lying next to her bed, and then ran downstairs where she met Sybs and her parents in the entrance hall.

"Are you sure, Mom," said Camilla, concern in her voice. "She hasn't fully recovered."

"Camilla. We've had this discussion. She's fine. She's with me." She squeezed Camilla's hands reassuringly in her own.

"Bye Daddy," said Tracy, hugging her father.

Harold kissed Tracy on the crown of her head. "You be safe, you hear?"

Tracy hugged her mother and kissed her on the cheek. "Don't worry, guys. We're just going for a drive. We'll be back soon."

Sybs winked at Harold and Camilla and then opened the front door.

◊ ◊ ◊

Tracy strapped herself into her mother's car as Sybs reversed out of the driveway.

"What's going on, Gran? Where are we going?"

"We need to get away, away from here. It's for their protection," she said, waving at the house.

"What do you mean? Are they in trouble?"

"I found them," said Sybs pulling away from the house.

"What do you mean? Found who?"

"Sabine and her grandmother. Her name is Selene."

"What? How?"

"I searched for them in the spiritual realm. They were waiting for me. They attacked me."

"What the hell? Are you okay?"

"Yes. I created a mirror image of myself and escaped."

"Why did they attack you?"

Sybs glanced in the rear-view mirror, took a deep breath, and sighed. "Revenge. Selene said that they're taking revenge for Sabbe."

"Sambethe's twin."

Sybs nodded. "She spoke about a prophecy that they are here to fulfil. A prophecy of doom, preordained by Sabbe thousands of years ago. As far as I understand it, she believes that they are here to wreak havoc on the world as a precursor to this prophecy."

"My dream. The visions. That's what I saw. That's what Sabine showed me before she injured me." Tracy's shoulder ached with the memory of the fiery hell that she witnessed. "Holy crap. What are we going to do?"

"We have to stop them."

"But how?"

"The flute. It's the only way. When I made my way back from my encounter with Selene and Sabine, I had a vision. You were with me, blowing the flute. Ships surrounded us."

"In the harbour?"

"Yes. It was here in Milwaukee. I recognised the Hoan Bridge."

"Is that where we're going?"

"Yes."

"Look," said Tracy lifting the velvet bag. "I brought it."

"Good girl," said Sybs.

"I just knew to bring it with."

"Intuition."

"I'm scared, Gran." Tracy had never seen her grandmother so serious before. It made her apprehensive.

"Don't worry. It will all be all right."

Somehow Tracy didn't feel assured. "But she has the other flute. How are we going to stop them?"

"I have a plan," said Sybs. "Trust me, okay?"

Tracy nodded. She stared out of the window, unable to get rid of the uneasiness that was beginning to build in her stomach.

◊ ◊ ◊

397

"Look. There it is," said Sybs as they approached the harbour.

Tracy gazed out of her window at the colourful display of lights that decorated the Daniel Hoan Memorial Bridge. Thousands of LED light bulbs had been installed right across the span of the bridge that slowly transitioned through a kaleidoscope of colours like a vivid rainbow. A two-year fund-raising campaign was put in place to illuminate the Hoan Bridge in recognition of the many acts of kindness, generosity, and service that give Milwaukee hope. Individuals and corporates alike were encouraged to sponsor a light bulb in honour of these unsung heroes, in return for being mentioned on the website running the campaign. The campaign was so successful that a portion of the proceeds raised was donated to a homeless shelter in the area.

"Wow. It's beautiful," remarked Tracy. "You know that this is the first time that I've seen it at night with all the new lights?"

"Me too," said Sybs. "Let's hope it's not the last," she grinned.

"Gran! Don't say that! Don't tell me..."

"No. Don't worry; I'm not going to die any time soon. This old bag 'o bones still has a good few years left in her."

"Good, because I won't let you go anyway," said Tracy, squeezing her grandmother's hand.

Sybs drove over the Hoan Bridge on the 794 and onto Jones' Island. She took the next offramp and pulled over in between an abandoned warehouse and the water's edge. In partnership with the City of Milwaukee, and planning to last around ten years, several organisations were currently involved in a massive refurbishment project to transform the Harbour District into a vibrant waterfront. Therefore, abandoned buildings, cranes, and other construction vehicles filled much of the area around them.

"You sure this is it?" said Tracy looking around apprehensively. "There's like no one here. Nadda. And it's dark."

"Over there," Sybs pointed at a spotlight attached to the

398

warehouse. "Tracy."

Tracy turned to look into her grandmother's grey-green eyes.

"Remember what I have taught you?"

Tracy nodded.

"Always focus on your crystal. It is more powerful than you know. Your intuition is everything. Go with your gut. And lastly, I love you no matter what happens."

Tears welled up in Tracy's eyes. "Oh, Gran!" she cried, throwing her arms around her grandmother. "I'm scared."

"There, there," said Sybs, patting Tracy on the back. "You're stronger than you think, you know. Just focus your intention, and the power will flow. You do it so well with that flute of yours. Close your eyes and imagine that you're playing it all the time. Come, it's time," she said, letting go of Tracy and opening her door.

The crunch of gravel beneath Tracy's shoes was the only sound in this desolate place. She felt the shape of the flute in the velvet bag and it gave her solace as she followed Sybs towards the warehouse. The warehouse door was ajar. Sybs confidently pulled it open and stepped inside. The shadows rushed up to meet Tracy, stealing the breath from her mouth as her throat constricted in angst. The orange glow of a single, flickering light at the far end of the warehouse banished some of the bigger shadows away, but the warehouse was, for the most part, pretty dark and gloomy. Tracy closed her eyes, brought her hand up to touch the crystal around her neck, breathed in deeply through her nostrils, and the constricted feeling slowly subsided.

Sybs raised her finger to her mouth and whispered, "They're here."

Tracy looked around, straining her eyes to see into the darkness. "I don't see…"

"Shhh. Close your eyes."

Tracy closed her eyes. Her ears pricked. It felt as if they were pressed up against a pair of conch shells, and she could hear the waves breaking on a distant shore. The sound of the waves morphed into a rasping voice that sounded like the wind blowing through a window that had been opened just a crack. *Traceeeee.*

Instinct forced Tracy to open her eyes, and there, standing immobile beneath the orange glow of the flickering light on the other side of the warehouse, were two cowled silhouettes. Tracy turned to her grandmother who stood silently by her side with her eyes closed and her brow creased in concentration. No. It was more like consternation. Tracy turned back to gaze upon the two robed characters and noticed that the one on the right was much shorter than the other. The figure on the left pulled back her hood, and Tracy immediately recognised her. The girl from her dream. Sabine. She moved forward towards Tracy and Sybs.

"Go," said Sybs. "Outside," she pointed at the door. "Lead her outside. Remember what I have told you. Focus. Use the flute. I will take care of Selene," she said, turning her attention back towards the hunched, hooded figure.

Tracy gritted her teeth and clenched her fists. *You can do this,* she told herself. *Come on. You can do this.* She shuffled her feet, stepping backwards towards the warehouse door, all the while keeping her gaze fixed on Sabine as she advanced slowly towards her. Tracy waited at the door until Sabine was about ten yards away before twisting around to run outside. Her heart was beating so hard in her chest that it ached. She stopped running and turned to face the warehouse. The spotlight outside was bright enough for Tracy to make out the ugly scars on Sabine's face. They seemed to writhe like they were alive; as if she was Medusa incarnate.

The back of Tracy's head began to tingle. The tingling spread down her shoulders, along her arms and finally into her fingers. She looked down at her right hand. She still had the black velvet bag in its grip. Instinctively, she reached into the bag, retrieved the flute, and brought it to her lips. Before she knew it, she was blowing gently into the instrument. She focused her intention on Sabine and blew harder. An invisible wind stirred and then began to grow in intensity until Sabine's black robe billowed out behind her. The force of the wind forced Sabine to take a step backwards and then another. She dropped onto her haunches and then placed her hands on the ground, fighting against the powerful force that threatened to propel her back into the side of the warehouse. Tracy quickly drew in another breath to continue her refrain. It was in this moment of pause that the turbulence around Sabine subsided enough for her to reach into her robe and withdraw the other flute.

Both Tracy and Sabine brought their flutes to their lips together and began to blow. The turbulent wind returned, but this time, it formed a mini maelstrom between the two seers; a whirlwind that fought with itself; two forces twisting around each other, caught in a savage stalemate. Tracy turned her attention to a pile of wooden crates behind Sabine. She focused on lifting the top one. It rose into the air, creaking in protest. Sabine turned to face the crate as it hurtled toward her. She blew a high-pitched note, and the crate shuddered in the air. It changed direction, plummeting down into the ground with such force, that it exploded into thousands of tiny fragments.

Tracy heard a loud, scraping sound. She turned to find a huge metal container flying towards her, rolling through the air as if it was a die being cast by a giant's hand. There was little time to react. She launched into a sprint and then dived into a roll, just as the container hit the ground with a tremendous bang, sending chunks of gravel and tarmac into the air. The container literally bounced as it hit the ground, flew right over Tracy's head and landed about thirty yards away, rolling harmlessly into a fence that buckled under its weight.

Tracy looked down at the back of her forearm. It was grazed and a little numb. She checked the flute, to find with relief, that it was unscathed.

"Join us, Tracy," said Sabine mockingly. "You cannot win. We are stronger."

Tracy ignored Sabine's taunting. She had an idea. She touched her crystal to centre her intention, closed her eyes, and concentrated on the body of water in the bay. She blew into the flute once more, gathering up the water, creating an invisible net; a forcefield of energy that lifted a swimming pool-sized load of water out of the bay and into the air. She opened her eyes, guided the water directly over Sabine, and released it. Sabine looked up and blew into her flute, but it was too late. The weight of the water dumped over her, knocked her down and washed her across the shipyard like a piece of flotsam. Tracy looked at Sabine lying face-down, unmoving in a puddle of shallow water. She walked towards her, wondering if she was still alive and then she moved, pushing herself over and onto her back. She coughed up a mouthful of water, sat up and reached for her flute lying a few yards away.

Tracy turned around, searching for a suitable object lying about to launch at Sabine. The sound of Sabine's flute sang though the air. Tracy started playing too until she had conjured up another whirlwind that she pushed towards Sabine. Tracy frowned. There was nothing stopping her attack. She encountered no retaliation as before. She pushed harder, and the turbulent wind tore at Sabine, threatening to push her back, but she pulled her hood over her head and continued to blow into her flute. Tracy wondered what she was doing until it was too late. She looked up in awe at a fifty-foot ship, floating precariously in the air. It hovered over Tracy, seawater pouring off its hull, and then as if in slow motion, it fell from the sky towards her. She took a deep breath and blew hard into her flute, until her cheeks began to burn, creating a protective forcefield of energy around her; an invisible barrier that miraculously absorbed the weight of the ship falling upon it. The forcefield acted like a cushion, slowing down the ship's descent until it came to a halt, just inches away from crushing Tracy, and then, like a trampoline, it pushed the massive ship back up into the air. The ship reached its apex and then began to topple over in the direction of the warehouse. It twisted in the air, dropping stern first, smashing through the roof of the warehouse and then collapsing sideways, falling across the entire structure in an explosion of brick and mortar.

"Nooooo!" Tracy screamed. "Granny Sybs!"

Sabine laughed in a high-pitched wail that echoed across the dock like the mocking cry of seagulls in search of food. In a flurry of movement, she pulled something long and slender from beneath her robes.

Tracy glimpsed the silvery flicker of something spinning through the air and then she felt it - a sharp, stinging pain in her shoulder. She looked down and discovered the hilt of a blade protruding from her collar bone. Instinctively she grabbed the knife and pulled it out, screaming in pain. The knife clattered to the floor. It sounded like glass. Blood poured from the wound, and her left arm felt limp and drained of energy.

Tracy gritted her teeth and with effort, lifted the flute to her mouth. She blew into the instrument, whipping up a vortex of energy. She focused on the shards of wood from the smashed up crate, lifted them into the air and shot them directly at Sabine like deadly darts. The projectiles whizzed through the air, striking their mark with such force, that Sabine was lifted into the air and propelled backwards, landing flat on her back with a thud. The splinters of wood had penetrated her robes, fatally puncturing her body in over a dozen places. Blood oozed out of the corners of her mouth as she writhed around on the ground, struggling to breathe. Tracy walked over to Sabine, picked up the flute lying beside her and gazed upon her scarred face with disdain.

Sabine pulled her mouth into a sneer. "You… are doomed," she said, coughing up a mouthful of blood. "The Armageddon is coming." She drew in another breath and coughed up more blood. "The Apocalypse. It's too late…" she wheezed one last time. Her head rolled to one side, and her lifeless eyes stared transfixed up at the moon suspended in the heavens above.

57 ~ Face Up

Sybs traversed the spiritual world with finesse, expending just the right amount of energy to follow her adversary. She focused her intention, seeing beyond the mundane and into the multiple planes of existence of what was, what is, and what was going to be. She touched her crystal to steady and focus her gaze upon the trail ahead, pushing harder to catch up to Selene as she drew Sybs deeper into the void like a spider to its lair.

A veil of mist permeated the air around her, and Sybs slowed her pursuit. She looked about, carefully scanning her surroundings for any sign of Selene.

Coward, she projected her voice into the gloom.

I am no coward, came the reply.

Then why do you hide?

I'm not hiding; you just do not see me. The mist swirled, and Selene appeared like a dark wraith from a macabre alien world.

I see you now, you old witch, said Sybs. *You will not survive this.*

Neither will you, replied Selene. She lifted her head and her hood fell to her shoulders, exposing her wild, wispy white hair and wrinkled old face.

We all have to go someday. Today is your time.

What is today? said Selene sardonically. *What is today if it is*

404

not yesterday or tomorrow? Today is now, and as of now, I'm still here, communicating with you. Today is not my time, cousin. Today is my path to tomorrow, to the end of days, to the Armageddon. It is coming, and no one is going to stop it. Not you or your cursed granddaughter.

Selene raised both of her arms and the mist around her began to swirl, concealing her from sight once more. There was a crackle of energy, and an arc of lightning exploded from the mist, striking Sybs in the chest. She was flung backwards, and rendered briefly unconscious with the force of the blow. When she opened her eyes, Sybs found herself hurtling through unfamiliar surroundings. She closed her eyes again, delicately touched her hand to the crystal around her neck and focused on her intention. When she opened her eyes once more, she was back amidst the lightly swirling mists that tickled her ankles as she moved.

Another arc of lightning exploded from the mist, but this time Sybs was ready. She raised her arms into the air just as the lightning struck her, but instead of catapulting her away, the electric current shot into her fingertips and coursed through her body in undulating waves of energy. It was as if her body itself became a conductor of lightning, channelling the electricity harmlessly through it. Sybs closed her eyes as the electric current charged her body with the power of the blast. She took in a deep breath and exhaled, riding the electric force as it lashed out of her body like an angry sting from a scorpion's tail, burning through the mist like a blast of pure sunlight and striking Selene with enough power to disable a horse.

Now that the mist had cleared, Sybs looked upon her adversary in astonishment. Selene was down on one knee with her left forearm over her head as if to protect herself from falling debris, while millions of tiny electrical sparks fizzled all over a defensive shield that she had conjured up just in the nick of time.

Selene rose slowly to her feet. *That all you got, little cousin?* She grinned a wicked grin, causing her eyes to fold into her wrinkled face like a snail returning to its shell. And then the whimsical look on her face all but disappeared as she concentrated on her hands. She brought them up to her face, cupping them opposite each other as if she was holding a small, round ball. A spark ignited a tiny flame in the space between her palms that expanded into a sphere of fire as she slowly pulled her hands apart. She drew her hands back and lobbed the fireball at Sybs. It hurtled through the air, leaving a black trail of smoke in its wake. Sybs brought her hands up instinctively as the fireball struck, quickly engulfing her in a fiery mass. The green-tinged flames continued to burn steadily with a life of their own.

Selene's cackling laughter echoed through the spiritual realm as Sybs fought assiduously beneath the suffocating flames that were fuelled by the darkest of magic. If it were not for the power of the ancient crystal around her neck, Sybs would have been consumed by the fire that burned steadily over her. With both hands firmly wrapped around the crystal, the only thing that stood between Sybs and obliteration was the incantation of protection that she uttered. Drawing on the crystal's power, she repeated the mantra over and over again, focusing her intention on preventing the flames from breaking through her steadfast resolve.

The flames flickered. The hungry, green-tinged tendrils had lost their appetite and began to change hue from green to blue until they snuffed out completely, sending hundreds of white, wispy tendrils into the air around Sybs' frame. Her face was red and puffy as if she'd been sitting in the sun all day and she looked exhausted from fending off Selene's assault.

Selene grinned smugly. I will destroy you now, she said. And you will know suffering for all eternity, trapped here in this place like a prisoner unable to rest. Selene waved her arms through the air, and the mist at her feet began to rise, twisting and turning in on itself, growing darker and thicker as it moved. She thrust her arms forward, and the mist obeyed her, shifting towards Sybs, wrapping its tendrils around her legs, moving up her body, tightening itself around her arms and chest. She tried in vain to move, but the mist had thickened so much, it had

taken the form of a matrix of connected, rope-like appendages,
preventing Sybs from taking so much as a step in any direction.
Gradually, the mist shifted higher, all the while growing denser.
It reached her throat and tightened its grip, squeezing,
compressing, choking her, until her face reddened even further.
Unable to stand any longer, she dropped to her knees and fell
over onto her side, completely incapacitated, unable to defend
herself from the onslaught of the dark, twisted mist, bent to the
will of a madwoman.

Sybs heard a melody - a song calling her name. She smiled,
welcoming the sound. She closed her eyes and saw Sambethe,
the first Mother, the powerful oracle of old. The Ancient One.
She let herself go, succumbing to the crushing grip of the mist
as it pressed the very life out of her. She felt the tendrils relax
their grip on her body as she ebbed away, taken by the melody
of the great seer Sambethe, as she returned her soul to the
source of all things.

"Granny Sybs? Can you hear me? Granny Sybs?"

Sybs slowly opened her eyes. It was dark, but she could
make out the silhouette of someone hovering over her. She
smiled. She was weak, tired. "Tracy?" she croaked.

"Yes! It's me, Tracy. Thank goodness you're okay."

"What... what happened? I thought... Sambethe..."

"You were trapped, tied up. Oh, God, I tried to help you."

Sybs looked at the silver object in Tracy's hand. "The flute.
It was you. You saved me." She smiled wanly.

"She... the old woman. She was hurting you. I had to..."
Tears streamed down Tracy's face.

"It's all right," said Sybs. "Thank you."

Tracy smiled, pulling her grandmother into a warm
embrace.

"You need to stop her," said Sybs. "The flute. It's the only
way."

"I thought you were dead," said Tracy, wiping her face and
looking about the warehouse. "The ship," she pointed at the
huge vessel lying across the expanse of the warehouse floor

amidst all the dirt and rubble. "It crashed down and… and… I thought… Oh, thank God you're alive!"

"You're hurt," said Sybs. "Your shoulder…"

Tracy looked at her blood-soaked top. Her shoulder throbbed. "It's nothing. Just a scratch. I'll be all right." She forced a smile.

"You must go back. Find her. The flute…"

"Yes, yes. Okay. You just rest here. Will you be okay?"

Sybs smiled. "I'll be fine," she whispered. "Go now, before she returns," she said, pushing Tracy away weakly.

Tracy removed her crystal from around her neck and placed it over Sybs' head.

"No. What are you doing? You will need this," said Sybs in protest.

"You need it more," said Tracy, placing her grandmother's hands over the two crystals hanging around her neck. "I've got this, remember?" said Tracy holding up the flute.

Tracy lifted the magical instrument to her lips, placed her fingers gently over the holes, closed her eyes, and blew. She became one with the melody, riding the notes into the spiritual realm like a cosmic surfer, gliding into the ether to find the old oracle. She felt no fear. Instead, she bristled with confidence, faith, and conviction in her abilities.

I am Tracy Sybil Barnes, a descendant of the great Sambethe, the original oracle, the prophetess, and I am ready to face my destiny!

The mists of the cosmos swirled in Tracy's wake as she traversed their milky depths. She knew exactly where to go. It was as if the map to her destination was carved out into the back of her eyelids. She gritted her teeth and pressed on, determined to make the old woman pay for what she did to Granny Sybs. She gripped the flute tightly in her hand, thinking back to her grandmother's words that echoed inside her head.

The universe is filled with music. It's made out of music. Celestial music. So when you hear the flute, it's connecting with the universe in song. Everything in the universe is music.

Right now, that's exactly how she witnessed the world.

Everything was connected in song; a great symphony, directed by the Great Conductor. The music filled her head, her very being, and she was in harmony with it as she roamed the universe in search of an anomaly, an aberration that she knew she had to expunge.

The silence was deafening. The music was gone, replaced by a vacuum that invaded Tracy's thoughts, suppressing her intention like constant, throbbing pressure. It was as if she encountered a powerful forcefield that drained her energy, sucking it up like a sponge. She knew it was Selene's doing, but she had no idea how she was able to do it. The invisible energy engulfed her from every angle, making her feel completely helpless and vulnerable.

You are no match for me, child. You are weak. I will crush you.

For the first time, Tracy felt fear. It washed over her like a wave. *Where are you?*

I am here. I am everywhere. This is my world, and I know its secrets. Did your grandmother not reveal them to you?

Tracy thought of her grandmother and her blood boiled. And then she remembered the flute. She brought it to her lips and blew, but nothing came out. There was no sound. Fear washed over her again. This time she could feel her heart beating painfully inside her chest. Her throat constricted, and she began to panic. She closed her eyes, and her grandmother's face appeared.

Focus on your intention.

Tracy took a deep, yet painful breath from deep down inside her tummy and blew into the flute, this time, with fierce purpose, and the music erupted from the instrument; liberated like a genie released from a bottle. It cascaded around her, like a fountain, washing away the pain, the fear, the pressure that she felt from all sides. She continued to blow, awakening her spirit, a fire deep inside her that began to build. And then she felt it again, the barrier, the forcefield. It pressed back like a wall, preventing her from breaching its perimeter.

Tracy heard a cackle of laughter. She opened her eyes, and

Selene stood before her. Her wispy, white hair fell about her shoulders, and the deep furrow of wrinkles on her face reminded her of Sabine and the scars across her cheeks.

She's dead, said Tracy. I killed her.

The look of dread on Selene's face was palpable.

You never knew, said Tracy. It is you who are weak. Not I.

I was distracted, said Selene. Your grandmother…

She will survive.

You! It was you and that flute. I will crush you!

Tracy brought the flute to her lips again and blew. She encountered Selene's forcefield again. This time it felt stronger than before. It began to surround Tracy, pushing her back into a corner. It was too much for her. She felt her defences begin to crumble. The melody of the flute wavered. She closed her eyes and she remembered her grandmother's words.

There is a balance in all things, Tracy. Disturb that balance, and there is an imbalance. Instability. Chaos. Find the frequency of the object or thing that you are trying to affect, connect with it, and you take control. You take control of that object, that physical thing. In the real world, when you find and connect with the frequency of a physical object, you can take control of it and move it. But when you connect to the frequency of an object in this world, the spiritual, you can change its very properties. You have the power to destroy things; reduce them to piles of ash.

Tracy took a deep breath. She consciously contracted the muscles below her abdomen, sucking in as much air as she could into her lungs. She felt her belly expand until there was no space left. She held her breath for a few precious seconds, focused her intention, and then exhaled, pushing the air from her lungs and into the flute. Her breath, her spirit, was pure energy, and the flute, the weapon that she used to wield it. She was a warrior of light, a paladin on a quest for justice and truth, descended from a long lineage of oracles, charged with the decree to protect the world from any threat that may befall it. This was her duty, her birthright. It had come to this. This was the moment that all of it made sense. This was the moment that Tracy understood why she had the power to see into the future.

This was the moment that she realised why the flute was so important and why she had to use it to protect all of humankind from Selene and her fulfilment of the Sabbe's prophecy.

The melody that poured forth from the flute was powerful. It was filled with conviction, integrity, and above all, pure intention. It melted away the forcefield like a blast of heat from a blacksmith's forge, carving a path towards Selene with ease. Tracy adjusted the tone, connecting to Selene's energy frequency, tapping into her very essence. Selene fought back, pouring everything she had into her defences in an attempt to shut out the powerful current of musical energy that melted through her resolve like a hot knife pushed into butter. The connection was complete. Tracy was in full control. She took one final breath and blew into the flute, moving her fingers rapidly over the holes until they became a blur. The chaos of notes that emerged, converged upon themselves, twisting and turning, subjugating Selene's spirit, dragging her down onto her knees in pain and confusion. She convulsed on the ground in fits and starts, yelping like a stray dog caught in a bear trap. The turmoil increased in intensity until her body began to shift and change shape. Her face distorted, stretching until it became unrecognisable. The musical mayhem continued to pour forth from the flute, and Selene's body continued to morph into a contorted mess of flesh and bone.

Tracy pushed out the last of her breath until the muscles in her stomach ached, sending a shudder through her body. She dropped to her haunches, exhausted from the mental concentration and physical effort she put into the ordeal. It was over. Sabine and Selene were gone. Sabbe's evil lineage was no more. Tracy closed her eyes and returned to the physical world, to the warehouse, to Granny Sybs and the flashing lights of Milwaukee's emergency services.

58 ~ Last Blast

"Hi Trace," said Josh, as Tracy opened the door. "I came as soon as I heard. You all right?"

"I'm fine, thanks. Just a few grazes."

"What happened? I heard that a boat smashed into the dock at the harbour."

Tracy smiled. "It's a long story. Come inside."

"Who is it?" said Camilla. "Oh, Josh. Hi. Nice to see you."

"Hi, Mrs. Barnes. How are you?"

"I'm fine, thanks. Come, we're all sitting in the living room," said Camilla. "Don't just leave him standing there, Trace."

"Mom! I just told him to come inside," said Tracy glaring at her mother who was already leaving the entrance hall. "Parents! They can be so annoying."

Josh followed Tracy as she led him towards the lounge.

"Hi, everyone," said Tracy. "You all know Josh."

"Hi, Josh," said everyone together.

"Oh, and this is Granny Sybs," said Tracy introducing Josh.

"Hello, young man," said Sybs with a smile. She winked at Tracy.

"Hi," Josh waved.

"Josh, please, sit down," said Camilla. "Dylan, shift up a

bit."

Josh shook Harold's hand before he sat down. "Afternoon, Professor."

"Call me Harold," he said with a grin.

"Hi, Lisa," said Josh.

"Hey," replied Lisa.

"Can I get you some tea?" said Camilla. "Juice? Water?"

"Some tea would be great, thanks, Mrs. Barnes," replied Josh.

"Tracy was telling us about the concert," said Harold.

"With the flute?" said Josh.

Tracy nodded.

"Oh, wow. I never knew you were that good. I'm impressed."

"Have you heard her play?" said Harold.

Dylan shook his head. "No."

"Neither have I," said Lisa, glaring at Tracy. "I never even knew that you played the flute."

Tracy blushed. "It's kinda a new thing. I got it in Turkey."

"But that was like two weeks ago," said Lisa. "How did you get so good in two weeks? I mean a concert? The school concert?"

Tracy nodded and then looked at her grandmother. "Practice, I guess. And some help from Granny Sybs."

Sybs smiled at Tracy.

"Did you ever find the other one?" said Harold.

"The other what?" said Lisa.

"The other flute," said Tracy. "There were two."

"What do you mean?" said Lisa in confusion.

"We got two flutes from Turkey," said Harold. "It's a long story, but one disappeared."

"No," said Tracy. "It's gone."

"Aliens," said Dylan. "Aliens took it."

"That's Dylan's standard answer these days," said Camilla with a sigh.

"Especially when there's no clear explanation," said Tracy.

413

"Okay. Just gang up on me. I've got an opinion too, you know!"

"Calm down, everyone," said Harold. "Dylan's right. His opinion counts."

Dylan stuck his tongue out at Tracy.

"But Dad!" said Tracy. "Aliens? Come on."

"*I* believe in them," said Josh, sticking his hand into the air. "I dunno. There are just so many unexplained things out there. And come on, with all the billions and billions of planets in the universe, there has to be life out there, right?" he looked at Tracy and shrugged his shoulders.

"I was having this conversation with Tracy just the other day," said Harold. "Aliens *could* exist."

"There, told you so!" said Dylan, jumping up, off the couch.

"I said 'could,' Dylan. There's no scientific proof."

"I'm still sticking with aliens. They're out there. Promise you they are."

"Aliens, shmaliens," said Lisa. "Who friggen cares? I just wanna hear Tracy play this flute of hers."

"Why don't you get it, Trace?" said Harold. "I'm sure that Josh would also like to hear you play, right, Josh?"

Josh nodded. "Sure," he said with a grin. He looked at Tracy, and she blushed again.

"Here," said Camilla, handing Tracy the black velvet bag.

Tracy removed the flute.

"Wow," said Lisa. "It looks beautiful. Can I see it?"

"Sure," said Tracy, handing Lisa the flute.

"It's so light," said Lisa, turning it around in her hands. "What's it made of?"

"Carbon-fibre."

"Amazing. It's beautiful. Why are the holes all over the place? Is it a Turkish design or something?"

"Fibonacci," said Tracy. "They're in sequence."

Lisa frowned, confused.

"The distance and spacing of the holes are based on the

Fibonacci sequence, the Golden Ratio. It gives the flute a unique kind of sound."

"Incredible," said Lisa. "Now I really want to hear you play." She passed the flute back to Tracy.

All eyes were on Tracy now as she brought the flute to her lips, closed her eyes, took a breath and exhaled, gently pushing the air into the narrow shaft. The sound was clear and pure. It filled the room, expanding, building, amplifying until you could hear nothing but its sound. It was a beautiful, enchanting melody that mesmerised everyone in the room. Through the magic of the flute, Tracy caused the air particles in the room to expand and vibrate at high speed, creating a blurred visual effect that forced everyone to gently close their eyes. Then she focused on the frequency of each and everyone around her and allowed the melody to touch them, one at a time, charging their spirits with energy, enlightening and illuminating their souls.

The sound faded, but the vibrational discharge lingered. Tears rolled down Lisa's face. She opened her eyes and stared at Tracy in awe. "That was… simply beautiful. Emotional. So pure. I felt…" She shook her head in disbelief and wiped her face. "Wow, Trace. You have such a gift. I had no idea. Amazing."

Tracy blushed. "Thanks, Lis."

Granny Sybs applauded, and everyone else joined in. Tracy's face turned crimson.

Josh stood up and threw his arms around Tracy. "I love you," he whispered in her ear.

Tracy's heart melted. She smiled and kissed Josh on the lips. "I love you too."

THE END

Thank You

I really hope you enjoyed reading my book. Thank you for reading it! Reviews are very important for authors. If you enjoyed the book, please consider posting a review on Amazon.com.

Please visit my website, richardgradner.com for more information about my other novels, *Return to Lemuria, Unicorn,* and *Servant of Memory.* By registering for my monthly newsletter, you will receive a link to download a complimentary digital copy of my first novel, *Return to Lemuria.*

Thanks in advance for your support!

Richard

UNICORN

Richard Gradner

1 ~ Mantra

Harappa, Indus River Valley, 4518 BCE

Their round, smiling faces appeared hazy, and the sound of their voices muted, as consciousness slowly returned to Halim.

"He has your eyes, Arja."

"And your nose, Shan. Awww. Hello, little Halim. You cute, cute baby boy. You're going to grow up to be a great warrior like your father, aren't you? Yes, yes, yes!" Arja tickled Halim under his chin. He squirmed his little body from side to side, pulling his face into a toothless smile.

"It's been seven days. It's time to do the test," said Shan looking askance at his wife.

"Yes. I guess it is," nodded Arja sombrely.

Shan reached into the folds of his cloak and pulled out a small, round, pale blue stone. It was smooth and shiny as if it had been regularly polished. He gently pried open the tiny fingers of his son's right hand and pressed the stone into his palm. Halim instinctively squeezed his hand around the stone. Shan gently placed his hands, one on top of the other, over his son's forehead, leant in close and whispered, "Halim. My son. By the power vested in me by my father and his father before him, I charge you with the might of the Peraja Stone. May the gods find favour in your chosen path and lead you forward to your destiny."

Shan carefully removed his hands and took a step back. Halim appeared to have gone back to sleep. A moment later, his eyes flickered open, and he began to cry; the shrill sound of his voice piercing the silence like the wail of a startled river bird. Shan pried the stone loose from his tight grip and carefully examined its surface. He smiled.

"The colour is good, and the energy of the stone glows with strength and power."

Arja moved forward for a closer look. The stone had changed colour, from pale blue to sea green. Tiny golden flecks covered its surface like the glittering reflection of the sun's rays on the great, wide ocean.

"Ah. So pretty," Arja beamed with pride. "The gods have blessed us." She turned to her husband, took his hand in hers and gazed up at him affectionately with a smile on her face.

◊ ◊ ◊

"Halim. Give your sister back her toy."

"But mama, I got it first."

"That's not the point, Halim. It's not yours."

Halim clamped his tiny hands over his ears, trying his best to shut out his sister Taja's high-pitched, wailing cry. He picked up the little, wooden unicorn carving and threw it at his sister in annoyance. The statuette clipped the side of her head, resulting in even louder fits of screaming.

"Halim!" Arja reprimanded. "That was unnecessary. Go to your room. This instant!"

"No!" he shouted boldly.

"By the gods, if you do not do as you are told, then you will be severely punished."

Halim folded his arms and stared at his mother in defiance. She glowered back at him. The tension grew but Halim stood his ground.

Shan walked into the room. "What is all this commotion?" he demanded emphatically.

Arja turned to her husband. "This child of yours is disrespectful," she said, pointing at Halim. "He made Taja cry, and now he refuses to obey my command."

Halim turned and ran away down the hall.

"Halim!" Arja shouted. "Where are you going? Come back!"

Halim ran as fast as his little legs would carry him. He ran away from his mother and the look of disapproval from his father. He ran until the tears dried on his face. He ran until his lungs burned from heavy breathing. He ran until he fell down on the soft earth of the forest beyond the walls of the city, rolled onto his back and stared up at the swaying boughs of the trees caught in the wind around him. A smile creased his little face, and the feelings of anger and resentment were gradually replaced by a peaceful serenity he could not explain. He watched as the trees acquiesced to mother nature's invisible force, his chest still heaving from the effort of the run.

◊ ◊ ◊

He was drifting, floating, flying. He was an observer, watching the history of his life from above; looking down on his journey, his adventure. He was beyond time. He was beyond space. He was learning. He was the learner. He listened. He was the listener. He became part of the conception that had already been, yet was also taking place now. The memories flowed, and he became a part of them. Again and again.

"Halim. Halim! Do you hear me, boy? Why are you not listening to my instructions? I told you to follow me, yet here you are again, lost in your thoughts." Shan fought to restrain his fury.

"I'm sorry, papa. I cannot help myself," replied Halim timidly.

"That's the problem right there, Halim," rasped Shan indignantly. "You're not focused. You're not concentrating.

What have your thoughts got to do with our practice? Hmm? Exactly. Nothing!"

Halim hung his head.

"Look at me when I talk to you, Halim."

Halim slowly lifted his head.

"That's better. Now. I know it's hard sometimes, but you must push yourself. Do not lose focus. What I'm teaching you is the foundation of the practice. If you lose your concentration, then rather lose it to the practice, not some obscure fantasy in your head. You must learn to live in the now. This moment is all that matters."

"Yes, papa."

"When you truly understand the importance of this lesson, only then will you see the value behind my instruction. Until then, you must listen to me, do what I do, and repeat. Constant repetition builds conviction and purpose. It's only once you have repeated yourself time and again, will you realise that this is the path."

"What path, papa?"

"The path to enlightenment, growth and experience," Shan continued. "You see, Halim, everything is constant, moving. That which stands still fades away and disappears like it never was. Our purpose is to find that which moves, and then move with it. Such is life - a constantly flowing river upon which we must sail and navigate. To sail on the river, we need to repeat the foundational practice until it becomes second nature, part of one's very being. Only then do we become worthy to join those that direct the ships of change. As a future Shakti Warrior, this is your destiny, my son."

"I understand papa. I will try harder," said Halim.

"Good. Now follow me. Observe, then do. Bring your hands together in a prayer mudra in front of your heart. Take a deep breath and fold forward. Breath out. Bend your legs, slowly sit down in a comfortable seat and close your eyes. Now, clear your mind and focus on your breathing, nothing else."

Halim closed his eyes and focused on his breathing as his

father instructed, imagining the air around him as a silver mist flowing deep into his lungs and then throughout his entire body, charging it with powerful Prana.

"Good, Halim. Excellent focus," said Shan, commending his son. "Now, just as we repeat the movements, we repeat the mantra."

"Why must we repeat the mantra, papa?" enquired Halim earnestly.

"When we use a mantra, by repeating it, we elicit vibrational energy. These vibrations permeate one's entire being, overcoming and diminishing the current vibrational energy that you may be subject to until all thoughts are replaced, leading to the silencing of the mind."

"So, we become what we chant?"

"In a manner of speaking, yes," replied Shan. "This is the magic of Yoga. We first prepare the body physically, pulling it this way and twisting it that, until we are soft and flexible like clay, ready to accept the vibrational power of the mantra that will shape us into the direction in which we would like to go."

"I don't understand, papa," said Halim, creasing his brow.

"The only way to truly understand is to experience it for yourself, my son. The sacred mantra that I will teach you today is known as laghiman, the power to cancel out gravity."

"You mean levitation?" Halim asked.

"Yes. Levitation. This is the lesson. Its foundation is the mantra. Study it, repeat it until the words become part of you, and then it will take effect. This is why I get upset with you when you lose your concentration because, without it, you become lost. It's all about your intention, Halim. Now focus and chant with me."

"Dish tyaw day vwah tan naw,
Tee awsh vwah sah jaw yah tay."

"Now repeat this next verse over and over again, and bear in mind your intention to levitate, to rise."

"Lah gahah yah yah jaw yah tay,
Ut kah lal lah jaw yah tay,
Ooh daw nah yah jaw yah tay."

(Thank you, Lord, for allowing me to stretch, to breathe easy, to become. To become light, to rise, to fly.)

Halim began to chant the mantra until it became a repetitive, flowing, melody. His father was right. Singing the mantra over and over again, created a vibrational energy, that began to shape itself around his body until he became the intention of the words being chanted. There was nothing else, just the mantra. The words of levitation. Halim could feel his body becoming light and buoyant the more he chanted. The weight of his physical body melted away as he gradually overcame the power of gravity. Both father and son chanting in unison, created a powerful intention, causing them to rise gently away from the earth.